THE BLIND SPY

THE BLIND SPY

Alex Dryden

WINDSOR
PARAGON

First published 2010
by Headline Publishing Group
This Large Print edition published 2011
by AudioGO Ltd
by arrangement with
Headline Publishing Group

Hardcover ISBN: 978 1 445 85834 0
Softcover   ISBN: 978 1 445 85835 7

British Library Cataloguing in Publication Data available

Printed and bound in Great Britain by
MPG Books Group Limited

To Mia, I love you anyway

'Everyone imposes his own system as far as his army can reach.'

Joseph Stalin, April 1945

'Don't you understand, George, that Ukraine is not even a state.'

Vladimir Putin to George W. Bush, April 2008

THE BLIND SPY

PROLOGUE

August 1971

Lieutenant Valentin Viktorov walked carefully and with evident hesitation through the labyrinth of Aleppo's covered souk. A keen-eyed observer perhaps might have described him as being lost, but, lost or not, it was clear that he had his mind on things other than his surroundings.

He was a tall man with short-cropped fair hair and an athletic build. His face was so finely shaven, his skin so smooth, that he looked almost too young to be shaving at all. He certainly looked far younger than his twenty-seven years, and gave off an appearance of youth that a teenage Russian army conscript on leave might have done, rather than the seasoned KGB intelligence officer that he was.

Despite the fact that he was not on official assignment on this summer morning, he was operating as he always did for KGB undercover work when he was outside the secret, closed and protected spaces of the Soviet spy elite, places like the embassy compound in Damascus from which he had set off before the sun came up. In other words, if anything went wrong, he was unprotected. He carried no identification from the embassy that would get him out of trouble if that was what he was heading into.

But the difference between a normal undercover operation and his activities this morning was that this was a personal mission—the

KGB had no part in it. It was his own solo, private operation, and one that would have drawn deep disapproval from his boss, should he have known of it, possibly bringing an end to his career altogether. He had no back-up for what he was about to do.

Dressed in the drab civilian clothes of Soviet Russia he seemed, like Russia itself, drained of colour and bereft of joy. In this he was clearly distinguishable from the bustling and colourful Arab throng in the souk. Not just his clothes and his height, but also his pronounced Slavic features set him distinctively apart from the Arabs.

He was distinguishable too—though more subtly so—from the few, mostly Western tourists who might look like him with their Caucasian features, but that was where the resemblance ended. Unlike Valentin, they were all staring wide-eyed at their surroundings and carrying armfuls of cheap souvenirs which they would be taking back home with them. Unlike nearly all of these other visitors to the souk that morning, Valentin seemed unimpressed by his surroundings and he carried nothing that was visible.

Only the thick packet concealed in his buttoned-down shirt pocket and the small emergency pistol tucked away beneath the waistband of his trousers accompanied him.

But there was something about his urgently controlled movements, the hard muscles of his body visible through the shirt and his alert and watchful eyes that anyway suggested he was something altogether other than a tourist. He didn't seem to belong in the souk, even as a visitor. He looked like a man prepared, and pre-paring, for some kind of sudden action that was in another order of things than merely a shopping expedition. There was, too, a sense of latent violence about him; his toned and muscled body appeared to reach out for a reason to be employed to the full. He was a pumped-up sportsman, a human missile ready to go off. He certainly didn't look like a tourist sponge soaking up the wonders of the place. He was a part of his surroundings, while also being apart. And unlike the tourists, he spoke fluent Arabic.

Valentin paused with the minute attention of a bookkeeper at the cupboard-sized shops on either side of the narrow alley. But he didn't really look at their contents. If his eyes were focused at all on what was around him, he looked without seeing. There was a nervousness about him, which expressed itself in small, tense movements. He repeatedly brushed his short-cropped fair hair with one hand and occasionally touched the buttoned-down pocket of his white shirt with the other. It was an anxious gesture made as if to reassure himself that the package was still there. The muscles of his lean jaw twitched every time he felt the package and after each contact with it he thrust his hands back into the pockets of his grey trousers as though to physically restrain them from the obsessive checking of the pocket.

Valentin walked on, blindly surveying the over-filled alcoves crammed up against the alley that was wide enough for a donkey loaded with panniers to pass by, but not much bigger.

What separated him too from the other visitors to the souk was that he looked at these little shops one by one, without any of the discernment of the

3

real, dedicated shopper. It was as if he were seeing them for the first time, even though that was far from the truth. Anyone who watched him closely would have said that he wasn't truly looking for anything, in fact; that he wasn't a potential customer at all, and that his mission was actually elsewhere than in the souk. The souk and its multitude of variegated delights were there to slow him down, to delay an arrival of some kind. And in his heart, he knew that he was stopping deliberately. And he knew that the reason for these pauses was in order to postpone his purpose—they were not the purpose itself.

The traders and hawkers who crowded the souk's alleys on either side of him were volubly selling their jute sacks of multi-coloured spices, green and mauve soaps piled up like sweet-smelling brick walls, lurid meats that dripped blood from hooks and butchers' blocks and which ran thickly away into the runnel along the centre of the stone alleyway. And then there were other shops that sold the red and white *keffiyehs* the Arabs wrapped around their heads, the silk and nylon dresses in gaudy gold and green, the striped woollen *jellabahs*, the sheepskins that betrayed the rancid smell of under-curing, the vegetables piled high in pyramids, the tin and brass lamps and lanterns . . . On it went, fifteen kilometres of covered market in all, a warren of commerce that sold produce from China and central Asia, the Levant, the Arab countries, Russia—even the West—in this place, Aleppo, the world's oldest of trading cities.

And in every direction in which Valentin flickered his sharp, electric-blue eyes, what he saw

4

were the photographs of the Soviet Union's ally, the stern president of Syria, Hafez al Assad, which, whether faded or new, looked down on the commerce and haggling, the conversation and coffee-drinking, like a looming superstition that threatened reprisal of some kind, rather than a figure of flesh and blood. Valentin was accustomed enough to the threatening faces that gazed down from walls back in his own country to hardly notice this one.

He stepped aside for a man with a frayed stick who was driving a donkey laden with baskets of green leaves along the covered narrow alley. The man, like all the Arabs, barely looked at him and, when he did—and then only briefly—it seemed to be done deliberately without curiosity. Was it fear of contact with foreigners that kept their eyes cast aside after the briefest of glances? No, he thought, the foreigner—whether a casual tourist or one of the Russian military and intelligence personnel like himself—was irrelevant to their daily lives. These people simply went about their business, that was all.

Not for the first time, Valentin was shocked by the freedom and social detachment which commerce brought to the people even under a dictatorship like Syria's—and which was absent in his own country where commerce was a dirty, even a criminal word.

In a moment of reflection that suddenly brought him into the moment, Valentin pondered that he was leaving all this behind him now anyway. He was well into the last week of his posting to Syria. Three years it had been since first he'd been sent down from Moscow. He'd graduated from the

KGB school at Balashiha-2 in The Forest outside Moscow, then he'd spent two years behind a desk. He'd learned Arabic and was taken under the wing of a rising star in the KGB's foreign intelligence department. This senior officer had then requested Valentin's transfer to Damascus, where this mentor had been made head of station. And now, in just over five days, Valentin would be returning to Moscow again for another posting, to another Arab country, he supposed—or maybe it would be just a desk job at the KGB's highly secretive Department S, in the Arab section, of course.

But it wasn't nostalgia brought on by his departure from the country that had drawn him up from the KGB station in Damascus to Syria's second capital, Aleppo. He hadn't come to say goodbye—not to the country, at any rate, or even just to Aleppo. He was perfectly aware that his slow progress through the souk was purposeful in its delay for another reason entirely. The private reason he had made this trip to the north of the country was hard for him to accomplish and he was postponing the moment a little longer. He was neither savouring it—this particular end—nor fearing it. Nevertheless, why he had come to Aleppo contained a finality that he wished to put off.

He turned to the left down another alley in the neat grid of the souk. Like all the others in this maze, it was filled with the conflicting sights and smells of spice and skins and alimentary produce. The sounds of an Arab lute came and went from a record player in a carpet shop. He stopped briefly at the shop and fingered some Kurdish kelims, but he didn't truly see them, either. His mind was

6

elsewhere and as soon as the shopkeeper tried to get him to buy something he walked on, stiffly smiling a thank-you, and pretending he couldn't speak their language. He fingered the packet in the buttoned-down pocket of his shirt once more to make sure that it was still there. The gun was cool against his skin and a constant heavy presence.

At the end of the alley, or perhaps it was at the end of the one after that, he saw daylight and headed towards it. He took a deep breath. He was approaching the moment. It was time to finish his business here and get back to the capital before he was missed. He certainly didn't want to have to answer questions from his station head, the truculent and volatile KGB Colonel Resnikov, and account for his time of absence from Damascus. He needed to be out of here within the hour and back to the capital. Suddenly he began to think more clearly, to take a grip on his usually incisive mind in order to carry through what he had come to do.

And then at last he emerged into the blinding white light of a busy street. The thick heat from which the covered market had protected him hit him like a suffocating mask, wrapping him in its intensity with a physical sensation that was almost like a dull, dry-fisted blow. With a muscular forearm bared from the rolled-up sleeve of his white shirt, he wiped his forehead as if to ward off the sweat that hadn't appeared yet. The heat was an insistent presence that demanded your attention, he thought, took over your thoughts.

He looked up and down. The street was a cacophony of horns and shouting. It was full of donkey carts with car tyres for wheels, and with the occasional cars and trucks that by some miracle still functioned vaguely as they were built to do. Exhaust fumes from a vegetable truck up from the country choked him as the driver pressed down on the throttle and its engine squealed agonisingly by him. The man should check his fan belt, he thought automatically.

The café he was looking for was a few hundred yards away. That was the venue they'd told him, the starting point for his real purpose this morning. He could just see it from the souk's exit. The men would take him from there. It was their own proposition, this meeting place, to which he'd agreed.

He stopped under a shaded awning before committing himself finally. He had come here against all good regulations, let alone good sense. What if something happened now? What if the men in the café had another agenda? They might try to stick a knife in him, he supposed. But most likely they'd let him go once he gave them the packet in his shirt pocket. It was his conscience, as well as his curiosity, that had brought him here and that was bad trade craft—no trade craft at all, in fact. He was going right out on a limb.

He saw them, three of them, sitting at the edge of the café—they were at a table nearest to the road. He knew only one of them, but guessed the other two were also her brothers. When he approached, warily, they didn't greet him, but they didn't look hostile either. Blank faces, cold, dark eyes. Neither trusting nor distrusting. But here they were in a public street. Maybe it would be different when they had him in some hidden place. He trusted, however, that they would take what they could get from him and that they wouldn't dare to harm a Russian from the embassy. He inspired respect from his physical presence, but at least they knew of his position—despite no actual identification—and it was that which inspired fear. Without a word, the men stood as he approached and indicated that he should follow.

The four of them walked for more than half an hour, away from the market and the ancient citadel of Abraham, past the *hammams* and the *khans* behind their old wooden doors, beyond the poor restaurants and bike repair shops, away from the commercial centre and on to the outskirts of the city.

Once they were clear and had reached a chronically poor residential neighbourhood, they finally turned up a small alley of mud houses and he guessed that it was here where the family house would be. But it was only a guess. Valentin had never been here before. He'd only met the woman once, in fact, that one time when she'd been dancing at the restaurant back in the direction from where they'd walked. She'd been a sudden attraction—he twenty-seven, she nineteen.

She'd danced for the three of them, all Russian intelligence officers up from Damascus for the weekend. When the others had left, he'd stayed, infatuated, lost, overturned by her beauty or by her movements or by the drink and the music—or all of those things.

He remembered now how it had been back then. One minute he'd felt like he'd been walking quietly and relatively enjoyably through life—albeit an Intelligence life of suspicion and paranoia—and the next, he was metaphorically hanging upside

9

down from a tree with a noose around his foot. That had been her effect, he remembered. She'd turned him upside down without warning. He remembered her eyes now, eyes that drew him into a whirlpool that was more of his own imagination than from any physical attribute of hers. She was a professional, after all. She was paid to use her eyes like that, as well as her body. Her charms were directed at everyone she danced for, not just at him. But it was he who had fallen for her.

They'd had sex in a room at the back of the restaurant which she and the other dancers used for changing. It was very sudden, unexpected, they'd hardly removed their clothes. He hadn't gone to the manager enquiring about her with sex in mind. He'd just wanted to see her. It was a vague, rudderless desire that was more about his fear of never seeing her again than anything else. He was infatuated. But the manager had let it happen either because of the money Valentin had given him to keep quiet, or because he was afraid of these Russians. And the woman—the dancer— why had she let it happen? He didn't know. She'd been a virgin. Most probably she'd seen in him some kind of salvation from the narrow and ever-shrinking opportunities of her life. And he didn't even know her name, he realised afterwards. Maybe sex with him had been some desperate throw of the dice on her part, an attempt to change her life for ever.

He looked ahead now, along the alley that wound up a slight dirt hill. The men didn't seem to be worrying that he wouldn't follow them. And now the three men and he, trailing behind them, seemed to be approaching the house that was their

10

destination. The movements of her brothers were slowing, their walk kinked a little to the left. He stepped over a pile of loose garbage. The alley was filthy, just like all the others. The smell was high with kerosene and stale, human sweat, rotting vegetables and open drains. Half-naked children and rib-thin cats played in the drain. The women were covered here. The secular state didn't reach into its dark alleyways. Nobody looked at him, nobody seemed to notice him. It was as if he wasn't there.

Why didn't he turn around now, leave this place and forget what had happened with the woman? He didn't even know her name, he thought again with incredulity. Was it really his conscience driving him or was it something else? He knew that most of all it was curiosity. He knew deep down that he wanted just once to see the son he would never see again. And he would pay for that in cash, as if it were his conscience paying. Perhaps then he would be able to forget the whole thing.

They told him to wait outside the broken-down mud house which they'd now reached. They'd be getting rid of the women inside, he supposed, sending them somewhere into the back. Then the one brother whom he knew—or at least had met when he'd made the deal—beckoned him inside. The man didn't waste any time and pointed into a dark corner of a bare room lit only by a shaft of intense sunlight coming through the half-open door.

'There it is,' he said. It was a deliberately brutal statement, Valentin thought; an insult.

Valentin looked to the far side of the room, across a flattened earth floor and into the near darkness. When his eyes had adjusted from the bright whiteness of the light outside, he walked towards a small, low wooden table, the only piece of furniture in the room apart from two home-made wooden chairs. There on the table he saw a crude wooden crib constructed from a vegetable box and in the crib, wrapped in dirty white swaddling clothes, was what he had come to see: his son. 'It', the man had called him.

He looked down and saw a small face with dark eye-brows, the eyes tight shut, fingers curled up around them. The baby would be just over twelve weeks old, he thought.

One of the other two men came over and flicked his fingers, his dark eyes angry and wary at the same time. With the relief of a job done, Valentin took the packet from his shirt pocket at last and gave it to him. The man swiftly counted the money, like a trader who is experienced at flicking quickly through bundles of bank notes and assessing their value instantly. He seemed satisfied. Then he looked at Valentin directly in the eyes.

'Now you take him,' the man said to him. It was an order.

Valentin looked back at him in surprise, then alarm and finally anger. At first he didn't understand what the man was saying, but then he realised he'd been right in the first place. It was the man who was gripped by a misunderstanding, not him.

'You don't understand,' he said at last, quickly. 'The money I've given you is to care for the boy. It's for his mother to look after him. I can't take him with me. It's impossible.'

The man shrugged. 'Either you take him or he

will be left,' he replied implacably.

Was he hearing right? Left? He meant left to die, Valentin realised with disgust. Left on the street for animals and strays to pick at. Or by the side of the road outside the city, or up in the mountains somewhere. 'The money,' he repeated precisely and slowly in Arabic. 'That is what it's for. To look after the boy.' He felt himself getting angrier. He realised that he'd like to throttle the man, hit him, knock his teeth out. He felt the gun nudging him to it.

'He is cursed by God,' the man said simply.

Valentin looked back at the twelve-week-old boy. What was the man talking about? He unwrapped his son from the filthy cloths and saw a perfectly formed human being. The boy didn't wake. He saw his tiny chest move with his breath.

'Why is he cursed by God?' Valentin said, without betraying his rising anger. He believed they were going to blackmail him for more money, but he had none. It had taken all his wits to get his hands on the local currency as it was.

The man stood beside him and looked down at the boy. 'He is cursed,' he said. He shrugged again. 'God has cursed him,' he said, as if it were perfectly obvious that this was the reason for not wanting the child, and for killing it.

And now Valentin knew. To these people, any defect in a newborn baby meant that it had been cursed by God—and they would reject the child, reject it with the finality of death. Looking down at the boy he could see no physical defect, however. So the child's defect must be him—Valentin—he supposed. A foreign father, and out of wedlock, too. Doubly damned. Otherwise the boy looked

13

healthy enough.

Valentin walked back across the room. The other two men were watching him closely. They were afraid, but there were three of them and one of him, and they were in their own home, surrounded by their own people outside in the street. If he'd been on official business in this God-forsaken part of the city, he would have threatened them, drawn the gun concealed under his waistband, but he was here in secret, unknown to his boss. He couldn't afford a scandal, so he kept himself under control. 'Where's his mother?' Valentin asked finally. 'I want to see her.'

'She's not here,' the brother he'd met before snapped in reply. 'That is not part of the bargain,' he added.

'Where is she?'

There was silence. He didn't like to go where his imagination was taking him. He didn't like to think what had happened to her, what they'd done to her in punishment. If sex with him had been a desperate throw of the dice on her part, it had certainly changed her life. But it was a change that would probably finish it for good, if it hadn't done so already.

Valentin stopped in the centre of the room and felt the possibilities that faced him diminish. He knew he was beaten. Condemn his son to death, no, that was not possible. 'What about an orphanage?' he said suddenly. 'Where is there an orphanage?'

The men talked among themselves. 'In Damascus. On Khalabbah Street,' one said finally.

'What about here? In Aleppo?'

The men shrugged. Either they didn't want the

14

boy in Aleppo, or they didn't know.

Valentin suddenly stopped thinking. 'Then I'll take him with me,' he said. Circumventing thought, the decision was made for him.

A few minutes later he was walking back down the street carrying the live bundle of his son and when he'd reached a paved street he took a private car that willingly converted to a taxi to take him back to Damascus. He was late, later than he'd planned to be, and he told the driver to hurry. It was a long journey by road.

On the way to the capital he ran through what he would have to do. He was clear now in his head; it was his only choice to save his son. But he also wanted to tell someone else, not just to leave the boy abandoned at an orphanage. If one other person knew, he considered, then he would be able to leave the country with a clearer mind.

There was one person he thought he might trust—just possibly. It was crazy, he knew that. After all, he was an officer in Soviet foreign intelligence. But he knew that the only person he could trust with the knowledge of his son was the wife of his head of station in Damascus, Natalia Resnikova. She was a good woman, a caring person. He believed she might understand. She was pregnant with a child of her own, after all. It would be born under a year after his son had been born. That is what he decided to do, no matter what the risk.

Having made his decision, the only other thing that preoccupied him on the journey to the capital was that his son didn't have a name.

When the car reached Damascus, they drove to one of the poorest parts, to the east of the city.

15

Behind a concreted area that served as a basketball pitch in a flat, grey suburb on the fringe of the capital, he dismissed the driver. Then he walked until he found Khalabbah Street. The houses were new here—mostly cheap, concrete, barely functional buildings to accommodate the influx of people coming in ever greater numbers from the countryside to work in the city. There was construction work going on over the whole area; cement dust rose in a mist from the rear of a truck, a bulldozer was piling the broken remains of old, destroyed houses into a heap.

Despite the noise of construction, his son seemed capable of sleeping for ever.

He saw the workmen were wearing white cloths to protect their necks against the heat, even now at six in the evening. The noise of machinery and the fumes filled the air around the waste ground they were clearing in order to put up more concrete housing blocks.

Valentin walked on through the dust until he reached an older building on Khalabbah Street made of yellowing stone. A former school or government building, perhaps? But whatever it was in its former life, it was now the orphanage. It was quieter here.

He put his son down in the shade under a portico at the entrance and took out a piece of paper. On it he wrote in Arabic. 'This boy has no parents. Please look after him.' They would know it was a foreigner's writing, and that bothered him momentarily. Then he sucked the pen for a moment and wrote again. 'His name is Balthasar.' Balthasar. He hadn't been able to think of a name throughout the journey from Aleppo, but now it had come to him in a moment. He liked the name. God protect the King. They had dramatic names and that was one of its meanings, in any case. Then he looked for some way of alerting the people inside the building. He found a bell-pull made of old cord hanging at the side of the door and pulled on it. He heard a distant chime. Then he walked swiftly away. Whoever ran the orphanage would be accustomed to the ring that announced the abandonment of another child.

He walked for a mile back towards the centre of the city and finally found himself at the Russian embassy compound. The White Houses, the Russians called the compound, in an unconcealed expression of racist superiority.

His mind, he found, was blurred, vague, as if he were in a film of himself rather than being the real Valentin Viktorov. But he went straight to the house of his head of station and rang the bell before he lost his nerve. There was no point in delaying.

It was the maid who answered the door. He asked for Natalia Resnikova. Resnikov's wife finally came to the door and invited him inside. She was an elegant, beautiful woman, but her eyes were usually shaded with sadness. Married to Resnikov, Valentin wasn't surprised. He smiled nervously at her and she returned his expression with calm, uncritical serenity. Then she nodded at him sympathetically. He liked this woman and, he liked to believe, she had a soft spot for him too.

Valentin saw at once that they were alone. He was relieved that his head of station, Colonel Resnikov, was in his study as usual, probably drinking foreign whisky. He would be able to be alone with Resnikov's wife and she was a good woman, a good person. They sat and took tea in a shaded patio at the rear of the house. When the maid had gone, Valentin told her everything; the night in Aleppo, the woman and their child.

She didn't reply at first. There was a silence, but it wasn't awkward. Then she called the maid and Valentin thought that she was going to betray him, but she simply asked for her knitting to be brought. He noticed the bump of her stomach that had grown in the past month, and she saw him looking.

'They will be almost the same age,' she said simply. 'I believe I will have a girl.'

'Just a year apart,' he said. 'What will you call her—if she's a girl?'

'I'd like to call her Anna.'

Valentin knew that Natalia Resnikova did good works in the city—that was why he had come to her. At least, she did good works when she could do so without drawing her husband's disapproval or disgust, or even wrath. Resnikov was a hard, bitter man who seemed to gain pleasure from nothing, even the Western whisky he somehow got his hands on.

The maid brought her knitting on to the verandah. The pregnant wife of his boss showed him what she was making. 'It's a sweater for my baby,' she said. 'I'll make another one for your son. Then they'll have the same.'

He nodded his thanks, suddenly overwhelmed by the thought that now his son would be a real citizen of the world, with a sweater made specially for him, not just an abandoned child living off hand-me-downs.

'And when Anna is born she and I will visit your

son when they are both old enough,' Natalia Resnikova said. 'Until then, I will go alone when I can. I know the orphanage quite well.' She finally touched his arm. 'It's a good place. And you did the right thing.'

Such unexpected understanding made Valentin's eyes moist with relief as well as with the grief he felt for his encounter with the doomed woman dancer and finally, underlying all, for the birth of his son whose life or death he had held so recently in his hands.

PART ONE

CHAPTER ONE

8 January 2010

The black s-class stretch Mercedes crossed beneath the Moscow ring road on Entuziastov at just after 5.30 in the morning. It was snowing harder outside the city, or maybe that was just how it seemed to the men inside the car. For once they were away from the protection of the city's buildings, the snow was free to hurl itself across the open landscape and a whirlwind of large, fluffy snowflakes rolled out of the eerie, monstrous white void only to disintegrate as they raced in to hit the car's heated windscreen.

With the ring road behind it, the official car kept up the same steady, regulation speed and moved on to the M-7 heading north-east out of Moscow in the direction of Balashiha.

They were two Intelligence chiefs who sat on the soft, sweet-smelling black leather of the back seat and the military intelligence driver was the other figure in the limousine, alone in the front. Both chiefs were the most senior generals, elevated to their positions by age, experience, duty, but most of all by the supreme skill of the Russian political intelligence class—a ruthless animal instinct for supremacy in the power struggles of the Kremlin's internecine bureaucratic wars.

In their late sixties, they wore uniforms almost comically bemedalled from past campaigns—real wars—that made them resemble highly colourful performers from a travelling medieval pageant.

These tiered ribbons of medals had been won mostly in Afghanistan after Russia's 1979 invasion of the country, and its disastrous and debilitating war there that had finally emptied the Soviet treasury and heralded the end of empire. They were the medals of defeat.

General Valentin Viktorov had been personally in charge of an intelligence team which, with initially magnificent success, had prepared the ground for the invasion of the presidential palace in Kabul at Christmas of that year. But those were the glory days, before the Soviet effort descended into stalemate and retreat in the subsequent years of brutal conflict.

Afghanistan. It was never far away from either of the generals' minds, even now, decades after the war ended. Just as the Second World War—the Great Patriotic War, in Russia's lexicon—had been the foul crucible whose hellish alchemy gave birth to Soviet might and to the greatest empire on earth, so Afghanistan was the insidious chemical formula that finally ripped the whole shaky edifice to pieces. For both the generals—as for many of the military veterans of that disastrous war— Afghanistan was the defining moment of their and their Motherland's loss of pride. Afghanistan was the fault line that severed modern Russia from its glorious past. The actual collapse—that of the Eastern European empire in 1989 and the subsequent folding of Russia's central Asian possessions after that—was just the inevitable consequence of the Afghan defeat. And it was Afghanistan that welded the psyches of the two generals and thousands like them into an overwhelming and unified desire for the recouping

24

of all of glorious Russia's losses since then.

But despite this psychological link between the two generals, it was notable that they sat as far from one another as the seating allowed, each pushed up against their respective rear doors. They were rivals and, in Russia's medievally clannish political and intelligence world, they had often found themselves working against each other. One of the two generals was from the GRU, Russia's Main Intelligence Directorate, the other, General Viktorov, was core SVR, Russia's First Chief Directorate and the successor to the KGB's foreign intelligence department.

The two men didn't talk and, indeed, the only body language between them consisted of the deliberate distance they put between themselves that strongly suggested a mutual antipathy. They also spent most of the journey looking away from each other and out of the windows on either side of the car, though the view was obscured almost completely by the white-out of driving snow. Only the thin, bunched-together trunks of birch and fir trees as they approached The Forest took shape, though dimly, through the otherwise white landscape and the snow-filled sky.

They also both wore tight-lipped expressions that suggested even sharing the same car was an imposition. But that was the way it had been arranged by the prime minister's office and they hadn't been given the choice to travel separately. It was as if this enforced journey together was a test of sorts in itself. 'You'll be working together'—that had been the order. But they had never worked together in any commonly accepted way.

The relative seniority between the two men was

25

hard to judge—not least by themselves—but their rivalry was evident in the tension that existed between them. The GRU general, Antonov, deployed five or six times more agents on foreign soil than the SVR and he personally commanded twenty-five thousand special forces troops, or *spetsnaz*. But it was the SVR that considered itself the elite foreign intelligence force and it was to the SVR headquarters in Balashiha—The Forest, in KGB parlance—to which they were going. General Viktorov of the SVR was also a central figure in the elite of elites—the directorate's highly secretive Department S. This inner clan of foreign intelligence officers was in charge of training foreigners to spy for the Kremlin, and then to commit terrorist acts back in their own countries. Viktorov's highly sensitive department had achieved several important assassinations in the past year alone.

But in addition to being at the heart of Department S, Viktorov had the vital advantage of having closer personal access to Prime Minister Vladimir Putin than his rival. The two of them were actually friends outside the day-to-day business of the intelligence world, and skied and hunted together. In Putin's baronial court where rank was often a secondary consideration after personal favour—and favours—this probably gave Viktorov the edge.

After crossing the ring road, it wasn't more than a few miles to Balashiha and The Forest. The snow ploughs had been out all night to keep the vital road connecting the Kremlin and its intelligence heart clearer than any other in Russia. Neither of the generals made any attempt to break the silence between them for the remainder of the journey.

Perhaps each was thinking over the purpose of this pre-dawn meeting with Putin, or perhaps they simply had little to say to each other without the catalyst of the prime minister's actual presence and his sudden call for them to meet him. But, more likely, each was thinking of his own strategy of personal pre-eminence when they met Putin, regardless of the purpose of the meeting. And each of them was certainly in a state of anxious speculation that the other knew more, had been briefed prior to this journey, had been taken into the confidence of the prime minister more closely. The usual fear of some loss of favour with Putin plagued them both. And that was how the Kremlin played its games. You never got used to that, Viktorov was thinking. Rule was administered through anxiety and fear, just as it had always been.

The car finally swung through the high gates—razor wire and gun turrets disappearing into the snow on either side—and the generals' identities were shown and logged by the guards. The Mercedes pulled up half a mile beyond the entrance, outside a long, low building, most of which was concealed beneath the earth.

It was Golubev the special assistant from the prime minister's office who was there to meet them. A chivvying young man with a foolishly small moustache, Golubev was a product of the new, post-Soviet era. He was a politician-lawyer rather than a soldier—let alone an intelligence officer—and therefore the kind of bureaucratic, ministry man who elicited little respect from either of the generals. His youth allowed no memory of the

27

defeat in Afghanistan or even of the collapse of the entire Soviet Union two years later, which that humiliation precipitated. Unlike the generals, Golubev looked to the future at the expense of nurturing the past and its humiliations. And, to the generals, he also looked to the future at the expense of redressing the balance that had been lost in the past twenty years since the Soviet Union collapsed. That balance—in the dreams of many like them—was the restoration of the Russian empire.

With a fussiness that disguised fears of his own, Golubev brushed imaginary dust from the lapels of his jacket, smoothed its sides and then led the generals through cream-painted concrete corridors to an elevator which took them down four floors into the earth and finally into a brightly lit room the size of a tennis court. It was one of many operations rooms in this core SVR building and Viktorov knew it well. It was here that many undercover missions had been planned, from the wars in Chechnya to foreign assassinations in the Middle East and Europe. Long, identical tables were laid out in neat rows, each with a harsh light over them, and at a casual glance the whole space might have suggested a snooker club.

Golubev proceeded to a table near the centre of this space and pulled up two high chairs for the generals that offered a view down on to the high table, and then one for himself, which he never sat on.

At once, Viktorov looked at several maps that had been opened on this long table. The particular map that caught his eye—it was in the centre of the table which was at the centre of the room—was of

28

the Soviet Union. It was a pre-1991 map, in other words, from a time before the Soviet Union had broken up. Viktorov was pleasantly surprised, as if he were looking at a recently discovered family treasure that had been uncovered in the clear-out of an old attic, and he took a greater interest. He saw another map of the period, and of equal size, next to it which was a close-up of part of the former empire. It had been titled 'Little Russia', but only by a scrawl on a yellow Post-it note stuck to the top. The name on the map itself, however, was 'Ukrainian SSR'.

'When is the prime minister arriving?' Viktorov asked, looking down on Golubev from the high seat. Golubev fidgeted uncomfortably. Viktorov was a big, muscled man, despite his age, and he took care about his appearance and his physical fitness. His eyebrows were artfully shaped to eliminate the wild-growing hairs that age unleashed and the skin of his face had a polished, pampered appearance. General Antonov, on the other hand was ruddy in complexion and had allowed the hairs of his advancing age to grow like weeds in an abandoned courtyard. The one general affected a modern, careful appearance, while the other seemed to seek the virtues of a rugged lack of vanity.

'You'll be meeting with some colleagues, first,' Golubev said. 'The prime minister has been detained.'

'Colleagues?' Antonov queried. 'For how long?'

'*Patriotiy,*' Golubev replied almost mutely, as if embarrassed at the mention of this informal, almost underground group which was definitely not part of his modern Russian vision. 'We are waiting for the prime minister's call,' he added.

'Ah,' Viktorov said. 'Our *Patriotiy* friends. That's the reason for the map, then.' He was pleased to be meeting with fellows and, no doubt, old colleagues too from the *Patriotiy*.

Golubev didn't reply. But the generals relaxed into their seats as the nervous ministry man ordered coffee to be brought.

The *Patriotiy* were the core, Viktorov ruminated as he waited for the coffee to arrive. They were the promise. They were like a rare seed preserved in one of Russia's frozen storage units that guarded the planet's ecological and agricultural future. Like these rare seeds, the *Patriotiy* were the guardians of Russia's past and the hope for its future. They were the only ones left with any power who were true to the memory of their own people where Russia's former might was concerned. And for a moment Viktorov felt a brief affinity for the GRU boss Antonov, a veteran like himself of Afghanistan.

The *Patriotiy* consisted mainly of these veterans from the Afghan war which had ended so bitterly for the Soviet Union and damaged its self-image so catastrophically ever since the 1980s. Most importantly in this all-but-secret society of the new Russia, members of the *Patriotiy* didn't believe that the loss of empire was anything other than a temporary historical mistake. In any democratic country, they would have been way outside the political process, on some semi-lunatic fringe. In the Russia of the twenty-first century, however, they were at the centre of power, though invisibly so to all but a few. Afghan veterans like himself and Antonov, who had risen in Putin's Russia through the organs of the security services, the

Patriotiy were now in control of several intelligence departments and government ministries and had brought their grudges of lost empire with them.

Coffee arrived, delivered by an attractive woman in uniform whom Viktorov smiled at with an avuncular look that didn't—and didn't intend to—disguise the lust that lurked behind it. And then the room began to fill up with a dozen or more men in their sixties or seventies and a few younger men. Most of them were in uniform; lesser generals, colonels, retired or not retired. Greetings were exchanged, old links renewed. Two more uniformed female assistants had now materialised to help Golubev distribute files to all the men. Viktorov gave his trademark smile to the woman who approached his table. He took a file and slipped a pair of reading glasses over his nose. The title in bold Cyrillic on the cover was: *Reappraisal. The Weakness of Ukraine—Political, Economic, Ethnic and Military.*

Viktorov and the others leafed through their files without yet reading them closely. 'Who wrote this?' Viktorov snapped at Golubev.

'A think tank at the Ministry of the Interior,' was the reply. 'Along with some of your own intelligence staff, General.'

Behind my back, Viktorov thought. The prime minister's mind games had begun. But he snorted loudly and confidently, though whether at the words 'think tank' or the fact that Interior people were in part the authors was unclear. Not that he despised the Interior Ministry. The Interior Ministry was one of several important ministries now controlled by the *Patriotiy* and its chiefs shared the same aims as people like the group in the

31

room.

For a moment, Viktorov removed his glasses and looked across the large room. He stared hard with unfocused eyes. So it was him. He thought he'd recognised him and he'd been right. It was his son, Dmitry. Or Balthasar—though only the two of them knew him by the latter name. He saw that Balthasar was talking to an older man—an officer in the Alpha Group, Viktorov thought. Viktorov couldn't take his eyes away from his son.

Then Balthasar broke away from a brief exchange with the officer and began to make his way through the throng. He walked with expert precision around three tables and paused to nod a greeting and say a few words to two or three other men. He looked assured, smooth in his movements, somehow modern, Viktorov thought, in that his proper deference to senior men was never at the expense of his personal pride and individuality. He was a colonel—also in Department S—and was now thirty-eight years old. But in this room he was a junior.

Viktorov watched Balthasar to see that he was clearly making his way towards him. With one hand he was lifting up a chair that was in the way, while with the other he shook greetings with colleagues. He looked directly into people's eyes.

Amazing—even now it amazed Viktorov. Such extra-ordinary power Balthasar had. Nobody who didn't know him would ever have guessed that he was blind. And, knowing that he was blind, nobody would have dreamed that he could be Russia's most senior and most-decorated intelligence field operative in all of the Muslim countries. Amazing, there was no other word for it. Sometimes his son's

32

strange abilities discomforted Viktorov—but there was no denying Balthasar's extraordinary, if uniquely bizarre, powers. For not only did he have an unerring geographical relationship with the people around him and with his surroundings in general—sensing the chair, moving it easily, knowing precisely where there was a hand to be shaken, understanding exactly where were the eyes his own sightless ones needed to 'look' into—but also, despite all of this supernatural power, to Viktorov's mind, Balthasar's real value was not that he could 'see' physical objects without seeing. It was that he could do what no eye and no electronic device could do—no matter how sharp or sophisticated. He had the ability of seeing inside the minds of those he was with. He had a sixth sense and maybe—who knew—a seventh and an eighth.

Viktorov cast his mind back thirty-nine years. The brothers of Balthasar's mother who he, Viktorov, had rescued him from all those years ago had said he'd had a defect. They'd interpreted his blindness as being cursed by God. This 'defect' had turned out to be a most precious, a most unique weapon. God had given him something far greater than normal sight. As it turned out, God had blessed, not cursed him.

Balthasar approached his father and, with the same direct accuracy, shook his hand, 'looked' in his eyes, and exchanged a welcome. To Viktorov, he seemed to be in some official position in this room—that was what his son's demeanour suggested. He appeared to be at the heart of the purpose of the strange meeting. Viktorov wondered why he hadn't known before about

Balthasar's presence. He was the chief of Department S, for God's sake.

So. This morning was the prime minister's party and his own position could be, and often was, usurped by Putin and a few others. Yet what did Balthasar have to do with the message on the table? The map? Ukraine was an Orthodox Christian country. Not Balthasar's area of operations at all. Balthasar was in Islamic operations, pure and simple. Ukraine was the birthplace of Russian Orthodoxy, the origins of old Rus. Ukraine was Russia's spiritual heartbeat.

'Look at this,' he said, pointing at the map, and then immediately felt foolish to be using a word that assumed working sight.

'I know.' Balthasar smiled, ignoring the mistake. He put his hand on the map, as if he could actually feel the terrain it represented. 'Ukraine,' he said simply.

If Viktorov thought he would draw out his son's reasons for being here by referring to the map of Ukraine, he was unsuccessful.

A trolley was now brought in by the two women who had distributed the files. It was 6.45 a.m. and there were several bottles of flavoured vodka and shot glasses on it. Not Golubev's idea of the right time for a drink and the ministry man was showing it with anxious glances. Not Putin's idea either, for that matter, so perhaps that was why Golubev looked so uncomfortable. But the glasses were distributed solemnly—like some sort of pseudo-religious, regimental ceremonial—by a one-legged *spetsnaz* hero who was apparently determined to show his infirmity made no difference. The toast, when it was raised by a fellow SVR general, was to

'Historic Russia'. All present drank and placed their glasses back on to the trolley which was wheeled away. One drink for the toast, that was it. The party, such as it was, was over. And they all knew that historic Russia meant Kiev, the capital of a Ukraine which had been independent from Moscow now for twenty years, after centuries of occupation.

Golubev's phone rang. He walked away from Viktorov and Balthasar, who reminisced in quiet voices. When he returned, he looked only at the generals, Viktorov and Antonov.

'You'll have to read it on the road,' Golubev said to the two generals, nodding at the document, and he clicked the mobile phone shut. 'The prime minister is delayed. He asks you to come to his dacha.'

As the Mercedes swung out of the gates and took the autoroute back to the ring road, Viktorov thought that none of this—the apparently pointless trip to Balashiha, the meeting with the veterans and even the enforced shared trip with Antonov—was unplanned. Clearly he would be expected to work with Antonov and the meeting at Balashiha was in the style of an underground regimental get-together, something like Nazi SS officers meeting in secret at inns in the depths of the Harz forest after the war. Except that here it was official and government backed. The *Patriotiy* were the establishment.

They were met at the imposing gates of Putin's dacha by a Kremlin car which would take them up the drive to the dacha where Putin worked, swam and practised judo. His family dacha was hidden further into the forest.

Inside the high reception room the two generals stood. Still they didn't talk. Finally after nearly half an hour, they were summoned to a long, lavishly furnished office the size of a small ballroom where Putin was sitting at a desk under the Russian eagle. He motioned them to seats in front of the desk, then, without preamble, leaned on his elbows with his hands clasped together and stared his blank, unblinking stare.

'We need greater co-operation,' he said. 'This war between two great services has to stop.'

Viktorov shifted uncomfortably in his seat. The latest skirmish between the SVR and the GRU had occurred just three weeks before, in Germany. The SVR had betrayed two agents of the GRU to the German intelligence service. Their reason was—from the SVR's point of view—that the GRU was transgressing on its own patch.

'We have important work to do,' Putin said. 'And I need full co-operation. Your jobs are at stake. Russia's future is at stake.'

The generals inclined their heads. Putin didn't seek a reply. Then he leaned in closer. 'The report,' he said. 'Read it closely. Elections in Ukraine take place in just over a week's time. The final run-off is three weeks after that. But the elections are irrelevant. Whoever wins, we want to make our arrangements with our friends in Ukraine. Redress the balance.' He looked severely at them and Viktorov wondered, not for the first time, if Putin actually didn't have any eyelids, if he was like a snake. Putin leaned back in his chair and stared at the two generals. 'You know, of course,' he said with finality, 'that Ukraine is not even a state.'

CHAPTER TWO

8 January 2010

The head rested gently between two reinforced glass clamps on the glaring white surface of a disinfected plastic tabletop. The table had gleaming, skeletal aluminium legs protruding beneath it and its aluminium wheels were locked in place at the bottom of the legs in the unlikely event that the trolley might roll away on the perfectly level, spotlessly clean, white floor.

The chill in the laboratory storage facility at the CIA's Forensic Investigation Department in Langley, Virginia was almost as great as the freezing winter temperatures outside the building and the two men and one woman who stood closest to the trolley table were still wrapped in the thick winter coats they'd worn for the short walk across the car park to the building. Three white-coated laboratory workers who stood behind them like pagan ceremonial guardians of the severed head wore Arctic thermal wear in here, for the greater freedom of movement of their arms.

The head was indeed like the graven image of some ancient god. Though it was a thing of flesh, it was not a thing of blood. Its dull, lifeless, fish eyes in the grey, dead flesh seemed to bring the temperature down still lower, as if temperature were a kind of mood that fitted the sombre circumstances.

The head had a plump face which showed a round-cheeked man, with bristling black eyebrows, slightly frosted from the deep frozen drawer that had contained it until the visitors' arrival. The bloodless lips were generous, the ears looked almost enormous. There was a scar on the left cheek that looked more pronounced without any blood flowing beneath the skin around it. The neck, foreshortened by a jagged cutting instrument, was jowly and flabby and the wild thick black hair that topped the head seemed frozen in a concoction of swirls and curlicues, as if the head were a still photograph of a man captured in a high wind.

It looks like a sculpture, Burt Miller thought—though he was thinking, not of a stone god, but of one of the modern pieces the British artist—something-or-other Quinn, he seemed to remember—made and which consisted of a plastic head filled with the artist's own blood. But the colour of the flesh, Burt mused with an art historian's appreciation, was more like the grey, dead-looking humanity to be found in a Lucian Freud, one of whose works Burt owned—at a cost from Christie's in New York of something in the region of ten million bucks.

'So, Theo . . .' Burt said breezily, exhaling a slightly frosted breath. Then, sticking to the modern art similes that continued to come and go in his mind, he said, 'Exhibit A.'

Theo Lish, the CIA chief, drew his coat further around his neck. 'Exhibit A–Z actually,' Lish replied moodily. 'It's all we have, Burt.'

'Not the usual headless corpse, but the less common corpseless head,' Burt said lightly and with his usual upbeat view of any situation that presented itself to him, no matter how complex and inconvenient it was. 'It's a message, then.'

'Presumably,' Lish said with a nod. 'They want us to know the man's identity. That's the significance.'

Burt looked to his left at Anna Resnikov, the only woman present in the lab. 'Normally, in an identification parade, we'd have half a dozen severed heads for you,' Burt joked. 'I guess the others just never turned up. You've got to up your fees if you want these identity parades to make a difference, Theo,' he said, turning back to Lish.

But his gaze returned to rest on Anna.

She didn't return his look. Either she wasn't amused or she was staring so hard at the head on the table that she hadn't heard his little witticism. That was the reason she was here, after all—to study, identify, bring her knowledge to bear. For she was not just Burt's highly valued lieutenant in his vast private intelligence empire that went under the cheekily named Cougar Intelligence Applications, she was also a former colonel in the KGB and—until her defection—right at its dark intelligence heart, Department S.

'How did it get here, Theo?' Burt asked, looking back to the CIA chief again.

'It was delivered to the home of one of our junior embassy officers in Kiev,' he replied. 'Young man, name of Bill Singleton, married, two small children.'

'What about security?' Burt shot back.

'In Ukraine all our staff houses have cameras, security alarms, early warning systems, sensors— you name it. The usual, in terms of the bare minimum. But Kiev isn't high up on the list as far as security threats are concerned. This'—he indicated the severed head with a nod from his own living one, '. . . this was left in the garden, actually, not the house,' he said by way of correction. 'The person who placed it there was caught on camera, but set off no sensors. Not close enough to the house, apparently. The film shows a man, we presume, wearing a balaclava. He enters the garden, carefully removes the head of the Singleton children's snowman, drops this one out of a sack, and replaces the snow head with it. The four-year-old daughter of the family found it next morning. Someone had been tampering with the family's snowman and she was outraged—in tears.' Lish sighed. 'Clearly it was delivered in that particular place because security allowed it to be. We don't have—or need—razor wire-topped, twelve-foot walls for all our Kiev embassy staff. But it was clearly left for us. So, yes, it's a message. They want us to know who it is.'

'And then?'

'Singleton called our embassy sweepers in straightaway. We kept the head in the freezer until it could be put on a NATO bus that was flying into Kiev from Afghanistan for refuelling that morning. It was here twenty hours later. Left as a decoration on a snowman on Thursday night—in this here laboratory by today at six a.m.'

'And if you know who the man is,' Burt said, 'what's the purpose of Anna's presence? What's she here to identify?'

He looked at her again to find she was tracing the man's scar with her finger, not quite touching the flesh, and her face only an inch or two from the head. Then she stepped back for another overall reappraisal. Burt was keen now to head for lunch, but it looked like that was some way off.

'He goes by the name of Yuri Saltyakov,' Lish explained. 'He approached one of our operatives in Kiev three weeks ago saying he had "information". We checked him out on all the Agency photo and data bases. No tags. Nothing. Nothing in London, either. Adrian was very obliging. No match to anyone we know. His story was that he had information on work being carried out at Novorossiysk port on the Russian side of the Kerch Straits, opposite the Crimea. He was a dock worker there, according to him. Wanted to sell us his story. But we never received any of the information about the port. His main interest to us was that he seemed to have quite detailed information about a ship called the *Forburg*. He described it as a "terror ship", whatever that means. We never got out of him what he meant about that either; was it carrying nuclear fissile material, nuclear triggers, other high-grade weapons, anthrax . . . who knows? We don't. We tracked the *Forburg*, however, having eventually picked it up on the Worldview Satellite off the coast of Burgas, in Bulgaria, to the western end of the Black Sea. The *Forburg* seemed to be heading for the Bosphorus, then presumably the Mediterranean, unless Istanbul was its destination, or it turned off early.' Lish paused, perhaps embarrassed by what he then had to say. 'Because then,' he finally continued, 'God knows how, but we lost the damn ship. That was three days ago. Radio contact disappears, somehow the satellite loses it. Presumably, again, it goes into port and reappears under new guise, or more probably does all that changeover at sea under cover of cloud, night, a giant mosquito net—all three . . . I've no idea. But it does disappear. Twenty-four hours later the head of the man who gave us the information turns up.'

Burt watched Anna. She was curling back one of the thick lips from the opened mouth. She was peering inside the mouth. Then she spoke for the first time. 'Russian dental work,' she said without looking at either of them.

She was, as always, Burt thought admiringly, completely unimpressed by anything or anyone, even here at the Agency's HQ.

'That's what we concluded,' Lish agreed. 'But we assume his name isn't Yuri Saltyakov and we have no other leads. That's why we wanted you to come in, Anna. On the off chance.' He looked at Burt. 'Thank you for being so prompt.'

'Happy to oblige, Theo,' Burt said magnanimously, allowing the implication of Cougar always being there, ready and helpful, to get the CIA out of a spot of difficulty, to hang gently in the air.

'He's Russian,' Anna said. 'But they left just the head because his hands would show he wasn't a dock worker. And a head is easier to transport. So it probably came from the south of the country. Not Kiev, but the Crimea itself, perhaps.'

'Perhaps,' Lish said uncertainly, slightly fazed by an analysis he hadn't, so far, received from any of his own team. 'Do you recognise him, Anna? Anything you can help us with?'

'No,' she replied. 'I've never seen him, or a picture of him, before.' Her voice measured, giving nothing away. You would never penetrate her thoughts, Burt told himself, unless she wanted you

42

to.

Burt looked at her quizzically. 'Sure?' he said.

'Yes. Sure.' She was looking at the place where the neck had been cut. 'It's not a Russian execution,' she said. There was a long pause in the room. 'Or, at least, it's not meant to look like a Russian execution,' she finally added.

Burt looked sharply at her this time, but he didn't want to pursue the implications of these appended words in front of Lish. That would be something for him and Anna alone, later.

'What kind of an execution is it?' Theo Lish enquired.

'It's like something the Chechens do,' she replied. 'It's a specifically Islamic execution. Or that's how it's meant to look,' she added, reinforcing the doubts she had already expressed.

Lish enquired no further.

They went upstairs in a warm elevator to the ground floor and all three loosened their coats until they'd warmed up enough to remove them.

'I'm going to have a chat with Theo,' Burt said to Anna. 'Do you mind waiting?'

She didn't mind. She never minded what was happening, Burt thought. It was his view of the world exactly. All that's important is what's happening. Forget the rest.

In an office on the fourth floor, which was not Lish's but which he cleared of two young men in crisp white shirts and ties, Lish sat in a swivel chair and offered Burt a comfortable-looking sofa that was more suited to his bulk.

'Do you have a decent cognac?' Burt asked, without a great deal of hope.

'I don't think we do, Burt,' Lish replied with a

softly apologetic tone, and Burt felt satisfactorily confirmed in his decision to leave the CIA ten years before, after a glittering career, in order to set up a private intelligence company awash with decent cognac and, more importantly, awash with government contract money.

He'd served with Lish in the Agency for many decades, more than three, anyway. They'd joined together back in the sixties—Burt, the maverick operative, Theo, the meticulous bureaucrat. Then Burt had left, sensing new opportunities for intelligence-gathering in the modern world. Three years into Cougar's existence, the company was turning over two billion dollars a year in the wake of 9/11, on the basis of several healthy government contracts. And then he'd lured Lish away from a senior Agency position in order to head up Cougar's Eastern European Section. Three years after that, Cougar was turning over twice that sum, nearly four billion dollars. Two years after *that*, Lish had returned to the CIA, with Burt's blessing, as its director, its chief, the Agency's main man who had the president's ear on all foreign security matters. But now he was Cougar's main man too, at the pinnacle of the government-run intelligence establishment that filled DC like an undigested meal. After Lish became CIA director, government contracts to Cougar increased and Cougar became the largest private intelligence agency in the world. And into the bargain Cougar quickly made itself indispensable to the CIA.

Burt settled comfortably into a pile of cushions. 'Ukraine,' he said. 'Cougar has a watch on Ukraine, Theo. Up-coming elections. As it happens, I was already sending Anna over there,

44

anyway—down to the Crimea too,' Burt announced. 'We have some other business to conclude in Ukraine's south-eastern sector. Crimea is its Achilles heel, if you like. And now it sounds like we have new work to do.'

'Why on earth send *her*?' Lish said. He was aghast. After the KGB's attempt on her life in Washington just over a year before, it was clear she wasn't even completely safe in America, and under Cougar's massive protection to boot.

'Because she's the best, Theo,' Burt said patiently.

'She's also on the KGB's most-wanted list. She was almost assassinated on our ground, Burt. For God's sake, she'll be wandering around in Ukrainian territory where you know there's a high-profile KGB presence. With their Black Sea fleet based there, the Russians are crawling all over Sevastopol. The base is also an excuse for them to insert all kinds of other, unconnected operations into the country. The place is completely porous to Russian operatives. She shouldn't be going.'

'Spoken like her fairy godfather, Theo,' Burt said. Then he sighed contentedly. 'But that's the deal made by her, not me. She's only mine—only Cougar's—if she's allowed to operate in the field, and against Russia. Otherwise I lose her and I can't afford to do that. I give her what she demands, that's all.'

'What's she going to do?' Lish said, exasperated. 'Go on fighting the Russians until she's scaling the walls of the Kremlin with grappling hooks?'

Burt chortled. 'Maybe, Theo, maybe. But she's grown-up enough to make her own decisions. And I can't afford to lose her.'

45

'Her recklessness is getting to be of comic book proportions,' Lish said. 'We could never employ her here, you know.'

'That's a lie and you know it,' Burt said good-humouredly. 'You'd snap her up immediately if she were free.'

Lish huffed. Burt was right. She was gold. But he was thinking of another argument. 'What about her child?' he said, going off on this new tack. 'Doesn't she want to stay alive at least for him?'

'We gave her boy a new identity,' Burt replied.

'I know. You told me.'

'He lives with a new family now, three half-siblings, on a nice farm in Connecticut. Four years old, or coming up. She goes to visit him once a month.' He looked directly at Lish. 'But the boy needs a new life whether she's working or not, Theo. It's irrelevant if she's a fully-engaged operative scaling the walls of the Kremlin, or a kitchen gardener producing new strains of purple broccoli. Either way, the KGB won't rest until they have her. Her picture is used for target practice out at The Forest. They hate her, and they're vindictive enough to let that obscure their vision.' He smiled. 'That's good. That plays in our and her favour. Aside from her obvious—and huge—talents, in some ways the Kremlin's hatred offers her a small amount of protection. They want her alive now—that's the information coming out of Moscow. They want her to be an example, not in public, perhaps, but in the intelligence community. They want to display her and that gives her a little immunity—at least from a bullet in the head in some backstreet.' Burt heaved himself sideways and his bulk crushed another part of the sofa. 'So

46

she may as well have a crack at the Russians since they'll be after her anyway. As we've already seen, her son is a vulnerable part of any trap they might set to get their hands on her. She knows his safety is assured if he's far enough away from her. And she knows she's lost him—effectively.'

'That's sad.' Unlike Burt, Lish was a confirmed Christian family man who saw most of the problems in the world as arising out of family dysfunction.

'And it's a fact,' Burt replied stolidly. 'We can't ignore the facts, Theo. So she pursues her revenge against her former masters in any way she likes, as far as I'm concerned. She's the best.'

'You think it's revenge? For her man they murdered? For Finn?'

'Partly,' Burt said, but he was deep in thought now. 'But in my opinion it's not revenge for Finn alone. Or even *mainly* about revenge for Finn.' Burt clasped his hands over his generous stomach. 'You know, Theo, for Anna, Finn was just the wrench that got her out of Russia. Sure, she loved him, maybe he was the only man she ever loved. But leaving Russia to make her life with the Brit wasn't just about her and him falling in love. For Anna, there was a far greater question that filled her skies. A decisive break from her background, her father, the regime in Moscow, the organisation she so successfully worked for. In her mind, coming to the West was a decision in favour of life rather than of half-life. It was about the shedding of entrenched and decomposed ideas, like a snake sloughing off its coat. It was complete reinvention. It was about the destruction of the social, political and family DNA that held her in its prison. Above

47

all, it was an act of extreme, risk-taking bravery. Finn was just the key that opened the door.'

'But what's the change? She's still doing the same damn job,' Lish protested, exasperated now. 'Just for our side, that's all.'

'She's smart. She knows it's what she does best,' Burt said simply. His mind turned to lunch once again. 'And she likes her steaks underdone, with or without purple broccoli,' he added.

And then Burt apparently tired of explaining the motives of the best operative he'd ever had in all of his long career, and he began to lay out for Theo Lish the real purpose of their little chat in this office. Apropos of the severed head and not, as with Anna's trip, pre-planned at all, he was also sending Logan Halloran to Ukraine. He ignored Theo's raised eyebrows. Separately from Anna's assignment, he told Theo that while the three of them had been in the laboratory, looking at the head, he'd decided Halloran would be going to Kiev.

He explained to Theo why he was sending Halloran, and that he wanted Halloran to have all the cooperation the CIA station in Kiev could give. Theo raised his eyebrows still higher. Burt explained that—who knew?—maybe the *Forburg* would turn out to be connected in some way to 'other stuff', as he put it vaguely. Maybe Halloran's mission to Kiev would dovetail with the story behind the appearance and then the disappearance of the *Forburg*. He artfully painted a picture of a fascinating possible array of connections and coincidences, real or imagined. Then, once more, he threw in Anna's assignment to the Crimea, pre-planned though it was, as another useful feeler worth extending in the hunt for the *Forburg*. Look for the connections, he said to Lish, even if it's only to eliminate them. As luck would have it, he said in conclusion to this pitch, his two most experienced field operatives in the Eastern European and Russian sectors would be on the spot. One in Kiev, the other in the Crimea. We'll find the *Forburg*, he concluded triumphantly. We'll track down this terror ship together, Theo. Burt now used the dead man's words as if they were gospel.

And now too, suddenly, the *Forburg* began to take form, as if the ship itself were appearing through a thick sea fret. It was a full-blooded terror ship now, not just in the opinion of some dead and little-known Russian operative whose severed head lay propped up on a table four floors below. But it was so in the opinion of the great Burt Miller, the intelligence guru who had the ear not just of Theo Lish—and through him to the president—but of most of the senators on the Intelligence Committee whom Cougar had carefully lobbied over the years and who also represented the interests of Cougar in Washington's intelligence hothouse. And when he'd established his position where the 'terror ship' was concerned, finally Burt wove a tapestry of co-operation and success between Cougar and the CIA which would bring glory to them both.

More or less in parenthesis, Burt then told Lish, in detail, what he wanted from the CIA and he eventually received a nod of agreement from the CIA boss—and his former employee. Lish's eyebrows, it seemed, could go no higher without taking leave of his head altogether.

CHAPTER THREE

Saturday, 16 January 2010

The moment she stepped off the boat, Anna Resnikov knew that she was being followed. They must have been tailing her when she'd boarded the ferry in Istanbul. One man, maybe more than one, she wasn't sure. But her conviction that she was observed came neither from belief nor suspicion, both of which were to her subtle distractions that she swiftly discarded in any analysis. She either knew something or she didn't, and in this case she knew.

She reached the foot of the clanking, rusted metal steps that led from the upper deck of the *Kalydonia* ferry to the dock and then waited in line with the other passengers on the windswept quay at Odessa's customs and border post.

It was 16 January. Tomorrow would be the first round of the presidential elections in Ukraine. That was a mere coincidence, as far as she was concerned. She had come to the country for another reason. She had come to make a contact.

There would be a prearranged drop-off, and then, if all went well, she would make the pick-up. If things went according to plan then it would be a two-to four-day round-trip for only a few minutes of active engagement. Her assignment was to return with documents—they were military blueprints, Burt Miller had told her. In any case, they were the kind of documents that could only be delivered by hand and not electronically, even if that were advisable in the porous world of electronic communication. The provenance of the documents she was to pick up was an agent of Burt's company Cougar Intelligence Applications, in Moscow. He was someone senior at the Naval Ministry, she'd been told. Someone high-up, she'd worked that out, and a former naval man, Burt had said, as well as a core KGB officer who had turned against his country and now supplied information to Cougar. But it wouldn't be the agent himself who made the delivery. The agent would have a courier and he or she would be making the drop.

Anna cast her eye around her fellow passengers in a non-committal way as she waited in the line on the quay. There were mostly Ukrainians and Russians who had been on the boat's manifest, returning from temporary jobs in Turkey or from shopping at the duty free malls in Istanbul with their greater choice of international brands. There were also a few Turks who, no doubt, had business of one kind or another in Odessa. Odessa had once belonged—way back in its history—to the Ottoman empire, the Porte of the Sultan, and the Turks still plied their trade here. But there were no tourists on the boat at this time of year. Odessa was a seaside holiday destination that burst into life in the spring and summer. Now, in January, the boat was only half full.

After taking a casual look at the passengers nearest to her, Anna didn't look around any further to spot who it was who was tailing her. She just waited quietly in the line. She'd seen nobody observing her on the boat but, nevertheless, she knew now. The line shortened and she neared the front—and the border post. She wondered if they

51

would act now before she was through. Most likely they would wait, she thought. Those would be their orders, she was now sure of that too.

At just under six feet in height, and with long legs that might easily give the impression she was an athlete or a dancer, she was taller than most of the others in the line. And she was evidently a lot fitter, more alert. Any other person feeling they were being watched would have been nervous, would have looked around, wanting to be sure, to see the evidence. But Anna didn't just act the part of unconcern—she was supremely aware of the danger of her situation—she actually *was* unconcerned. In her core, she knew any anxiety now would interfere with the clear passage of her thoughts. Hers was a cold awareness.

She distrusted belief and suspicion. They were the crevices into which the credulous and ignorant fell. For an operative, they might easily prove fatal and for a long time Anna had left such things to others. Belief—and disbelief, for that matter—she viewed as a decadent luxury for those free from imminent threat. And suspicion was just another fallible mental process that confused fact with fear. Fear was the enemy, in any walk of life, but particularly in hers.

Now, as she reached the head of the line, the Ukrainian border guard almost snatched her false American passport, then studied it closely and made a great play of staring at her face. It was a face that men stared at without such an excuse; a face with a pronounced bone structure that took the eye from her curved, full mouth over a fine Slavic nose to the high cheekbones on either side, and then to her eyes, deep blue and penetrating, so that the guard found he could not look back into them for very long. She had blond hair, cut to the top of her shoulders, and it hung in a single thick fold. She stared back at him and, for a moment, he felt as if it were she who was deciding whether to admit him in to her country, rather than the other way around.

But though she stared back at him, she barely noticed him. The danger—if any existed at this moment—was behind her, not from the guards at the post. They would be Russians behind her and who were watching her, not Ukrainians. Hers was now a purely animal reaction, tensed, ready for action. It was a sense that existed somewhere beyond her five regular senses, that bypassed unreliable mental processes and was hard-wired to certainty. Someone was watching her and they were watching her, not like the guard, for how she looked, but because they were under orders to follow her.

After much exaggerated raising of his eyebrows and rocking back in his seat, without a smile the border guard finally allowed her through and on to the territory of Ukraine.

She casually slung her backpack over her shoulders and looked ahead towards the town. Beyond the border post, there was a wide boulevard that ran perpendicularly along the whole length of the quay. On the far side of the boulevard, she saw a small cobbled lane that ran up a hill through the old port and into the town. She crossed the boulevard and entered the lane.

With the knowledge that she was being watched came a sort of calm. She now let her mind relax and her tensed muscles followed. She continued to walk purposefully up the short hill, leaving the boat and its passengers behind her. She looked neither right nor left nor behind her. She didn't need to see the tail yet. She was only thinking of one thing at this moment; that it always made things more straightforward once a potential assassin—or maybe there was more than one out there in the city's undergrowth—came to you.

Throughout the voyage from Istanbul she had remained mostly in her cabin, emerging only very early in the morning at the restaurant for breakfast or in the quiet hours after midnight below decks, behaving in a manner that any observer would, perhaps, have described as pacing or even prowling. Otherwise she'd had food and drink sent down to her first-class accommodation. A storm had lashed the Black Sea for the duration of the crossing—it had been an uncomfortable voyage—and, like her, many of the passengers had stayed out of sight. Her absence wasn't noticeable. The upper deck, the sea deck, had anyway been put out of bounds by the captain due to the storm, and the regular partying and drinking that was a common feature on the crossing to Odessa was muted.

At the top of the short hill that led from the harbour she came to an intersection of the cobbled lane with a main thoroughfare and she crossed to the other side. Even bending her head and now covered with a long hooded jacket that came halfway to her knees, she was a commanding figure compared to the other pedestrians. On this crowded boulevard her height was distinctive. But it was the way she walked that drew attention as much as anything else. She walked with a smooth stride as if on a long trek, and she seemed to insinuate herself along the pavement, as if her feet barely touched the ground. Hers was a cat-like walk. Prowling was not a bad description.

Bare trees, their branches carefully pruned back to the trunks, lined this second boulevard on both sides. She looked curiously to left and right. She hadn't been in Odessa for several years, from before the time she'd defected from the KGB. But Odessa was as she remembered it had always been: a stylish city, its pride deriving from its past first as a Russian imperial naval base, then from its heroic Soviet resistance against the Nazis when much of the whole city had been destroyed. More recently, since Ukraine's independence in 1991, this proud history had come to be mixed with modernising influences that sought to bring the city into the twenty-first century. A civic pride that actually derived from the city's military standing bloomed here, publicly on the streets, more than in most post-Soviet cities.

Despite her commanding presence, she lost herself head down in the crowds of pedestrians. The clean, swept streets were busy at this time of the morning. People were going to work. Like her they also walked head down in the rain, and those who passed her on the pavements were huddled up in coats and hats. It had started to rain as she got off the boat but now it was coming down harder. She pulled the hood of her jacket further over her forehead. She walked along the busy morning pavement quickly.

It was time to take matters into her own hands. If they hadn't stopped her at the border post, it was a virtual certainty that her observers were not from the SBU, the Ukrainian secret service. In which case, they must be Russian. Of that she was sure now. They would need to conceal their activities from the sovereign Ukrainian guards, on whose sovereign territory they were conducting their operation. She decided she would find a narrow, uncrowded space now. That way it would be easier to identify her tail.

As soon as she saw an alley that led off to the left between two nineteenth-century buildings—two of the few that had survived the Nazi onslaught in the Great Patriotic War—she turned into it and quickened her pace, feeling the eyes upon her. She walked fast, still not looking behind her, betraying no anticipation, let alone fear, until the alley dog-legged to the right and she could stand out of sight from her pursuers behind a stone-porticoed entrance from where mildewed steps led down to a dank basement filled with bags of uncollected rubbish.

She carefully watched back up the length of the alley towards the boulevard from where she had turned off. She could just see the boulevard now, framed by the narrow entrance to the alley. And there in the frame she saw there were two men who had entered the alley and whom she could just see only from the edges of their flapping coats. They'd stopped, she saw. No doubt there would be others out there. Six or more, maybe up to twelve in a full-blown operation and, for the prize of having her, the KGB might just be throwing in everything.

She craned further out from behind the pillar. The men were talking to each other, not facing down the alley towards her. One of the men wore a grey cap and a khaki coat and his black hair came out over the collar. The other had a longer, black raincoat and wore a fur hat. The men were talking urgently, one also into a mobile phone, and then the one with the fur hat finally turned down the alley in her direction. Anna descended the steps to the basement and waited.

Less than a minute later she caught the sound of the man tailing her as his raincoat swished in the downpour that was now hitting the alleyway above her head. She heard his shoes slapping against the wet paving stones. She emerged from the cover of the basement on to the steps. From the back as he passed, she saw his coat flapping back over itself in the wind and the fur hat spotted with rain. He had passed her by.

One of these two men whom she'd seen on the street would be on the bus later, or maybe they would send a third man who hadn't been exposed in the street. She decided now to lower the odds against her.

She left her pack in the basement and climbed back up. Emerging from the steps that led up from the dank basement, she walked behind the man, closing the distance rapidly. The alley ahead narrowed between two high buildings so that it was only wide enough for one person. She looked behind her for the first time. There was no one else in sight. She saw the man hesitate where the alley narrowed, wondering perhaps whether to continue through the narrowed passage or to contact his colleague first. He came to a halt and, as he started to turn—perhaps sensing a presence behind him—she put her left hand around his eyes, digging her fingers into them, and her right forearm into the nape of his neck. Preoccupied with the agony in his eyes—and before he could struggle enough to dislodge her—in a swift, jerking motion she had bent his neck back over her forearm and snapped it with a dull sound like the breaking of a damp stick.

She quickly dragged the body into another basement, hauling it down more moss-covered and mildewed stone steps, and dumped it behind some ancient piles of building material leaning up in a corner, which were disgorging their contents of solidified plaster and cement. Then she rifled through the pockets of the man's jacket beneath the black raincoat. There was an FSB identity card. They were Russian intelligence, as she'd assumed. She took the card and a gun that was loose in the inside jacket pocket and then carefully mounted the stairs. She was glad of the gun. The way she had come into the country through a legal border post meant that it had been impossible to be properly armed. She looked both ways up and down the alley. There was still nobody visible. She picked up her backpack from the first basement and then she walked back up the alley from where she had come and back again on to the boulevard.

She knew she should abort the assignment now, save herself as best she could. That would have been what Burt would have ordered. He hadn't wanted her to take the assignment in the first place. It was too dangerous, for her in particular— a former KGB colonel and a defector on the KGB's most wanted list—to go anywhere near the territory of Russia. But she'd insisted on it, threatening to resign and leave the employ of Burt's intelligence company, Cougar. Burt didn't want to lose her from this vast intelligence organisation—an empire that now challenged the CIA in its breadth and influence—and she'd banked on that. She knew Burt wouldn't have dared to risk her leaving Cougar. He didn't want another agency—the CIA itself had courted her regularly—to gain her talents, and so he'd reluctantly acquiesced.

But, in any case, Burt wasn't here, in Odessa. She calculated the risks. She accepted at once that either they would follow her to the bus, or they already knew she would be taking it. They'd known she would be on the boat, that was for sure. If they knew, too, that she was heading for the bus, then there was unmistakably a leak, and she faced greater danger than she was in already. But if they'd known she was on the boat, there was probably a leak anyway.

Suddenly she felt an unwelcome memory returning. It was the first time she had been this close to Russia since her defection four years before. A memory of why she had left back then began to surface in her mind—of her father, the retired General Resnikov, and her hatred of him; of the spies with whom she'd once worked and who had now once again taken control of the country she loved; of the evil nexus of the spies and their mafia allies who sought to subjugate the Russian people under their jackboot. And then she thought of her grandmother who had died two years before, and of her mother who had finally left her father and was working for the Sakharov Foundation. Women—it was usually women—who seemed to be the good people. But then she repressed the memories that threatened to divert her from her task.

59

The bus station was situated at the side of the railway terminus where trains departed for Kiev to the north. A few dilapidated buses stood with their engines running, rain pouring down the windscreens. The rain was now cascading in rivers along the sloping gutters and there was a huge pool where a drain must have been blocked. She watched the ticket office, cast her eyes across the expanse of concrete, looked for the destination signs, and then saw the bus that would take her to Sevastopol. For a second time, she questioned the wisdom of going through with it now. Her arrival was blown, but was the pick-up in Sevastopol compromised also? Would she be able to evade her pursuers? Or did they know about the pick-up too? And then, decided, she walked across several lanes, past the waiting buses to the ticket office, and bought a return ticket.

The slow, ancient bus departed twenty minutes late for the twelve-hour journey and wound its way out of Odessa to the east. Low grey cloud hung over the mountains until the country was closed in by its embrace. Beneath the clouds a fine spray of mist came in off the sea. There was no view either of the sea or the land. Everything existed at close quarters. Her mind similarly ratcheted down to the immediate: a field outside Sevastopol, with coordinates provided and memorised, just beyond the edge of the town; a stone barn that stored root vegetables and perhaps the odd piece of agricultural equipment; and a courier she would never see, the agent's cut-out who would make the drop.

She took a seat near the driver in order to be the first out, knowing that behind her was a watcher, and perhaps more than one. The bus's heater wheezed, and pumped a mixture of engine oil and stifling air into the enclosed space. They wouldn't make a move yet—her watchers—she knew that now. They would want to know why she was here in Ukraine. The real prize for them was certainly her. The KGB had been obsessed with finding her for more than four years. But first they would want to discover who she was meeting and what she had come to find. She would have to lose them once the bus reached Sevastopol—unless she lost them before her destination. Above all she had to protect the courier, their link with the agent. But that was twelve hours away over the long slow bus route to and then across the Crimea.

The seats were small and the bus full. She was squeezed on the window side next to a man in a thick padded jacket and workman's boots. He fell asleep almost immediately. On the seats directly across the aisle were two plump women. She guessed from their rural appearance that they came from a village along the way. They talked purposefully to one another, never pausing. She didn't look behind at anyone else seated on the bus. For a while she pretended to doze, but she remained alert for any movement in the aisle. Time stood still.

The bus climbed and descended the undulating land, stopping at a few villages and sometimes out in the middle of nowhere, until they reached Nikolayev. There was a stop for fifteen minutes and Anna watched the two women, but while one or two passengers boarded or got off the bus the two women stayed where they were, chatting endlessly. Then they set off again, across the

61

Roskovsky Straits at Kherson. There was another stop there and then another stop and another leg to the bridge on to the Crimea at Krasnoperekopsk. As they entered the Crimea, they were about two-thirds of the way to Sevastopol.

After nearly two hours beyond the city of Krasnoperekopsk, and now well into the Crimea, the bus pulled into a service station at a remote crossroads that served as a stop. They would have the usual fifteen minutes, the driver said. There was a grim-looking café and a couple of pumps. The two women across the aisle from her picked up half a dozen heavy plastic bags and made for the door. It was their stop, she realised.

Anna put on her backpack and got off the bus quickly in order to catch up with the slow-moving women. They were now walking in a waddling motion from side to side with the weight of their bags. They were still talking without pause. A change of plan, Anna decided, a change of mind. That was a sign of intelligence, to be able to change your mind. When she drew level with the women, she smiled at them and offered to carry some of their bags. The women were struggling to keep hold of everything.

'I've come to visit my grandmother,' she said.

As she took three of the bags she still didn't look behind her. She would leave them to guess whether or not she was aware of their presence.

Around the rear of the service station, there was an ancient pick-up with peeling dark red paint, where the bare metal itself wasn't showing through. It had its engine running for warmth. One of the two women indicated that the truck was where they were going. A man was sitting in the driver's seat, Anna now saw—a brother, a husband, perhaps?

'Where are you going?' Anna asked.

'Voronki,' one of the women replied.

'I'm going to Vihogradovo,' Anna said.

'It's not on our way, dear,' the second woman replied.

'Perhaps you could give me a ride to the Vihogradovo road?'

The women didn't know.

The man in the driver's seat didn't get out or offer to help. The women opened the passenger door and put their bags in first, then one of them began to climb in ponderously over the high sill of the truck.

'I'm going to the Vihogradovo road,' Anna said to the driver.

He shrugged. 'These women take up all the room.' They were squeezed on to a double seat next to the driver.

'I can sit in the truck bed.'

He stared at her.

'I'm here to visit my grandmother. She's dying.'

'We're all dying,' the man said.

'Not so quickly, I hope,' she replied.

He didn't take his eyes away from hers. 'You want to sit in the rain?' he said as though he couldn't care less. Then he shrugged again. 'It's up to you,' he said and looked away.

She threw her pack into the back of the truck before he could change his mind and climbed in using the wheel as a step. As the truck pulled away, she looked back for the first time. The second man she had seen in the alley near the boulevard was now talking into a mobile phone. She saw the grey leather cap and the black hair coming out at an angle over the khaki collar. They had lost one man and now they had no back-up but him on the bus. Perhaps there was a vehicle following the bus, but for now he was alone. Like her, they would now have to improvise. The man didn't look at her but she knew it was him.

As the truck pulled away from the main road and up into the hills, the thin mist turned to fog.

The road wound its way through villages and across moorland. The journey was slow, the old truck dropping to low gears for the slightest climb. Two vehicles passed them, though she couldn't identify who was in them. And then after nearly an hour she saw a car, far enough behind them to be tailing the truck. The truck was so slow the car should have overtaken them, but it hung there emerging then disappearing, as the fog rolled across the hills. An hour later the truck she was in came to a crossroads high up in the Crimean peninsula.

The red truck stopped. She glanced back at the car. It had pulled over, just visible where the fog was closing on the road. She looked around for an escape, but she could only see less than a few hundred yards. The land absorbed the colourlessness of winter, but the rain had eased leaving a dampness that hung in the air. The truck was going straight ahead across the road. Anna had told the driver she was going along the road to the left, that was the way to Vihogradovo. She climbed down and the woman sitting nearest to the window opened it.

'Thank you,' Anna said.

'It's another twenty-five kilometres,' the driver replied.

'How will you get to Vihogradovo?' one of the women asked.

'I'll get a ride. If not, I'll walk.'

The driver wasn't going to offer her a ride.

'Good luck,' one of the women said and patted her arm through the open window. The truck pulled away and disappeared over a ridge and into the fog.

She stood alone at the crossroads and looked back. She saw the car pulling out on to the road behind her and watched it approaching slowly. The moment of truth. She saw now that there was only one person inside it. She had upset their plans, confused her pursuers. She waited by the road where it turned to the left on the way to Vihogradovo and the car turned too and began to approach. The man would have to make a decision; drive on by and risk losing her, or stop. If he didn't kill her in the opening few seconds, it would be fatal for him. And she knew they wanted her alive. They'd wanted her alive in the four years since she'd defected from the KGB. She was to be paraded at The Forest before her interrogation began. That they wanted her alive was now their biggest and most deadly weakness.

She put out her hand in the pretence of hitching a ride and the car hesitated. The man was there to watch her, she knew, not to come into contact with her. But then the car pulled over towards the verge and crawled the few yards to where she stood before it stopped. It was the man with the black hair that came over his collar. He wasn't wearing the grey cap now, she saw it on the passenger seat.

65

Through the window, she could see indecision in his eyes. He needed help, orders, this was beyond his knowledge. He didn't want to act alone, or maybe he couldn't. Her approaching him—that was not in the book—she was supposed to be running *from* him, leading him to her secret destination. There was no preparation for this. It seemed that it was suddenly too big for him. And then she saw in his eyes the possibility of personal glory, to be the officer who captured Anna Resnikov.

She opened the passenger door. 'Sevastopol,' she said. 'I'm going to Sevastopol.'

He stared at her and she saw confusion, then fear.

'Can I get in?'

He looked at her wide-eyed as if she were a bomb that was about to go off.

She got into the passenger seat. The other man's gun that she'd taken was hard to draw in the confined space. She slid a knife down her arm invisibly from inside her jacket and into her left hand and, in the same movement, thrust it with the precision of a butcher under the man's ribs on the side of his body furthest away from her, where his heart was. Then she forced it upwards, driving the honed blade into the centre of his heart. He rocked back then forward violently. His fisted hand flailed at her and struck her hard in the face, drawing blood. But his life was already leaving him.

Anna withdrew the knife and climbed out of the car. She wiped her bloodied hand and the blade on the grass and put the knife back into her sleeve. She checked the road was empty and then she hauled the dead body across the seat and out of the open door. She turned out the pockets of his coat: a wallet with an FSB identity card, another gun which she gratefully took, some money and keys. She took the money. Then she dragged the body a few yards on to the grass and left it, deliberately visible from the road. She got back into the car, in the driver's seat, put the car in gear and pulled away.

She drove fast along the road until she saw a farm track a mile or so away and to the left. There were deep tyre marks on the track, from a tractor most likely, and she drove with the car's wheels in the tyre tracks until she found a cutting in the hill to the side where she could conceal the car from the road. She pulled over into the cutting, double-checked that the car couldn't be seen from the road, and closed the door. The man's phone on the dashboard had started to ring. When they found the body, they would look for the car. Their first assumption would have to be that she was driving it towards Sevastopol. She opened the door and disabled the phone, flinging the batteries into a pool of water. Now they couldn't locate the car from his phone.

As soon as she'd got clear of the car, she began to run, up towards a ridge that was slowly forming above her through the fog. She kept running, up through soggy grass meadows and into the hills that rose to the north. It was a long climb that finally took her over a high ridge and down into a valley on the other side. There was a village there, sufficiently far away from the road they'd travelled along, away from any pursuit. And she knew they would look for the car first.

67

Just over an hour after she had been dropped at the crossroads by the truck, she entered the single street of the village. There was a store, a service station with a single pump, some bedraggled scavenging dogs that combed the gutters and doorways. But she saw few people. She entered the service station and inside found a boy, fourteen or fifteen years old, she guessed. She asked him how far it was to Sevastopol.

'Four or five hours if you've got a decent car. There's no bus from here.'

'I need a ride. I'll pay.'

The boy shouted into the back and a man she took to be his father emerged. He wore oily overalls and looked like he'd been fixing a car. He had a bad-tempered expression and said something abrupt to the boy. The boy repeated her request to him, then disappeared into the back, and the man stared at her.

'I can give you a hundred dollars,' Anna said in Ukrainian. 'My grandmother is sick.'

'How did you get here?'

'Friends brought me this far.'

The man looked at the mud on her trousers and at her wet hiking boots. 'Make it a hundred and fifty,' he replied too quickly.

Half an hour later, and having paid in advance, she was on a small rural road that would take them eventually to Sevastopol. The man drove fast and in silence, as if he were unwilling to earn the money, or just disapproved of being paid by a woman.

After driving for nearly five hours, the city of Sevastopol lay in cloud below them. Mountains soared to the north and east. The great natural harbour, gouged eight kilometres into the land, was once the Soviet navy's warm water port. Now it was the naval base for the Russian Black Sea fleet which shared the facilities with their Ukrainian naval counterpart. She saw ships at anchor out in the roads and in the near harbour itself. Other naval vessels were up against the quays or in dry dock. They were the Russian and Ukrainian fleets which now shared the port with an ill grace that was growing by the month into something uglier. It was inevitably a source of tension between Russia and its former possession. Ukraine had won its independence two decades earlier and the Kremlin didn't like it.

The drop was outside the city just beyond the outer limits; a barn in some unfenced fields that climbed the hills fringing the town. Anna told the driver to leave her just over a mile, she guessed, past the track that led up to the barn. By the time he dropped her she was nearer to the centre of town than to the barn. She would walk back once the man had gone.

He turned the van around without a word of goodbye and headed back in the direction from where they'd come. Once he'd disappeared, Anna returned back up the road and walked fast until she found a break between a row of houses. This was the place. She walked behind the houses and, once she was through, she studied the approach to the barn. Then she walked up through the fields beyond the houses until she found a small copse of trees. It was a shelter of sorts, both from the weather and from unfriendly eyes. Later, for the approach, the fog higher up the hill would be good cover. And soon darkness would fall anyway. She decided she would wait until then.

CHAPTER FOUR

Masha Shapko exited from Sevastopol's rail terminus and followed orders. First she took a taxi into the centre of town. She carried a battered black leather bag with its colour fraying down to the bare leather where it had been bent from use and she wore a thick pink padded coat that had faded with age and Moscow's harsh weather. On her head she had a black rabbit fur hat. She was dressed in clothes which had been appropriate for her departure from Moscow two days before. It had been twenty degrees below zero when she'd boarded the train at Kursky railway station.

She followed her orders to the letter: a taxi to the centre of the town, then she would catch a bus towards its western end, then a walk of a few miles until she reached the outskirts of the town. But on the way to the drop, her boss had told her, find the time to stop, to look, to watch. So when the taxi dropped her off on the central boulevard, she stopped at shop windows as she strolled towards the heart of the town. First she entered a second-hand clothing shop, then she bought a coffee at a café in the square and sat away from the window. And all the time she watched for any familiar face from the train or from Sevastopol's rail station. Satisfied at last that she wasn't being followed, she finally moved on to join a line for the local bus that went to the western end of town.

She was late—nearly a day late, in fact. The train had been held up for twenty-four hours as it entered the turbulent regions of the south, where

70

separatists were detonating bombs with regularity. 'A terrorist threat' was the announcement on the train and they'd stayed at a halt on the line and watched the OMON police and local FSB walking beside the tracks, then questioning people on the train. She'd been afraid they'd discover what she was carrying, but her papers were in order, her father was a prominent figure in Moscow's KGB, and she, too, carried an FSB card of her own. They gave her only a cursory check. Four other passengers, without their papers in order, she assumed, had been handcuffed and removed from the train.

Her orders were not to contact her boss in any circumstances. But she knew that the delay was cutting it very fine. Whoever was making the pick-up would be expecting to do so this evening, in a few hours' time, in fact. She knew it was touch and go whether she would make it and, if she did, whether there would be a risk of crossing over with the person, her opposite number. But all she could do now was try, she supposed. Her orders hadn't factored in a twenty-four-hour delay.

She had been well trained in various institutions of the KGB inside Moscow and outside at The Forest. She was still a rookie, certainly, but she'd completed all the basic training required to enter the lowest-ranking echelon of officer recruits from two years before when she'd passed into the intelligence agency with flying colours. She had been top of the class, in fact. After she'd finished school, she'd been educated at the Moscow Power Engineering Institute, intending to become a manager at the national electricity grid. But then, while she was looking at the options, she had been approached by a friend of her KGB father to make an application to join Russia's security services. She was inducted into the FSB after eighteen months of training.

At just over twenty-four years old, she had married a fellow officer recruit two months before. This was her first solo operation and she was proud to be serving her country, without having any idea of what it was she was doing. She had been given no indication of what was concealed in her bag.

She had a small, delicately pretty face with fine features and grey-blue eyes with the depth and intensity of deep ice pools; so her new husband had told her. They were eyes like an Arctic animal's, he'd said, and she assumed the description was one of admiration.

She'd been chosen for this mission, her boss Volkov informed her, for several reasons. One important factor for her cover was that she had family in Ukraine. The family owned a farmhouse outside Sevastopol and that's where the barn was located. It was cover of sorts. And so the ostensible reason for her trip was established as a visit to a cousin, Taras. Though he lived in Kiev, it had been arranged that she would actually meet Taras at a club on Odessa's waterfront by the name of the Golden Fleece. The reason why she was going south, to the Crimea, rather than straight to Kiev, she'd worked out with her boss, after she'd told him about Taras's family's farmhouse. Her cover would be that she was first of all visiting the place of her childhood holidays when she'd stayed with Taras's family outside Sevastopol. Taras's father had bought the farmhouse there as a holiday place, in the 1990s after some post-Soviet business deal. So the trip to the Crimea was to be a detour of fond nostalgia, before heading to Odessa and spending a few days with her cousin.

But there were reasons other than the convenience of the farmhouse for her being picked for the mission. Her boss had also lavished praise on her as an up-coming intelligence officer of a new generation whose rise was guaranteed, he said, not just because of her family connections in the security services, but also due to her own skills and intelligence. Her performance to date had been favourably noted, and Volkov flattered her enough so that she didn't question that she'd been chosen. Promotion—that had been the word her boss had used finally to catch her with. And now, as she sat on the bus that crawled westwards out of the town, she knew she'd certainly like the money promotion would bring. 'It's an easy drop, straightforward,' her boss had told her. 'Just the thing for your first assignment.' The drop was intended as a little help for 'our friends in Ukraine', he'd said. These 'friends' were Russian patriots like her and though, technically, they were of Ukrainian nationality, they shared hers and Moscow's interests. These 'patriots' saw no difference between Russia and Ukraine, he'd said, and rightly wished to return the country to Mother Russia. The Kremlin would know of her mission, her boss finished with a flourish of patriotic fervour. Her mission would therefore be a small feather in her cap, but a feather nevertheless. And Masha had ended up feeling proud to be chosen out of her whole graduate class and to be doing something for the new motherland.

But no operation is ever without risk, her boss had added. She had been issued with a gun, a GSh-18 military pistol, the latest one the GRU used, the military intelligence people. Just a normal precaution, he'd said, but whatever happens, you will avoid being taken alive, he told her gravely. In those circumstances we'd kill you quickly if we could, but they'll take a lot longer, he'd added grimly. They'll want information and they'll never believe you don't know more. That was the nature of torture, he'd said, and it had frightened her, as he'd intended it to.

She felt the gun in the pocket of her coat now. So the gun was only there to use on herself.

The city bus crawled up from the central square, stopping regularly. Mostly there were people getting off. Fewer and fewer boarded as they got closer to the end of the line. Masha held the leather bag close to her, on her lap. She had no idea what it contained, only that a thick, sealed plastic envelope was buried in a small, sealed plastic bag of garden fertiliser inside the case. It was to be left in a barn, so that made sense.

When the bus reached her stop, the end of the line, she was the only passenger left. Masha alighted and walked for half a mile. Then she saw the road she was to take, to the right, and twenty yards ahead. It turned up a steepening rise in the hillside away from the main road. She followed her orders to the letter. It led up past a row of houses and then turned into a track that wound away into deserted countryside. The fog seemed to have crept lower, or maybe it was simply that she'd come up higher, but it didn't matter. Darkness had almost arrived.

Masha suddenly felt afraid now. The excitement of her mission evaporated as darkness fell. She thought about her husband and their small apartment off Gruzhinskaya Bolshaya. She began to feel that she wasn't up to even a task as small as this. She felt a panic rising up inside her. And a regret that she'd ever imagined she was suitable material for an intelligence officer. She wanted to get it over with, then reassess her whole life. She wanted to be someone small, insignificant, and she wondered what on earth had got into her to make her believe she was fit to face danger. But she forced herself on, the shame of failure greater than the fear.

Once on to the track she walked with a false determination up the hill until she reached the shed she'd been told about. She was pale with fear now. The shed was some way behind the houses, far enough away for it not to be seen—and just where it should have been. As she pulled open a broken wooden door, she saw she was about a hundred yards below the copse of trees. Everything was exactly as it should have been. She entered the shed and, trembling, she quickly took off her coat, fumbling the buttons in her haste. Then opened the leather case. She removed the sealed bag of fertiliser and some old agricultural clothes stuffed in around it. She placed her pink coat and black fur hat to one side and put the farm clothes over the clothes she wore. Then she screwed up the pink coat and put it and the hat into the leather case and tucked it behind a pile of broken boxes that looked like they'd been there for years. 'The shed isn't used any more'—the words from her briefing repeated themselves in her head, but her

75

head was also a jangle of other things there and suddenly she hated the gun she was carrying.

But Masha was now glad of her orders. They were suddenly the only thing that kept her focused. They were imprinted in her memory and she ran through them again as if they were her friendly companions and a talisman against failure. 'Lose the leather case in the shed, change into the clothes, then head up the hill. Once you are at the top of the hill, first leave the plastic fertiliser bag in a safe place, half a mile or so before you reach the drop. The barn. That's when you reconnoitre the barn itself. In that way, if you're intercepted—God forbid—but if anything does go wrong at the barn, you won't have anything compromising in your possession. Then, when you've seen that all is well at the barn, return with the fertiliser bag.' The drop-off was a niche in the wall inside the barn, under the third beam from the rear, on the right-hand side. She felt the heat of fear, rising towards panic.

Masha left the shed and took a circular route through the fields behind the houses, taking her away from the drop at first, then she followed the curve of her own circle, past the copse, until she came up behind and above the barn, a little over half a mile away from it. By now the sky was dark and night had come. She looked at the time that glowed on a cheap watch on her wrist. It read 6.35 p.m.

She removed the small bag of garden fertiliser from inside her tattered working coat. Then she looked for somewhere high off the ground, above the eye line of humans or dogs who might look for it. That was the procedure, leave it high up.

Perhaps she could quell the fear by concentrating on procedure.

There wasn't much she could see in this bare hill landscape. But standing against the skyline a hundred yards away to her right and at the same height as where she stood on the hill, she saw a lone tree, its branches bent and gnarled by the wind. She walked towards it and saw a crook in the trunk ten feet above her where four branches began their angular reach towards the sky. Climbing up on to a knot in the trunk, she could just reach the crook with her outstretched hand. Her hand trembled as she pushed the fertiliser bag into the crook. Then she climbed back down from the tree, returning to a spot directly above the barn. As she descended the hill above the barn, she suddenly felt cold, as if she had a fever. But this was it, she told herself. It was nearly over. She vowed she would resign as soon as she returned to Moscow. She couldn't face something like this again. She thought about after the operation. Her mind focused on Taras and the club where they were meeting. She felt an overwhelming sense of love for her cousin. She would take the flight to Odessa from the Crimea's capital, Simferol—just inland from Sevastopol—and meet with him, a day late perhaps, but soon she would be there.

When she was twenty yards away from the barn, she stopped once and listened. She was completely exposed against the open hill but felt protected by the darkness. When she heard nothing she set off again, covered the remaining ground to the entrance of the barn in less than a minute.

There was only one high, broken wooden door remaining in the arched stone wall of the barn. It creaked slowly in the wind. The other door was missing. It was just as her boss had told her. She entered the dark interior through the gap and, when her eyes had become accustomed to the almost pitch blackness inside, she began to make out darker shapes against the feeble light of the night sky entering from a hole high up in the wall where a window had once been. She switched on a small torch with a fine narrow beam that shed no light to the sides. In the light of the torch, she picked out the edges of straw bales, a beaten mud floor, and cobwebs close up to her. As she played the torch along a beam to the left following the wall of the barn, she saw the third roof beam from the end. The beam of the torch came down to reveal the niche beneath it, itself a tangle of cobwebs and dust. All was well. It was time to leave and then return with the plastic fertiliser bag.

As she began to turn, there was a small bang like an explosion, which she realised a second later was an engine suddenly bursting into life. She felt her heart thump violently and almost stop. Even without the shock it gave her, the sound of the engine was suddenly deafening in the small space which before had been so silent. And with the engine came a light, just a split second later. Standing in the centre of the barn she was suddenly illuminated by blinding washes of floodlights that must have come from arc lamps up on the roof beams. It was a generator, she thought dimly, the engine was a generator and the lights came on automatically with the generator. She was blinded, her senses confused. And then she heard a single voice.

'It's not her,' a man shouted, and this was

78

followed by a curse in Russian.

Masha followed orders. It seemed to take the men inside the barn completely by surprise. She drew the handgun from inside her jacket, pointed it towards her head, and pulled the trigger.

CHAPTER FIVE

In the evening of the same day that Anna Resnikov entered the country at Odessa's port and Masha was crossing over from Russia, a meeting was taking place in the capital Kiev. Being the night before the presidential elections not everyone present was in an agreeable mood to have their time taken up with non-election matters, particularly here. The four men and a woman sat around a smoked-glass table in a safe room at the American embassy on Mykoly Pymonenka Street and the atmosphere was not friendly.

They were not diplomats or trade representatives or visiting senators and congressmen. In fact, all of them worked for the CIA station attached to the embassy, except for one of the men, Logan Halloran. He was an employee of Burt Miller's tauntingly named Cougar Intelligence Applications, the multi-billion dollar American private intelligence corporation. And it was Logan—backed by the might of Cougar —who had summoned the CIA on this Saturday evening, not as one might expect the other way around.

Sam MacLeod, the CIA station head, was the most senior figure at the table—at least officially—

but orders from the CIA's director in Virginia, Theo Lish, had requested—this was the careful word used—that MacLeod make every effort to accommodate Cougar's wishes. Cougar 'had something that needs conveying at once', was the opaque way that Lish had put it to his station chief. After his meeting with Burt three days earlier, Lish had requested that they make every effort to accommodate Logan. In his usual, cunning way, Burt Miller had introduced a question that now hung in the air unanswered, but that Lish knew had to be investigated with the greatest of vigour.

A suave, close-shaved and neatly tonsured man in his late fifties who wore impeccably cut pinstripe suits, MacLeod was visibly irritated before the meeting had even begun and his irritation stemmed from being summoned by, of all people, Logan Halloran. Simply put, he didn't like Halloran and he didn't intend to even look Halloran in the face, despite the fact that they were sitting directly across the table from each other.

Halloran himself was unmistakably MacLeod's sartorial opposite. Despite Burt's efforts to make him appear like the corporate figure he was, long, thick, light-brown hair flowed erratically over Logan's shoulders, and was perhaps not as clean as it could have been. He wore a crumpled faded pale green suit that had seen much better days and the collar of his shirt was open, with tufts of chest hair emerging from the neck—'like some eighties pop star', MacLeod had witheringly told his second in command, Sandra Pasconi. On top of Logan's insultingly dishevelled appearance, MacLeod couldn't help noting, despite his determination not to engage in eye-to-eye contact with him, that Halloran had a deep tan in the middle of the Ukrainian winter. A fake tan was something that MacLeod, a traditionally down-to-earth Texan, found profoundly un-masculine. It didn't occur to him that Halloran had been lying on a tropical beach only the week before. But either way, to Sam MacLeod, a man's appearance was either respectful or the reverse—there was nothing neutral in between—and to him Halloran demonstrated a casual approach that smacked of disrespect.

It wasn't so much his physical appearance, however, that riled MacLeod the most, nor the gross inconvenience of it being a Saturday night and the fact that he was just on his way out to a pre-election cocktail party. Nor was it that he should suddenly find himself at the beck and call of a private intelligence company—albeit one that commanded almost the same level of resources as the CIA itself. It was Logan Halloran's past life that was topping the list of the affronts that irritated MacLeod this evening. Apart from his slovenly appearance, with an attitude to match, Halloran had once been a CIA officer in Bosnia back in the 1990s until he'd been fired by the agency many years back now. Yet here he was practically giving orders to one of the CIA's station heads in one of the world's intelligence hotspots and on the CIA's own ground, to boot.

Was it Burt Miller's idea of joke to send Halloran? Probably, MacLeod thought. At any rate, he wouldn't put it past him. Burt Miller walked the corridors of power in Washington with effortless ease, thanks to Cougar's generous dispensation of lobbying fees. He operated like some private satrap at the heart of power. Since 9/11, Cougar had grown from a regular intelligence outfit into Washington's most influential intelligence hub, with the power and money to show for it. And, if he knew little else about Burt Miller, MacLeod understood how Miller enjoyed flaunting this power and wealth.

But MacLeod also knew that Cougar's power on this particular evening at the embassy in Kiev was now replicated in other American embassies around the world. Cougar—which had employed the CIA head Theo Lish until two years before—was now able to issue orders on more than an occasional basis at CIA stations throughout the world. Lish had been a board director of the CIA, then was poached by Burt Miller to be CEO of Cougar, and had now returned to the CIA as chief, apparently giving Miller access to whatever it was he wished. It made MacLeod almost visibly seethe with indignation.

The others sitting around the smoked-glass table consisted of MacLeod's junior officers, all in their mid twenties to early thirties. Younger than MacLeod, they were more overtly angry at this indignity. Sandra Pasconi, the only woman present, was the senior of these three young spooks and she spoke first, as arranged beforehand. Macleod had dictated before the meeting that he wanted to stay in the background, as befitted his position, and not stoop to liaising directly with Halloran. He affected a position of not acknowledging Logan was in the room at all.

'Isn't it a bit premature to have this meeting the night before a presidential election?' Pasconi asked acidly. 'We don't know what Ukraine's going to look like, yet. The election tomorrow is just narrowing it down to two candidates. Then there'll be a run-off in three weeks' time. That's when it's appropriate, if ever.'

Logan smiled back at her without replying. He felt a supreme self-satisfaction that the CIA was at his bidding after his mistreatment at their hands. He still had scores to settle with his old organisation over his dismissal. The resentment he felt towards the agency looked like it would never die and he now felt a dangerous desire to rub their noses in it. Yet at the same time, if you were to study Logan's erratic motivation—something he didn't do himself with any great zeal—he had a great need for acceptance by his old employer at the same time as he nurtured resentment against it. He wanted them to recognise their mistake in ever dismissing him. He wanted to extract love from humiliation.

'But we all know what the result of the election's going to be, don't we, Sandra?' Logan replied. 'The current president is out. It's between Yanukovich and Timoshenko now. That'll be decided in three weeks. And we all know Moscow's favourite, Yanukovich, is going to win. It's practically a done deal. The Orange Revolution is over. Russia holds the cards.'

Pasconi bristled at the use of her first name. 'Look, Halloran,' Pasconi continued, 'we know just how important you are—or Cougar is, in any case,' she almost sneered, 'so you don't have to push your weight around, OK?'

Logan was delighted at her angry response. Hostile, that was what Logan had expected, and that was what Burt had told him to expect. 'Let them be hostile.' But Logan wanted to exacerbate that hostility. It only made his enjoyment at their predicament all the greater. He'd already noticed that MacLeod refused to look at him, while the other two younger men seemed to be waiting on the edge of their chairs with an eager fixation in his direction, like terriers ready to rip his throat out. He smiled benignly, but in his heart he felt the old anger surfacing.

Logan paused to let the sarcasm in Pasconi's tone of voice dissipate into a flat silence that had the effect of leaving the tone, rather than the words themselves, hanging in the air.

'The question is,' he said smoothly, 'what is Ukraine going to be in three weeks' time? Burt Miller sees it this way,' he said quietly. 'He believes that Ukraine is moving to the top of our concerns. Your boss in Washington apparently agrees with him,' he added. 'Miller's convinced him that this is priority, red alert. And he simply wants the agency to be fully in the picture.'

'Our instructions are to listen to what you have to say,' Pasconi said. 'That's all. There's nothing here about Mr Lish agreeing or disagreeing with Miller's thesis on Ukraine.'

Logan leaned back in his chair before replying and delayed his reaction, like a sportsman who lowers the pace of his game in order to upset the urgency of an opponent. 'Cougar sees it that the Ukraine will soon become a front line of sorts,' he said finally. 'More so than it is now. Ukraine is an independent, democratic, pro-Western country under threat from its more powerful, belligerent and anti-democratic neighbour. Soon it will have a pro-Russian president. Yanukovich has made that clear enough. And Cougar sees it that Russia's geopolitical intentions may be viewed most clearly through the prism of Ukraine. It's not just about Ukraine, it's about all the former Soviet republics.' Logan leaned in. 'Moscow wants them back and Ukraine is the jewel in the crown.'

'That doesn't explain why now, why this evening of all times,' Pasconi snapped and Logan felt that she was flailing in the wind. 'It's damn inconvenient,' she added. 'Pointless, I'd go as far as to say.'

Logan opened the file he'd brought with him— the same file he'd distributed to the others in the room and which they had studiously kept unopened. 'We didn't think it should wait,' he said flatly, with a trace of contempt and without acknowledging Pasconi's hostility. 'Intelligence is coming in all the time and it's of a very disturbing colour.' He looked up with what passed for a helpful expression on his face, but everyone else saw it as merely cheeky. 'Cougar is very conscious of the fact that our embassies around the world want to know anything with any terrorist implications immediately. They want to know like the day before yesterday. And, naturally, the terrorists are aware that our defences are most likely to be lowered on occasions like a presidential election in a foreign country, as well as on our own national holidays.' He paused. 'We want to set the agenda here, not allow them to. Cougar didn't want our embassy here to be caught napping.' He leaned towards Pasconi. 'We're just trying to help.'

The nerve of this approach was lost on none of

the others in the room. Pasconi bristled again, her face contorted in an ugly grimace, but she stayed silent. MacLeod himself was feeling a deep resentment at the incursion of Cougar on to his territory, never mind that it had been endorsed by his chief. The implication that, without Cougar, the agency—and his station, in particular—would be caught napping now infuriated him and he struggled to retain his studied aloofness.

Logan watched a similar struggle competing on all of their faces. But he was following Burt's instructions to the letter. Mention terrorism right at the top, Burt had told him. Then they can't afford to ignore you. The potential blow-back is too risky for them.

'When you care to take a look at this,' Logan continued smoothly, indicating the file, 'you'll notice that Russia has been ramping up its hostile, or potentially hostile, actions in Ukraine over the past few months. And they were high enough already. You have all the facts, I'm sure. But Cougar also has evidence that smuggling across the—'

'Smuggling what?' Pasconi loudly demanded to know. 'Smuggling terrorists!'

'Perhaps. And it could very well be so. But I'll get to that later. Right now I'm talking about the smuggling of materiel. And what kind of materiel is something that Cougar is currently investigating,' Logan replied, unruffled by the interruption.

'So you're saying the KGB could be smuggling paper towels, or pork fat or spare parts for jeeps.'

'Unlikely,' Logan replied. 'Unless Russia's *spetsnaz*—specific-ally the Vympel division—have fallen on very hard times.'

There was a prolonged silence in the room this time. Then Pasconi, who seemed to be the only other person in the room with a voice, spoke.

'What's the evidence? What's the threat? What have Russian special forces got to do with terrorism—even if we could disengage that from their normal activities?'

Logan paused, a change of pace again. 'We have satellite pictures from our own hardware, and we've also had a piece of luck. Or what Burt Miller, in his great wisdom, calls a dodo.'

Logan enjoyed watching the expressions around the table change from hostility to bemusement. He was getting into his stride now; a pleasantly nasty thought crossed his mind that, if he didn't pass on Burt's instructions, they might all, like he had once, lose their jobs when some crisis blew up. But he continued in a relaxed voice.

'A dodo, according to Burt, is the reappearance of something that you thought doesn't or couldn't possibly exist. In this case, the dodo is a face recognition from satellite pictures of one of the officers who took part in these border missions. This KGB officer is leading the smuggling operation. He's a colonel in the Vympel Group— the special forces teams based at the KGB's headquarters east of Moscow known as The Forest—who was jailed two years ago for atrocities committed in Chechnya in the late 1990s. His jail sentence was one of Moscow's regular transparent attempts to make us believe they are abiding by the rules of international law. However, this colonel served only five months for the murder and torture of Chechen civilians in Russia's last war there. His

87

release was kept secret from everybody. But one of our senior analysts and field personnel recognised him.'

'You mean Resnikov,' Pasconi demanded.

'I can't reveal who,' Logan said. But everyone around the table knew that only Anna Resnikov would be able to recognise a colonel in the *spetsnaz* Vympel group from a satellite picture.

'What else?' Pasconi said, evidently unwilling to be denied an answer for a second time.

'Burt Miller is setting up an operation on the ground with the intention of intercepting one of these border smuggling operations.'

'Resnikov again,' one of the terriers said triumphantly.

Logan looked at the young officer with a pitying contempt. 'So you have a tongue that doesn't just hang out,' he replied, and received an evil look in return. Then he turned back to Pasconi.

'We hope to have evidence from on the ground in the next two weeks,' Logan continued. 'In view of any terrorist implications, Cougar is requesting that the CIA offers its help. But with or without your help, we believe the Russians are preparing something from across their border with Ukraine.' He leaned in now. 'The background to this leads in one direction only, Miller believes. For years the Kremlin has been interfering with oil and gas supplies that have to come through Ukraine before they can get to Western Europe. Threatening Western European energy supplies, in other words. On top of that—and in another theatre of their Ukrainian operations entirely—there are tensions in the south, mainly in and around the Crimea. These tensions are deliberately being raised by

Russian actions on the ground. The Russians' provocation of the Ukrainian border police there, and even the Ukrainian military, is on the rise. Russian foreign intelligence teams have been on the increase in this southern sector too. While this is going on, up in the north-east of the country—in the Donetsk region—there are reports of weapons caches and planned artificial labour strikes. Some of these reports suggest that these preparations are being made in order to disguise an armed uprising against the government in Kiev. A labour strike followed by a "spontaneous" armed rebellion.' He paused to let this sink in. 'It seems the Russians are throwing a bewildering number of different strategies at Ukraine in order to destabilise the country.' Then he dropped his voice so that the two terriers in black suits had to lean closer from the end of the table to hear him. This was his coup de grâce, and it was the real reason Burt had called the meeting together this evening. This is what they really *want* to hear, was the way Burt had put it. Logan looked at MacLeod directly as he spoke. 'But we believe the most alarming aspect of all of this Kremlin-inspired provocation is the ongoing information we're receiving that suggests an al-Qaeda-backed group in the Crimea is being armed by the Russian foreign intelligence service for an attack on the Crimean parliament.'

Logan sat back slightly in his chair and casually watched the reaction of the group that sat around him at the table. He could see immediately that he had hit his mark dead on. As Burt had anticipated, it was a bullseye.

It was undoubtedly known to the agency's Kiev station that the Ukraine's semi-autonomous territory of the Crimean peninsula, which jutted out into the Black Sea, was a region of seething discontent. In fact, that was common knowledge in the media, whenever editors applied their desiccated attention to the subject. As with most of the current problems in the former Soviet Union, the Crimea's problems dated from Stalin's time. Hundreds of thousands of Crimean Tatars had been deported in 1945. Then, since 1991, a quarter of a million of them had returned. The Tatars were Moslems, not extreme Moslems and not even all practising ones, that was true. But they were Moslems, nevertheless. The building of mosques and madrasahs on the peninsula had increased tenfold in the past few years. Burt had briefed him—though God knows on the basis of what information—that the region was ripe for trouble from various different quarters; Russians with their military and empire-building interests in the region; a restless, growing and politically marginalised Moslem population, and a general desire for Crimean self-rule, apart from Ukraine, among its pro-Russian population.

At some point in the pause that followed Logan's final remarks, MacLeod finally looked up and back into Logan's eyes which hadn't left him.

However they treat you at first, Burt had told Logan, once you introduce the words al-Qaeda, you'll have their attention. It doesn't matter if it's true or not. Just plant the seed. 'But is it true?' Logan had asked him. 'I said it doesn't matter,' Burt had replied, rather testily for him, and Logan was none the wiser.

'What group do your intelligence reports point to?' Pasconi said disbelievingly.

'Qubaq,' Logan replied.

'They're a non-violent Islamic organisation,' she shot back at him immediately. 'They've never committed a single attack.'

'Exactly,' Logan replied. 'The perfect peaceable Islamic organisation. Something in the West we should be courting, but alas we haven't been. And something the embassy and the CIA have consequently taken their eyes away from.'

Once more, the other four in the room bristled with indignation at the implications. MacLeod's face growled back at Logan. So Burt Miller was powerful enough to go behind their backs to the CIA chief and then send his minion—his disgraced minion—to push Cougar's weight around and insult him in the process.

And now Sam MacLeod could no longer remain aloof. The idea that the station in Kiev wasn't doing its job properly was too much for him. 'Kind of reverse logic, isn't it, Halloran?' he said acidly. 'Because someone has done nothing fundamentally wrong, then they must be on a suspicion list.'

Logan didn't hesitate this time. 'I think the point is, Sam, that the Qubaq support others who do perform terrorist acts,' he said, knowing that the use of the station head's first name would rile him more. 'That's the question. If someone supports terrorist acts, even tacitly, then they're complicit. That's the dictum. Qubaq also supports the re-establishment of the Caliphate, sharia law, a unified Moslem world. The question is, surely, what are they doing promoting radical Islamic culture in a secular country? Ukraine isn't the northern Caucasus. It's an Orthodox Christian

91

country.'

But Logan could see the Pavlovian reaction he was getting simply from the mention of an Islamic group that Cougar believed came under some suspicion. The CIA will take it from there, Burt had said. All you have to do is cast suspicion. The last thing the CIA dare risk is to be upstaged by a private intelligence company, let alone ignore a potential terrorist group. Once we reel them in, we can use their resources and direct the play.

Logan continued now, confident that finally he had broken down their refusal to listen. This was the final play of the evening. 'We are receiving information that funding for Qubaq is coming from the Centre in Moscow, right from Department S, in fact, the secretive heart of the SVR. It's coming from the very top of Russia's foreign intelligence operations, in other words. We also have information that Russia's military intelligence, in the form of the GRU, is actually now recruiting agents from within the Qubaq group. It's common knowledge that the GRU and Department S recruited Moslems in Chechnya and other parts of the northern Caucasus, not to mention the Middle East. It's a potent combination, Burt Miller thinks—Russian foreign intelligence and a radical Moslem group with a clean record.'

'Evidence?' Pasconi demanded.

'Page eleven,' Logan replied and at last the four CIA employees opened their files.

The initial part of the thesis was Anna's. She had seen the training of foreigners, and particularly radical Moslems, at first hand when she'd been the KGB's darling at The Forest. The thesis began with a history of the KGB's and, specifically, Department S's involvement in the training of foreigners—in this case Moslems—to commit terrorist acts back in their own countries. Then it narrowed down into an account of Moslems being trained at The Forest outside Moscow to commit terrorist acts specifically in Western countries deemed hostile by the Kremlin. Finally, it was brought up to the present day with several of Cougar's inside agents' accounts from Russia of how this training continued to be performed in the highly secret 'Foreigners' Area' of the Russian intelligence services outside Moscow at Balashiha-2. One such trainee had been abducted by Cougar's heavy boot brigade in Jordan and had given much interesting insight into the methods and purpose of such KGB training. This man was now under lock and key in one of Cougar's private military bases in the United States. The report didn't mention what kind of pressure the abducted man had been put under in order to get him to reveal the information.

Pasconi was reading avidly, looking for objections. 'No mention of Qubaq here,' Pasconi said, looking up from the report.

This was always going to be the most difficult moment for Logan to carry off. Burt had refused to put the name in writing. Logan found that disturbing. Did the group really have a connection, Logan wondered, or was Burt just unsure? And why, anyway, did Burt want the CIA's resources? Cougar had more than enough of its own. Normally, in fact, Burt strained to keep the CIA at arm's length from Cougar's operations. This was evidently one of Burt's long and opaque games,

93

and he hadn't given Logan any more information than was in the file and in his personal briefing to Logan.

'There's hearsay, there's rumour, there's suggestion and, finally, there's the record of the KGB's activities in this field,' Logan said and pointed casually at the file. 'All of that is what, initially, an intelligence agency needs to pay attention to. That is how an alert comes into existence and how ultimately the evidence will be found. This group needs to be on a watch list—at the very least.'

'Bit circumstantial, isn't it?' Pasconi said.

'Follow every lead, Sandra.' Logan smiled in acknowledgement. 'That's been our country's mistake in the past. Leaving stones unturned.'

Pasconi in turn looked absolutely furious that Logan addressed her once again by her first name.

MacLeod put his elbows on the table and clasped his hands together. 'Perhaps when you see Burt Miller, you'd tell him that we aren't exactly idle here,' he said coldly. 'And we aren't exactly stupid. So. If Russia is going to get what it wants with a new president of Ukraine,' he said, 'assuming Yanukovich wins in three weeks, then why would it be going to the trouble of stirring things up?'

'Cougar is working with evidence that it is stirring things up,' Logan replied. 'Read the report, Sam.'

'Seeing as how you're just the messenger boy here, perhaps you'd convey my question anyway,' MacLeod said dismissively.

After the meeting had broken up, Logan left the embassy and walked into the freezing night. He

94

decided to continue walking rather than take a taxi. He admitted to himself that pinning the agency's station chief to the wall like a captured butterfly had caused him a rush of adrenalin-filled satisfaction that came from his resentment at the treatment meted out to him by the CIA ten years before. But this rush was quickly followed by enervation and finally a feeling of emptiness. MacLeod's parting jibe didn't help his falling mood. For that was exactly how he felt himself to be—Burt Miller's messenger boy. While all the time, Burt's favoured individual, Anna Resnikov, seemed to get all the glamorous, headline-grabbing jobs. One day he wanted to be Burt. But all the glory at Cougar nowadays went to her, his one-night stand in New York two years before, who had then cast him off. Unlike Burt treated him, Burt treated her as an equal.

Once he had shaken off the hostility and unfrozen the atmosphere of the meeting in the freezing cold outside he was left with a feeling of deep discontent. Burt didn't recognise him for the smart agent he'd been and, in that sense, Burt was no different from the CIA.

He walked on, aimlessly at first, trying to digest his sudden dissatisfaction. He guessed that this meeting was only one of Burt's plays in the country, and that he was just getting into his stride. Indeed, Burt had given him another task to perform in Kiev, one that was more long-term than the meeting. Logan's presence in Kiev on behalf of Cougar was two-fold and now he looked at his watch and decided it was time for his second rendezvous of the evening. He turned off to the left and headed for a bar just off Independence

Square where he'd planned to meet his recently made Ukrainian contact, Taras Tur. Burt wanted information from the Ukrainian side and Taras was an officer in the SBU, Ukraine's secret service, who might be willing to accept some extra money for a little work on behalf of Cougar. Logan had met him twice already—they'd drunk and dined and visited a few clubs, two men in their thirties and on the loose. He was a rather formal man, for Logan's liking, and didn't enjoy the pursuit of Kiev's teenage hookers as Logan did, but Logan liked him and he felt he was beginning to insert a wedge into Taras's reluctance to become close to a Western agency. Tonight, he hoped he'd gain a little more leverage.

Taras was Logan's favourite among the contacts he had attempted to make in the previous few months. There was something oddly honest about him. He treated Logan with respect, was grateful for the material Logan fed him now and again— and at Burt's instructions—and occasionally bought him lunch or a drink. He was generally a civilising influence in Logan's resentful life. And so Logan was glad that it was Taras he was meeting now. The Ukrainian would, perhaps, revive his spirits.

He turned on to Dymitrova and walked the short distance on to Independence Square. Then he crossed the road that took him into the centre and walked across until he saw the street he was looking for. He crossed this road on the far side from where he'd entered the square and walked up Chervonoarmils'ka and entered the bar that was their prearranged rendezvous. At that moment he noticed his mobile phone had a message. It must have come while he was in the meeting. He sat at the bar and ordered a large Macallan malt whisky and took two satisfying slugs before he turned back to his phone. He opened the message box and read a brief text. It was from Taras. 'Not possible tonight,' it said. Damn him, Logan thought, and he finished the whisky and ordered another.

CHAPTER SIX

Hidden in the copse, Anna had seen the woman an hour earlier and she immediately thought she looked nervous for an operative. She looked more like a teenage girl than a woman. She picked her up as soon as she'd passed the houses from the roadside and entered the fields behind. Anna then watched her emerge wearing different, farming clothes, walk up past the copse and circle back in the direction of the barn. After that it had got too dark to see without the night vision binoculars.

She decided to remain in the copse and wait. The woman, this girl, was definitely the courier, but something was wrong. Despite the obvious nervousness of the woman's movements, it was the change of clothes and the surreptitious way she moved through the field that gave her away. She must be very inexperienced. Was this the best the agent could do?

The other thing wrong was that she was very late. She should have been here earlier in the day, made the drop and departed long before there was any chance of a crossover. That was not good, it was highly unprofessional, in fact. There should be no possible identification between the person making the drop and the one doing the pick-up. But against that, Anna knew she wouldn't have long to wait now before she made the pick-up. The less time a drop was left in place, the better.

At six-thirty she walked carefully over to the side of the copse nearest the barn. There were no lights in that direction, but she knew from the reading on the binoculars that she was just under a quarter of a mile away and only open land with two ditches in between separated her from it. She would give it an hour, maybe an hour and a half. Let the woman make the drop and get clear. Maybe the courier would return by the same route she had come or, more likely, she would return by a different route, perhaps straight down the track that connected the barn with the road. Neither of them should see the other. But Anna decided she would leave at least an hour before she moved.

She listened again. The copse was quiet, the birds had stopped singing, but there was the sound of traffic from the road below. She sat on some dry wood and waited. Once she thought she heard the low growl of a military truck, but it could have been a commercial vehicle.

Just before seven o'clock—she remembered later that she'd checked on her watch—Anna heard the sound of a diesel engine starting. It was unmistakably a diesel engine and seemed to be coming from the direction of the barn. Then she saw a bright light coming from the barn and after that she heard the truck engine she'd heard before, the deep, growling truck engine. She was sure now it was a military vehicle. Suddenly the barn was ablaze with light, through what looked like half of an arched doorway. Then she saw a truck's lights swinging fast off the road and heading up the hill along the track towards the lighted barn. Anna ran out of the copse and, crouching low in the darkness, headed towards the barn. When she was just over a hundred yards away, she sunk down into a shallow ditch and caught her breath. As she looked over the lip of the ditch, three things happened simultaneously; she saw a big vehicle— the truck she'd heard—pulling up outside where the blazing light came from the barn. Its engine died, but the headlights stayed on; she heard shouting and curses coming from inside the barn; and finally she heard a shot.

She ran back to the copse. She turned and saw the shadows of men in the truck's lights. She heard orders being snapped out. Taking the night vision binoculars from her pack, she picked out Russian soldiers. She was certain they were Russian. They were Airborne judging from their caps, but the *spetsnaz* disguised their identities with the blue Airborne caps and epaulettes. Either that, or they wore the uniforms of units stationed nearby. She couldn't see any other insignia from this distance. Did they have dogs? She watched the uniformed men fan out. Some were highlighted against the light of the barn, others faded into darkness on either side. Through the binoculars she could see they were facing her and were starting to walk slowly in the direction of the copse, towards her. Then torches were switched on and now she could see the positions of all the men from the torches they carried. A line of soldiers, maybe twenty or thirty. They were beginning to make a sweep across the fields towards where she was hidden.

From the edge of the copse nearest to the barn, she watched their slow progress from four hundred yards. As she was about to make her retreat, there was suddenly the sound of another military vehicle and she looked down towards the end of the track from the barn where it reached the road. Two military jeeps were racing up the track and a truck swung in after them and stopped. It turned square on to the track and blocked the exit to the road. The jeeps raced on, lashing their gears until they slid to a violent halt next to the first truck beside the barn. Eight soldiers jumped out of the jeeps, weapons drawn. There was shouting and she heard the sound of small machine guns being armed. The new arrivals were levelling their weapons at the Russians outside the barn—two officers, she guessed; they were *spetsnaz*, that was unmistakable now that she studied them through the binoculars.

The line of soldiers halted their advance, then turned raggedly, the torches swinging around in the darkness. Anna watched the men from the jeeps. They wore green-grey uniforms and had Ukrainian insignia and shoulder patches. There was evidently a disagreement. The Ukrainian officer in charge was shouting at his Russian counterpart. 'Illegal, illegal'—she picked out the single word repeated. Russians making covert operations on Ukrainian territory, that was what he meant. It wasn't the first time. Tensions were high outside the barn, but they were high wherever Russian troops and naval personnel were situated on Ukrainian soil. This looked like an illegal Russian intelligence operation. And the Ukrainian officer was making threats of arrest, despite being outnumbered six to one.

Anna ran through the low scrub trees until she'd reached the far end of the copse. Returning to the road was out of the question. Now both sides would have it covered. She would have to head higher up, away from the town. She remembered roughly where the courier's route had been on this side of the copse and thought she would follow it before the soldiers found it, if they returned. There was still a chance of completing the pick-up. If the courier had followed the rules, she would have left the drop hidden somewhere while she reconnoitred the barn. Unless her arrest was, in fact, her second visit to the barn. But now, did she even have time to save herself, Anna wondered, let alone look for a small bag hidden in the darkness?

The land was soaked with rain on the far side of the copse. Her feet sank into it, it was almost marshy here. Her footsteps would be found, but she could also find the courier's steps too. With no light, she crept low over the grass until she found the indentation she was looking for, a footstep that led up the hill. She followed, placing her feet as well as she could in the courier's steps. She went in a wide circle, at an angle to the hill, until the steps turned straight upwards, then back around above the barn.

She stopped and watched the soldiers' lights. They'd returned to the barn and there seemed to be a stand-off between the Ukrainians and Russians. She watched through the binoculars as the Ukrainian commanding officer spoke into a radio. Calling for back-up, she supposed. But they were all below her now. And there were no dogs that she could hear.

She reached a sandy part of the hill where there

were low, scratchy bushes. The footsteps were going in all directions. Had the courier stopped here? To find a place to stash the fertiliser bag while she made a reconnoitre, perhaps? But she saw nothing in the scrub, feeling with her hands in the darkness. The bag of fertiliser wasn't there. Had the courier taken it with her already to the barn? She looked down the hill again. The soldiers were still facing each other. And then she saw other vehicles arrive at the foot of the track—more Ukrainian jeeps, she guessed. Internal security. The truck that blocked the track pulled back and let them through, then blocked the track again.

They were too busy with each other to find her footmarks soon, or the courier's tracks she had followed. Maybe the Ukrainians would order dogs to be brought up, once the dispute was resolved. She had a little time, and a little space to manoeuvre. There was no cover for the courier to hide anything, except a tree she saw in the distance, maybe a hundred yards away, at the level of the hill she was on. She felt a great urge to get away. But first she went towards the tree and found the courier's footsteps again. It wasn't the direction the courier would have taken to the barn. Up in the crook was a plastic sack that looked grey in the darkness. Standing on a knot in the tree, she snatched it and ran now, up the hill until, higher up, she could find rocks to obscure her tracks.

As she fled through the rocks, she knew that if the courier hadn't been late, it would have been her the Russians caught in their lights.

*   *   *

102

Anna smelled the sea before she saw it, and heard the persistent, low roaring noise the sea makes even in the calmest conditions. She guessed she was roughly a mile away from the rendezvous, but then there was the cliff to descend before she could make the beach and she had no idea how long that would take. It was nearly twenty-four hours since she had escaped from Sevastopol and the time for the rendezvous was approaching. But if she didn't make the time agreed with Burt at their briefing, then Larry and the others would activate the plan to get her out off the beach on the next day, or the one after that, and at the same time.

She looked down the long slope of a hill that fell away gently to some high, sharp cliffs that flanked a small cove. She was roughly halfway between Sevastopol and Yevratoriya. In the gathering darkness, the walls of the cliffs where they curved around and away from her were a shade lighter than the fields above them and the sea below, and she knew she was in the right place, even if the GPS hadn't told her so. There was no road to this place, that was why they'd picked it. It was isolated from people. She'd walked through the night and all that day after the pick-up. As the crow flies, it hadn't been so bad. Tonight would be the first chance of rescue.

Overnight on the long walk away from the city, she had fished out the thick plastic envelope from the plastic bag of fertiliser, thrown the bag away, and stashed the envelope in her jacket. She had enough food for three days, maybe four if she eked it out. That was so she could go underground in the event of trouble and there'd been nothing but trouble since she'd arrived at Odessa. There was more than one opportunity for a rescue and it could be days before they felt they could come in. She looked out to sea now. The fog had lifted, that was a pity. Maybe they would wait for more bad weather to arrive. Maybe they would wait until the sea cut up again, or maybe there wouldn't be time for that. All she could do was to make the rendezvous, then her fate was in their hands.

When it was completely dark, she descended the hill slowly, watching all the time. If her arrival had been known, and the drop itself was known, would they also know the fall-back plan for her ex-filtration from the country. It didn't matter, either way there was no other chance now. She'd seen Ukrainian soldiers combing the outskirts of Sevastopol, and the ports and other exit points would be heavily guarded.

As she descended she thought about the stand-off between the Russian and Ukrainian military at the barn and wondered what the Russians had told the Ukrainian government—an escaped prisoner from their naval base, perhaps? But there was only the woman—a girl, really, from what she'd seen. And the Russians were unlikely to be believed in the highly tense atmosphere that existed in Sevastopol. It depended who had gained the upper hand at the barn. If it was the Ukrainians, then they would want to know the identity of the courier, once she was revealed to them, as much as the Russians did. The Russians would try to concoct a story that made the Ukrainians seek common cause with them, perhaps, or just curious enough to heed their requests for a search of the city and its environs. It depended on those few seconds at the barn—with diplomacy the Russians might have convinced the Ukrainian military to work with them. No doubt the spectre of terrorism would be invoked, the convenient lie for all unwelcome events.

She reached the top of the cliffs and now clearly heard the waves breaking two hundred feet below. There was an old path fit only for animals, she'd been told in the briefing. But nobody had actually seen it. It was said to have been there for more than two and a half thousand years, since the Greeks occupied the peninsula. Suddenly it sounded uncertain to her, unplanned. They hadn't even known for sure where it began its descent from the top of the cliffs.

She decided to walk to the left along the cliff edge first. It was pitch-dark now, the sea blacker below except where the waves broke. She didn't know if she'd see the path even if it was there, and she couldn't risk using a light. So she walked carefully, stopping often to study a change in the shades of darkness that might reveal the existence of the path. After an hour, examining every possible opening and once almost falling over the cliff, she thought it couldn't be on that side. She walked back to the centre of the cliffs where she'd started and began again, this time pacing slowly to the right. She was losing valuable time just finding the path—if it existed at all. But she was calm, as she always was in any extreme situation—calmer in those circumstances, if anything. Even the prospect of being left alone on foreign soil and with half an army out there looking for her wasn't enough to drive fear into her thoughts. Everything—as long as you were free—had a solution.

After twenty minutes searching on the other side to the right, she saw a break between two rocks. The ground was overgrown, but they'd said the path was unused. That was its advantage. Carefully, she dropped down between the rocks and saw a tiny ledge. Below her and the ledge she saw the white crests of the waves rolling on to the beach. It looked like a sheer drop, but she edged out along the ledge and then saw that the lighter streak widened down below. There, ahead of her, she saw a snaking, sandy-looking area that might indicate a way. It seemed to wind its way past other rocks and stones and that was a good sign.

She crept ahead using the narrowest of footholds, in almost complete blindness. The sound of the waves was beating in time with the blood in her head. But once she'd reached the furthest point of the ledge she saw a step off it on to small stones where nothing grew. She looked down on to another almost sheer drop. Below her, another lighter-shaded and twisting shape of what seemed to be a path wound around the near-vertical cliff face. In the darkness it was like a loop that appeared and disappeared in ox-bow curves. This must be it, she decided, but even a goat would have trouble traversing it.

She slid and climbed, mostly backwards and using her hands against the cliff face, for over an hour. She clutched on to the jagged edges of rocks when she felt herself going, until finally she stepped out on to a shingled beach. The salt smell of the sea hit her first and then the smell of seaweed and tar filled her nostrils. She slumped down on the pebbles, exhausted suddenly. Her heart was racing. She didn't know how she'd made it.

Her watch said it was eighteen minutes after midnight. She wanted to sleep. She was hungry. But she put away her fear. Fear was the enemy. From a pocket in her jacket she withdrew a key-sized plastic tool and flipped a switch. A tiny beam lit beyond the edge of the beach where the water broke. She flashed it three times in a south-south westerly direction, then three times in a south-south easterly direction. She repeated it twice more and sat down to wait. If the Russians or the Ukrainian coastal patrols were looking for her out there, they would see it too. She was getting colder. And she wondered if she'd be able to get back up the track if Burt's team didn't come.

As she waited, she cast her mind back to the scene at the barn once again. There'd been the shot. She'd thought about that at first, wondered who had fired it, until she'd seen what followed. For before the Ukrainian jeeps had arrived and before she'd turned up the hill to escape the soldiers, she'd watched a body being carried from the barn; two soldiers, one holding the arms, the other the legs. She'd seen the courier's long hair— a woman's hair—hanging down and dragging along the earth. She'd looked like a dead deer being carried on a pole. It could only be that the woman had killed herself. They would certainly have wanted her alive. But she was certainly dead from the way they carried her like a hunted animal and if she were dead, it meant the agent was safe. The courier had sacrificed herself to save the agent, even though she didn't know it. She wondered if the Ukrainian officer had demanded to look inside the truck and what he would do when he saw the body of the courier.

As Anna sat, numb, and listened to the surf, she wondered for the first time about the courier; she'd been a young woman. Anna thought about her young life, her past, what the mission had meant to her. It seemed she'd been a novice from everything Anna had seen. Perhaps it was her first time. Anna felt a deep, wrenching sadness at the waste of life. And she wondered what it was the agent had told her to ensure that she'd killed herself: that this was a KGB operation, certainly; that it was for her country, for the new Russia—that would have been his message to disguise the truth. It was not for the courier to know that she was delivering material that might damage her country. The young woman undoubtedly believed she'd been delivering a package for her bosses in the KGB, not for a Western intelligence agency.

And then, when she'd been caught at the barn, she'd shot herself. There seemed to be no other explanation. Her captors certainly would have wanted her alive. But the agent would have made as sure as was possible that she didn't allow herself to be taken alive. The agent had deceived her well—so well that she was dead by her own hand. Anna sat and thought again about the young woman; first deceived into delivering material that was treasonable, then deceived into taking her own life in order to protect the agent. Unlike the detached, clinical thoughts she'd had for the two men she'd killed the previous day, Anna now felt a deep compassion for the young woman, duped by all sides, and a friend to no one. She'd been everybody's fool. Something Finn had once said to her came into her mind. 'If there were no spies,

108

there'd be no need for any spies.' It was true. The facet of espionage that troubled her most was that it existed entirely for itself and was self-fulfilling. Finn, too, had died for that, for the pursuit of an uncertain goal in the small bubble of an alternative, fake world.

The waves crawled up and back on the shingle beach with a monotonous regularity that began to make her sleepy again. There was hardly any moon, the sea was dark in the small bay and beyond. And then she saw it: an object darker than the water that nudged up against the shore at the corner of the cove where the wave motion was broken by an outcrop of rock that shielded it from the sea.

Anna kept to the top of the beach and crept slowly towards the object as it gingerly approached the beach, until she saw the black prow of a rubber boat. There were three figures in it. One stepped over the side as it came in close and pulled the boat a little further on to the shore, just to keep it from being dragged back, no more. Then a light flashed. A torch on the boat flickered twice, a pause, then three times and a pause, then twice again. Anna flashed the torch three times, then a break, then three times again, and repeated it. She was only thirty yards away now. It was them, she was sure of that. But she drew both the guns she had taken from the dead men and waited for a few seconds. With one gun aimed at the figure in the centre of the boat, and the other ready to fire in any direction necessary, she walked at an angle across the pebbles until she could see the men's outlines clearly. They wore balaclavas. The man in the centre removed his and she recognised Larry.

Nobody spoke.

As she reached the sea's edge, Larry hauled her into the rubber boat. Then the two other men pushed the boat sluggishly away from the shingle and it crept away from the shore with muffled engines. Once they were clear of the shore they crossed the bay at speed and headed out to sea. Still, no words were spoken.

In just under an hour from the rendezvous the boat pulled up beside the rusting hull of a small Nigerian-registered freighter and a ladder was dropped. Anna went up first, feeling the package pressing into her chest as she climbed.

CHAPTER SEVEN

The Golden Fleece nightclub on Odessa's waterfront was not a regular haunt of Taras Tur. In fact, no nightclub anywhere on the planet was even an irregular haunt of his. He wouldn't have been here at all if it weren't for his cousin Masha. It was her suggestion that they should meet here. That was supposed to have been yesterday evening. She was a day late—not at all an unlikely event for Masha—and so he'd decided to return here a second time in the hope that tonight she would arrive. Nevertheless, her non-appearance troubled him.

The choice of venue he put down to her youth. She was younger than he was by a decade and she still liked the nightclubs even now that she was married. As for him, even in his youth Taras had never enjoyed places like the Golden Fleece. He thought about this for a moment and decided that he simply didn't *believe* in them. Taras was not an escapist. He liked to know what was what and, until he'd met his wife ten years before, his previous girlfriends had either become hurt and angry by his organised, rational mind or teased him for it.

He looked at his watch again. It was nearly ten o'clock and she had said she'd be here by nine the evening before. Well, that was Masha. She'd told him by phone from Moscow a week ago that she would be in Odessa the previous afternoon. She was arriving from Russia the day before that—that would be two days ago—then making a brief and, he assumed, nostalgic visit to the farm outside Sevastopol. She should have taken the plane from Simferol to Odessa yesterday afternoon. It had all sounded quite organised for Masha, in fact. But she wasn't answering her mobile, a whole day later, and the feeling of unease crept over him again.

Taras looked around at the dressed-up girls and women in the club and guessed that Masha was probably in some cheap hostel in the town, still choosing what to wear, putting on make-up— whatever young women like her did before going out for the night. And he felt a moment of fondness for his young cousin.

He took another sip of cold Czech beer and settled in again for the wait with his elbow on the bar. He didn't intend that they would stay here if and when Masha arrived. He would steer her to a quiet bar behind the port where they could talk.

A stockily built, handsome man of thirty-five, Taras's angular face reflected the sickly, pulsing shades of the club's multicoloured lights. He'd

111

worn street clothes rather than the gaudy outfits Odessa's youth had dressed up in for their usual Saturday night of hedonism. His face, freckled in youth, had now absorbed the freckles into the background as he'd got older so that his face was slightly darker than the rest of him, as if he spent a great deal of time in the open air. He had broad shoulders and a big frame which, on close inspection, was made up principally of hard muscles and which came from the rigorous training of his job, but also from regular games of squash. He was the SBU squash champion. His expression—even outside situations like this one that he found a little strenuous—reflected life's knocks. There was a lived-in look in his eyes, exaggerated by a dolefulness from his heavy eyelids that slanted downwards towards the outside. They gave him a seen-it-all look. But the pupils were hard points that seemed to bore into whatever took his attention.

He wasn't on duty tonight and had arrived wearing a ski jacket, now hung on the stool beneath him, a blue sailing sweater and jeans. But he suspected he still stood out as being a cop, even though that was only half right. He was an officer in the SBU, Ukraine's intelligence service, with a stalled career due to his father's murky business dealings, and a stalled ambition to match. But perhaps cops, security officers and spies all looked the same to the carefree crowds of youth at the Golden Fleece.

Despite not being on duty, he still looked at the faces and studied the attitudes of the club's occupants. There was a workmanlike look about him, as if he'd come straight from an office. But his square jaw, heavy hands and stern expression suggested a man who took life rather more seriously than the young crowd at the Golden Fleece did. They were all just ordinary young people, mostly in their late teens, out for an evening of drinking and dancing at the clubs that were putting on special shows on this pre-election night.

Looking around him now at the relaxed groups of Odessa's youth flailing in the flashing lights, there was one persistent thought that wouldn't leave Taras's mind: they'd all been too young to vote in 2004. When the Orange Revolution had swept through Ukraine, toppling Viktor Yanukovich from an illegal election victory, and installing Viktor Yuschenko, the current incumbent, most if not all of the club's occupants had been barely teenagers. And yet though the Orange Revolution was only six years ago, as far as the youths in the club were concerned it might just as well have been half a century ago. The Orange Revolution was something remote to them, like a black-and-white film or a pop song that was now derided for its old-fashioned, museum quality and—let's face it—naivety.

The world and his own country with it had moved on with astonishing speed and the kids in the club had grown into their voting years under the shadow of the failure of that revolution. What they knew about politics, if anything, was the disappointment of those expectations; the continued corruption, the economic failure and—as the inevitable consequence of that—the political exclusion of Ukraine from the European Union and NATO. There was a sense of national

113

humiliation which came from Ukraine being defined by the outside world for its faults.

Taras had been brought up from childhood in Odessa, but in his teens his father had bought the farm outside Sevastopol in the Crimea. That was the reason he and Masha decided to rendezvous in Odessa rather than in Kiev where he worked. His father, now dead, had been a *buzinessman* in the early years after the country's independence. Taras didn't know exactly how that had happened, but remembered one night how the house they'd lived in next to Odessa's Ilyich Park by the Provoznaya Market had suddenly become full of boxes of electrical equipment brought in from Turkey: almost-the-latest computers, some of which worked, hi-fi, kitchen goods—anything, in fact, his father had been able to get hold of. The whole thing seemed to have taken off in a few days when the rules were relaxed. His father was suddenly at the centre of affairs, just like that.

Odessa had always been a great trading city, but within a few months in 1991, Taras's family had moved to the Crimea, into the farmhouse outside Sevastopol, and the Odessa residence became his father's office. By that time, his father had warehouses in Odessa and other offices in Kiev, thanks to payments in the right places. The family—minus his father—had moved out from the fringes of Odessa to a place his mother loved and where, Taras suspected, his father was only too happy to keep her out of the way. It was for their protection, as his father had put it, and after that the family hardly saw him when the business took off.

How had his father done it? Connections, of

course. His father had also been with the SBU and was able to capitalise on the looser commercial rules quicker than most. From being a company man in the SBU he had elided into another, this time commercial, company with ease but one which consisted of business entrepreneurship. His father, however, had a natural talent for rising in the new economy that had made him rich where others with the same opportunities squandered them.

It was his father who had eased Taras's way into the country's intelligence services, but he'd failed to interest him in making money. From the elite school of intelligence, his father had created what he'd hoped would be a place in the elite school of business—and a dynastic continuity. But Taras had found himself more interested in working for his new country than stacking up money. Money for what?

And then his father had died, shot on the streets of Berlin in 1994. He was murdered by the Chechen mafia, voices at the SBU had said. Creditors had arrived. And then all Taras had left was the farmhouse outside Sevastopol and his job. He had no interest in, or talent for, business.

He looked around his surroundings now and thought that he'd come about as far as he was ever likely to go in the intelligence world, too. Even without the suspicion with which he was regarded by the intelligence agency after his father's murder, he feared that he lacked ambition. And he certainly lacked the greed of his fellow officers for turning his privileged position into cash.

Tonight the Golden Fleece nightclub in Odessa was summing up all he didn't like about the quest for money. He casually looked at the cocktail card on the bar top. The kind of place that served cocktails with names like 'Blow Job Shooter' wasn't his kind of place of all.

Taras was by nature as well as by profession a student of the subdued, the grey and the nondescript. God knew, he had spent enough evenings like this one, propping up bars in various states of repair—both himself and the bars—and waiting for someone who might, but more often than not didn't, show up. But the Golden Fleece nightclub was like no other meeting place he had ever been in his career so far.

No venue that Taras could recall—no billionaire's club, no flashy joint or grubby dive or bootlegger's den he had ever visited—had achieved anything quite approaching the individual mix of astonishingly vulgar wealth openly on show with the extreme, outlandish kitsch that the Golden Fleece displayed on this particular January evening.

He looked around with a cool expression of disinterest that bordered on disapproval at the mass of humanity writhing on the dance floor. It was no place for an intelligence officer to be, of that he was sure. It screamed public 'excess' and 'display' at him which he found uncomfortable in the extreme.

From the snaking menace of the reflective aluminium bar top, dotted with flashing diamonds of light, which disappeared some indeterminate distance away from where he stood into clouds of purple and magenta dry ice; to the walls of glass that changed colours in giant banks of plastic green, yellow, orange, red and blue; to the glass

116

dance floor, ringed with small explosions of fireworks and similarly flashing livid circles of coloured light from below; and then right on up to the cages suspended above the dance floor, Taras looked for some relief from the brightness and the hideously unnatural tones that bore no relation to anything he recognised in nature. And all of these eye-numbing, brain tissue-scarring sensations that besieged his brilliant, meticulous, though underused mind assaulted him before he could even begin to take in the ear-splitting cacophony of techno-funk to which the bodies and the lights and the artful, flashing explosions of glittering fireworks that flanked the dance floor paid homage.

Not for the first time his eyes lingered for a moment on the cages that hung from a ceiling too far above him to see. Inside each cage writhed a mostly—no, looking more closely now—an entirely naked girl. They were even more beautiful than the Kiev girls. The designer topiary of their pubic hair was apparently adorned with real gold dust, mined from the gold fields that belonged to Viktor Aaronovich, the billionaire Russian oligarch from eastern Siberia and the owner of the Golden Fleece. At least, that was what it said on the club's website.

For a moment the massed gold dust of contorting female pudenda above his head, which—indelicately, he thought—gave the Golden Fleece its name, made him feel giddy and slightly sick. He looked down swiftly, only to be met once again by the writhing bodies on the dance floor, the rich and extremely rich of Ukraine's youth who were here to dance and drink and drug and—who

117

knew—probably fuck, until dawn. Lucky them, he thought—though Taras wondered about the truth of that. In any case, there was no way he could possibly put himself in their thousand-dollar shoes and therefore imagine what it would be like to be them, lucky or not. His family had nothing left apart from the farmhouse after his father's death. Mysterious creditors had arrived and they'd had no respect for his position as an intelligence officer in the new Ukraine.

In the midst of this deafeningly glitzy freak-beauty show of Ukraine's gilded youth—and in the case of the girls in the cages, literally gilded—Taras drank stolidly from the bottle of beer.

He thought about the meeting in Kiev with Logan Halloran that he'd almost forgotten to cancel. Halloran was a strange figure. He'd been sacked by the CIA, according to his research at the office, then had worked as a freelance. And now he was working for an outfit called Cougar whose annual returns the year before were counted in the billions of dollars. Halloran seemed to him a peripatetic character, however, rarely at ease, always striving for something he didn't have. He was too hungry, Taras thought, that was his problem. But he had a soft spot for Halloran, after their two or three meetings. Perhaps it was because few people in the intelligence world in Kiev seemed to like him. Taras wondered if he just liked him out of pity, or if he was really interested in the inevitable offer he expected Halloran to make him. He knew Halloran's interest in him wasn't out of friendship.

He looked in the mirror behind the bar and casually surveyed his appearance as closely as he dared. As someone who rarely looked at his reflection, he was surprised. Instead of the slightly formless creature he took himself to be, he saw a well-built man who was only let down—in here at any rate—by his clothing. When he looked back at the crowd of mostly girls at the bar he decided that they weren't grimaces of contempt after all, but smiles, some of which now seemed quite seductive and enticing. It was his clothes that were weird, not the club itself, he decided, and they were making him the most noticeable figure in the entire place. That was what unnerved him as much as anything. He wished Masha would arrive and they could go somewhere else. He liked to remain in the background. The small bar he had in mind, somewhere behind the port, would suit him better.

He turned towards the barman and ordered another beer and noted the man only spoke Russian, not Ukrainian. Unless he was refusing to speak the national language.

Taras sipped from the neck of the bottle. Always a bottle, and opened in front of him, that was the rule. You never could tell what else might be tipped into a glass.

At least no one tried to talk to him. He was gratifyingly shunned. He was stationed at the end of the aluminium bar, at the appointed spot nearest to the entrance—which he preferred to think of as the exit. He wondered briefly how he had even been allowed into the Golden Fleece in the first place. If anyone was designed to be rejected by the thugs on the door, who exercised the strict *feis kontrol* that excluded the uncool and the obviously unattractive, as well as the gangsters, from such elite nightclubs, it was him. He knew that, and he didn't care.

As he drank the straw-coloured beer he looked up from his thoughts to the huge wall that stretched the width of the club behind the dance floor. Once again, the whole wall had turned a pale white. The blur of thumping noise and flashing light was interrupted every half-hour by what was, Taras considered, the most bizarre apparition of all on this January night in 2010—the night before the first round of the much-awaited presidential elections. Either at some pre-determined, computerised moment, or at the whim of the club's billionaire owner seated invisibly somewhere in a private room, the glass walls would fade to white. And then, across one side of the entire club, a back-projected face would appear, fifty feet by fifty feet—the extraordinary and extraordinarily beautiful face of Yulia Timoshenko. Tonight in the club—and in the previous few weeks more behind the scenes than he was in here—Viktor Aaronovich was repeatedly flaunting his support for her bid to be the next president of Ukraine.

There, up on the wall, the face now appeared and would remain for some minutes, and the cheers from the dance floor at this apparition almost exceeded the noise of the techno-funk.

It was a face that said not just 'purity', but 'Ukrainian purity'; not just success, but highly glamorous success; not just money, but ship loads of the stuff. Her pale cream-coloured facial skin drawn over high cheekbones was crowned by a halo of corn-coloured hair plaited severely yet entrancingly over her fine head. It was a look, a hair arrangement, that Halloran had told him was described in *The New York Times*: 'It curls around her head like a golden crown, a rococo flourish that sets her far apart from the jowly men she has challenged'. It was a face—and a body to match—that had appeared on the cover of Ukrainian *Elle* magazine. A Ukrainian woman's beauty was judged by the thickness of her braided hair, 'like wheat', he'd explained to Halloran, and this effect had certainly reached its apogee in Yulia Timoshenko. Even to Taras, a happily married man who was sexually satisfied by his wife, she seemed like the Corn Goddess, the Goddess of Fertility, the divinity who would make Ukraine and Ukrainians fertile, rich and, maybe even, more sexually appealing.

In what was sure to end up in a two-way election, Yulia Timoshenko was undoubtedly the glamorous choice, but she was not only that. She was also by far the richest of the three main candidates. On both counts she was a natural for the wealthy, fashionable, thrusting youth of Ukraine now cavorting on the dance floor—if anyone in the Golden Fleece this evening bothered to vote at all. Her beauty could be clearly seen, at face value, and during one interview with a cheeky Western press corps, she had even let her hair down when it was suggested that the corn braid was a hairpiece. She had made her fortune in the energy sector back in the 1990s, then joined the political arena during the Orange Revolution of 2004 that saw off the Russian-backed candidate in favour of the current, Western-looking president.

But now, in 2010, she stood against both the failed president from those heady days, with whom she had once been linked, and the returned Russian-backed challenger, the *éminence grise* of the previous six years who had waited in the wings and was still supported by the Kremlin. Against both this Putinist would-be president and the current incumbent, Yulia Timoshenko's credentials were immaculate. She was a highly successful businesswoman, she wore the badge of a democratic revolutionary from 2004, and on top of everything she was also a goddess—all this rolled into one. How could she possibly fail, Taras wondered. She'd get the western Ukrainian vote, yet it was looking bad for her in the country as a whole.

The apparition faded once more, like some ethereal being in a science fiction movie, and Taras looked at his watch; 11 p.m. He would wait another half an hour, though he was sure that Masha would not make an appearance now. She must have missed her connection.

A little too relaxed after six beers in a couple of hours, he idly glanced around the waves of throbbing bodies clad in Gucci, Prada and other, hipper labels he was unfamiliar with.

Would he even notice Masha, if she did arrive? he wondered.

Taras looked towards the entrance a few feet away from his end of the bar and, for a moment, he, Taras Tur, was the only person in the Golden Fleece who felt a wave of impending doom. It washed over him suddenly and unexpectedly. What was it that he'd seen? Nothing. It was, he realised, something he hadn't seen and that should have been there. The four thugs on the door who picked out the prettiest girls and the richest, cutest boys had disappeared. All four of them. That was impossible. He looked at his watch a second time;

11.20 p.m. And he decided that now he would go. Something was wrong. That was what his mind was telling him loud and clear.

But he swigged from the bottle another time—finish it, why not?—and tried to collect his thoughts. Then he glanced towards the door again in the hope that his unexplained fear would be placated. But the thugs were still not there.

At that moment he went deaf and began to lift into the air. Or maybe it was a second later. Maybe he heard the roar of such extraordinary ferocity it could be heard a mile away—in any case, maybe he heard it for just the split second before it deafened him. He could never quite tell later whether he'd heard it or not. Maybe he saw the ball of flame and the sheets of glass and jagged metal struts that erupted through the dance floor and shot forty feet into the air, first licking up into the cages where the beautifully clipped golden crotches writhed, and then engulfing them completely. Or maybe the blindness like the deafness overtook him at once. Again, later, he could never quite tell. But for another, split second nothing seemed to happen. The moment froze. And then, movement and sensation returned like a movie film reel freed from some obstruction in the projector, and he found himself being hurled upwards at great speed, and at the same time blasted backwards by some horrific force, then smashed over the aluminium bar and finally dumped down on its other side with an agonising thud behind a massive refrigerator. Then the refrigerator seemed to explode upwards and disappeared, the bar that protected him caved in completely and seemed to dematerialise, simply vanishing into nothing.

Visions of hell began to swim through all this blindness. A hell beyond anything he had ever experienced. Body parts—that was what the newsmen always called them, using the antiseptic language of the hospital. But amid the crash of falling beams, the explosions of glass, the roar of flame and high explosive, and the screams of people, what he saw was nothing so antiseptic as 'body parts', but severed limbs, ripped chunks of bodies, torched feet and hands freed from their usual places, flaming torsos, flesh-stripped skulls and, once, a severed head that flew with such force from the direction of where the dance floor had once been that the force of it killed the lone, standing barman stone dead.

As the post-blast furnace began to cook, then melt the club and its occupants, Taras crawled out from behind where the fridge had once been. He felt air on his face—the exit—and began to drag himself blindly towards it. One side of his face was hanging off, he thought. But he carried on, smoke choking his lungs, the heat scorching the tan blazer off his back. He'd never get past *feis kontrol* looking like this, he thought dimly. He reached a once-red velvet curtain that swayed from a collapsed rail, and he felt the roar of angry flame behind him reaching, like him, for the air in the street. A siren in the distance; screams subsiding, new screams beginning, the roar of fire, the fizzes and bangs of cracked pipes, the tearing sounds of structural wreckage—they all swam through his fractured consciousness as he gained first the lobby, then the outer entrance, then an open door and the pavement. Still he crawled. He saw feet around him, feet in heavy fire boots and thankfully

124

attached to legs, and then he saw fire hoses. He dimly glimpsed flashing lights—blue, orange—and he heard shouting, before he slumped finally against a wall and felt a hand place an oxygen mask over his mouth.

He lay, dazed, leaning half to the left against the wall like a drunk. He felt burned, torn, fractured, frozen—all at once. Terror, he thought, that was what we call a terror attack. Terror, the crasher at the party, the vengeful handmaiden of a modern election. But whose terror? he wondered through the haze of his shattered mind and through the smoke that poured from a hole in the wall to his left. The Russians? Or was it factional, a Ukrainian terror? Or perhaps terror committed by one of the mafias on either side, Russian or Ukrainian? Who knew? And did it matter? Terror was just terror, wasn't it? Terror terrorised as much by its anonymity as by the exploding bodies that resulted from it. Now, it seemed, it was always terror, the only game in town. Terror that stalked democracy as if both had a compulsive need of each other; terror, against which, in the twenty-first century, freedom was now defined. The alternative to freedom was no longer confinement, it was terror. But terror was also freedom's corollary. They had joined the same coin, were stamped at the same mint, and apparently were now the world's only means of barter.

And then he rose up from the pavement and found that the pools of blood surrounding him weren't his own. He walked unsteadily away from the club, declining offers of help and removing the oxygen mask. Thank God Masha hadn't arrived.

125

CHAPTER EIGHT

A few hours before Taras Tur entered the Golden Fleece nightclub—and at roughly the same time that Anna was making her escape from the field behind Sevastopol and Logan was holding his meeting at the American embassy—Laszlo Lepietre stepped out of the French embassy at number 39 Rue Reterska in the country's capital, Kiev. An embassy car that had been waiting inside the gates for an hour was now idling its engine a hundred yards from the building's entrance. Those had been the driver's orders.

As he walked towards the black Citroën, Laszlo watched for any interest that his exit might have aroused from watchers on either side of the street. But this was only from habit. He didn't expect to attract much attention from the Ukrainian secret services on the night before the first round of the presidential elections. But he watched in any case and he knew his back-ups would be sweeping the pavements behind and ahead of him and checking for any vehicles that might follow the Citroën. The watchers had been trebled for his exit from the embassy. For whatever happened this evening, he couldn't afford to be followed.

Thomas Plismy, the head of the Russian desk in Paris, at the French foreign intelligence service, or DGSE, had insisted—after an unusually swift analysis, Laszlo thought—that this evening's meeting was a genuine dangle, not a hoax. Having been dragged over the coals the year before for losing a valuable KGB colonel—and a beautiful

126

female one at that—who was under French protection and on French soil, Plismy was now looking for something juicy to boost his damaged reputation.

Laszlo walked outside the embassy's wall with a light, boxer's walk, the emphasis on the balls of the feet. A blustery wind now blew the beginnings of a sleet shower directly down Reterska Street and into his face.

At forty-one years old, he kept a trim figure, and made sure its shape was well-advertised to the rest of the world. The hard muscle tones of his medium-height body were accentuated by a cashmere coat over a tight-fitting dark suit, with a white silk scarf draped artfully low around his neck. Even the careful haircut that swept his thick blond hair in a mop to one side seemed to exist only in order to show off the lean, carved face, with its well-oiled and spa-pampered skin. His hands were recently manicured and his clear blue eyes, with their curiously expressionless gaze that bordered on the defensive, seemed to have some neutralising gauze stretched over them. His was a deadening expression, as though any hint of character or personality might upset the physical impression Laszlo wished above all else to convey.

To achieve this physical fitness that was, incidentally, beyond the call of duty, Laszlo spent his spare time climbing mountains, riding in cycle races, skiing and sailing a catamaran off the coast of Brittany. In Kiev he'd had to make do with an expensive gym. To achieve his tough but well-looked-after appearance, some colleagues suggested, required a narcissism of quite exceptional dedication.

With a final look up ahead of the Citroën to check for other parked cars, Laszlo stepped into the rear seat. The retired sous-lieutenant from French special forces who was his chauffeur for the evening pulled out into a steady stream of traffic that was headed out for a Saturday night's entertainment in the clubs and bars of Kiev. It would be a pre-election binge, Laszlo thought with slight disgust, a brain-numbing drink-fest designed to lay to rest the disappointing inadequacy, the lack of achievement in the six years since the Orange Revolution of 2004—and prepare the way for a hoped-for change. Drink to forget the past, that would be it. And drink to welcome the future. The King is dead, long live the King. Whoever won the election, at least there would be change, even if it only meant a few more names added to the list of corrupt Ukrainian industrialists on the new government's books.

As the car threaded its way towards Independence Square, Laszlo wondered how his new posting to Kiev might affect his career, the only aspect of life that he devoted as much attention to as his appearance. Perhaps it would depend on the meeting tonight, he thought. Precious little else had happened since his posting to Kiev that could offer him a moment of glory. Until six months before, when he'd been posted to Ukraine, he had spent five years stationed in Moscow. There, he had made many lasting contacts who were now interested in his new posting—Russians, both *buzinessmen* and KGB officers to whom, unlike the Americans, the French had left an open door of communication.

Laszlo was, principally, a Russo-phile, like his

boss Plismy. And Russia was the biggest game in town if you were in the east of Europe. On top of that the French had special interests in Russia that pre-dated even Napoleon's disastrous defeat in 1812. Russia and France were natural allies, and always had been, despite the embarrassment of that distant invasion. Laszlo believed that France and Russia had a special relationship that would bear fruit now in the twenty-first century. France's energy companies were making great headway in the allocation of contracts by the Kremlin and the Russians were favouring them over the British, let alone the Americans.

But before that, before his posting in Moscow, Laszlo had been stationed at the *Outre Mer*— Overseas Department—of the French Republic's former colony of Guadeloupe. And it was there that in his twenties, as a young, ambitious and comfortably amoral intelligence officer, he had learned the merits of election-fixing. That experience, he thought as the car turned left over the Dnieper river, had served him well in Putin's Russia and—as he fully expected—it would serve him well as the world watched the unfolding of events in Ukraine in the following three weeks, first in tomorrow's elections and in the final run-off between the two leading candidates. At the end of which the final victor would be revealed.

For a moment, a slight sneer marred Laszlo's otherwise blandly smooth countenance with its strange, unwelcoming eyes. The Americans and the British would be out in force tomorrow—as well as in the final vote in three weeks' time—to ensure that the elections in Ukraine were free and fair. The Anglo-Saxons were always there to impose their hypocritical conditions, he thought. As if the American elections were free and fair! But as Laszlo knew, whichever way the Ukrainian elections were viewed in the outside world by the West's electoral observers, behind the scenes the corruption and fixing would be of the usual gigantic proportions. And that was why this meeting tonight intrigued him. He was hoping that it would be an insight into what was really going on in and outside Ukraine to influence the elections.

'Take a couple of turns,' he said to the driver. He spoke little and when he did his voice was flat. The sous-lieutenant obediently went twice round Independence Square.

Laszlo had been many things in the past eighteen years besides an intelligence officer: soldier, journalist, trade representative, election observer, though all the time the underlying reason for these diversions was his job as a DGSE intelligence officer. But he seemed to have no friends from his previous incarnations. He was unmarried. Ambition seemed to be absent from his considerations, but only seemed so. Tonight he felt that here was the moment he'd been waiting for; an opportunity for advancement. Like his boss Plismy, he sensed that he was close to something crucial, to something that would, ultimately, bring him the power that all his patience, self-control and disinterest in other human beings had prepared him for.

The driver finally turned the Citroën away from the square and it made its way smoothly, though by a roundabout route, towards the Theatre of Russian Drama not far from Kreschatik. They crossed the Dnieper river twice more, turned

130

around in a U once, stopped to buy a magazine from a kiosk by St Sophia's Cathedral, and stalled deliberately at a crossroads further up the street, holding up angry drivers who flattened their hands to their car horns. And on each occasion, driver and passenger observed the similarities and differences in the street landscape, without forming the conclusion that they were being tailed.

Finally, the Citroën pulled up outside the theatre. Laszlo stepped out of the car without a word to his driver. He entered the theatre, checked his coat, bought a ticket for Tchaikovsky's *Queen of Spades*, and then entered the auditorium. He saw the two fire exits on either side near the stage and passed down on the right side to a fire door that led to a side street. He took no notice of the young usherette who asked him where he was going. Within a minute of walking out of the theatre, he'd checked all the possibilities and concluded he was on his own.

He walked briskly, not least because of the cold. Though prepared for walking with no coat—he wore a silk thermal vest under his suit—January was not a month for an evening stroll through Kiev's streets. First he retraced part of the Citroën's route back in the direction of Independence Square. The billboards he passed in the capital's streets were dominated by election themes and by the eighteen candidates for the opening round of the next day's elections. Sixteen of them would be gone by tomorrow night and, with them, their investment. There were only two candidates who had a chance of passing into the last round.

The city had slowly filled with foreign election

observers in the previous days but, unlike in the heady period of the Orange Revolution six years before, the signs of electoral interest from actual Ukrainians on the streets was minimal; there were no crowds as he entered the square, just a few minor rallies, that was all, mostly extremist groups largely made up of pensioners from the old days of the Soviet Union and a smattering of far-right nationalists with skinhead views. After six years of disappointed dreams under the incumbent president, Viktor Yuschenko, Ukrainians seemed to believe that their political views no longer made any difference.

Laszlo crossed the square and made for a café in a side street that was to be the meeting place.

He entered the Reprisa café at 8.25 and, buying a short black coffee, he retreated to the back of the orange-coloured space and took a stool screwed to the floor and against a wall. There were a dozen or so people in the café, the strip lights were shockingly bright and seemed designed to put a customer off from staying too long. He withdrew a newspaper from inside his jacket and, with his back to the rest of the café, began to reread stories he'd read earlier in the day. He was patient and seemed incapable of boredom. Life, he thought, held few surprises, even a secret life.

He had read the paper from cover to cover and drunk two more short coffees before his elation at the thought of the forthcoming meeting began to be replaced by a feeling of anticlimax. He'd looked around the café from time to time. There were three high school girls sitting at a table. They looked at him, spoke in whispers, laughed occasionally and self-consciously in his direction, then returned to their own affairs. A man in a slightly grubby black suit sat in a far corner. There were two other men still wearing their hats and coats as they sat at the counter, and other, scattered groups dotted elsewhere who seemed to have no plans for the evening. But by 9 p.m. the café was beginning to thin out. Everyone who had any plans was heading off for their evening's entertainment. In half an hour, only the lonely would remain, and then the café would close anyway.

It was not, Laszlo thought curiously, a good place for a meeting anyway; it was too bright, too sparsely populated, too public. And the small window in time for the meeting was unusual too. There was just a half-hour in which it could take place before the café closed; 8.45 until 9.15 was the time the contact had dictated. For a moment Laszlo felt unnerved, uncertain about his hopes for the evening.

He reviewed once more what they knew about the proposed contact on this evening, 16 January 2010. That he was a contact from the Russian side, Plismy seemed to be sure this was the case—though why he was sure was anyone's guess. Codename: Rafael (chosen by the contact, not by them, not by Paris—the contact had insisted on that). Sex: male. Age: in his late thirties or early forties. Nationality: Russian, Middle Eastern or from one of the former Soviet republics in the Caucasus mountains. This seemed unnecessarily vague, though agents often obfuscated details of their identity, for obvious reasons. Usefulness: unknown, but rumoured to be in possession of some highly sensitive information regarding the

Kremlin's intentions in Ukraine. Purpose of contact: find out those intentions. In other words, clear-cut, straightforward and simple. At least, that was what it should have been, Laszlo thought. All he needed was for the damned contact to actually show up.

Laszlo now sat half-turned towards the entrance to the café, willing 'Rafael' to enter in the dying moments left. To his vague surprise, at just after 9.15 p.m., he saw a face he recognised. The man was walking head down, almost obscuring his identity, along the wet pavement outside the rain-streaked window. Laszlo had exchanged information with this man before—the man worked in the intelligence communications section at the Italians' Kiev embassy. Behind him, at a distance of some twenty-five yards, Laszlo now saw a Romanian intelligence officer he also recognised. Coincidence? Possibly. Was the one following the other? Likely, he supposed.

Kiev seemed to have become a front line of sorts for the world's intelligence agencies, and in particular those of Western Europe. The whole country was crawling with spies—officers, agents, informers . . . Kiev appeared to have become what Vienna had once been in the Cold War. It was bang up against Russia, as Vienna had once been before the Soviet collapse and the Russian retreat from Eastern Europe. And now, after twenty years of its own form of capitalism, Russia now transported its energy supplies at great profit to Western Europe's hungry nations. And with its vast network of pipelines, Ukraine held the key to Western Europe's energy needs. Without Ukraine's willingness, or ability, to transport

Russian oil and gas, the EU countries were beggared. That was why Russia's meddling in the country was of the greatest interest to all.

The two men passed outside the window and out of sight. Laszlo turned away, back to his study of the wall two feet away. A plasticised picture of the Orange Revolution met his gaze, a kind of photographic negative, tinged in orange. It seemed almost quaintly out of date—after only six years.

France's view, he knew, was to bypass Ukraine's interests and befriend Russia. Soon, anyway, there would be pipelines directly from Russia underneath the Baltic that would curtail Ukraine's importance as a go-between. But France had its own, and possibly unique policy. The Anglo-Saxons seemed intent to keep the two countries separate, to keep Ukraine independent of the Kremlin. Good luck to them, Laszlo thought—but in his opinion, that wasn't going to happen. The forces against it were too great. So the intelligent thing to do—France's secret policy—was to prepare for the eventuality of Ukraine's return to Russian rule—direct or indirect was unimportant—after more than twenty years of the country's independence.

By 9.30, the last moment for the meeting had passed. Now that no one had showed up and when he was alone in the café with only the two men in coats and hats, Laszlo realised that his expectations for the evening were not going to be met. The café was closing. There was no fallback venue, that was odd, too. It was over, at least for tonight. The contact, he guessed hopefully, must simply have been delayed.

Laszlo paid now, for his three coffees in an

hour, and he left the café just as a woman with a broom swept up the day's detritus from beneath the chairs and tables. He decided to walk and ended up back at the theatre where he retrieved his coat.

*   *   *

The non-appearance of the man who called himself Rafael was a recurrent theme in Kiev on that night of 16 January, and not just in Kiev. In other towns and cities across Ukraine—not to mention one proposed meeting by a lakeside near the Russian border which the unfortunate head of intelligence at the Chinese embassy pointlessly attended—Ukraine's spy community was coaxed to attend meetings that never took place. Rafael turned out to be a chimera. In total, the embassies of fourteen different countries sent out their intelligence officers on this wild goose chase. Rafael had spun his web so effectively that none of those contacted knew any more by the end of the night than what Rafael had chosen to give them— which was very little and even that, it was assumed, would turn out to be false.

But with the intelligence community living on top of itself in the city and though meetings between the officers of different agencies were largely covert, soon the rumour began to pass around the watering holes and restaurants of Kiev that everyone had fallen for Rafael whom Rafael had contacted. It started with an apparently innocent question from an intelligence officer at the German embassy to his opposite number at the Spanish embassy: 'Come across a source who calls

136

himself Rafael?' was the casual remark. Then the question was repeated in bars, until it left the street talk of the spies and graduated to informal chats between the chiefs of the different national agencies involved.

At first there was reluctance. Nobody wanted to admit they'd been fooled until someone else admitted it first. At first nobody even admitted to knowing anything about anyone called Rafael. But soon everyone grew to the understanding that they had all been set up, equally and with no shame, and then the discussions between rival and allied agencies became more open. Rafael made it on to the agendas of inter-agency meetings, he was tagged by NATO, and he was openly discussed now in the bars and restaurants of Kiev whenever any two officers from different countries crossed paths, either by design or by accident. Rafael was an embarrassment, then he became a joke, an anecdote, until finally he was filed away at the very back of the fine minds who'd been taken in, to be forgotten at the earliest possible convenience. Why did he do it? Whoever this Rafael was. It was generally assumed that he was just some clever student who, instead of hacking his way into national computer networks, preferred a more earthy approach in order to mess around with the world's intelligence efforts. And so, finally, Rafael was laid to rest, and the world moved on.

On the following day, a Sunday, all eyes in Kiev and in the political world at large were anyway focused on the first round of the elections. Of the eighteen candidates who were standing, by the end of the first round two remained for the run-off in three weeks' time—Yulia Timoshenko and Viktor

Yanukovich, the man who had benefited from the fixed elections in 2004 which had led to the Orange Revolution. He was Russia's preferred candidate for ultimate victory, it was noted, while Ms Timoshenko appeared to be available for wooing by all sides, west and east.

At the American Embassy in Kiev, at number 6 Mykoly Pymonenka Street, the Rafael affair, or incident—or spoof, as it was commonly known—caused a similar confusion, and then an irritation, as it had caused elsewhere. Sam MacLeod, the CIA's station head had, in fact, despatched a relatively junior officer to a meeting with Rafael at a small town in the Carpathian Mountains—a day trip that was enjoyed by the officer despite its lack of success. And, as elsewhere in Kiev's intelligence community, Rafael was swiftly relegated to an elaborate prank by the Americans.

But on that very morning of the elections, 16 January, however, a letter had been delivered to the embassy, sealed in a quaintly old-fashioned way with red wax, on which there was an impression of a bird. The letter was addressed not to anyone at the embassy, but to Burt Miller, head of Cougar Intelligence Applications, which had foisted Logan into MacLeod's presence. Burt Miller was known throughout the CIA community at a national level. A senior ex-CIA officer himself, then a director at the CIA, he could now be said to call the shots on certain matters of national intelligence, due to the enormous wealth of Cougar, as well as the expertise and the ensuing government contracts that Cougar netted annually. And in the East, from Kiev to the Tajik border with China—including the vast landmass of

Russia—Burt's name was very well known indeed in certain circles. It was here in the empty regions of central Asia that had been his original stamping ground. As a man in his early twenties he had begun his explosive intelligence career over forty years before in the great central Asian plains and mountains.

Because of his—and Cougar's—importance to the CIA and general good regard from its chief Theo Lish, the unopened letter was put on a morning plane to London, where Burt Miller was meeting with the head of Britain's Secret Intelligence Service, Adrian Carew, before they both attended a meeting of NATO intelligence chiefs in Brussels in the following week. During a brief break in his talks with Adrian Carew, Burt carefully slit the top of the envelope, avoiding causing damage to the seal, and withdrew a single sheet of paper. On it he read, 'Rafael will not be meeting tonight'. He stared at the message for a long time and then replaced the sheet back into its envelope.

When he returned to the meeting with Adrian, Burt hadn't the slightest clue to the meaning of the six words, or of who Rafael might be—if anyone. But Burt Miller was a man who allowed his instincts full rein, and they were usually good. On this occasion he felt a growing sense of excitement that these instincts—this time for an intelligence coup of some importance—told him was genuine. This instinct, he regularly told his juniors in briefing sessions, and using the third person to describe himself like any autocrat would, was 'Burt's line to God'.

CHAPTER NINE

Sunday, 17 January

The view beyond the table and through the porthole from aboard Burt Miller's 302 foot yacht *Cougar* was of Tower Bridge and the City of London. Anna looked through the round glass and saw the skies were a uniform battleship grey. A light rain was spattering the glass of the porthole and the wide panoramic windows on either side of it in a needling sort of way. The irritable flecks of rain glancing off the glass seemed to be an insistent reminder that London's monochrome winter wasn't going away.

Inside, however, the artificial lighting in the sumptuous operations room of the ship was almost too bright by comparison and was particularly focused over the large, square mahogany table. It was almost the size of a small room in itself and stood with a kind of magnificent defiance right at the centre of the deck-wide space. Burt Miller was standing by the table, while Anna sat to the side on a high upholstered stool and pensively drank from a cup of coffee.

Burt grinned at her as he made a great ceremony of opening the plastic envelope she had delivered. There was a boyish glint in his eye as if it had been a birthday present Anna had given him and she was his lover rather than an employee of Cougar Intelligence Applications who had brought him secret intelligence documents.

He finally drew out a sheaf of folded papers and

140

carefully opened them up until they could both see there were three large, light-blue sheets in all, each four feet by three feet in dimension. Burt triumphantly laid out the three photocopied sheets of what would have been, in the original, drawings on architectural white paper. He placed them on the mahogany desk in a row, one after the other. Burt surveyed the plans with an air of satisfaction. Then he looked at her and grinned a second time.

'Plans for the port of Novorossiysk,' he said triumphantly and looked back at them as if they were a map of buried treasure. 'Or the development of the port of Novorossiysk, shall we say. Highly secret. Very restricted. Our agent has done very well to obtain them.' Then he looked at Anna. 'And you, my dear, had an even more difficult task, I hear from Larry.' He beamed his wide grin that creased the flesh of his face upwards until his eyes were almost invisible. 'You are the best there is.'

Anna was sitting on the high stool that gave her a view from higher up on to the table and the plans. She'd arrived at the yacht only an hour before and it had been just over ten hours since they'd picked her up off the beach in the Crimea. With Larry alone, she had been helicoptered off the Nigerian-registered freighter to Ankara, where one of Burt's private jets was waiting to take them both to London. She'd slept little on the flight and then Burt had wanted to see her immediately. She would have been happy to send Larry with the delivery without her. She'd done her job. She took pride in being just a field operative. But she knew Burt wouldn't leave her alone until she agreed to share with him the contents of the package. As with most things in his life, Burt enjoyed the ritual, the ceremonial element, and her company was an essential ingredient for both things.

Now he stood in a pair of navy-blue trousers and an extravagantly tailored Gilbert and Sullivan-style yachting blazer that seemed to her to be a deliberate mockery of maritime pomposity. Perhaps it was. Burt liked dressing up—it was playacting—she knew that. She'd seen him in many such incongruous situations and disguises and the yachting paraphernalia was undoubtedly a disguise and one that he had donned simply for his own amusement. On this ship, he was the eccentric Edwardian billionaire owner. When he was at his mansion in Connecticut he was the English gentleman in tweeds and plus fours who owned his own fox hunt, had his clothes made to measure in London's Savile Row, but he couldn't actually ride a horse. At his vast ranch in New Mexico he dressed in the manner of a nineteenth-century American cattle baron. And in the corridors of power in Washington he was the ultimate flamboyant corporate owner in silk suits and hand-made shoes. Wherever he was, it seemed he simply enjoyed living any dream he felt like living, and which his enormous wealth could effortlessly make a reality.

His big, round face glowed like a ripe apple and his rotund, well-fed form seemed itself to stretch the imagination. There was nothing too big for Burt, apparently. At least that was the effect of his outsize physical presence and the outsize personality that kept in lock-step with it. Now he smoked a large cigar, a Churchill, another almost permanent accessory in his props cupboard, and which, for the moment, was fuming quietly on its own in a large bronze ashtray shaped like an anchor. There were other half-smoked or quarter-smoked cigars of great commercial value that could be found discarded wherever it was that Burt was currently passing through life and Anna could see at least three of them now lying like unexploded ordnance in various ashtrays around the room.

She didn't respond to his knowing enquiry. Burt's questions and interrogatory remarks were in general of a declamatory nature and usually didn't require a reply.

But Burt wanted to relish the moment, to extract the maximum amount of suspense from the presence of the architectural plans and, before he took a close look at them, he went over to a refrigerator, plucked out a bottle of Krug champagne and opened it. Another largely ceremonial gesture, as he would drink perhaps half a glass at most.

A big man—though at just under five feet eight inches he seemed bigger than he was—Burt was, to Anna, exuding his usual warmth and confident bonhomie this afternoon, though it was tinted as always with a subcutaneous level of granite. The geological strata of Burt began on the surface with a sunny, welcoming, friendly terrain, while underneath it the bedrock was absolutely unyielding. And his smile usually left room for this hard power to be always visible behind it.

The combination of the two effects—the sweet and sour of Burt—would have been equally appropriate in a mafia boss attending his daughter's wedding, or a casino owner welcoming a high net-worth client. Welcome to my World, was Burt's usual *modus operandi* and he treated others largely as if they were present for his own entertainment.

Burt handed her a glass and raised his own.

'To a great partnership,' he said. 'I have everything to be grateful for that I ever came across you.'

'Thank you, Burt.' She drank. 'You know we lost the courier. I believe she shot herself.'

'Larry told me.'

'Apparently in order to save the agent,' Anna said. 'He must have trained her well.'

Burt allowed a moment of silence, more to allow the evaporation of the awkwardness of the news than in respectful memory of the girl.

'We have to protect our agents,' he said simply. Then he looked back at the table and the event was forgotten.

'Let's see what we have here,' he said, beamed, and put his glass down on the table. He fingered the left-hand sheet and read the title, which Anna had already studied while he was displaying his relaxed self-assurance and opening the champagne. 'This one, the sheet on the left, is what exists already. Port facilities, refuelling capacity, open water anchorages, quays and dry docks, as well as land transportation to and from the port.' He walked eighteen inches or so to the right and the next page. 'And these two,' he read the Russian Cyrillic writing on the legend at the top of the second and third sheet, 'these two are the proposed developments, signed and sealed by the Ministry of Defence in Moscow, approved by the navy and the security services, rubber-stamped unseen by the Russian parliament and ultimately ordered by Czar Vladimir Putin. So what do we see?'

Anna stayed on the stool. She knew Burt and knew she was expected to join the little dramas in which he chose to perform. But to her, the drama of the plans in front of them seemed overblown. They were plans of a relatively minor Russian naval military installation and commercial port on the far side of the Kerch Straits and across the Black Sea, to the east of the Crimea on Russian territory. Novorossiysk was just a Russian port, that was all, across the water from its old possession, Ukraine. She wondered how the plans could possibly have been worth the death of a courier, an innocent, deceived courier at that, not to mention her own near capture and the execution that would inevitably have followed back in Moscow.

'Well?' Burt said almost gleefully.

She got up from the stool now and, walking up to the table, leaned forward to study the drawings.

'They're architectural engineering plans that show proposed extensions to what's already there at the port,' she said. 'The proposition seems to be a deepening of the harbour. Most of the quays and loading facilities look like they're being upgraded, there are new oil storage tanks, two new roads leading in to the port, and upgrade of the rail track.' Anna looked more closely. 'I guess it's an expansion of the port by maybe twenty per cent.'

'Exactly. Twenty, maybe thirty, per cent,' Burt said. 'And that's not enough, is it?' He beamed at her triumphantly.

'Enough for what?' she said.

145

But Burt wasn't going to be drawn on this point, not yet in any case. He ran his finger down the lines of the drawings as if he were studying some old masterpiece and trying to judge its origins. He was a collector of art, mainly modern British art in the past few years. That suited his general anglophilia, which he had developed over forty years before as a Rhodes scholar at Oxford. But at his other homes in the United States, Anna remembered seeing a Picasso sketch hanging in a bathroom, a Turner on a staircase and one old master she couldn't recall in a study somewhere that was reputed to have cost Burt sixty-five million dollars.

'Tell me about Novorossiysk, Anna,' he said.

Anna returned to her seat on the stool and gave him a brief description. 'It's a southern port of Russia's on the Black Sea. A warm water port, one of very few Russia possesses, and therefore strategically important. Russia's and, before that, the Soviet Union's Mediterranean fleet has used it more or less in its present form for more than fifty years, though it was always second to Sevastopol in Ukraine. Sevastopol's always been the big base. Until the Soviet Union collapsed, Sevastopol had a hundred thousand men stationed there. Now it's more like forty thousand. The Russian Mediterranean fleet has been largely inactive since the 1990s. Many of its ships are going out of date, rusting away, and being decommissioned. But now Putin wants to expand it again, to patrol the Mediterranean, go up against America's Sixth Fleet once more. Novorossiysk was—is—mainly a commercial port, with some Russian navy facilities. In the days of the Soviet Union, it was the main exporter from the southern republics. But oil and gas was its main export. And that's been on the increase. Oil and gas from the Caspian. Now that's being diverted into pipelines, so the importance of Novorossiysk will undoubtedly decline. There isn't much else that Russia exports from there. Some timber, foodstuffs from the southern republics. That's about it.'

'It's in decline as a commercial port, then,' Burt said. 'And as an alternative? Is it an alternative to the Russian Black Sea fleet's base in Sevastopol?'

'It could be, but unlikely.'

'After the upgrade that these plans demonstrate, perhaps?'

'Yes, but it would need more development than these plans show. Besides, Sevastopol has a natural deep-water harbour, bays five miles deep. It's one of the best harbours in the world.'

'Exactly,' Burt said again. 'And that's what makes these plans so interesting. They're just what I expected.'

Anna got up from the stool again and walked to the far end of the room. She looked out at the Thames through one of the wide panoramic windows, two of which flanked the porthole that was really just for show, it seemed. She began to tot up what Burt had spent on this operation in the previous days: the freighter which was presumably hired, Larry and the others in the boat, a helicopter to Turkey, then the private flight to London. And herself, of course. She didn't take into account the death of the courier, it was unquantifiable. Yet all this money and the girl's death had been for a few drawings of port improvements at Novorossiysk. None of it made a

147

great deal of sense to her.

'Larry treat you all right?' Burt said.

'He was on time,' she replied.

'He'd never be late for you, Anna.' Burt grinned. 'Even on a windswept beach in the Crimea. None of us would be.'

He seemed to enjoy her coolness, she thought. The perfect complement, perhaps, to his own flamboyance. He'd as good as said so when he'd made her a director of Cougar. As a former KGB colonel in special forces and in the highly secret Department S, she'd caused quite a stir inside Washington's beltway. Specialist magazines had wanted to write her profile, though largely, it appeared, in order to show pictures of her. Burt paid them not to by taking several large and expensive corporate advertising spots.

'It was a wise move to come out off the beach,' Burt continued. 'Much better than risking the border posts.'

Was this remark disingenuous? she wondered. Did he really think she'd have risked so much in order to rendezvous with a boat on hostile territory? She turned towards him, but all she saw was his big beaming expression.

'It was the only choice,' she replied. She looked across the room at him and held his eyes. He looked back at her with a quizzical expression now. 'There's a leak, Burt,' she said. 'They were following me from Istanbul. On the ferry. They also knew about the pick-up. They had the barn staked out. That's why the courier killed herself.'

Burt raised his eyes and looked at her. 'You didn't mention this to Larry.'

'No.'

'And you still got the goods,' he said in admiration. He always focused on the positive, sometimes to the point of foolish optimism, she thought. Once again, the courier's death went unmentioned.

'There's a leak, Burt, perhaps at Cougar,' she repeated firmly. Then she looked straight into his eyes until he could no longer return her gaze with equanimity.

'They were there? On the boat from Istanbul?' he said, seriously now.

'More importantly, they were there at the barn. They knew everything about my movements from the start. It was only because they wanted me alive that I got out at all. They could have taken me any time.'

Burt picked up a phone and immediately connected with a switchboard. 'Get me Bob Dupont. In here.' He replaced the phone. 'We'll see what Bob has to say. I had no idea, Anna. This is serious. I'm sorry.'

'Never be sorry,' she said, repeating one of his own maxims.

He grinned at her.

Bob Dupont, Burt's head of internal security, entered the operations room a few minutes later. Tall, silver-haired, his running joke at Cougar was that he was the only person in the company who was older than Burt. He greeted Anna, nodded at Burt, and came over to the table. He looked down at the drawings. Burt poured him a glass of champagne which he didn't touch. Dupont didn't drink, Burt knew that perfectly well. Sometimes Anna thought that Burt just liked to have two glasses available for himself, even though he didn't

149

drink them. Life is about expansion, he liked to say.

'I went to Novorossiysk over forty years ago,' Burt said as Dupont studied the plans. 'Twenty-eight years old, just married, and working for the agency.' He grinned at Anna's questioning look. 'Before you were born,' he said to her. 'The height of the Cold War.'

'These are what Anna's returned with?' Dupont asked.

'That's right,' Burt answered. 'And only I knew what the delivery consisted of. Not even Anna.' He walked over to stand beside Dupont. 'But how many people in Cougar knew of Anna's assignment, Bob? The details. And who outside Cougar?'

'The three of us. And Larry—but none of the other boys with him.'

'Did you tell the Russians, Bob?' Burt said mischievously.

Dupont looked momentarily wrong-footed, before realising that this was Burt's usual line of humour. He didn't respond.

'The three of us and Larry,' Burt said. 'Who outside?'

'You informed the CIA,' Dupont pointed out.

'But not the times or dates, just the general outline.'

'The general outline, but they could have looked more closely if they'd wished. They might have been checking out the hiring of the freighter, I suppose, and found it was ours. We disguised it, of course, but you never know. They might even have been tracking Anna. It's possible.'

'Why would they do that?'

'Professional jealousy, that's the only reason. You know how the agency feels threatened by Cougar. And you also know, Burt, how they like to know everything.'

'Lish is our man,' Burt said.

'But who knows if he passed it on to anyone. Watching us, or Anna, is in the normal run of things for the agency.'

'Get him on the phone.'

Burt picked up the cigar from the ashtray and champed it between his teeth.

'Why are you asking this?' Dupont said.

'There's been a leak. Anna could have lost her life.'

'And the courier was killed,' Anna reminded him.

Dupont looked shocked. Against Burt's easy acceptance of the status quo he was visibly disturbed.

'Don't get in a state about it, Bob. Let's just deal with what's happening.' Burt's mantra was always the same, familiar refrain to Cougar employees and, before that, to CIA recruits whom Burt had once taught at the CIA's training centre, known as The Farm, in Virginia. 'The only thing that matters is what happens'—no regrets, no self-chastisement, no anxiety—just act in the frame of what happens, that was Burt's time-honoured method. 'What happens is King, God, and all you need to know.'

'You want to talk with him in here?' Dupont asked.

'Yes, call Theo from the dedicated phone. I want to get him right away, give him no time to consider it.'

And so Dupont put a call through to Langley

from Burt's yacht and the CIA chief, Theo Lish, came to the phone after a minute or two. When Burt took the phone from Dupont, he walked away from the table towards the stern of the ship and spoke to him from the far end of the operations room. After a five-minute conversation he returned, handing Dupont the phone as if he were unable to put it down himself.

'I have my own ideas about this,' he said, but he didn't expand, nor did he relay the contents of the conversation he'd just had with Lish. 'Now, let's have an early dinner. You must be tired, Anna, and there's something else I want you to do before the NATO meeting next week.'

It was the reason for Burt's presence in Europe, a meeting of NATO intelligence chiefs in Brussels that took place every few months and to which Cougar was now invited. Burt's influence had brought him to the national level of intelligence consultation and, in truth, Cougar rivalling the CIA in importance carried considerably more weight in the international intelligence spectrum than many of the sovereign states in NATO.

'By the way, I want you at that meeting, Anna,' he said. 'Alongside me.'

Dupont looked questioningly at him.

'Not this time, Bob. This time I'm taking Anna. She's going to make a presentation.'

He looked at her, expecting a question, but she wasn't going to give him the easy satisfaction and, once again, she saw he liked her self-contained coolness.

They dined on board the ship. The *Cougar*, as well as the ranch in New Mexico and half a dozen other possessions of importance to him, had a crew of forty-five, and eight of them were chefs. 'It's the best food in the City of London,' Burt boasted, though clearly without intending anyone to believe him. Burt's world was one of endless positive beliefs. He was the epitome of positive thinking no matter what the situation was.

Throughout the three-course meal, with the usual accompaniment of excellent wines, he regaled Dupont and Anna with stories of his youth in the CIA, stories both of them had heard before but which Anna listened to each time in order to spot the occasional inconsistency. Burt liked to elaborate—or fabricate—much of his experiences in the field. She doubted, in fact, that he had ever been to Novorossiysk at all.

After dinner, Dupont left the ship and Burt suggested that Anna should stay and sleep on the *Cougar*, instead of at the company apartment. She readily agreed. Pouring himself a brandy in the saloon, Burt sat in a large armchair.

'You were too young to have worked in the days of the Cold War,' he said.

'I joined the KGB in 1990,' she replied.

'And now the world is reshaping itself again,' he said. 'Who will come nearer to the top of the pile and who will drop back?'

She didn't reply this time, knowing that these conversational brushstrokes were his way of getting to the point.

'The new Cold War is different from the old one only in terms of geographical location,' he said. 'Once it was worldwide; arming African and South American potentates, spreading our rivalling ideologies thinly across the globe. Now the new Cold War is being fought in the former states of the Soviet Union. In central Asia it's about oil and gas supply, as well as Russian and American military bases in countries like Kyrgizstan. American wars in Afghanistan and no doubt beyond Afghanistan before long require us having bases there. The Russians see our soft spot and try to exploit it. In the Caucasus, Russia invaded Georgia to prevent NATO expansion there. And then there's Ukraine, Russia's soul. That's where we must look now.'

'Endless conflict,' Anna murmured.

'We find out who our enemies are in times of conflict,' he said. 'And that is why we need conflict. Conflict cleans out the stables, reveals what lies underneath history's layers. Conflict is necessary to see the enemy.'

'Haven't the Americans had enough conflict?' she said. She got out of her chair and poured herself a brandy.

'America has made mistakes,' he answered. 'America always sees the obvious at the expense of the obscure. It waited until it was attacked before it addressed the *jihad*. Now it talks of wars of prevention, of pre-emption—as if that were a new concept, but it's always tried to pre-empt. Central and South America are one long, and generally disastrous, episode in America's pre-emptive struggle against its enemies. But they were small fry. Deposing the odd dictator in the Third World doesn't even sharpen the teeth. No. America has got scared of its real enemies. Maybe it always has been. Maybe it has only ever reacted against its real enemies, rather than acted. The Cold War was one long reaction.'

'What are you saying? That they should have

nuked Moscow?'

Burt laughed. 'No, nothing of the sort and you know it.'

'There were enough proxy wars to fill an encyclopaedia,' she replied. 'What else could America have done?'

'I'm not interested in history, let alone potential history,' Burt said. 'History never taught anyone anything. I'm interested in flushing out our enemies now. And I want you to pursue this theme for Cougar. In the field, if you insist. Though I'd rather you were directing operations.'

'You know the deal. I'll only work in the field. That's where I'm best.'

'I know that.'

'And you mean against Russia.'

'Yes. But the purpose is two-fold. Russia is becoming the enemy again. But of equal importance, I want to know who are Russia's appeasers in the West. I want to flush out Russia's intentions but also find which way certain other countries in Europe will jump. With us—with America—or with Russia.'

'What has this got to do with Novorossiysk?'

'Maybe something. But that's for down the line a little. I need to send someone into Ukraine again. If it's you, you need to leave tomorrow in order to be back in Brussels in time.'

'Is it important that I come to Brussels?'

'I'd like you to be there.'

She didn't enquire why.

But for once Burt explained. 'I think you'll have something bang up to date from your trip—if you decide to go.'

And then Burt stood and withdrew a set of maps

155

from a chart desk. They were aerial and satellite maps, as well as regular ones for roads and terrain.

'These are the interesting ones,' Burt said and pointed at a pile of satellite photographs which came with the maps. 'From Cougar's own satellite in the past two weeks. And this one from the US World View satellite.'

She didn't ask him how he'd obtained the latter but stood and looked down on a faux chart table on which Burt had placed the maps. The maps were high-definition studies of Ukraine's border with Russia, but to the north of the country, far away from the Crimea from where she'd just returned. They focused on the Kursk area on the Russian side and Sumy on the Ukrainian side. In each of the satellite pictures, two unmarked military trucks, in various states of magnification, were shown proceeding towards the Ukrainian border from the Russian side and by various roundabout routes.

'The interesting thing', Burt said, 'is that they seem to be receiving privileged passage on the Russian side from Russia's border patrols. They go unmolested by small roads and tracks to a mile from the border. Then they stop.' He looked at her. 'What I want to know is what are the intentions of the men inside them? Satellites can't tell us that.'

CHAPTER TEN

19 January

The two unmarked gunmetal-grey trucks were displaying no lights as they moved slowly along the track towards the no-man's land of the border zone. After the deliberately roundabout journey from Kursk which had taken four hours instead of the usual two and a half, the men inside had finally reached their first destination, the jumping-off point, and they pulled up just over three miles from the border. For the next three miles from here towards Ukraine was traditionally accessible only with military or KGB passes. In the brief period of democracy in the 1990s, Russia had handed over border control from the KGB to regular border police. Now, since Putin had been in power, the KGB had been given back that control.

The muffled engines of the trucks went quiet and the men inside sat in silence, three in each truck, while the dusk drew in around them. It wasn't a long wait. When the darkness had deepened into a cold January night all six men then stepped out, stood near the trucks blowing on their hands and stamping their feet. But all the time they looked towards the border.

The men wore combat fatigues and, like the trucks, they had no insignia to identify them as officers of military counter-intelligence from the Russian 3rd FSB Division. But all the men displayed the word *Patriotiy*, written in black, across the shoulders of their jackets. It was more of a gang slogan, an embroidered tattoo, than any identification. Each man had sewn on the word himself.

As the last of the sun's light faded from the distant horizon, the vast flat steppe around them absorbed the night and disappeared.

The older of the men, a veteran colonel in his forties, pulled open the driver's door of the first truck and took out a back pack. There were no spoken orders. It was evident they all had their tasks and it had been rehearsed meticulously. The colonel stood for a moment and listened. The night was still. There was no sound to disturb the silence, no wind, no water, no human or even animal presence. The moon was four days old, a thin silver sliver in the eastern sky that offered no light even when the clouds briefly parted. The veteran looked into the blackness. Three miles ahead of them and to the west, now lost in the darkness, was the 1200-mile-long border that separated Russia and Ukraine.

He checked that there were no lights that shouldn't be there, no random border patrol vehicles on either side. They should have all been pulled back to let his mission through, but you never knew. The Forest's chain of command was obsessed with secrecy, even when it was necessary to be open enough to keep away prying eyes. He was looking with his naked eye for lights first of all. He already knew there was no human habitation along this stretch of the border—that was why it had been chosen—and the only lights he could see were the sparsely placed border posts which displayed a few glimmering yellow arc lamps in the far distance. But the border posts were two miles to the north and south of where the trucks were going—where they should be. The colonel spat on the frozen earth. In any case, it was a border that the six men—and their masters in Moscow—believed shouldn't be there at all. The *patriotiy* wanted the border removed, so that Russia and the historical birthplace of Old Rus were one again. To the colonel and his men, the darkness and the thinly stretched border posts seemed to exist for the sole purpose of tempting men to cross without papers.

Without a word, the men climbed back into the trucks and now in the cover of darkness drove a further two miles down a more derelict cart track this time, and always towards the border.

The mission had been planned in great detail, just like all the others. Four days before this particular night, at Kraznomenniy Street in Moscow, a building secretly owned by Russia's Interior Ministry, the mission had been laid out before the six men. It was the shortest time line and one that left as little room for error as possible. Three Interior Ministry officials were in attendance. The ministry officials were the formal representatives of the *patriotiy*, which were a wide, shadowy grouping of KGB officers that reached from the lowest ranks to the senior leaders of the intelligence services. For the purpose of this meeting at Kraznomenniy, the three officials were typical of the leadership type. They were all either in or approaching their sixties, all ranking KGB veterans of the Russian war in Afghanistan launched on Christmas Day 1979, and they all nursed the anger and resentment of Russia's

159

intelligence services and special forces at the motherland's humiliating defeat back then. In the intervening period up to the present day they and their colleagues had ascended the ranks of the ministry, thanks to their KGB backgrounds, and now controlled a powerful clique inside the Interior Ministry, one of Moscow's more powerful centres of authority. The ageing officials were gifted with powers that ranged from control of Russia's prisons to censorship of the media, and 'special operations' on Russian territory.

And for the purpose of this mission—code-named with utmost simplicity 'Repossession'—the independent state of Ukraine, a land with its own culture and language and with an application to join the European Union, was considered by all concerned to be part of Russia's territory.

Inside the higher echelons of the KGB, the interior ministry clique was openly known as the *patriotiy*. But outside it, they were only the subject of gossip in street cafés, rumour and conspiracy theories. The clique was an unofficial branch of Department S, however, itself a highly secret body within the KGB responsible for aggressive measures on foreign soil. In the usual arrangement of the structure of Russian dolls regularly adopted by the KGB's special forces, a discreet distance was placed between the actual perpetrators of terrorist attacks on foreign soil and their ultimate controllers. There were the men on the ground— in this case, the six men. Above them were the interior ministry officials. Then came the shadowy figures from Department S, then an irregular KGB committee set up for the purpose that itself answered to the head of the intelligence service,

160

then a Kremlin intelligence liaison, and finally the prime minister himself, Vladimir Putin. If anything went wrong with this mission—a high-risk smuggling operation on to another country's sovereign territory—the six men would simply be declared independent *mafiosi* out for their own commercial gain. The men were happy enough with that denial, even though it meant they might take a big fall if they were caught.

The senior official, a KGB general from the ministry, had convened the meeting on a day in early January when an intense snow flurry that developed into a blizzard had dusted then clogged Moscow's chilled streets. The sky had then cleared, the sun had appeared and, for a moment, the city seemed to dangle the promise of spring before its inhabitants. Icicles that formed on the eaves began to melt and occasionally fell dangerously from the eaves of high buildings, exacting their usual, fatal, toll on unwary pedestrians. But by the evening of the day of the briefing, winter had exerted its grip once more.

In his introduction to the six men, the general echoed the words of Russia's Prime Minister Putin almost exactly two years before, in April 2008.

'Ukraine is not even a nation,' he stated. In the ornate wood-panelled room in the secret government building on Kraznomenniy Street, the general thus gave the men the righteous cause for their mission—a terrible injustice done against them personally and against the integrity of Russia. Like Putin before him, the general explained to the six men that Ukraine consisted partly of Eastern Europe and was partly a gift from Russia—mistakenly made—in 1991. Now, in the depths of the winter of 2010, it was time to redress this terrible wrong.

Sitting at an over-sized and heavily built polished desk under the Russian eagle, he told them: 'Your mission is crucial to the future greatness of Russia and a decisive step in atoning for past mistakes.' Words like 'justice' and 'atonement' were central to the hurt suffered by Russia's elite spy community and to the mythologising of Russia's mission. Kiev, Ukraine's capital, was the birthplace of Russia a thousand years before, the cradle of Russian civilisation.

But the general didn't mention that this mission which the six men were to perform was just one of tens, perhaps hundreds, of similar operations. For the six men, it was as if they, and they alone, stood between Russia's historical greatness and another humiliation similar to the ones they believed they had already suffered. For them, it was a chance to begin the reversal of a process of retreat that had seared the Russian soul for more than twenty years.

Three of the six men had been released early from prison for the mission, including the colonel commanding the mission. But they had been given the lightest of sentences for conducting illegal killings, massacre and torture in the Chechen wars. Theirs had been a new type of Russian show trial whose purpose was the opposite of the usual show trials. It was in order to find their innocence—or lack of culpability—not guilt, while at the same time appeasing Western calls for justice in Russia to be free and fair. Firstly, then, their trials were a pretence to Western observers that justice in Russia was working. But in reality they were a clear signal that things were back to how they had been under the Soviet Union. No matter what offences they had committed, the KGB would look after its own, welcome them back into the fold after their derisory short sentences, and then swiftly promote them through the ranks.

The other three men were fully paid-up officers of the Vympel Group, the special forces team engaged in 'social warfare' based at The Forest.

The general laid out the broad purpose of the mission and the historical rightness of it. Then when he had departed, he left his two lieutenants to lay out the details on the ground. It was, in essence, a straightforward smuggling mission across the lightly guarded border between Russia and Ukraine. The porous borderlands between the two countries were regularly travelled by commercial smugglers who transported anything from pork fat—a delicacy beloved by the Ukrainians—to nuclear materials. The lieutenants from the ministry brought out maps and grid references, set out times, distances and moon phases and, finally, the methods of communication with a team of two or perhaps three men on the other side of the border in Ukraine.

Out on the steppe, the advancing night had turned the temperature to well below freezing. The leader of the six men nodded to the driver in the first truck and the vehicle pulled up a second time, now just a mile from the border. The truck behind pulled up in line. The leader stepped out, looked inside the truck, and motioned silently to the two men remaining. In the second truck, a similar silent order was given. The six men descended, opened the muffled rear doors of the

163

trucks and waited again. Either they would be met tonight on the far side, or they would return on the following night, and then the night after that, until a way was clear.

The leader now withdrew a pair of Baigish night vision binoculars from inside his pack and surveyed the terrain between the trucks and the border. He was no longer looking for anything as obvious as lights. The land between him and the border was a flat expanse of grass steppe which stretched across to the other, Ukrainian side. In both directions he therefore had a wide and long field of view. The lake that straddled the border was to their left. They had no need of maps. Everything was contained inside the colonel's head. When he was satisfied they were alone, that no unlit human presence lay ahead of them, he signalled to the men without words.

Two ramps were slid out of the rear of the trucks. From each truck a light amphibious vehicle was then wheeled down the ramps. Each vehicle was fully loaded and fitted with electric engines. As the colonel swung the binoculars across the terrain a second time, the other five men checked the batteries on the vehicles for the third or fourth time that evening and gave the strapping that attached the loads a final twist. The leader then let the binoculars hang on their straps, stepped back into the truck and opened a metal case. He took out a computer, opened it up and tapped in a code. Then he waited. There was a pause of maybe seven to ten minutes. Finally, he received the coded response they were hoping for. So it would be tonight. He shut down the computer, removed the hard disc, and placed it in a lead-lined box.

164

The electric engines on the amphibious vehicles were switched on, and the men climbed aboard. In almost total silence they then headed into the blackness towards the lake and the border.

CHAPTER ELEVEN

The road that followed the borderland on the Ukrainian side of the border was no more than a cart track. The grass where it appeared through the snow was grey and brown and grew down the centre of the track, providing a visible line to follow in the failing light and would also do so when darkness fell. Ruts created by farm vehicles in the previous autumn had frozen into deep, hard crevices and the ice in them was thick enough to walk on. The snow lay across what would be deep green meadows when the spring came, and these would-be meadows undulated on either side of the track.

Anna looked up ahead. Through her frozen breath she dimly spotted the large lake, which barely stood out in a colourless grey shape in the winter light against the dark sky that threatened another snow storm and against the paler snow. She saw that the lake was fringed by thick reed beds that waved from the motion of the water rather than the wind. There was no wind. The lake seemed to wind its way through low-lying, water-logged islands—darker than the water—so that it seemed more like a river. She stopped on the track and looked behind her. To the north of where she'd stopped, the forest steppe stretched away for three hundred miles while, to the south, steppe grasslands flattened the landscape for another eight hundred miles to the Black Sea. To her left, eastwards, was the border.

Anna set off again and kept to the left-hand, deeper rut of the track and walked southwards at a steady pace. The GPS told her she was six miles north of where Burt believed, from previous satellite pictures, that a rendezvous was to take place; another smuggling operation across from the Russian side.

Three-quarters of a mile out to her left, she occasionally saw glimpses of the border posts on the Ukrainian side and beyond that there were another few hundred yards to the *Kontrol* signs that marked the territory of Russia. Then there was the no-man's-land inside Russia, which varied in depth, depending on which part of the huge frontier you were on; some parts were considered more dangerous to Russia than others and had a deeper Russian no-man's-land.

When she crossed the border illegally, she carried a small pack and wore hiking clothes. She had a tent in a roll at the bottom of the pack, despite the unlikely existence of hikers or campers in the area in January. More importantly, she also carried the bare minimum of small arms: a Thompson Contender handgun with a 12 inch barrel and a separate silencer, ammunition, a bowie knife, and two grenades that might provide enough mayhem to distance herself from any trouble if things went wrong.

The sun, when it appeared, gave off a feeble light—it was the semi-darkness of a late winter afternoon with a storm-laden sky. But the sun was

166

now anyway sinking to the west and the winter air was turning to a deep chill that would probably, she thought, fall at least ten degrees below freezing after darkness fell. But now, as the sun began to set, the sky was turning a soft pink between breaks in the clouds and the landscape was becoming clearer, more delineated without the flat white winter light, like a photographic negative. She found a hollow on the right-hand side of the track, scraped out the snow, and squatted down out of sight until the sun disappeared altogether and the lights of the scattered border posts were switched on and then glittered across the cold steppe.

Rumours; that was how it had started, Burt had told her. That was how it always started. Or perhaps the antecedent to the rumours were the belligerent statements of the Russian government that had inflamed, cooled, and then inflamed again the tensions between the two countries for twenty years, ever since the Wall fell, the Soviet Union collapsed and Ukraine became independent of Russia for the first time in centuries. But though these inflammatory words of Russia's KGB leaders had kept conflict rumbling just beneath the surface, the initial cause of Anna's assignment to this remote border area were the rumours. It was only when they had circulated through the border areas and finally reached the corridors of Cougar that Burt had concentrated one of Cougar's spy satellites on the region.

While Vladimir Putin had declared that Ukraine was not a real state, Yuri Luzhkov, Moscow's mayor, had said it was time that Russia seized the Ukrainian Crimea, way to the south of where she was now. But recently the rumours and stories had

167

hardened into inescapable facts, thanks to Anna's and Cougar's own sources on the Russian side. The rumours were now beginning to flesh out the Kremlin's aggressive words and the pictures Anna had studied on Burt's yacht began to bring out the rumours into solid facts. First, the Russians were said to be distributing Russian passports to the Ukrainian population in the east of the country that bordered Russia. The purpose of this, if true, was to provide an excuse for Russia to defend its own in case of crisis. And Burt had said it was undoubtedly true.

It was the same tactic the Kremlin had used as a casus belli to invade the Republic of Georgia two years before.

Then came stories of weapons caches in the border areas, and an infiltration of Russian *spetsnaz* troops, disguised as farm workers. After that, it was said that the Russian workers at the Malyshev Tank Factory in Kharkov on the Ukrainian side were to stage an uprising, initially disguised as a labour dispute, but then developing into full-scale violence.

But the rumour that drew Anna to the borders on this particular evening in January at Burt's behest was that a consignment of unidentified materials was to be smuggled across the border in one of the long stretches of land where the border posts were stretched to the limit. It was the fourth or fifth such consignment that Cougar knew of. American satellites, including Cougar's, had detected unusual movements on the Russian side for months, but Burt Miller never put his trust in technology. The ubiquitous eyes in the sky were supposedly all-seeing, but even the giant American

Worldview satellite which could pick out a car number-plate from space, was, in Burt's opinion, highly flawed and relied upon to an insane degree by the CIA. How many remote control Predator missiles did it take to kill one suspected terrorist in Afghanistan? Up to half a dozen—and this because the all-seeing eyes didn't see all.

Anna drank some water from a flask, then strapped the Contender on to her body inside her thick jacket, its barrel extending behind her and over her waist. It was strapped for a rear draw, her favoured stance when shooting in tight circumstances. But the length of the barrel necessitated that anyway. It would have been impossible to walk with the gun strapped to the front. Then she stood and, once she was satisfied that it had got as dark as it was going to get, she strapped on the pack and began to walk the remaining miles to the rendezvous.

Burt wanted intelligence on the ground, human intelligence, not push-button intelligence from a video console in Virginia, and Anna was the best operative he'd come across in more than forty years of intelligence work, whether with the CIA or now with Cougar.

Anna continued to follow the rut on the left side of the track at first, its lighter shade of ice against the slightly darker snow making it just visible, and the tufted broken line of grass down the centre showed the way. After three miles she took out night vision binoculars and surveyed the terrain for three hundred and sixty degrees around her position. Finally satisfied she was alone, she turned off the track and, in almost complete darkness, set off at an angle in the direction of the border where copses of trees afforded some protection as she approached the foreseen rendezvous. She made the next three miles at a slow pace, in just under an hour, stopping at regular intervals to search in the dark with the aid of the binoculars. Then she found herself at the edge of another lake, bigger than the one that she'd passed earlier, and which, she knew, was the one that straddled the border itself.

She made a hollow in the reeds on the shore and, when she was satisfied she was concealed from all sides, she took out the night vision binoculars once again. She trained them first on the Ukrainian side. She needed to know first that she was well protected behind her.

To her alarm, she immediately picked out what looked like an old wooden agricultural cart of the kind still used by farmers in the area. It was stopped at the edge of a wood on a slight incline about a quarter of a mile behind her and above the lake. It was less than half a mile inside Ukrainian territory. At first she thought it had simply been abandoned there for the winter, but, on closer inspection, she picked out a horse grazing on a bag of hay tied around its neck, a little further away from the cart. She wondered if her arrival had already been seen.

Anna stayed in the cover of the reeds. One advantage of the cart's presence was she now believed she needed only to observe it if the rendezvous took place. It must be connected. At just after nine o'clock, several hours after dark and with the temperature now well below freezing and still falling, she saw movement up in the wood. There were three men wearing what appeared to be camouflaged jackets and caps. She studied them closely to see if there were any insignia to say they were from the Ukrainian army—border guards in some kind of rear position, perhaps. But she could see nothing of any such detail through the binoculars. They were dressed as hunters, she guessed, not military, that was the reason behind the camouflage. They were using the cover of hunting.

She watched as one of the men took a piss in the grass at the edge of the wood and then he walked to where the horse was standing passively chewing, took away the hay bag and led the horse towards the cart. Then he harnessed it to the cart, while the other two men began to descend towards the lake. They walked slowly, purposefully, apparently knowing where they were going. They reached the edge of the lake about two hundred yards away from her and now she noticed they were carrying fishing rods.

She turned in the cramped space of the reed nest to look in the other direction, across the lake towards the border. She listened for the sound of an engine, but the stillness was complete and the silence unbroken with the exception of a duck calling in alarm from where the men stood.

The first sign she had of anything coming from the border was the light outline of water pushed up apparently by the prow of a boat. Then another white line appeared just behind the first. The binoculars began to pick out the darker shape of a craft against the water, and then a second craft. She fitted the silencer to the handgun, placed the two grenades in a pocket of her jacket and began to crawl through the reeds just above the waterline. It would be best if she could allow the transfer to take place, and let the Russian side of it retreat to the border. That way she would have only three men to contend with.

As the craft drew nearer, she recognised they were tracked amphibious vehicles, but there was no sound of an engine. Only now did the wave caused by the boats begin to ripple outwards and finally to reach the water below the reeds where she crawled. She was thirty yards away from the men on the shore.

She dimly made out the shadows of the craft as they silently pushed through the reeds and finally rested on the snow with solid earth beneath it. She saw six men disembark, three from each of the craft, and then turn the craft around to make it easier to unload the cargo. When the covers came off she thought there were four boxes on each.

In her intense study of the bank ahead, and the contents of the craft, she hadn't noticed that two of the men had walked to either side of the boats and were searching the area with binoculars. One of them was now approaching along the bank, on the other side of the reeds where she was hiding. She held her breath. The man came closer and finally stopped, standing just two feet away from her still concealed by thick reeds. She waited, considering the options; by remaining silent she would almost certainly be unobserved. But there was still a risk. She quietly drew the bowie knife from its sheath on her leg. The man didn't move. It seemed as if this was his prearranged station. She gripped the knife and drove it into his calf muscle.

With her free hand she pulled him down by his wounded leg and, clamping one hand around his mouth, she drove the knife again into his throat. But the brief cry had already escaped his lips before she could silence him. She lay in silence on top of the dying man and felt the blood seeping from his throat and covering her hand. At last, he lay still.

She rolled away from him and snatched up the binoculars, training them on the spot where she'd previously been looking. She saw all the men stationary, looking in her direction. They were professionals, she now saw—special forces, not amateur smugglers. Nobody panicked. Nobody called out the dead man's name. She watched as they went into crouched positions and drew weapons. She saw the leader wave his arm. Two of the men began to crawl fast on their bellies up the hill towards the wood and the cart. Two others crawled along the edge of the reed bed towards her. She couldn't see the other four men. They might be with the men coming towards her, but behind them and invisible to her. Or they might be coming through the water, making use of the reed cover. Despite the nearly freezing temperature of the water, that was the way she would have done it in their position; form a pincer movement, even if it meant descending into the freezing lake where ice was now forming. Wherever they were, she watched what she believed to be a highly skilled formation growing around her.

The men who had gone up the hill were now separated and, twenty yards apart, were coming down the hill directly above where she lay. They had some height and were covering their fellows at the water's edge. If she turned for an escape route now, she would lose sight of the formation—and there was nowhere to go, anyway.

The men coming towards her on their stomachs alongside the reeds were now less than twenty yards from her. Then the men on the hill skirted around again and were behind her. She sensed a man, certainly more than one now, somewhere out there in the water. They were slowly surrounding her position.

When the men had formed almost a complete circle around her she realised that now their firing line went directly through her towards each other. In any exchange of fire they would be firing at each other as well as at her. It was a brief moment of advantage, perhaps the only one she would get. Her other advantage was that they didn't know what was happening and, if there were a trap laid for them, how many opponents they had. But now she also saw a way to confuse them.

Making no noise as she fitted the silencer, she put a round into the barrel and fired a single shot into the water where she believed some of the others to be. She then fired in the opposite direction, up the hill, a direct shot that entered the cheek of one of the crawling men and came out through the back of his skull.

She unscrewed the silencer and now fired two more rounds at the water and the hill. The sudden explosion of noise without the silencer blew apart any pretence of her position. She thrust the gun and one grenade into the water-proof pack. Then she lobbed the second grenade towards the water, waited for the explosion, then slid off the bank like a snake and disappeared under the freezing surface.

Despite their training, the men reacted with an

174

instant display of fire which they swiftly realised was dangerously close to becoming a fire fight between the two groups. The guns went silent almost immediately. In the distance, over by the Ukrainian border posts, a searchlight came on and panned across the sky.

Anna swam under the water and bumped a half-submerged body above her. She kept swimming until she felt the bottom of the first craft. She felt her way underneath it and came up for air behind the second craft. The men were all behind her now, she supposed. But whatever happened in the next minute or two, she knew that the remainder of the men would, at some point, return to their cache of smuggled goods. She retreated behind the cover of the second craft, and then realised her muscles were seizing from the icy water.

She didn't know how she could survive in the water. Her body was becoming completely numb. Soon her muscles would be useless. Most worryingly, her hands were almost frozen now and her finger wouldn't be able to clamp around the trigger. She had to get out of the water to stand a chance of survival.

She broke away from the craft and swam into another bank of reeds behind it. She could barely move her arms and legs. She crawled into the reeds, found the bank jutting out inside them and dragged herself on to it. She began to rub her arms and legs. It took five minutes for any feeling to return, and still none of the men had returned.

She took the binoculars and found a gap in the reeds where she could get a view up to the wood. The cart was still there, the horse harnessed to it. There was no sign of the men. She wondered how many she had killed in the water with the grenade and what their fall-back position would be. There were, she thought, still three men out there somewhere, but no more. She also wondered how long it would take for a border patrol, alerted by the firing and the explosion, to reach the remote spot. At that moment she saw twin headlights approaching from maybe a mile away, then another pair, and another.

She crawled towards the craft again. With the knife, she cut away the straps from one of them that bound the boxes. She picked up one box. It was heavy, the contents packed tightly. But it fitted in her pack. She was sure now that the men who were left alive wouldn't risk returning to the craft, not with the patrol approaching. They would have another means of escape.

As the lights approached from far away, she began to crawl up the hill to the shelter of the wood. She would have very little time before her now exposed figure would be picked up, either by any of the smugglers who remained or by the fast approaching patrol itself. She stood and began to run. A shot fizzed into the earth behind her. Then another. It wasn't coming from the border patrol vehicles, but from somewhere behind her. She reached the wood and continued running in pitch blackness as the lights of the patrol swung towards the lake and picked out the two craft beached in the reed bank.

CHAPTER TWELVE

Two days after the the first round of the elections, at just before nine o'clock on the Tuesday morning, Taras walked down the short street that led to the SBU offices. They were contained in a large building, described as 'The Annex', which was a short walk from the much smaller building in Volodymyrska Street that was the public face of the SBU. He hesitated, then stopped at the outside gate to exchange comments and a cigarette with the guards about the two remaining presidential candidates who would run against each other in three weeks' time.

'So it's between Yanukovich and Timoshenko,' Taras grunted, inhaling the smoke from a Ukrainian-made Marlborough.

'And Yanukovich will win,' one of the guards said—with a sense of triumph, Taras thought.

'You think so?' Taras drew heavily on the cigarette to avoid reacting angrily and swept his eyes around the yard inside the gate, anywhere to avoid literally facing the opinions of the guard.

'Of course he will. He should have been president six years ago,' the guard continued. 'If it hadn't been stolen by the revolutionaries.'

The second guard was silent, Taras noted. Like Taras, he was avoiding comment. It seemed that those who supported the Moscow-backed candidate talked openly about victory, while the democrats inside the security service were embarrassed to express an opinion; including himself, he was forced to admit. He ground out the cigarette under the toe of his shoe and bid them good morning.

Though he worked for the SBU Taras liked to think he was unlike either his father or his uncle Boris in Moscow and he was in most ways correct to think so. Despite the failures of the past six years, despite the forgotten promise of the Orange Revolution, he believed in a new, independent Ukraine, tied in with Western Europe and NATO, speaking its own language instead of Russian and able, at last, to stand on its own feet after centuries of Russian rule. But his Intelligence family here at the SBU didn't all share these views. Even within some Ukrainian families the country's right to be independent from Russia was disputed. And so he kept his nationalist feelings from all but a very few close friends at the SBU headquarters who, like himself, believed in Ukraine for itself and not for the Kremlin.

Taras passed through the internal security screens, and was patted down—unusually—by a heavily armed soldier. Then he entered the building and walked past some worn wooden reception desks into a long corridor lined on the ceiling with an unbroken line of strip lights and on the floor with worn brown and yellowish linoleum, the colour of ancient nicotine stains. In general, the building had a colourless air about it, as if all of nature—and all joy—had been sucked out of it completely. He almost felt an approaching pallor wash over his face to match the surroundings.

But he was too worried this morning to give the surroundings his usual feelings of contempt and headed straight to his office on the third floor. His cousin Masha had evidently disappeared. There

178

was no other conclusion. He'd heard no word from her since her planned arrival on Saturday evening—and that was nearly three days ago now.

Walking down several corridors towards the stairs at the rear of the building, he greeted one or two colleagues, and finally turned left at a T-junction in the warren of passageways. Then he walked another thirty yards on more faded and broken yellow linoleum, before reaching the broad well of stone stairs. He wanted movement rather than taking the lift. As he walked up the steps two at a time, he deliberately stretched the muscles in his legs as if it were a training exercise. He noted the grey walls, the bland cheap paint chipping here and there, and thought that the spy buildings were like hospitals. Perhaps the difference was simply that their aim was to anaesthetise the truth and operate on the soul rather than the body; the spy buildings existed to fix the ills of the body politic. But to whose advantage?

He entered his office with a spring in his step that came from a decision to find Masha. And he would do what his usual decorum usually prevented him from doing in personal matters; he would use his position and all the resources at his disposal, which his position gave him. He refused to allow the familiar grey of the room to dishearten him: dusty paper blinds on the windows; a plain desk and a chair, another wooden chair for visitors that looked like it had come from a car boot; a shelf of books—manuals and regulations; a shabby lamp and the ubiquitous strip lights in the ceiling. It was more like a cell than an office, he thought. There was just the bare minimum—enough to remove any colour from its occupant and render him a grey servant of the grey state. He flicked open the blinds to allow some low, winter light into the room and found an unwashed coffee cup on the bookshelf. Nothing is as it seems, he thought, but he didn't know what made him think that or what the thought even meant.

He walked out of the office and down the corridor to the coffee machine. The dark brown liquid filled the cup, he put two heaped spoons of sugar into it and stirred it with a dark-stained spoon. Then he returned to listen to the messages on his internal phone which he'd noticed had been blinking as he'd entered the first time. He saw there were three messages on his internal phone, nothing on the outside line from Masha or anyone else, and when he pressed the Play button all the messages turned out to have been left by Kuchin, the chief of counter-intelligence.

When he'd listened to all three, he was left in no doubt. The words 'Immediate', 'Now' and 'At once' dominated all of them. Go to Kuchin's office, was the message. Do not pass 'Go', do not speak with anyone, do not do anything. Just get upstairs. Now.

Taras delayed. Before he went to see Kuchin, he wanted to run over what he'd discovered so far. Two days after the aborted meeting with Masha at the Golden Fleece—and once his hearing had begun to recover from the effects of the explosion—he'd put in a call to the airline Masha was taking from Simferol to Odessa. There'd been only one person left in the airline offices, despite the fact that it wasn't even four o'clock in the afternoon. But he'd told the man who he was and there was a five-minute pause while the official checked with SBU headquarters. When he came

180

back on the phone, he asked Taras for a code. When he was satisfied Taras was who he'd said he was, the man told him that Masha Shapko had been on none of the flights from Simferol to Odessa in the past five days. That was when he'd begun to feel that something bad had happened. She hadn't called him, she was off the map. Masha had disappeared.

Taras now picked up the phone, dialled Kuchin's extension and got his secretary. 'Tell him I'm on my way,' he said. 'He's there?'

'He's waiting for you,' she answered. Taras thought he heard an amused tone in Yelena's voice, something he'd noted before and put down to a flirtatiousness on her part. Whether it was for him or for anyone Kuchin was dragging over the coals, he didn't know.

Taras sat down and sipped the scalding coffee, which burned his mouth, until the urgency of Kuchin's order overcame his need for caffeine. It wouldn't do to take the coffee up to Kuchin's office. So he burned his mouth some more, before putting down the half-full cup. Then he left his office once again to take the lift this time, to the fifth floor.

He wasn't kept waiting more than a minute in the room with Yelena, which was highly unusual—almost unprecedented, in fact—and, when he entered Kuchin's office, he saw there were three other men in the room as well as Kuchin, who was sitting bolt upright behind a large desk with a Ukrainian flag on it. Behind him on the windowsill was a photograph of Viktor Yanukovich, the Kremlin's choice for president.

'Sit down,' Kuchin said abruptly. 'Where have

you been?'

'It's nine-fifteen in the morning,' Taras replied. 'I've been on my way to work.' He wondered why, if this was so urgent, they hadn't called him on his mobile.

Kuchin unfolded a piece of paper and then dropped it on top of another sheet as if to hide it from Taras's eyes.

'What were you doing on Saturday night?' Kuchin demanded without preamble.

'Several things,' Taras replied.

Kuchin's eyes flared for a moment then settled into an expression of dull antagonism. 'Between seven-fifteen and ten-thirty in the evening,' he said.

'I was in a club in Odessa,' Taras replied. 'A bomb went off.'

'Why?'

No sympathetic concern, Taras noted. It was simply a pedantic question. But Kuchin was never either subtle or sympathetic.

'I was drinking and waiting for someone,' he answered.

'Waiting for whom?' Kuchin said.

'My cousin.'

Kuchin looked at some notes. 'Two days later you made a call to the airline offices at Simferol airport,' Kuchin said. 'They checked with us here. The shift security told them what to ask you and what reply they should expect. Then you gave them the correct code for the day.'

Kuchin looked hard at him.

'Yes, that's right,' Taras replied.

'You asked for travel details on one Masha Shapko, a Russian citizen.'

'My cousin, yes.'

Kuchin at last leaned back in his chair, as if he'd had a steel rod removed from his spine, and an exhalation of air seemed to empty his chest. It appeared that he'd been holding his breath all this time.

'Your cousin . . . ?' he said. It was something they didn't know, Taras realised.

'Yes, she's my cousin. She's supposed to be visiting me. I was meeting her at the Golden Fleece. But she didn't turn up and she still hasn't turned up.'

'Yet she was in Sevastopol.'

'That's right. Then taking the Simferol flight to Odessa.'

'Why?'

'She'd decided to go to the country outside Sevastopol before coming to Odessa. My family has a house down there,' Taras replied.

'So she was visiting your family.'

'My father's dead,' Taras replied, 'as you know. Masha wanted to see the house. There's no one there right now. It's a summer house.'

'So why was she going there, then?'

'She wanted to go and see it for old times' sake before coming to Odessa to meet me.'

'Why?' Kuchin said.

'She used to holiday there with us in summer. Fond memories of childhood. Maybe she just wanted a holiday too.'

Taras recalled the first time he had met Masha, his mother's sister's daughter. He'd liked her from the moment they'd met the summer after his father's death. He'd been more like an uncle to her than a cousin. His little cousin from Moscow, twelve years younger than him, had been fun to have around. After that first holiday she'd come every summer to get away from the heat of Moscow and spend a few weeks by the sea. Her mother had married a Russian, Boris Shapko. Shapko had been stationed in Kiev with the KGB, but their home was always in Moscow and he had become a naturalised Russian back in the 1980s. Masha's father Boris was now a firm Russian nationalist, a loud supporter of Putin's United Party, and a member of the Duma, the lower Russian parliament. Masha's father—like the whole male side of the family, it seemed—was rooted into the intelligence world. And like others who originally came from the Soviet republics, Boris Shapko had become more Russian than the Russians, perhaps to prove his loyalty. Boris believed that Ukraine itself was part of Holy Russia and not an independent country at all.

'A holiday?' Kuchin said, interrupting his thoughts. 'In January?'

'It's the only time she was free. She's working now, in Moscow.'

'Yes, we know what she does.'

'Her father is a KGB officer and a member of the Russian Duma,' Taras said openly. 'And she's also worked in the security services in Moscow for the past two years now.'

Taras wanted another cigarette. He looked at the other men in the room now for the first time. Kuchin's intense questioning had kept him focused on his boss. Two of them looked like internal security people. Grim-faced, single-minded, unspontaneous. They were professionally humourless men, whether they were in here

184

'guarding the state' or swinging naked from chandeliers, he imagined. 'I'm still trying to track her down,' Taras said. 'Has something happened to her?'

'Yes,' Kuchin replied. 'Something has happened to her.' But he wasn't going to say anything that might alleviate Taras's concern.

'Why else would your cousin go to Sevastopol?' one of the internal security monkeys snapped at him.

'That's the only reason I know of,' Taras replied. 'She loves the place and she particularly loves our house there. The first time she came there she was twelve years old and she'd never seen the sea. It has a kind of magic for her, I guess.'

'She's got herself into trouble,' Kuchin said mysteriously.

'That sounds like Masha,' Taras replied, deliberately avoiding an over-reaction to Kuchin's insinuating tone of voice. 'What sort of trouble?' he enquired. He looked at the other three men in the room properly now. The third one was Ukrainian special forces, he was certain of that now, and the other two were in civilian clothes. Undoubtedly internal security people. Spies who watched the spies. He wondered who watched them, and who watched the people who watched them. No level of paranoia would be too great, of that he was sure anyway.

'Why was she carrying a gun?' Kuchin said. 'If she was going on holiday.'

So. They knew her whereabouts. Perhaps they were holding her. 'I've no idea,' he replied. 'Maybe she carries one because she's allowed to.'

'It's the latest GRU pistol.'

'Well, she works for Russian intelligence. Why do any of us carry guns?'

'We don't take them across the border into Russia without notifying the authorities.'

'I can't help you, Colonel,' Taras answered. 'All I know is that she was coming to Odessa after she'd visited our place in Sevastopol. Where is she now?'

Kuchin paused, for a moment disoriented by being asked a direct question himself. He turned to the man in Ukrainian special forces who was sitting closest to the desk.

'Lieutenant-Colonel Babich,' he said, 'tell Tur what you know.'

Babich put his arms on the desk and looked at Taras with the neutral expression of someone who has been brought in to a situation he doesn't like.

'We picked up information that a team of Russian soldiers, who we now know were from the FSB and special forces, were heading out of the city. Sevastopol, that is. It was suspicious because they hadn't notified us as they should have done. That's the agreement we have with the Russians. So we put a tail on them and when we saw where they'd regrouped, we sent our own team, of which I was the leader. There was an uncomfortable stand-off at a barn outside the city. They were very tense, threatening. So we called up reinforcements and eventually they backed down. It was a close thing. Then we saw they were holding someone. This Shapko. Your cousin, apparently.'

'Check it,' Taras said angrily, and then regretted his outburst. But Babich ignored him.

'She was in the back of one of their trucks,' Babich continued smoothly. 'We demanded they hand her over. They said she was a Russian citizen and we told them they were in Ukrainian jurisdiction on Ukrainian territory and had no rights outside the militarised zone around Sevastopol harbour. When our reinforcements arrived, we effectively forced them to hand her over. She'd apparently tried to shoot herself, but we don't know for sure. She hadn't made much of a job of it. The bullet had gone through her cheek and smashed her jaw before exiting fairly harmlessly. She was alive, in any case,' he said harshly. 'But much longer, and she might have been dead from loss of blood.'

Taras stared back at Babich.

'What makes you think it was her who'd fired the shot?' he said eventually.

'The Russians told us she had. But, to be honest, that's what it looked like. Not a good attempt.'

'Where is she?' Taras asked.

'She's in hospital. She's stabilised.'

'In Sevastopol.'

'Yes.'

Taras suddenly liked Babich. He was just telling what he knew.

'So that's why you didn't meet your cousin,' Kuchin said. 'She was involved in something other than a nostalgic visit to your family house.'

'Is she conscious?' Taras asked, but to Babich.

'In and out, when I last saw her.'

'The question is,' Kuchin said impatiently, 'what was she doing attracting the attention of Russian special forces? We have to work with them. We don't like going up against them like this. It causes trouble at the highest levels.' He looked angrily at Babich.

Babich didn't comment.

'Do we know it was her who was attracting their attention?' Once more Taras looked at Babich. 'Maybe she just got caught up in something. If all this happened at the farm.'

'That's a good point,' Babich said reasonably. 'One of the Russians made a slip, perhaps. He told me, "It wasn't her." I'm certain he meant they were expecting someone else.'

'But why did she try to shoot herself if she was innocent?' Kuchin snapped, evidently either disagreeing with this interpretation or merely wanting things to be neat, tied up and off his desk. 'She was involved,' he added

'Maybe,' Babich conceded. Kuchin glared at him for his lack of full support.

CHAPTER THIRTEEN

22 January

'Coalition Interoperability' was not an expression that Adrian Carew was likely to find anything other than blind stupid. It was American, of course, he told himself. The multilingual NATO intelligence committee conducted its business in American—or an 'international' version of English, as they called it—and that didn't help his mood. But in his view this sort of jargon was generally typical of the way the English language had become so hopelessly mauled that it was now being used either to cosh the listener senseless, or to obfuscate a situation to the point of meaninglessness. Incomprehensible language had become a substitute for clarity, and in Adrian's opinion a lack of intelligent decision-making was bound to follow. But worst of all, the language bored Adrian in the same way that reading the excruciatingly translated instructions on a Chinese-made vacuum cleaner might have done.

'Do you mean "working together"?' he interrupted and his lips tightened as if they were gripping a straw. He had a sudden notion that, as head of the British intelligence service, good English usage—or any other damn language for that matter—was the prerequisite for good international relations.

Most of the other figures around the large, perfectly oval, polished cherry wood table—it had reportedly cost over fifty thousand euros—looked at him as if it were he who had just uttered sounds in some as yet undiscovered language. Osvald Kruger, the head of the BND, Germany's spy agency, in particular looked like he was completely at home with 'Coalition Interoperability'. It was simply the norm. It was international English, his raised eyebrows seemed to say—at least they seemed to say so to Adrian. There was an uncomfortable pause.

'It's not, actually, exactly the same thing, Adrian,' the CIA head Theo Lish said at last in a patiently hushed voice, and then gave a little cough, either from a sense of linguistic superiority or simply from awkwardness. He had been drawing to the close of a complex exposition of the latest NATO strategy for combating cyber warfare and had now lost his thread.

'I know it's not *exactly* the same thing, Theo,' Adrian retorted. 'But at least everyone understands what it bloody means. It's Anglo-Saxon English, not some bureaucratic bloody gobbledegook.'

Lish now reddened in anger.

Only one of the thirty or so figures sitting around the table wasn't remotely ruffled by this disturbance. And he announced himself with his trademark loud guffaw from the opposite side of the table to Adrian. Whether from the loudness of the laugh or from its diversionary opportunity, the small explosion afforded an exit from the momentary impasse Adrian had created. Burt Miller banged the table with his chubby pink hand as a sort of percussion accompaniment to his boom box laugh, and looked around the table with a twinkle of mirth in his eyes.

'The Brits never agree on the wording,' he announced to the assembled espionage chiefs and with a broad grin on his face. 'That's the way they've lied their way around the world for five hundred years.'

This time it was Adrian who reddened. He looked across the table at Burt with a mixture of fury and concealed admiration that contorted his expression for a brief moment into something resembling a squashed cartoon.

Adrian then saw that the head of France's DGSE, Thomas Plismy, was obviously enjoying his discomfort and actually had a slight but deliberate smirk on his face.

Next to Burt, as always these days, Adrian noted, sat the Russian woman, the former KGB colonel Anna Resnikov. She had remained expressionless throughout Adrian's encounter with Lish and now looked across the table at Adrian with a level stare. The contrast between Adrian's rough and claret-tinged face and her smooth, finely textured features was like two Renaissance paintings, one of a bawdy house in downtown Venice, the other a pastoral Elysian idyll. The cool terrain of her personality seemed to wash over Adrian in an attempt to extinguish him with a single glance. On top of everything—for some reason this crossed his mind—she was taller than him by an inch or two. He searched her face for any sign of contempt, caught himself doing it, and felt angrier than before.

The consultative meeting between national security chiefs of the NATO countries was a regular event that took place several times a year and was held either in Washington or, more usually, as this time, at NATO headquarters in Brussels. The thirty-one nations sent their spy masters to confer, compare notes, pursue the alliance's common aims—and, with familiar regularity, to hide, withhold or obscure anything from each other that was considered by their respective governments to be of greater national importance than something to be shared between notional allies. It was a forum of supposedly common aims and strategies, but where conflicts of interest were everywhere and everyone knew it, though no one openly mentioned them.

In recent years the get-together included not just the heads of the thirty-one national intelligence services of NATO countries. Occasionally a few very select intelligence gurus, like Burt Miller, who owned their own private spy companies were also invited. There were one or two of these companies which had become indispensable to the American national effort and therefore to NATO. Burt headed up the biggest private intelligence-gathering organisation on earth and was here because his company now competed on more or less an equal footing with the CIA. Indeed, it was almost a branch of the CIA, some said, and one that in the past year controlled a budget nearly as large as the CIA's own. It had become the tail that wagged the dog, in Adrian's opinion. A kind of reverse takeover had taken place. Directors and officers left the CIA, joined companies like Cougar, then turned around and gave the CIA advice and even, on occasion, instructions. Then, when they'd served their time at Cougar, they would rejoin the CIA at the highest level and award Cougar intelligence contracts. Lish was just one of them. It was practically a protection racket, as far as Adrian was concerned.

But the other side of Adrian wished for himself the wealth that private intelligence gathering had sumptuously bestowed on Burt.

The woman, Anna Resnikov, only rubbed salt in this particular wound. A year before, she'd been under the threat of extinction. It seemed that somehow, inevitably with Burt's help, she had effortlessly turned that around. After her brilliant coup de grâce in the previous year when she had exposed a KGB spy ring in Washington and nearly been killed for her pains, she'd become some kind of a hero to the Americans. She was now Burt's associate vice-president—another meaningless expression which, to Adrian, was just Burt's method of getting her to accompany him on trips across the Atlantic like this one. In a year, Adrian seethed, she'd probably earned more from Cougar than he'd earned in two or three as deputy, and now head, of MI6.

With a finality in his voice, Burt looked up the table at Theo Lish. 'Damn fine run-down of the situation,' he said supportively, as if the cyber warfare question was now done with. 'Let's get back to the table refreshed for the afternoon session.'

As the meeting broke for lunch, Burt singled out Adrian.

'We're going to the Trois Couleurs,' he said. 'Why don't you join us?'

What did he mean by 'we', Adrian wondered. 'We've only got an hour,' he grunted, however. 'It'll take fifteen minutes to get out there and it's the most expensive restaurant in Brussels.'

'And the best,' Burt replied. 'What's more, it's pre-ordered and on me.' He grinned. 'We'll eat the best food in this town—some of the best in Europe—and be back here only a few minutes late.'

*   *   *

Outside the NATO building, a large, black, armoured limousine awaited Burt. He ushered Anna first into the long back seat—as if she were the bloody Queen, Adrian thought—and then stepped in himself, leaving Adrian to follow. There was nobody else invited, Adrian saw.

The pre-ordered lunch was brought to the table in the time it took them to be escorted by the maître d' from the entrance of the restaurant to their seats at a private table in a room at the rear.

A bottle of Pomerol 56 had been decanted and was now poured. Burt waved aside the opportunity to taste it and the sommelier smiled as if in complicity with Burt's apparently transcendental appreciation of the vintage and its quality.

'Expect it to be good, and it will be good, eh, Adrian?' Burt said, and raised his glass.

Adrian was nonplussed. Burt's curious combination of earthiness and, to Adrian, fanciful, airy-fairy, New-Age remarks like this one never failed to confuse him. 'To lunch!' Burt toasted, ignoring Adrian's demurral and, tucking a four hundred-count linen napkin somewhere into his chins, he began to enjoy the *boeuf en croûte*.

To Adrian's surprise, the conversation was minimal and he began to wonder what was behind this invitation after all. Indeed, why were they in a private room if they weren't here to talk? But Burt seemed intent on enjoying the *dégustation* and in no mood for talk, formal or otherwise. It was only when the bill had been invisibly paid—pre-ordered and on account, Adrian supposed—and they were heading back in the limousine for the afternoon session that Burt beamed at Adrian in a way that suggested something was coming.

'Know what's on the agenda this afternoon?' he said.

Of course Adrian knew, they all knew. 'Iran. For the umpteenth time,' Adrian replied patiently. 'And then a general discussion about the perils of scaling down in Afghanistan. What the intelligence role in that eventuality will be.'

'Ukraine,' Burt said. 'Russia and Ukraine. That's top of my agenda.'

'But it's not on the agenda at all, Burt,' Adrian

protested.

'I think you'll find it is.' Burt leaned slightly towards the MI6 chief. 'And, Adrian, I know you'll instinctively give your support for my—actually, for Anna's—thesis. She's been doing fine work in the past months. Particularly in the past few weeks. Work on the ground. And I just want you to know that your support will be a thing of great value to me.'

Adrian looked past Burt's bulk at Anna, but she didn't seem to be listening. She was staring through the side window of the limousine somewhere into the distance. The long profile of her face was caught by the sun flashing behind the trees as they drove. She seemed to cultivate an impenetrable, enigmatic identity.

Not for the first time, Adrian wondered what she was like in bed. She'd been Finn's woman until his death, and after that she'd picked and discarded at least one other man in the past year that he knew of. Including Logan Halloran, he recalled. Unlike the girls in his office, who he felt regarded him as the leader of the herd, she gave him nothing. Once, when Finn was alive, she'd come with Finn to Adrian's and his wife Penny's house in the country. He'd made it clear to her what he wanted—practically in front of his wife— and she'd looked at him as if he were a piece of dirt.

He snapped himself out of the memory. 'A thesis about Ukraine?' he said, momentarily baffled.

Anna then looked round at him at last, fixing him with her expressionless gaze, and he felt the infuriating calmness of her presence once again.

'Yes, Adrian,' she said. 'The second largest

country in Europe which borders Russia to the east and the European Union to the west.'

'Don't tease Adrian.' Burt grinned, and looked like he might pat her on the knee, but then thought better of it.

With this arcane exchange completed, the limousine drew up outside the NATO building and they were in their seats just ten minutes late.

Back in the committee room, Burt and Theo Lish drove a 'cookie cutter'—in Burt's words—through the Afghanistan question, dicing it into bite-sized pieces that concluded the intelligence role there was all but finished.

'Intelligence is a matter of pre-emption,' Burt summed up flatly. 'Intelligence protects, and intelligence is the tool to flush out our enemies. Afghanistan is over the edge. There's no longer anything to pre-empt. We know our enemies, and our enemies are winning. We're on an irreversible slide there. The White House knows it, even if it won't admit it yet, and the Europeans know it.'

Lish didn't disagree and the European intelligence chiefs seemed almost relieved the Americans were leading the retreat.

Then there was an hour discussing the latest intelligence in from Iran; its increased uranium processing facilities, the timeline for its nuclear weapons capability, Chinese support of the Iranian government, the illegal imports of material, the mindset of the ayatollahs and their political puppets, and the fledgling resistance to them. Finally, Theo Lish shuffled some papers and brought a sheet to the top.

'The added agenda,' he stated. They all shuffled papers and brought the swiftly printed sheet into view. 'Events concerning Russia and Ukraine.'

Burt rested his hand on the back of Anna's chair and introduced her to the rest of the committee, as if most of them didn't already know her and the rest didn't know her by her considerable reputation.

CHAPTER FOURTEEN

Anna sat composed and still. The thin northern European light on this January afternoon slanted in through a window where the blinds were only half shut and made a pattern across the table that was elongating with the sun's fall.

She was aware of the effect she had in the room; the only woman among more than thirty men. She was aware of their curiosity and their attention, and she was equally aware of the resentment that emanated from some of them. But she had been accustomed to such undisguised male attention for as long as she could remember and had long ago developed a quality of absorbing it that was neither a barrier nor an encouragement, but just a kind of neutralising aura.

According to Burt in a conversation with Lish earlier that day, which she had overheard— perhaps by design—she was the personification of Russia itself. In the kind of typically sweeping assessment of a person or event that Burt was fond of making, he had summed her up as follows: 'Anna', he had told Lish, 'will tactically withdraw until the opponent is weakened, desperate and all out of ideas. Then, if she chooses, she picks him off. She's like the history of Russia and its enemies, withdrawing into an endless interior until they're exhausted and beaten.'

Now, in the committee room, she effortlessly deflected the underlying motives of the men back in their direction and—brought face to face with their own conscious or subconscious thoughts about her—they experienced an uncomfortable moment of self-revelation. She destabilised the baser or more simplistic thoughts they held about her by exposing them in some sort of mirror.

Looking at them in the long silence she'd allowed to settle following Burt's introduction, the fractured group of Intelligence chiefs seemed a fragile defence against any single-minded, powerful and united enemy. Certainly the upper echelons of the KGB had never been this democratic, let alone this diverse. These were a strange group of people, brought together by an old war seventy years before and then—after the Berlin Wall came down—augmented by the incorporation of Europe's Eastern states, which had formerly been under the heel of the Soviet Union. Twenty years after the Cold War had ended—in the fond hopes of the West anyway— the Eastern European nations were now at NATO's table.

This committee, she thought, was as porous an institution as you could find, yet it was made up of the highest minds in the countries it represented, men who possessed the most secret and privileged information.

Anna knew—they all did—that someone had been passing on to the Kremlin details of America's proposed missile shield in Eastern

Europe. But the committee had been unreliable for a long time. During the Yugoslav wars in the 1990s, a French officer had passed NATO secrets to Serbia. Some people suspected Greece of doing the same. And the Estonian Defence Ministry security chief, Herman Simm, had been convicted of passing NATO secrets to the Russians. It was not surprising therefore that the nations represented around the table withheld their most private intelligence information.

Her presence, she knew, would be reported to The Forest by someone—and maybe more than one of the men in this room. What she had to say now would be read at The Forest within days, if not hours.

Not for the first time, she wondered what Burt's game was. Burt knew the score where the committee's trustworthiness was concerned, as well as anyone. One thing she was certain of, however, was that in this presentation he'd asked her to make Burt was undoubtedly making a play. He was putting a divining rod into the earth, as he liked to call it, to see what he would find. 'Intelligence is a tool to flush out your enemies'— his words from earlier in the week flashed across her mind. And our known enemies' intentions, she'd silently added to herself. 'We need conflict because that is where our enemies are revealed.' And if this were a play of Burt's—as it undoubtedly was—Anna could assume that the CIA was in on it, the Canadians, almost certainly, and Adrian . . . ? That was why Burt had openly solicited Adrian's support in the car after lunch. Burt always played a long game and he never told everyone everything, her included.

There was a hush of anticipation and of curiosity—even admiration, in some cases—both for her unique presence in this room and for her known exploits in the field. She was also the youngest of them by at least fifteen years and the only one who was still active as an operative.

She leaned forward imperceptibly and her stillness and quiet drew the others' attention even more. Theirs was the rapt concentration afforded to a person who speaks in barely audible tones. Anna's cool demeanour and measured forcefulness was as effective, in its way, as Burt's loud, bulldozing style. And the men in the room could not separate her skills and experience from her beauty.

'The Kremlin is upping the ante,' she began quietly. 'It's been well known to all of us here for a long time that the mood among Russia's leaders has become increasingly belligerent since Putin came to power in 2000. Two years ago, Russian forces made their first military adventure outside Russian territory and invaded the sovereign republic of Georgia. There were complaints from the West, but no action. In other words, the Kremlin got away with it. Thus the appetite of the men of power, the *siloviki* and their allies among the *patriotiy* in the intelligence community, was whetted for a far bigger prize. Something the Kremlin wants more than anything. That prize, we believe, is Ukraine.

'For the past ten years the Kremlin has engaged in a series of actions intended to destabilise its neighbour. The Orange Revolution in 2004 prevented the Kremlin's stooge Yanukovich from gaining power in Kiev, but the Ukrainians' democratic choice for president was nevertheless poisoned by the KGB, almost fatally. In the east of Ukraine, next to the Russian border, there is a large Russian community from Stalin's time and before, which is sympathetic to Russian rule. This, combined with the great resentment among Russia's intelligence community that Ukraine is an independent state, is creating a flashpoint which we believe the Kremlin intends to exploit. Today, from reports on the ground, as well as satellite pictures and KGB sources who are unfriendly to Putin's KGB clan, we have formed an increasingly clear picture, but it's still far from certain what exactly the Kremlin plans to do.'

'If anything,' Plismy, the French chief, said acidly. It was Plismy who two years before had 'lost' Anna to the Americans.

The historical precedent of a female, former KGB officer addressing an internal NATO intelligence committee did not intimidate all of them and Plismy was one of them. Plismy was her enemy too now. She'd run from French protection two years before—'protection' which had almost got her killed after she'd fled from Russia—and into American arms in the person of Burt and Cougar. The French were unlikely to forgive her.

'Do we get to see the evidence of this clear picture you talk about?' the head of Spain's National Security Service, Jorge Barrius, enquired.

'All the satellite evidence is available. Reports on the ground and from KGB sources are, of course, source-protected.'

'How can we assess its reliability?' This time the objection came from Ton Van Rijn, the head of the Netherlands intelligence agency, a trim man in his early sixties with a small moustache and sensible shoes like a schoolteacher's or a policeman's.

'As it's material that originates from Cougar, you can expect it to be of the usual high standard,' she replied smoothly. 'We have networks of agents in Russia and Ukraine that national agencies and the rest of the world would envy.'

Burt grinned amiably. Anna paused to invite further questions, but none came.

'First,' she continued, 'Russian interior ministry officers are handing out passports to citizens of Ukraine near the Russian border, as well as in the Crimea. This was a tactic they employed in Georgia and subsequently used as a reason for the invasion there: the defence of Russian citizens. Second, unusual movements of small numbers of military vehicles on the Russian side of the border in the Kursk sector seem to be connected to smuggling activities into Ukraine. Third, there is an obvious flashpoint for Russian anger to spill over into violence inside Ukraine, or result in direct military action. That flashpoint is on 20 May. On that day, the Ukrainian government is expelling all Russian intelligence officers from the Crimea. Up to now, the port of Sevastopol has played host to the Russian Black Sea fleet and its Ukrainian counterpart. That arrangement is set to continue until 2017. But by constant provocations on the ground, in and around Sevastopol, the Russians have finally forced the Ukrainian government to take a strong line. Hence the forthcoming expulsions. Again, provocation and a replay of the Georgian war. In my opinion, we in this room should be looking at offering our services to Ukraine's government, whoever becomes president. And Europe and America should be ready to draw a line in the sand. That line should be to prevent Ukraine from becoming another Georgia, or worse. In other words, to stand up to Russia.'

She paused, knowing that questions would come.

'But that's a political point,' Kruger, the head of Germany's BND, objected eventually. 'Our remit is to look at intelligence matters only.'

Everyone looked at Burt, expecting him to come to his protégée's aid. But he just sat back, apparently enjoying the show.

'The role of intelligence is principally to prevent conflict by knowing what our enemies are doing. It is also to provide our governments with the necessary ammunition to expose our enemies' intentions. Thirdly, it is to help our allies. Ukraine is an ally of Europe and of America.'

'Are you saying Russia is our enemy?' Thomas Plismy said. 'We import half of our energy resources from Russia.'

'We buy oil from Iran, too,' Anna replied. 'But Ukraine is closer to home. If Russia were to invade or effectively annex Ukraine in some other way, it would cause a split inside the European Union. East versus West. With good reason, the Eastern nations view Russia's intentions with greater concern than the Western nations do. They have a history of Russian domination and they note Russia's threatening stance towards them today with increasing alarm. In 2005 Putin stated that the greatest geopolitical tragedy of the twentieth century was the collapse of the Soviet Union. The nations to the east don't take such remarks lightly.

But any Russian move against Ukraine can be pre-empted, perhaps—certainly disrupted—by pooling our intelligence resources to expose whatever it is the Kremlin is planning to do. Revealing its hand will go a long way toward pre-empting any plans it may have to destabilise Ukraine.'

As ever with questions of Russia, there was a deep division between Eastern and Western Europe, as Anna herself had expressed. There were twelve Eastern members of NATO, all formerly subjugated to the Soviet Union, and fourteen Western members, including the United States and Canada. Standing united, the Western members would always outvote those from the East. But Burt had successfully persuaded the CIA head to put America behind the Eastern vote, levelling the score, and now everything rested on Adrian. Despite Cougar's power, Burt did not have a vote at this national level.

Evidence was passed around the table, including the satellite pictures which Anna knew—and knew they all knew—were inconclusive. Russia could move its own military vehicles—unmarked or not—wherever it wanted to on its own territory. Evidence of Russian ministry officials naturalising citizens of Ukraine with Russian passports was provided, but this, too, provided a glimpse only. As the intelligence chiefs looked at the pictures and written evidence, Anna further explained the developing crisis in Ukraine.

'The situation in Sevastopol has been spinning out of control for some time. There are the small things; like the street fights between Russian and Ukrainian sailors whose fleets share the same port. But full-scale Russian intelligence activity there has been increasing enormously in the past two years. Their agents and intelligence officers are everywhere. The policy from the Kremlin seems to be one of provocation. And the Ukrainians, provoked, predictably react. Their military personnel hold up Russian convoys that use the port for refuelling and rearming. In turn, the Russians react angrily. The heat is raised, the ratchet is tightened. That is why Ukraine has made the momentous decision to expel all known Russian intelligence personnel. What will the Russians do when that happens?'

Anna reached down to the floor and picked up a metal case. She placed it carefully on the table and opened the locks. From inside, she carefully lifted out a small aluminium flask and placed it on the table.

'This was picked up just over the border from Russia, inside Ukraine. It was part of a smuggled consignment of a dozen flasks like this one. Their origin is the KGB laboratories in Moscow's Leontevsky Pereulok.'

'That's the actual canister?' Lish said.

'No. This is a dummy. The actual canisters are contaminated.'

'With what?'

'That's what we're finding out. But it's some kind of poison, type unknown.'

When it came to the vote, the Eastern nations didn't, as Burt had hoped, vote as one. The Czechs, Poles and Romanians voted for sharing intelligence where it concerned Russia's borders with Ukraine and the Crimea in its entirety. Others dithered and finally came down on their side. Hungary voted against.

The deciding vote was left to Britain. For a moment, Adrian considered upsetting Burt's plans. Later it would be said that this was the key decision Adrian made in his entire career, from his younger days as an SAS officer to becoming head of British Intelligence. Burt looked on calmly. Adrian fiddled with the new sheet of paper dealing with the Ukraine issue and weighed his power over Burt's. It wasn't often that he found himself in a position to overturn Burt's aims—nor in a position to extract a quid pro quo in return for Burt's gratitude, for that matter. He cast his mind over what he would demand from Burt in return for his support and then, finally, he cast his vote in favour of the East—and of Burt—who beamed proudly at him as if he'd just won a race.

There were those in London who would whisper later that Adrian had crossed the Rubicon, finally putting his own interests—a foot in the door at Cougar and the wealth which that promised—ahead of his country's.

And although the meeting of intelligence chiefs was a consultative one only, it was accepted that each service would report back the views of the committee to their respective governments with a strong recommendation.

CHAPTER FIFTEEN

9 February

Anna asked Larry to drop her at the foot of the farm's earth driveway. There was some old bare and knotted wood rail fencing that stretched either side of a sagging gate and disappeared to the right over a rise in the land. She would walk up from there, she told him, and then arranged for him to return in three hours' time.

'Enjoy him,' Larry said.

She watched him go. Larry liked her son, had looked after him in the safe house in New Mexico two years before, and would have liked to have seen him. But the time was too precious and she wanted him all to herself.

She turned and looked towards the farm. To the right of her was paddock with around a dozen horses bunched up together with the car's arrival. A small circular pen was attached to the paddock for separating them out. Bales of hay were split and scattered near the fence and she saw a horse trough in which ice had been broken and was now floating in thick wedges on the surface. It was cold up here and recent snow still lay in patches on the fields. The horses stood and watched her, heads up, eyes wild, huffing big breaths from flared nostrils in the cold morning air. Then they tossed their heads and began to canter around the paddock in a group, kicking up their back legs in celebration of a new morning.

There was a pond in the paddock to the left of

the gate. Ice had formed there too, thick enough to walk on, she thought. The driveway ahead climbed a hill between the two fields to a wooden house a quarter of a mile in the distance and, behind that, woodland surrounded the top of the farm on two sides and ascended a high hill to the north. A stream flowed out of the wood down through the field to the pond and then on below to a river they'd crossed in the car.

As she always did when she visited her son in his new home, Anna thought it was a good place for him to grow up, to begin a new life. She'd seen many times now how much he loved the place and how he had fitted so easily into his new family.

Before she began the walk up the drive, she paused to take in the view. It was a beautiful place, the kind of rural paradise that brought on a wave of nostalgia for the simplicities of lost childhood. Though the country was nothing like the dacha in the forest where her grandmother had brought her up, Anna was reminded whenever she came here of that life. Anna thought of Dostoyevsky's reflection that there was nothing higher and stranger and more wholesome and good for life in the future than some memory of childhood, of home.

But this was a working farm, too, and that made it more than just a pretty picture or a vague, rural dream. Little Finn loved the animals in particular. There were mainly cows on the farm, which were now shut up in barns until the winter ended. Then there were the long sheds on wheels she could see higher up and that housed the chickens. The farmer moved the sheds around the fields so that the land was fertilised naturally. Some pigs rooted in the woods. And there were the horses, which the family used for their own recreation and which, in the summer, became a riding school under the tutelage of the farmer's wife.

Little Finn's new family had three small children of his own age. The farmer and his wife were in their mid thirties and had retired young from Cougar, deciding on a new life away from the secret world and its normal business targets and promotional ladders and the expectations of others. They'd bought the organic farm with Burt's help—she suspected it was Burt's way to smooth Little Finn's transition too—and were now supplying local communities within a twenty-five radius with meat and milk. It was a physically hard living, offered little money, and the two of them were content in the choice they'd made.

Anna waited until she felt still inside. It was necessary for her to arrive composed and quiet, to calm her generally turbulent emotions about the visits she made here. She had come to this farm in Connecticut more than a dozen times before, but even so she always felt the same way; a flutter of anxiety, a yearning, maternal connection that fought the physical disconnection between her and her son. Sometimes she felt she shouldn't come at all, that her visits were a source of confusion to him. He had this new family now. She feared she was becoming like a distant relation to him, rather than his mother. But always Burt urged her to cast these thoughts aside; it was important that he had a real contact with his mother, Burt said, and to know about his dead father, Finn.

But what good could it do him, she wondered, to be presented with a second, visiting mother, even though she was the real one? However things worked out she was satisfied she had brought him to the right place to live his early life. He had a new name, a new identity and was safe—that was all that was important.

But as she continued up the driveway, she felt the same hollow feeling in her stomach that she always felt when she came to visit the boy. Burt had decided—and she'd agreed—that for his own safety her son should be given protection against the threat of KGB retaliation. Her own life—as witnessed in a KGB attack on her in Washington two years before—was in danger and, if they couldn't reach her, they would find the boy an ideal hook with which to reel her in. So it was decided, after great heart-searching, that Little Finn would be given a new life. But it meant that she would lose him. One day, she knew, this family would become his own family and she would be his mother only in name. If not today, then one day, he would look on her as a virtual stranger.

She arrived at the top of the drive and walked up two wooden stairs and tugged the bell pull. Her presence hadn't yet been noted by the family inside, thanks to leaving the car at the foot of the drive. That was the way Anna preferred it. The door was opened by the farmer's wife Naomi who greeted her as always with a welcome whose fulsomeness seemed intended to forestall any doubts on Anna's part. Though neither of them had ever broached the subject, it was silently understood between them that Anna's visits were a strain to her most of all and Naomi went out of her way to welcome her as part of their family. Perhaps she could empathise with her position, Anna thought. Perhaps any mother could.

They went into the kitchen and Naomi began to make coffee.

'The children are playing outside somewhere,' she said. 'They're probably with Tom.'

'I'll have a coffee first,' Anna replied. 'Thank you.'

Normal conversation was never a choice. She couldn't talk about her job, what she'd been doing—even who she was. Naomi and her husband didn't even know she was Russian, let alone that she'd defected and was hunted by the KGB. All they knew was that her son had needed a change of identity and that was enough. The small talk between Anna and this family circled around and avoided the subject of herself, focusing only on the farm and its progress, the seasons, and the children.

'How is he?' Anna asked.

'He's fine. As I always say, he's added something to the family, Anna,' Naomi replied. 'He's bright and, to be honest with you, I'm grateful to have him with us. The others love him, they all get along well.'

It was the same in all her previous visits. She'd seen before how Little Finn adapted quickly to new surroundings when they'd been at the safe house. Now he was easily adapting to his new family. He wasn't plagued with thoughts of loss. He wasn't even making the best of it, she thought, he just happily accepted what was good. There seemed to be no clouds at all in his life, and she was grateful for that, despite the fact that it could only mean a widening distance between the two of them.

They walked up into the fields after they'd finished their coffee.

'They'll be up near the wood,' Naomi said. 'Tom is doing some coppicing up there. If he's not keeping an eye on them, I am,' she reassured her.

But the only thing in Anna's mind was that Little Finn would be four years old in three weeks' time. That made her think of Finn, as well as her son. Finn's death at the hands of the KGB, just over four years before, nudged itself into her mind whenever she saw their son.

They found the children where Naomi had said they'd be, playing up near the wood where the stream emerged. It was a beautiful cold winter's day, the few white clouds had cleared and the sun stood still in the sky, as if frozen itself.

When Little Finn saw her, he stopped what he was doing and stared at her, as if he wasn't quite sure. Then he leapt up from the stream bank and ran towards her and she caught him in her outstretched arms.

'He'll always be yours, Anna,' Naomi had told her many times and at moments like these she dared to believe it.

Little Finn immediately tugged at her arm and pulled her towards the stream where the other three children were playing. He showed her a small earth bank they were building 'to catch fish', he explained seriously. They played together by the bank until it was time for breakfast and then all of them walked back to the house. Tom kissed her on the cheek and squeezed her arm like a brother, as if he, too, knew the difficulty of her situation.

Over breakfast, Anna took out Little Finn's birthday presents and all four children gathered round to watch him open them. She'd bought him a few useful things—clothing mostly—and then the big prize, a farm set with animals and tractors. Suddenly she felt foolish to have bought him a replica of the real place where he was living. But he was interested in it—interested in everything—and the children went off to a playroom solemnly carrying all the pieces one by one and began to put it all together. He was absorbed, his thoughts only with his new family, and she didn't follow immediately.

'Is there anything you need?' she asked Tom and Naomi.

'No, I don't think so. We have everything,' Tom replied. 'We'll let you know if he needs something,' he added. The tension of demonstrating he was well-provided for and at the same time allowing her to feel involved was never absent.

'We love him very much,' Naomi added, and there was a sudden awkwardness in the air, as if his own mother couldn't provide this element of his upbringing, but only material things.

Before she left, Anna went into the playroom and sat with him. They hugged each other once and he showed her how they'd put the farm together. But already he was eager to be off. He'd seen his mother and now he had more important things to do. She let him go with a kiss and a Russian blessing. Then he scampered off back up into the fields with Tom and the other children. She felt bereft, forgotten and guilty. But, by leaving him, she knew she'd done the right thing for him, the only right thing.

'Come whenever you can, any time,' Naomi said before she left. 'You must come and stay. You know you're always welcome here, Anna.'

Always welcome in her son's new home. She fought down a painful feeling at the irony of that. But she knew that this was how it would always be. Little Finn was safe, that was all that really mattered, she knew that.

'I'd like to do that very much,' she said. 'Thank you.'

Larry was waiting at the foot of the drive, the engine running.

'How is he, Anna?' he said with his broad, uncomplicated grin.

'He's good,' she said.

The car swung back down to the road and Larry took her to the small private airfield nearby where one of Burt's smaller planes waited to take her to Washington.

CHAPTER SIXTEEN

20 April

The terror ship *Forburg* left the port of Novorossiysk for the second time on the first of April,' the CIA chief explained. 'We've found her.'

Theo Lish nodded to one of his fresh-faced assistants from the Threat Matrix team, an extremely tall and close-cropped Harvard graduate and basketball player who looked like he might also do toothpaste commercials on the side, and who went by the name of Archie. Unnecessarily, to Burt's mind at least, Archie indicated the port of Novorossiysk with a wooden cue, despite the fact

214

that its name was marked in three-inch-high letters on the electronic map that took up half a wall. Perhaps a metal cue would have caused an electrical short-circuit, Burt mused, and brought the whole bunker complex to a complete halt, leaving America defenceless.

The port of Novorossiysk was on the right-hand side of the back-projected electronic map on which red lights were blinking here and there to indicate something or other. On closer inspection, the flashing red dots now seemed to be ports on the Black Sea, as far as Burt could see, though due to the overall ponderousness of Theo's explanation, his mind was wandering and he wasn't willing to display a great deal of interest. He was already way ahead of Theo's analysis, in fact, and knew roughly what was coming.

Otherwise on the map there were cream-coloured, glowing lines of light that appeared to track the ship's movements out of Novorossiysk, and which extended slowly across the Black Sea as if driven solely by Theo's explanation rather than the ship's own engines. As Theo grew into his dissertation on the ship's movements, Archie from Threat Matrix moved across in front of the map with his cue, like an agitated spider, as if he were directing armies into battle. It was too much empty excitement for Burt's mind.

They were down several floors below ground level, in a well-appointed nuclear bomb-proof bunker at the CIA's Threat Matrix centre at Harper's Crossing, Virginia; Theo, Burt and Adrian—the CIA, Cougar and MI6—in that order. Theo Lish had made this order clear to Adrian in an unnecessary emphasis of the line of command that was guaranteed only to irritate Adrian's sensibilities.

For his part, Adrian was still seething at having been asked to strip down to his underpants in order to enter this holy of holies in the first place. He, Adrian Carew, head of MI6, had been requested with much polite deference and many apologies by two armed, uniformed and highly polished special forces soldiers to strip off!

'But I'm head of the British Special Intelligence Service, for Christ's sake!' Adrian had protested. 'Your bloody boss has invited me here!'

But it was all 'I'm sorry, sir', 'Regulations, sir', 'We all have to do it these days, I'm afraid', and 'It won't take a minute, sir'. If this was how the Yanks treated their allies, no wonder the world was full of their enemies, Adrian had thought. And for a moment, Adrian wondered if Burt had been made to go through this ritualistic humiliation. He somehow doubted it and that only made him angrier.

The room was decked out with the sort of deep leather armchairs that induced a pleasant afternoon nap in old-fashioned libraries, but other than the leather chairs it flashed its high-tech purpose over everything else, including the other furnishings which were all curved aluminium and glass. It was 20 April, more than three months since the first departure of the *Forburg* had been noted by the agency's Ukraine source whose head had wound up later on a snowman and which still lay in a frozen drawer at Langley. And it was more than three months since the ship had disappeared.

Burt looked at the huge electronic chart and considered—not for the first time—that the whole

216

set-up at Harper's Crossing was more like the world's best computer game than real life, and that its abstract nature merely distanced those of them in the room—and anyone else, for that matter—from the actual events on the ground.

'But now she's not called the *Forburg*,' Theo intoned with a triumphant note in his voice. 'She's called the *Yekaterinburg*.'

'How do you know it's the same ship?' Burt asked, considering that asking the obvious question would help him to endure the process by calming his mind.

'By a very complicated process of matching the lines of the original ship which were taken from our satellite photos with the current apparition,' Theo replied. 'It all then gets computerised and drawn up with an exactness of shape and size down to less than an inch. We're certain.'

'And now she's the *Yekaterinburg*,' Burt said, but only in order to nudge Theo on with the story.

'From there,' Lish continued, as if even he were now becoming bored by his own voice, 'from there—from Novorossiysk—she headed west in a diagonal straight line across the Black Sea and docked at Istanbul four days later.'

The cream-coloured line dutifully tracked across the Black Sea. Archie focused the cue on the word Istanbul in three-inch-high letters, with its corresponding flashing red dot.

Adrian cleared his throat loudly. It's like some early learning lesson for the educationally sub-normal, he was thinking.

'The fifth of April, in other words,' Lish continued and now pointed—with ever-increasing lack of necessity to Burt's mind—at the huge chart of the Black Sea on the wall and then back down on to a large polished wood table between them and the wall which dwarfed the several paper charts and satellite pictures lying on it and that were also being used to track the vessel's progress. On the paper charts, now that Burt and Adrian looked, a thin red pencil line had been drawn to indicate the ship's progress, as if the electronic map needed any back-up, or might fail at any time.

But the photographs from America's World View satellite indicated a ship and then a close-up of the name *Yekaterinburg*. Some of the pictures were so detailed Burt could make out a moustache on one of the crew members and a scar right the way down the left-hand side of the face of another.

Burt picked up a cue himself now, but with the grip on its handle of someone who was about to use it for breaking heads. He waved it dangerously. Adrian, he noticed, was tapping the wooden table irritably with the forefinger of his right hand.

A British foreign secretary in the nineteenth century, Burt recalled, had once said that a study of maps could drive a man mad. Whether you were looking at satellite pictures and electronic charts in the twenty-first century or whether you had studied medieval maps adorned with sea monsters in the court of Elizabeth I, what tended to happen, in Burt's opinion, was that the brain became disengaged—a distance developed—and the mental processes were diverted from hard internal analysis to a theatre in which objective appreciation of a situation replaced real intelligence. The ability to work out why something was happening rather than simply that it was happening was postponed, blurred and, finally,

218

became conveniently irrelevant. Maps and satellite pictures were the toys of the back-room boys—the computer geeks, of whom, no doubt, Archie was one—whose need for the tangible was a reassurance rather than of any actual use. The fog of war began here, in the operations rooms of Washington, Moscow, London or Paris.

'Russian registered, is she?' Burt asked, waving the cue from side to side like a deranged conductor with an outsized baton. But it served to urge the process on.

'So far,' Theo replied with a deadly seriousness that made Burt want to laugh out loud. 'But we'll get on to that,' Theo added mysteriously.

'She left on April Fool's day,' Burt chortled. 'I like it.'

'They don't actually have April Fool's day in Russia,' Theo replied pedantically.

'They don't have Christmas Day on Christmas Day either,' Burt replied. 'But that never stopped the Russians from using our calendars to perform their nefarious deeds. What then, Theo?'

'She unloaded a cargo of timber in Istanbul which was loaded previously at Novorossiysk. Want to see the pictures of that?'

'I think I know what the wood will look like,' Burt said, and Archie seemed disappointed at the missed opportunity for further visual extrapolation, as well as oblivious to the sarcasm.

'OK,' Lish resumed. 'Two days in port at Istanbul, that's all. Then she's off again, headed out through the Bosphorus and into the Mediterranean.'

'Who's watching her on the ground?' Burt asked.

'The British.'

That explained the presence of Adrian, then.

'We have two Special Boat Service teams tracking the ship,' Adrian said in a clipped voice. 'Round the clock, out of radar range.'

'What makes you think the *Yekaterinburg* is carrying ordinary radar?' Burt asked. 'Or that anyone interested in her like we are—like your boys in their rubber boats—aren't also being tracked but on someone else's satellite? If she's so important, if that's what this is all about, the Russians will know just where you are.'

'They keep below range,' Adrian replied. 'Small boats only, but I grant you there's nothing we can do if the ship and the area around it are being tracked from space by their side. Whoever their side is,' he added.

'Dashing around the high seas in little rubber boats,' Burt said with great enthusiasm. 'Great stuff, Adrian.' But in his mind he was satisfied that there was no one better for the job than the British special forces. They liked a fight.

'So. What then?' he said.

Theo moved another chart and satellite map over the first one on the table. Archie flicked a switch on a console in the hand that wasn't holding the wooden cue and projected a new electronic map on to the wall which now showed the eastern Mediterranean.

'First stop after Istanbul is Alexandria—Egypt,' Theo said, again pedantically to Burt's ears.

'I didn't imagine it was Alexandria, Virginia, Theo.'

'Detail's important,' the CIA chief said. 'No slip-ups, no misunder-standings. Step-by-step.'

220

Not this sort of detail, Burt thought. This was just flannel, stuffing, something to fill out reports with.

'Pick up a new cargo in Alexandria, did she?' he enquired, concealing his impatience with a trademark smile.

'Yes, she was loaded when she left. Down to the Plimsoll line. But we don't know what with. Or we didn't.'

'So?'

'She chugs off up the coast of the southern sector of the Med. We have our Sixth Fleet now supporting the British in the area. Refuelling and so on. Rotating crews from the SBS, Britain's Special Boat Service, sent out from the UK. She then docks in Algiers, three days later. Unloads a cargo of scrap metal, as it turns out. That's what she picked up in Alexandria.'

This was taking an awfully long time for Burt's liking. So a Russian merchant vessel left the port of Novorossiysk just like hundreds of others did every year. 'What about it?' he said mildly, concealing a growing testiness beneath his same trademark grin which, as usual, contained all the potential of a drugged and swaying cobra.

'This is where it gets interesting,' Theo said. 'Adrian?'

Adrian shuffled the two or three inches available to him in order to get closer to the charts and the satellite pictures on the table. There she was again on the maps and in the photographs, the *Yekaterinburg*, but now she was heading west along the southern littoral from Egypt. The line of light on the wall indicated her progress. It was an entertainment, Burt thought. And then he

221

remembered that it was the Walt Disney Corporation which had designed the CIA's Threat Matrix centre.

'She disappears,' Adrian said. 'That's what happens.'

'Disappears?' Burt queried and raised a mocking eyebrow. 'You don't mean into thin air, presumably.'

'Put it this way, Burt. Our teams are watching her. We have a four-man team on shore in Algiers and others out at sea. Supported by your Sixth Fleet, as Theo says. Our shore team can't get into the actual port area, but they have a view, shall we say. They overlook it.'

'Well done, Adrian,' Burt said, and Adrian tried and failed to pinpoint an unmistakable tone of mockery in his voice.

'On the morning of the fifteenth of April,' Adrian continued, 'she's no longer alongside the dock in Algiers. She's vanished. That's what I mean.'

'But your teams picked up what vessels left port during the night,' Burt said.

'Yes. Five ships left overnight. Between nine p.m. and nine a.m. We think the *Yekaterinburg* was one of them. In fact, she must have been, and we can show it.'

'That would make excellent sense,' Burt said. 'If she wasn't there any more she must have either left or sunk. What's the proposition?'

'Two SBS teams at sea tracked all five ships, until they finally reduced the search to one. If it's the *Yekaterinburg*—and we're certain it is—she was re-registered overnight under the flag of Tuvalu, and re-named the *Pride of Corsica*. Paint job, new

222

numbers, a few little differences to the outer appearance, but the superstructure's the same. My watchers are experts.'

'I'm sure they are,' Burt agreed. 'So she starts off as the *Forburg* in January, turns into the *Yekaterinburg* in April and then swiftly becomes the *Pride of Corsica*. Sounds rather over-elaborate, don't you think?'

'That depends on how elaborate they think it needs to be,' Theo said. 'Evidently concealment is of the utmost importance.'

'What then?' Burt said, and found he was now warming to the chameleon ship.

Theo now walked away from the table as if for some oratorical effect. Then he turned. 'So the boat we're sure is the *Forburg/Yekaterinburg* still heads west. But now she's under a new flag and named the *Pride of Corsica*. This time she's going to Libya.'

'And this time we see she has bodyguards on board,' Adrian said.

'Armed guards,' Burt murmured as a statement rather than a question, and as if in some way suddenly approving of the operation. 'What provenance?'

'We don't know. But they're crawling all over the deck. They must have boarded in Algiers, or just possibly under the cover of darkness out at sea. They looked like they were preparing for something.'

'But not a tea party.' Burt looked at Adrian. 'What sort of preparations?'

'A great deal of ordnance. Heavy stuff. Anti-aircraft, anti-submarine, you name it. Plus an arsenal of small arms that could bring down a

223

small country.'

Theo now brought up satellite pictures of the deck of the ship with a clear view of about a dozen men, Burt thought, armed to the teeth with Kriss Super Five sub-machine guns, and wearing balaclavas and combat gear. He now saw there was a stern-mounted anti-aircraft emplacement, plus one in the bow. He thought he detected what Adrian had called anti-submarine devices, too.

'And who's she registered to now?' Burt asked.

'She was originally registered—when she left Novorossiysk—to a shell company in the British Virgin Islands. We traced the account numbers of this company's bank to the BVI and then beyond. We think we have a match to a brass plate company in Omsk, Russia. Now, however, she's registered to another company in the BVI which we've traced to another, brass plate company, this time in Cyprus.'

'Who are the beneficiaries?'

'We're pretty certain they're also Russian,' Archie chipped in for the first time—as if they were nearing the kill. It filled the dramatic pause Theo had left while gearing himself up to reply and the CIA chief looked momentarily peeved. 'It would certainly make sense,' Archie added.

'Ah. Yes, Archie, it would certainly make sense,' Burt said.

'The name of the new, Cyprus company is Fennerman International,' Theo said. 'Telephone number, box address. Nothing there. But behind this shadow company in Cyprus there's yet another company, in the Turks and Caicos Islands, and behind *that* company there's a further company in Cyprus.'

224

'The mother ship,' Burt said. 'So who's behind that?'

'Work in progress,' Archie said eagerly.

'But you're satisfied that this company in Cyprus—the second one—is the end of the line?' Burt asked.

'Most likely. Ultimate beneficiary is, again, a company registered in Omsk, Russia.'

'Same one as before, or different?' Burt said.

'Different, but at the same address in a run-down warehouse building on the edge of town. We've had people take a look at it. It's empty but for a few hundred boxes of cigarettes.'

Omsk, Russia. Burt wished Theo wouldn't keep insisting on giving them a geography class. More of the same kind of report-filler, he thought, rather than useful information.

'Beneficiaries,' Adrian said. 'What are the names behind the company?'

'Don't know that yet, Adrian,' Theo replied.

'So. She docks in Tripoli—Libya,' Burt added in deliberate imitation of Theo's style, 'and then picks up another cargo there,' he said.

'Right, Burt. But this is the important thing,' Theo replied. 'She isn't what you'd call laden coming out of Tripoli, if you know what I mean. Whatever she picks up there has no effect on her waterline.'

'So how do you know she took anything on?' Burt said.

'Our teams have pictures,' Adrian said, and Archie brought them to the surface of the paperwork on the table. 'Wooden boxes, three in all,' Archie said. There were pictures of large wooden crates, big enough to hold two men, and

225

well insulated by the look of them. They were being lifted on to the deck and then dropped down into a hold out of sight.

'Something small and valuable, then,' Burt said.

'We think so.'

'And then there are the bodyguards,' Adrian chipped in. 'What are they there for?'

'What indeed?' Burt said. 'So, Theo, what then?'

'She returns by a roundabout route back eastwards again, across the Med. Docks in Piraeus first of all, then at Tartous on the Syrian coast. Then she turns north to the Bosphorus again, enters the straits . . . '

'And is now?' Burt interrupted.

'Our teams have her pinpointed at Lat 44.53 Long 32.65,' Adrian replied crossly.

'Around fifty miles off the coast of the Crimea,' Burt said, to both Theo's and Adrian's astonishment.

'I didn't know you were so familiar with the Black Sea,' Theo said. 'Or with the exact co-ordinates in the area, for that matter. You didn't know all this all along, did you, Burt? I haven't been wasting my time?'

'No, Theo. Just what you and Adrian have told me.'

It didn't look like either of them believed him.

'So what's the thesis?' he pressed on.

'That's what we now need to pursue,' Theo replied.

Burt thought for some moments. Then he walked away from the table so he could get the maps and pictures and names and numbers out of his head, and think. Finally he turned around.

'Kind of an obvious trail, isn't it?' he said.

'Not at all, Burt,' Theo replied primly. 'It's just that we have the capabilities to follow it. Simple as that. We've got every smart device known to man trained on this ship. Plus the British teams,' he nodded in Adrian's direction. 'Celebrate our ingenuity, Burt, don't cast suspicion on it.'

So that was it. We're cleverer than they are, Burt thought. We're smarter than the Russians. Somehow he doubted that. Nevertheless, what the *Forburg* or *Yekaterinburg*—or now the *Pride of Corsica*—was actually doing was as obscure to him as to the other two men.

'What's your take, Adrian?' he asked.

'The ship picked up something in Libya. Something small, something valuable and, most likely, something deadly,' Adrian replied. 'Now she's standing well off the coast of the Crimea. We can perhaps assume the two are connected.'

'What are we doing to discover what her cargo is?' Burt asked Theo.

'It's difficult,' Theo admitted. 'We have agents on the ground in Libya, of course. They're doing the best they can, but it's not exactly easy. The whole loading operation took place in a well-guarded and separate part of the port. Plus the fact that we think there was a special army loading team on the case, not the usual dock-workers. And it's not exactly a friendly environment in which to be asking sensitive questions.'

'But they are,' Burt said. 'Asking sensitive questions, I mean.'

'As best they can,' Theo replied, awkwardly, Burt thought. Even Theo Lish, the CIA chief, found human intelligence difficult to factor in these days.

'Well, good luck to them,' Burt replied.

Outside in the unusually warm spring air of Harper's Crossing, Burt took Adrian aside and invited him to lunch. They took a limousine that had been waiting for Burt and travelled in towards Langley and a restaurant named Rocco's where Burt seemed to be well-known enough to be given a prime table by the window and receive the attention of half a dozen waiters. When they had sat down, Burt didn't wait.

'What do you make of it, Adrian?' he asked.

'I think it fits in with other intelligence,' Adrian replied. 'Dangerous stuff coming over the border from Russia into Ukraine that you've detected. The only difference is that this is aimed from the sea.'

'If only we knew what "this" was,' Burt said.

'We're treating it as high priority,' Adrian replied. 'The highest. Just as the CIA is.'

'Then it must be important,' Burt replied drily.

CHAPTER SEVENTEEN

Burt and Anna were to take a Cougar executive jet from Washington Dulles Airport for the flight south. Larry was at the wheel of a Porsche four-by-four as they drew up outside a hangar at the private end of the airport and she saw the plane gleaming in the early spring sunshine.

She saw that, like all Burt's fleet of planes, it had been highly polished. It looked like an outsize model ornament destined for a giant mantelpiece, or a sculpture belonging to a proud collector and which only needed a pedestal to mount it on. The jet had the cleanliness of an anaesthetised surgeon's knife, nothing like the dirty, oiled, mechanised tool that was a commercial plane. And that was how Cougar liked to present itself to the world, she thought: as a clean, pure white and beautiful instrument. Like Cougar—like Burt—the plane was a thing of ideological and even moral certainty.

Larry unloaded the bags from the car and carried them on to the plane. Burt turned to her before they stepped out:

'How was your boy?' he said.

She had just returned from her monthly visit to see him.

'How is Little Finn? Enjoying life, I trust,' he said.

'Very much so,' she said. 'He misses seeing Larry and the boys, I think, more than he misses me.'

Burt looked at her. 'But he's in the right place, you're sure of that? Anything more we can do?'

'Oh yes, he's in the right place,' she replied easily, but she betrayed none of the hollowness that her visits to him always left her with. And Burt didn't press her, as he never did, about anything. 'He's very well,' she added unnecessarily, more to convince herself than him, and then she looked away, out of the window across the tarmac.

'He'll always be your son, Anna,' was all he said.

They boarded the plane, Larry chatted to the pilot, and then they took off into a startling blue sky that seemed as if it had been designed by Burt to receive his pristine jet.

Burt was relaxed as ever on the journey. Never a care in the world, a world which to him, anyway, it seemed to her, was like a Roman circus prepared for his own carefully planned shows and games, rather than the dangerous and inconsistent place it was to others and which forced its constantly changing flux on them. Burt, the ruler of the world; a plump caesar who this morning wore bright yellow slacks, a blue blazer and expensive suede loafers. And as always puffing on a half-smoked cigar.

When they were settled at their cruising height and food had been served, Anna turned to him. 'What will you do when you're too old?' she asked him. 'Who's going to run Cougar then?'

'We train youth teams.' He beamed. 'Just like the football clubs.'

'But there'll never be anyone like you,' she said. 'You are Cougar, aren't you?'

'And Cougar will therefore change,' he replied. 'It'll become a bureaucracy like the CIA, perhaps, with all the dead hand that implies.' He smiled broadly at her. 'A company can only be as good as its leader. And it can only be a dictatorship like Cougar when you have a benevolent dictator,' he said, and laughed his rolling laugh. 'And that's true. There'll never be another Burt Miller.'

It was an honest assessment, she saw, rather than simply smug self-satisfaction.

He looked at her seriously for a moment. 'Anna, I've offered Logan the Russian and East European Desk. What do you think?'

Anna felt a chill of bewilderment, then astonishment. Logan wasn't management material at all, in her opinion, let alone the right person to be put in charge of Cougar's second largest division. Over and over again, he'd shown himself to be unreliable, not even completely loyal. Burt knew this and she didn't understand. Burt continued to give Logan chances which he always saw that Logan wasted. She found she couldn't reply.

'It's OK. He turned it down,' Burt said.

'Why?'

'No reason. What do you think, Anna? What do you really think?' Burt asked again.

It was unusual for Burt to ask for advice about something outside another person's area of expertise. It was out of character and Anna's interest was always piqued when someone—particularly someone in Burt's all-powerful position—behaved out of character. She wondered whether to tell him what she thought, but knew that Burt only and always wanted honesty, no matter how difficult it was to hear.

'If someone rejects a part of something, it often means they want the whole,' she said. 'Logan fits that model. To me anyway, Burt.'

He didn't reply, but grinned at her, just to show he didn't take offence. But she saw he'd filed away her remark and that it conflicted with something in him outside the logic of usually clear thoughts.

On a wide circular table in the centre of the plane, Burt unfolded an old copy of the *Wall Street Journal* at the page which detailed the results of the final round of the Ukrainian elections. There was the Russian-backed candidate, Viktor Yanukovich with his arms raised in victory. He had beaten Yulia Timoshenko by three percentage points for the presidency. There were pictures of

231

him with a grim face even in victory—just like the Politburo used to look, Anna thought. And underneath were pictures of Timoshenko with her corn-braided hair wrapped tightly like an ornamental towel around her head. Her face was set in defeat but she said she would contest the results. Yanukovich had received a warm welcome from the Kremlin, however, and was already forming a cabinet, with an Economics Minister who spoke only Russian and had no Ukrainian.

'Theo says we can take our eyes off Ukraine now,' Burt said. 'It's almost a relief to the CIA that the Kremlin stooge has won. They'd rather have a Russian proxy president than a democrat who might raise Russia's ire.'

She didn't reply, but read the report and saw that most of eastern Ukraine nearest Russia had voted for Yanukovich while most of the western part of the country had voted for Timoshenko.

'Theo reckons that this result will lower tensions between Ukraine and Russia,' Burt said. 'Their man got in, so that's it, Theo says. And—wonder of wonders—they were declared free and fair elections, according to international electoral monitors. Timoshenko protests but doesn't have a leg to stand on.' He looked across at her. 'What do you think, Anna?'

She looked away and out of the window at the endless, intense blue of a sky that seemed to share nothing with events in Eastern Europe. Then she turned to him. 'Why does the CIA think that?' she asked.

'Theo reckons the Russians have got what they want in Ukraine now. The Kremlin can relax. And therefore so can we.'

'For now, maybe. But it's just the beginning,' she said. 'A temporary respite at most, in my opinion. But what then? When the dust settles, Yanukovich may prove to be not just their ally in the Kremlin but also their Trojan Horse in Kiev.'

He looked at her questioningly.

'I don't agree with Lish and the CIA,' she said simply.

'Neither do I,' Burt replied. 'I agree with you, Anna. A Trojan Horse—I like it. But we'll discuss it—the three of us—when we see Mikhail,' he said.

They were flying south-west and Anna slept for the rest of the journey. She was used to taking sleep when there was any window of opportunity. In just over three hours after they'd set out they landed on the long runway at the edge of Burt's vast ranch in northern New Mexico.

Cougar emblems decorated the watchtower—a mountain lion rampant, like some medieval jousting symbol—and they drove away from the strip towards high Spanish-style gates that announced an intensely guarded area at the centre of the ranch. Security guards were everywhere in evidence, a small private army in the semi-desert.

There were discreet, concentric circles of defence around the hundreds of thousands of acres of land and the circular defensive lines shrank in size eventually to a sort of fortress climax at the centre, though even this was still discreet. Another Cougar emblem reared its raised paws in bas-relief on a giant bronze tableau at the inner ranch gates. And Burt's private army, increased in size for the purpose of guarding his most prized asset— Mikhail—wore embroidered cougars on their shoulders, but were otherwise armed more effectively with MP5N machine guns. Any further Russian attempt to wrestle Mikhail from his chosen exile at Burt's ranch was not anticipated, but, nevertheless, planned for. Burt liked to 'futurise for all the eventualities', as he put it, like a seasoned general before a battle.

They walked across the high desert gardens that separated the parking area from the house. There was snow on the distant mountains and there was a scattering down here on the mesa. A frost gripped the land and it was two degrees below zero. The desert plants and cacti, like bristling steel gun emplacements, were dug in, biding their time for the short and almost invisible burst of growth that would begin in June.

Burt withdrew an envelope from the inside of his blue, silver-buttoned blazer and held it casually in the hand that also clutched his cigar. The sun was bright in the sky, but made little difference to the temperature in the depth of winter.

He hadn't shown Anna the message from the man who called himself 'Rafael' and which he had received from the American embassy in Kiev two months before, but he had it in the envelope he was holding now and the way he held the envelope showed off its wax seal of a bird, bright red and firmly imprinted in the dried wax that had flowed outwards at its edges before it had solidified. Something told him that Mikhail—as well as providing insights into the developing situation in Ukraine—might have something to say about it.

They found Mikhail sitting on a verandah at the rear of the sprawling ranch house. The verandah was heated by a line of gas heaters like an outdoor restaurant.

Burt's staff were everywhere in evidence; wheeled trolleys with coffee and cold drinks stood within Mikhail's reach; uniformed maids appeared to be polishing windows inside a drawing room behind them, and gardeners were covering the roots of shrubs with further mesh and straw against frost which lasted as late as June up here in the mountains.

Anna looked at the two gardeners who were working in her sight and saw the bulges beneath their arms. Burt didn't just have armed guards, he had armed gardeners too.

Mikhail was sitting in the wheelchair he'd been confined to for a year and a half now, ever since the KGB's assassination attempt against him in a Virginia park, across the river from Washington, DC. Anna, too, had been wounded in the firefight, the attempted abduction of Mikhail and of herself by the KGB. She'd taken a bullet in the shoulder, but, unlike Mikhail, she had made a full recovery. Despite the attention of the best doctors Burt's bottomless fortune could provide, however, it was by now conceded—not least by Mikhail himself—that the effect of the Russian bullet which had entered his spine on that day in 2008 would not now be reversed. Only Burt's faith in the ever-developing and banned medical technology of stem cells allowed the question to remain open. Burt never gave up his endless optimism for the prospect of Mikhail's improvement and full recovery. Mikhail never gave up hope regardless of any situation he found himself in—whether he was to remain permanently crippled or cured—and his injury seemed to concern him less than it did Burt. It was a mere detail for Mikhail. It didn't interfere with his brain, and that was all that seemed important to him.

They pulled up cushioned leather seats next to Mikhail. Anna kissed him on both cheeks, three times in the Russian way, and Burt raised his hand casually. Here down at the ranch, Burt would shortly adopt another of his many disguises, this time as a nineteenth-century cattle rancher—despite the fact that he had never sat on a horse.

'What news from the front?' Mikhail said. 'Where is the front these days, anyway?'

He was a tall man; even in a wheelchair it was possible to see that. His once thick, black hair had turned to grey in the eighteen months since he'd been shot. But his face was finely cut like soft and weathered stone and his eyes were piercing and dark. He had several newspapers opened on tables surrounding him, including the *Journal*.

'I believe the front is still Ukraine,' Burt said. 'Never mind that Yanukovich won. But I'm apparently in a minority. At least out there,' he waved his hand vaguely at the world. 'The CIA disagrees.'

'The Kremlin's choice has won, that's true,' Mikhail said. 'How will that make the spies in Moscow feel? And will it tame the monster? I'll tell you, Burt. If the monster gets one square meal, it won't think they'll come regularly, on time, every day, believe me. The Kremlin won't view this victory as satisfying its ambitions in Ukraine. It's just the beginning. It will just want more. It will see the Yanukovich victory as a sign of weakness among its enemies, not as a sign of its own strength. And that is always an indication of the most dangerous of enemies. The paranoia of the

236

self-pitying and wounded animal always looks to its opponents' weaknesses, it never enjoys its own strengths.'

'Then the three of us agree,' Burt said.

Anna looked into the eyes of the old spy and wondered if Mikhail was sliding into becoming like other exiles and defectors from the KGB she'd met in the West—an intransigent, hectoring and bitterly entrenched mind that would always see the Kremlin from now on as a two-dimensional enemy. But what she saw was his old intelligence and far-sightedness that could only come from calm contemplation. Neither his injury nor his exile, she realised, would ever blunt that. He spent most days entirely alone, Burt had told her, despite Burt's attempts to entertain him with arranged visits from friends and colleagues. Some made the trip down from Washington or Virginia for three days in order to meet the West's greatest double agent for a generation, and left without ever seeing Mikhail. He devoted his time, it seemed, to solitary contemplation. He was like a monk. But did he think of the past, his past as the West's great source in the Kremlin? Or was it contemplation of the future? Anna guessed the latter.

'Anna says this victory might just give the Kremlin what she calls a Trojan Horse inside Ukraine,' Burt said. 'That far from being the end it's the beginning.'

'If the Russians want to repossess Ukraine— really repossess it like in Soviet times,' Mikhail said, 'then Yanukovich can be their useful fool, yes. He can weaken the structures from the centre— from the inside—in line with the Kremlin's plans.'

Burt didn't reply or acknowledge Mikhail's

remarks for now, but simply turned over the envelope he'd taken from his blazer pocket as they walked to the house and put it on the table in front of Mikhail. 'Take a look at it too, Anna,' he said. 'Your two heads are better than an army.' Anna got up out of her chair and stood behind the wheelchair, looking over Mikhail's shoulders.

But before either of them could comment, Burt explained the provenance of the envelope and the antics of its sender, the ghost who called himself Rafael, in summoning most of the world's intelligence agencies who had a presence in Kiev to meetings that never took place. 'As far as I know,' Burt said, 'I'm the only one who received a message from the mysterious Rafael that said there would be no meeting. Even though there had never been a meeting in the first place.' He poured himself a glass of squeezed orange juice and took another Havana cigar from a leather case in his jacket pocket, even though the one he'd been smoking wasn't yet half-finished. Then he sat back in a semi-reclining position and appeared to be tanning himself, fully clothed, under the heater, eyes closed, while puffing at the cigar and sipping from the glass at regular intervals.

Mikhail and Anna read the six words of the message. 'There will be no meeting tonight'. And then Mikhail put the envelope on top of it, its back facing up, and with the seal facing him and Anna. The bird had a longish beak and long legs, a water bird, it looked like.

'It's a snipe,' Mikhail said. 'In Russian we call it *bekac*. In French it's *becasse*.' He looked up at Burt. 'They emigrate from Russia to Western Europe—for the winter.'

'I thought it was some kind of snipe,' Burt said. 'Good to eat then, if we can catch it. So. Who sends wax impressions of snipe through the mail accompanied by arcane messages? It was mailed in Novorossiysk, by the way. Not that its geographical origins have much to bear on the situation, I'm sure.'

'Maybe they do in this case. It's the ferry terminal from Russia to the Crimea,' Mikhail said. He handed the envelope to Anna with the seal facing her. 'Have you ever seen this before, my dear?' he asked. 'Recognise it?'

She looked again. 'No, Mikhail. But the message is in the seal, yes?'

'Yes.'

Mikhail sighed. 'It's a message that he's coming West,' he said slowly, and all the time his mind seemed to be working, thinking of the implications. 'Like the bird migrating. And it was sent to you via your embassy in Ukraine?' he asked.

'Yes. Coming West?' Burt said. 'You mean he's defecting?'

Mikhail thought for a long time. 'I don't know, but I doubt it's as simple as that,' he said finally. 'I think we can assume, perhaps, that he's coming there, only as far as Ukraine. Only that far West. For the time being, in any case. Maybe he's keeping his options open.'

'And maybe he's luring us to believe that he's open to our offers,' Anna said. 'Maybe it's a sting.'

'That's also possible,' Mikhail replied. 'We have to be very careful.'

'The snipe is coming West, to Ukraine,' Burt said in the mock dramatic tones of someone delivering a badly coded sentence. Then he laughed robustly. 'So what do we do? Shoot it? Eat it? Put it in a cage?'

Mikhail looked sideways at Burt, but he didn't—and rarely did—enjoy Burt's easy mirth. 'No. We do none of those things. We should give it a feather bed,' he said. 'We should guard it with our lives. The snipe might bring us good luck, or at least insight. For you, for us. And it might bring us very bad luck indeed. It depends on the circumstances.'

For Burt, luck was something you used, not something that used you. 'It depends, as always, on what happens,' Burt said, and repeated his favourite dictum: 'What happens is the only God there is.'

'You're a pagan, Burt,' Mikhail said and Burt roared with laughter. He surveyed the mesa with its mysterious rock formations that contained the petroglyphs of ancient Indian cultures. 'Out here it's a good place to be a pagan,' he said.

Mikhail leaned back against the wheelchair and left the envelope on the table without taking any further interest in it. Then he looked at Burt again and patted Anna's arm. He was the only man from whom she ever seemed happy to receive such casual physical contact, Burt noted.

Mikhail was the friend of her former Brit husband, the MI6 officer Finn, who was now dead. Finn had been murdered by the KGB four years ago now. Little Finn's father. Perhaps that was it, the friendship between Mikhail and Finn. But Finn had also been Mikhail's closest and indeed only direct contact with the West in the years when Mikhail had acted as a double agent inside the Kremlin. Finn had been the only person Mikhail allowed to know him when Mikhail was still at the top in Russia. Finn had been Mikhail's handler and so there was a bond with her dead husband through Mikhail.

'My guess is', Burt said slowly, 'that you know who the snipe is, Mikhail.' And his eyes—slits at the best of times—narrowed slightly.

Mikhail sighed and leaned back in the wheelchair. Now he, too, let his eyes wander over the jagged rock bluffs behind which the sun was turning a burning red in the freezing atmosphere and starkly illuminating their eerie profiles against the sky.

'I'm cold,' he said. 'It's time to go inside.'

Anna wheeled Mikhail inside and Burt came out from under the heater and followed them. There was a roaring fire in the sitting room with its floor-to-ceiling windows that gave them as good a view of the mountains as if they'd been outside. Burt threw more wood on the fire and asked a member of staff to bring champagne. Anna sat on a sofa away from the fire while Mikhail wheeled the chair closer to it. Burt seemed impatient and didn't sit.

'There's a man called Dmitri Respin,' Mikhail began. 'Dmitry Viktorov—and many other names he goes under. He, I believe, is the bird on the seal. A truly unique intelligence officer. In fact, he's one of very few non-Russians at the heart of Department S—he's half-foreign anyway—our most secret foreign operations unit in Russia. He was recruited from outside Russia originally and then was brought to Moscow and trained as would have been normal, initially in the Foreigners' Area of The Forest. His training was regular—for the purpose of conducting operations back in his own country. It consisted of sabotage, mostly. That's what we trained the foreigners to do back in their own countries. That and terrorism too.' The champagne arrived and was opened. Burt insisted on pouring it into glasses and politely dismissed the woman who'd brought it.

Mikhail sipped from his glass before continuing. 'But then his obvious qualities and his half-Russian ancestry elevated him to Department S, where he came under my watch at the start of the nineties.' He paused. 'But I get ahead of myself.' Mikhail pulled himself up against the back of the wheelchair and took another sip from the glass of champagne. 'He—this Dmitri Respin or Viktorov—was educated from the age of sixteen at Vishka—The Tower—in The Forest.' He looked up at Anna. 'The same place you were educated for the KGB,' he said. 'And the place where I have so far failed to achieve my own greatest ambition, the defeat of Putin's Russia. Like you, my dear, I was a part of Department S, but as we all know now, in the nineties I went on to control all of our agents in Western Europe. The apogee of my double career.'

Anna thought back over the years to a time when Mikhail had stood behind Vladimir Putin at a small service in the Kremlin's chapel after Putin became president in the year 2000. In the new, democratic Russia the archbishop had proclaimed 'God Bless the KGB', near the end of the service. Putin was photographed inside the church looking reverently towards the altar, for the benefit of Russia's newly enfranchised religious population who would be expected to support him in future, via the archbishop.

In the photograph, Mikhail could only be seen

with half a face in the subsequent pictures published by all the important Russian newspapers. But only if you knew Mikhail well would you have known it was him. At her interrogation by Burt, after her own defection to the West, Anna had been shown this picture, the only picture that was ever taken of Mikhail in public. When she had identified him by his known name, one of Burt's team, Logan, had recognised the face, even though none of them knew his identity as an MI6 agent through Finn and Finn alone. Logan had asked her then, 'Why is the Deputy Railways Minister seated behind President Putin? Why is he there at this most important occasion—the marriage of the KGB president to the religious masses the KGB has persecuted for seventy years?'

For Mikhail's cover in Department S had been the role of Deputy Railways Minister, a position that allowed him wide access to agents across Western Europe under the guise of marvelling at its railway systems. 'Why is such a lowly figure right behind the President?' Logan had asked her.

And that was the beginning of her long withdrawal from defending Mikhail's secret identity. She had protected him as best she could. She didn't want the Americans or anyone else to have him unless it was by his choice. And so she had met him in secret—twice—once in New York City, the second and final time in the park across the Potomac from Washington when they'd been ambushed by a KGB snatch squad. She had been shot in the shoulder, Mikhail in the spine, before Burt's legions had rolled over the horizon and settled the fight in her and Mikhail's favour. And

243

that was how the Americans—in the shape of Burt and Cougar Intelligence Applications—had come into the possession of Mikhail.

Burt stamped around the room, impatient for Mikhail to continue.

'Dmitri Respin or Viktorov was highly regarded inside Department S,' Mikhail continued. 'That was why Department S took him on in the first place. As I say, he was unique. He had what they call second sight. Or, at least, so they believed— and I have to agree with them.' He looked at Anna. 'As you know, our psychologists, psychiatrists and scientists were endlessly creative when it came to developing agents. It was only the rest of the country they let down with their services. Respin is about your age, Anna. A year younger, I think.' Mikhail settled himself back and a member of staff appeared and whispered to Burt that dinner could be served whenever he wanted. He waved the woman away and told her they would get their own supper this evening.

'You can all leave,' he said in dismissing her.

Mikhail drank slowly, savouring the champagne. 'Loosen the tongue but not the brain,' he said to Burt.

Then he continued. 'Respin was trained in every aspect of training that you'd expect for a foreign intelligence officer. He was always meant for deployment in the southern, Muslim republics and they are the most dangerous. Many of our agents were lost there in the brutal wars we fought, and are still fighting, against the separatists. So he had to be good, the best. But his vital advantage was this so-called second sight, not just his native grasp of languages or his weapons handling and combat

244

training, or his code work or his analytical mind. He was highly valued because he had something that no one else had.' He looked at Anna who was now sitting on his other side. 'Or rather he lacked something that everyone else in Department S did have. He lacked sight. Dmitri Respin was blind. And uniquely it was his blindness that gave him an edge. His blindness gave him a different kind of sight. He'd either had this second sight from birth or he developed it later. It was a talent for knowing things at a mental—maybe psychic—level that you and I have to see with our eyes in order to understand. And even then we only see dimly with the eyes compared to Respin's abilities. He had something more than eyes can ever give us. Dmitri could tell what someone was thinking. A huge talent.' He looked at Burt. 'As you always say, Burt, that's something that all the satellites and technology in the world can't achieve.'

Then he looked back into the fire. 'And that was just a part of the talents that came from his blindness. Far-sighted is a word you can use about the blind, and Dmitri was far-sighted.' Mikhail sipped from his glass of champagne again and Burt, eager for something to occupy himself with, filled all of their glasses. 'I had him working for me before I took over our agents in Western Europe,' Mikhail continued. 'It was during the first Chechen War in the mid-nineties. Dmitri went into Chechnya and he was unlike any other officer of the KGB. He went into that country as a friend to the Chechens, and as someone who didn't fear them.' He looked at Burt now. 'His name is not Dmitri, of course, and he is not a Russian. At least he's only half-Russian. He was born in Damascus

245

in 1971, the son of a Syrian dancer and a then young KGB officer by the name of Valentin Viktorov. Viktorov worked at the Soviet embassy compound in Damascus when your father was head of station there,' he said to Anna. 'His son, to whom we gave the code name Dmitri Respin, was left in an orphanage there when he was a few months old. His father Valentin was being posted to Moscow at the time and he took the boy away from its mother's family and placed him in the orphanage. I think he probably saved the boy's life by his actions.' He looked hard at Anna. 'You were there, Anna, in Damascus, and a child at the same time.'

Anna's mind reeled. It took her back to more than twenty years before to the KGB compound in Damascus where she'd been brought up until the age of fourteen while her father was the KGB's station head. After her fourteenth birthday she'd been sent to live with her grandmother in Moscow.

She recalled the old brute of her father—and then her mother who'd been his antithesis, a kind woman who seemed in everything she did to be atoning for her husband's sins. A kind of martyr, she supposed. Her mother's martyrdom was the driving force for her own desire to be a strong woman, untethered to a man's career.

And she recalled the orphanage her mother had taken her to visit in order to gain sympathy with the dispossessed and the unloved. But the blind boy she remembered hadn't been called Dmitri.

As if reading her thoughts, Mikhail continued. 'His name wasn't Dmitri then, of course,' he said. 'It was Balthasar, and probably still is. He used another name in Chechnya—neither Dmitry nor

Balthasar.'

And now she remembered him. He was an uncanny child, a year older than her but with a face which, though blind, held the wisdom not just of an adult but of an unusually intelligent adult, and beyond that he'd had a seer-like quality—so her mother had described it, anyway. Sometimes on their visits his presence was so powerful, it was as if it was he who had come to visit her and her mother, rather than the other way around. He had that kind of power, that made her think she was a supplicant.

'I remember my mother telling me he had a Russian father,' she said. 'And that was Viktorov? Now General Valentin Viktorov?'

'Now General Viktorov, yes. Then he was just a lieutenant or lower, I don't remember.'

'Balthasar,' Burt said. 'God protect the King.'

'That's right. And in Chechnya, they worshipped him. They thought he was a wise man, a magician, a religious mystic. They thought he would be their saviour.'

'And he fed the KGB and the Russian military the information that led the Chechens to the slaughter,' Anna said.

Mikhail paused. 'At first, yes, he did,' he said. 'But then I noted—though no one else seemed to—that he was beginning to avoid doing quite the same thing. He became like a hunter who loses his taste for killing and who doesn't shoot quite straight for fear or dislike of killing a rare or beautiful animal. He still fed information back to Moscow—back to The Forest—of course. He had to, in order to survive. But I noticed it had become much more selective. It seemed he was identifying

Chechens who were as dangerous to their own country as they were to Russia, but not the true nationalists and nation-builders who the Kremlin also wanted to destroy. He was giving us only the most extreme elements of the Chechen resistance—the fanatics of God, the men for whom the people are mere instruments—and I began to suspect that he was protecting the vast majority of the rebels and their citizens in that country; the people who we Russians would run down with our tanks, murder and torture, tear up from their roots. Just as Stalin did in 1944, the innocent and the good swept into the trash with the so-called guilty.'

'And now?' Burt said. 'What is Balthasar now?'

'That is hard to say. He's an extremely dangerous man. That I do know. A fanatic himself of sorts, perhaps, but a fanatic who is not attached to any cause, just to his own genius. Perhaps he is a mystic, I don't know. I do know that he is still deep in the black heart of Department S and that if he's coming to Ukraine, there is a deeply black purpose to it.'

'Why does he tell me he's coming?' Burt said.

'That's the question,' Mikhail replied. 'Is it a trap or is he genuinely putting out a feeler, trying to establish contact for other reasons?'

There was a prolonged silence.

'Why come to me?' Burt repeated. 'To Cougar?' And then he turned to Anna. 'Is this another Russian play to get their hands on you?' he said.

'Perhaps Balthasar knows that it is Anna who will respond to his overtures, yes,' Mikhail agreed immediately.

'So Balthasar is just the latest in their attempts

248

to abduct her.'

Mikhail turned to look at Burt. 'Maybe. But only maybe,' he said. 'That is the risk. It's possible that it's true and it's possible the opposite is true—that Balthasar is testing the waters. That he's finished. And that Anna is the only person he trusts. In my opinion, yes, he wants to meet with Anna, but whether as a trap for her or as a way out of Russia—that's impossible to say.'

'There's only one way to find out,' Anna said.

'No,' Burt said. 'I can't have you taking that risk.'

'But I will,' she replied. 'And with or without you, Burt.'

PART TWO

CHAPTER EIGHTEEN

22 April

The passenger ferry *Kerchinsky* was released from its mooring lines but stayed motionless for a moment, as if unwilling to depart. Then Balthasar felt the effect of the bow thrusters pushing gently away from the quay and the boat at last slowly turned and headed out into the Kerch Straits.

It was a clear day in early spring, and cool, but the sky reflected on to the water the deep blue of the coming summer. The mostly Ukrainian passengers, returning from visits to relatives in Russia, seemed to sense that a long winter had come to an end. They were chattering, breaking open bottles of vodka, and unwrapping Caucasian cheese bread as if they were going on a long voyage rather than the few miles back home across the straits. Ahead of them, spring meadows beneath the towering cliffs of the Crimea were greening and there were yellow daffodils in bloom, a flower the party of orphans on a vacation from the Russian Far East had never seen and would later mistake for onions and attempt to eat.

It was a brief trip from the Port of Kavkaz on the Russian side to Port Krym on the Ukrainian shore. After the ten-hour flight from frozen Magadan in the east, to Moscow, and then another six hours from Moscow to the Black Sea, the children, so it seemed to Balthasar, only now sensed their vacation was beginning, with the ferry's departure from Russian soil.

He had accompanied the orphans from the starting point in Magadan. That was his cover and it had been thought best that he should be known to them—and to their real teachers—for a period of time before meeting at the ferry terminal. Already an easy relationship had developed between him and the children at any rate, even if their teachers might suspect he was not who he was meant to be—a teacher with experience of orphans and also of the country to which they were travelling on holiday—and they consequently kept a discreet, if polite, distance from him.

And though accompanying the orphans, Balthasar himself stayed apart from the others. He stood leaning against the guard rail on the port side, away from the other passengers in general as well as the excited children. Leaning on the rail, he felt the gentle breeze of the boat's motion on his face, smelled the salt air and the diesel fumes and sawn timber, and listened to the bow wave's continual break, along with the cries of children and seagulls. Eleven children—he already knew that—and five seagulls, he was sure of that.

He felt the proximity and even the individual natures of other passengers further along the deck, as well as sensing a fishing boat nearly a quarter of a mile away and heading out to the Black Sea for its catch. And though he could not see any of these things—his dark, unseeing eyes flickered meaninglessly—he was as acutely aware of his surroundings as the prehistoric fish that hunt and eat their prey in the pitch-black canyons of the deepest ocean. His other four regular senses were highly tuned. But his predominant sense overrode all these and, despite the scepticism of some scientists, it was this sixth sense that afforded him a picture of people of which others were deprived. His own perceptions left others with perfect eyesight in the dark.

As he stood on the deck and felt the cool breeze running over his face, he reflected on why he was here, on this boat from Russia. Like so many journeys before, this one was for the purpose of another mission; dozens—maybe even hundreds, he'd lost count—that had sent him from his adopted country abroad. Each had its own fine-tuned purpose, each made some small adjustment to affairs that related to Russia, and most of the time each resulted in death and injury, the sowing of instability and fear and distrust among Russia's enemies. He was the most decorated officer in the history of Department S. And now that he contemplated this mission, as always he wondered whether it would be his last. But this time, this thought did not come to him just because of the dangers that lay ahead, but also because maybe it was this mission that he, Balthasar, would choose to be his last. Maybe this time he would end the cycle of betrayal and mayhem that he usually left behind. Maybe this time he would choose to follow this life no more.

On the breezy deck of the ferry he also contemplated his journey from his birth in Syria, to an orphanage there, to the discovery of his Russian roots and the meeting with his real father, and finally to his covert work for Department S. But to Balthasar these events and actions were manifestations of himself and his identity that he considered to be the paint on the wall of his person, not the wall itself. In other words, what he

255

had done and what he represented were of little consequence to him compared to the inner life which his sightlessness had afforded him and which was a richer realm of truth than anyone could imagine.

Perhaps that was why he liked the sea so much. His world was as invisible to other people as the world beneath the sea was. His was another life, another world entirely, and it was as colourful and rich as the regular vision of normal people was grey and drab.

It always surprised him how other people's eyes gave them only so much, just enough to make errors of judgement; some facts about their surroundings, perhaps, but even then the facts could be tricked. The camera could, after all, lie. Earlier in the winter, he recalled, he'd been present when the Russian 14th Army were placing inflatable tanks along the border with Lithuania in an exercise designed to intimidate the small country. Satellite pictures had shown them as if they were real. Warnings rumbled from Washington and the European Union, the government of Lithuania began to take defensive measures. And in Balthasar's mind the eyes of the world's satellites and its actual eyes deceived all too easily. Eyes without awareness depicted only a tiny proportion of a world. Eyes were tools, not knowledge.

He held on to the guard rail that ran along the deck and sniffed the salt in the breeze once more. His life had been a long road and its twists and turns—the twists and turns of anyone's life, he suspected—were nothing but normal to him. His normality was simply being without eyes. There

256

were fewer distractions if you couldn't see and if you saw it like that. That was how he'd begun to discover his own powers, simply by not being distracted by the ability to see things. It was a valuable lesson in solitary detachment.

Having no parents and no roots had afforded him even further detachment from the cruder, visible world than his own increasingly refined one. Brought up from scratch in an impoverished orphanage that depended for its knife-edge existence on donations, his early lessons in Damascus thirty-eight years before had consisted of bypassing the visible into what some, over-mystical people in his opinion, called another dimension; the dimension, however, was simply understanding what was in other people's minds. That was not a dimension or, to him, a mystery. It was a skill that he'd developed by necessity and that had once been common to everyone. In Balthasar's belief, in fact, anyone could do it—if they believed they could and if they weren't distracted.

And somehow these developed skills of his had led to his current incarnation—for many years now—as an officer in the most secret department of Russian intelligence. It seemed incredible to many of his colleagues, and yet nothing that happened was anything other than credible. Why did the mind insist that someone else's normality wasn't normal? It was because the world operated on a system of comparison, Balthasar considered. It was a ruthless and inefficient system, in his opinion. People compared their own lives with other people's whom they perceived more 'normal' than their own. Some kind of default mechanism.

Their purpose in doing so was simply to feel better about themselves when they perceived another as less well off than they were, or to harbour resentment and aspiration if they perceived the opposite. It all led to conflict and somehow his life's path had been at the hard centre of the conflict between people and nations. Had he now reached a time in his life when he could break his own pattern, be free of his masters?

And now Balthasar's thoughts had arrived at the present moment. His mission to Ukraine was straightforward—to implicate a group of people of Islamic faith in some strategic, Russian atrocity. He decided to make it his purpose, however, to also find what atrocity it was his masters were trying to conceal. In good time. For now, he would pursue his mission, but he would look for an alternative this time. And then perhaps this one would be his final assignment. Perhaps this would be his swansong. Whether it was done his way or theirs depended on how events unfolded. But whichever way the assignment went—whichever way he decided it would go—this was the end.

It was not so much a decision, just something that had come to him in the unfolding logic of his fate and whatever took place in the coming days or weeks was something that he accepted. He had no idea what the future would bring, no plans, no specific exit strategy. Either he would complete this mission as his controllers wanted him to, or not. That too was undecided. It depended on a number of things; what his masters were implicating these Muslims in, for one. He was no longer theirs to point in any direction they liked. But also it depended on the woman, Anna, and who she had turned out to be after nearly forty years. That was a concrete consideration certainly.

His thoughts of her cast his mind back to the beginning, or almost to the beginning. Up to the age of sixteen years old he had remained at the orphanage. The women and few men who worked there were unquestioningly kind and even loving. He had been given an education, he had played the few sports available outside in the cramped concrete yard, despite his blindness. He recalled a man who had been in the Syrian basketball team who had taught them basketball—the KGB's favourite game as it turned out later—and who was especially attentive to him. He had excelled academically and was considered to be a startling and intelligent pupil. But the children at the orphanage were also taught a practical education —weaving or jewellery-making, wood and metal work, basket-making, tailoring, pottery —whatever each child felt was his métier or simply interested him or her. The purpose was that they would be able to provide for themselves in the wide world outside the orphanage. At sixteen they were let go, supervised up to a point in their new life on their own, but set up in a small way with their skills out there in the capital Damascus. Many of them, it turned out, were better prepared for a life lived on their wits than children who had been brought up in the protective custody—or crushing vice, depending on your point of view—of the Syrian state.

And there had only been one contact with the outside world throughout all that time. He wouldn't have wanted any other, now he thought about it. She was a Russian woman, Natalia

Resnikova, who had visited him from the beginning, with her daughter Anna, who had visited him regularly from the age of five. He suspected the Russian woman had made small financial contributions to the orphanage. Hers was a kind of adoption, he'd been told by one of the women at the orphanage, and that no doubt meant some financial contribution, no matter how small. The Russians weren't rich after all. But the Russian woman Resnikova told him she was always there for him, surrogate mother, as long as her husband remained in Damascus. Her little girl, Anna, had played with him, hugged him, even told him he was her brother on one or two occasions. The two of them had visited him once a week, when Anna was old enough and unless something prevented their arrival.

In his own mind, through them, Balthasar had come to possess a family of sorts. When he was fourteen years old he thought he loved the girl Anna. And then she'd disappeared. Her mother still visited him after that, but she told him that Anna had gone to live in Moscow with her grandmother. Resnikova told him about Moscow, painted a picture of the dacha where Anna lived with her grandmother. She'd painted these pictures in his mind and Balthasar had never forgotten them or her.

Then one day, just before his sixteenth birthday, a man had arrived at the orphanage. He was a very important man, he'd been told, and a Russian too. He was a general, the women had told him, and he was Balthasar's father. General Viktorov. He made a gift to the orphanage, quite a substantial one, Balthasar gleaned from the mind of the head of

260

the orphanage. This man seemed interested in him, not just because he was his son but because of what the teachers told him about his abilities. They called them his 'abilities'. The ability to see without seeing, to know things, like the colour of a dress that he couldn't possibly have seen. Or the weather for the next day. But these were just cheap tricks to Balthasar, a conjuror's basic tools. What was not any kind of trick was his ability to know what someone was thinking; or the size and position of objects in a room. Many such things. His teachers spoke, fearfully it seemed, of a Third Eye. But to Balthasar all the hushed talk of his 'gifts', his 'abilities', even superstitious talk of a Third Eye, was just a normal aspect of his existence.

The man who came—his father, for what it was worth—took a greater and greater interest in him the more he witnessed Balthasar's behaviour. Viktorov had only intended to make a donation to the orphanage and then leave, but when he'd heard about Balthasar's gifts, and then seen them for himself, he had formally adopted his own son. They returned to Moscow together, a frightening time, Balthasar recalled. And there a new and unpleasant education had unfolded that treated his gifts as just something for others to use. He was confined in a kind of mental hospital at first, then a scientific institute outside Moscow, and he became the object of scientists' experiments. He was put through a series of tasks with the application of increasing stresses, physical and mental, to test his endurance and the endurance of his gifts. After two years, when they'd deemed that the tests were apparently successful, he'd been inducted under his father's wing into the highly secret department of the KGB, Department S. The year was 1989. President Gorbachev was in power and within two years the Berlin Wall would fall and the Soviet Union collapse.

And by now, in 2010, he had been of great use to his organisation. His Arab looks and speech were simply an added advantage, on top of his far more important powers. There'd been the wars in Chechnya in which Department S had played a most secretive role. There'd been the relentlessly perennial Middle Eastern blow-ups; and there'd been the rise of Islamic fundamentalism and the subsequent American push into Afghanistan, Iraq and Central Asia. Balthasar had been a bit-part player throughout the Caucasus and the Middle East. And now here he was on another mission, this time to Ukraine. It was not his usual area of operations, and indeed it was a mission so secret he had been briefed by his father alone and told very little even then. But there was still one secret Balthasar possessed that his masters at the KGB didn't know and hopefully never would. It was his contact with the spy and traitor 'Mikhail' who had now fled to America.

Balthasar turned over in his mind his new assignment once again. 'Reports are coming in . . . tensions along the border . . .' The stock phrases from the morning's radio news programme in Kavkaz reverberated in his mind. It was as if the low-level stubble fire along the Russian border with Ukraine that had flared and backed down to a glow for twenty years since the Soviet Union collapsed was finally on course for an all-out conflagration. Isolated hostile words and actions—

262

from the Kremlin's threat to seize the Crimea for Russia, to Russia's disruption of oil supplies into Ukraine and on to Western Europe (and even the detention of fourteen Ukrainian circus camels at the border) seemed to be coalescing into a single course for military conflict. The new Ukrainian president Yanukovich made preposterous objections to Russia, but in reality—as Balthasar knew—these objections were just for the consumption of Ukrainians and the West. He did nothing to face Russia down.

Ukraine and Russia, he thought, were entering another fateful dance between two mutually loving and equally loathing partners. They were, it seemed, historically united, even if that unity was primarily one of conflict. Balthasar turned the phrase over in his head. From a psychological point of view, an embrace between the two countries could only be under arms, he believed, like wrestlers.

And now, with a few weeks to go before Ukraine had announced it was to deport all Russian secret service officers from the Crimea, the Kremlin had set in motion a long-held plan to infiltrate a swarm of *spetsnaz* troops disguised as civilians and an equally impressive battalion of foreign intelligence agents from the KGB's Department S into the Crimea.

He let go of the guard rail now and walked over to the party of orphans, his cover for entry into the Ukraine. Balthasar was an orphan himself and today his guise of a teacher with the party of orphans was simply a natural cover.

Standing on the deck now, he recalled Vladimir Putin's recent words spoken brazenly in public at last: 'Ukraine is not even a state'. Everything about Russia's intentions was expressed in those words, but would the West see it that way—and if they did, what would they do about it?

The *Kerchinsky* slid across the remaining section of the straits and entered Port Krym.

When the boat had docked, Balthasar joined the orphans and the teachers. He stood in line at the sign which read *Kontrol* and offered his passport to the border guard. The Ukrainians were making it more difficult by the day for Russian visitors, but his association with the orphan party averted the usual anti-Russian mood. They were through. Balthasar patting a small boy's head as a teacher should.

The bus which was to take the orphans up into the green lands of the Crimea waited belching diesel smoke. He boarded with the party. The other teachers glanced occasionally at him with a mix of awe and distrust. For once they were deep inside Ukraine, they suspected that Balthasar would be parting company with them and another man would return with the orphans at the end of their vacation. This man would have the same name and age and passport number as Balthasar. The KGB was taking the greatest precautions in the movement of its agents across the border.

CHAPTER NINETEEN

Preparations for infiltrating Anna into Ukraine a third time were of an even higher order than for her previous operations. Her cover identity for the first entry, into Odessa, was evidently blown and a second identity had been provided for her operation on the northern border. Now Burt provided two more passports for this third entry. One identity she would use for passing through border controls and into the country, while the other was to enable her to change identities once she was across the border—and then only in an emergency. The first passport Burt had procured was American and the second, emergency passport gave her British nationality. Adrian in London had been, as ever, most obliging where Burt's requests were concerned.

Under the first, American identity she was to enter the country as a tourist exploring the byways of the Crimea just as the summer season was beginning. She would be a camper, a walker, a bird-watcher, with an added interest in the ancient Greek sites along the coast and a diploma in archaeology to match. This identity was designed for someone to roam the huge national parks behind Sevastopol but principally to give her ready access to the area around its port. And she would be able, if necessary, to retreat into the mountains behind the city. In the second, British passport—to be used in dire circumstances only, and only once she was inside the country—she was an investor in tourist infrastructure representing a British hotel company that was looking for opportunities on the beaches of the Black Sea coast for developing its hotel trade. Burt gave Anna a full back-up of business cards and an office address in London corresponding with a genuine tourist investment company Cougar owned and kept for special purposes on the shelf. Phone lines attached to this known company were arranged. All calls for her from the Crimea—if any checks were made by the Ukrainians—would be diverted from the company's offices to a special command centre Burt had also arranged in Mayfair. For this identity, she would take a different set of clothes, a different mobile phone and suitable business accessories which she would bury on entering the country.

'What are we going to do when every country introduces biometric passports?' Bob Dupont commented.

It was a question that all spy agencies were wrestling with. The days of a simple change of name and profession, with a clean passport and even full sovereign government support, were coming to a close. Soon, once you had entered a country, whether as an ordinary visitor or an undercover operative, there would be no opportunity for disguise on further visits. DNA would be the means of identification.

'I guess we'll find a way to change the human itself,' Burt said. 'Create an obstacle and we always come up with a way to subvert it, you can be sure of that. Our scientists are working on it now, believe me.'

But it was the thin fall-back plans should Anna make contact with Balthasar that bothered everyone the most. Burt had arranged a back-up team who would also infiltrate the country, Larry in charge as always. But of necessity this back-up team would have to remain in the background and steer clear of coming under observation themselves, should a meeting take place. Identities and further back-up had to be provided for the back-up team too.

'There's only so far you can be in the rear before you become completely useless,' Larry objected. 'I don't like it.'

But Anna insisted that his team should remain at arm's length. She was certain that she needed to act in an all-but-solo fashion, or there would be no meeting at all. Balthasar was treated by everyone with respect, but by Anna most of all. They all agreed that contact with him would be extremely sensitive, at best.

'He's used to operating in deepest cover,' she pointed out. 'In Chechnya. To survive years there without detection, his antennae are the surest there is.'

The third problem was with Balthasar himself. The idea of making contact with a highly skilled operative whose main intention might be to abduct her was hard enough to prepare for. But the added significance of an opponent who knew what you were thinking—as Mikhail insisted time and again was the case—created completely unique field rules. For two weeks, with the aid of three of Burt's company psychologists, Anna practised controlling her thoughts and even her perceptions. Her role as a camper, a tourist with the exploration of Crimea's beautiful parks as her sole aim, had to be perfected in a way that even an operative as

267

seasoned as she was had not anticipated. Once she made contact with Balthasar—if that was to happen—no other thought could even enter her brain that could upset the carefully designed cover they were preparing for her. For long sixteen-hour days, then seventeen- and finally eighteen-hour days, she practised this mind control until, one day, she'd asked Mikhail. 'But can he tell if you're controlling your thoughts? If he can, then all this is a waste of time.'

'I don't know, Anna,' was all Mikhail was able to tell her.

Burt's concentration on Sevastopol and the area around the Russian Black Sea fleet base was also a mystery to all of them except Burt himself. Why not Odessa? Both Larry and Anna asked him to no avail. And if the Crimea was the focus, why only the Crimea? What about the northern borders with Russia where she had found the canisters? But Burt was adamant, for reasons he didn't yet divulge, that Sevastopol was the key, not just to a meeting with Balthasar, but to any Russian move into Ukraine.

'That is the weakest point,' he told them, but he didn't explain the significance of their other discoveries of Russian infiltration into other parts of the country.

'They're all secondary to Sevastopol,' Burt stated emphatically. 'In my opinion, they're anyway just diversions,' he added vaguely.

Then, three days before her departure, when they were meeting at a safe house of Cougar's in the mountains of North Carolina, Burt laid out the operation itself and its background.

There were five of them in a long room in the

huge, wood-boarded attic of a clapboard house that overlooked the sea: Burt, Anna, Mikhail, Larry and Bob Dupont. Logan was explicitly excluded from the meeting. 'He'll join us later,' was all Burt said. 'When we've discussed what we need to discuss. Logan is involved only in one aspect of the Ukraine operation. What I'm about to say is for our ears only. And most importantly, Balthasar is for the ears of only those of us in this room.'

They sat at a polished oak trestle table that was more than thirty feet long. It was covered in maps, three dimensional terrain models, maritime charts, air, train, ferry and bus schedules for the Crimea, long-range weather reports in the northern Black Sea area; there were real-time TV screens on the walls that followed events in the Kiev parliament and news channels from Odessa and Sevastopol; and there were full moon and new moon tables and times and dates of the low-range Black Sea tides—though these last were left unexplained by Burt and, it was assumed by the assembled company, they were there just to provide any and every piece of information that could be extracted from the region.

Then Burt looked around the long room. It was illuminated by windows at either end, with strip lights tracked along the length of the ceiling. A coffee machine bubbled in a corner, there was a wine rack and cooler, and one of the staff below had laid out plates of sandwiches and biscuits, fruit bowls overflowing with every kind of fruit that would never be touched, and at the far end of the table near where Burt sat there was a modest humidor with a full selection of his favourite cigars. Burt placed his chubby hands on the table, the palms down, and commanded the attention of all of them.

'On the twenty-second of January, three months ago,' he began, using no notes, 'Anna retrieved a set of naval department blueprints secreted from the Russian Defence Ministry that show Moscow's plans for a modest enlargement of the port facilities at Novorossiysk, on the Russian side of the Kerch Straits from Crimea. Some days later, a severed head was delivered to a US embassy staff member in Kiev. The head belonged to a man who was a recent, and unidentified, Russian informant of the CIA station in Kiev. This informant reported what the CIA calls—using the informant's words—a "terror ship" that had recently left the port of Novorossiysk. It left the Black Sea, changed its name twice and returned with what was apparently a secret cargo. It now lies fifty miles off the port of Sevastopol.' He reached for a cigar, but used it merely as some kind of prop, stabbing the air with it, waving it as if he were drawing a picture in the air. Then he continued. 'A week after the ship appears on our mental screens, Anna captured a reinforced steel canister on the Russian-Ukrainian northern border. It was one of several batches being smuggled into Ukraine by Russian special forces troops. From our sources in Russia, we believed it to contain toxic substances.' Burt paused. 'And then, to cap things off perfectly, we received, from usually reliable sources in Moscow, stories of a Moscow-backed plan to implicate an Islamic Tatar group in the Crimea, by the name of Qubaq. The idea—apparently—was to create a set of circumstances that would destabilise the Crimean region and then blame this group.' He looked around the room. What he then said surprised his audience. 'What—if any of this—do we believe?' Burt stated with the majesty of a judge in the summing-up of a long case.

But without waiting for an answer—as everyone around the table was accustomed after one of Burt's rhetorical flourishes—he continued again. 'The general background to all this is that Russia has been agitating in Ukraine since the country's independence. This has been the case mainly since 2000, when Putin came to power. In more recent years, agitation has developed into what might be called a concerted subversion of Ukraine's political, military and intelligence structures. That began in earnest in 2004 when Moscow tried to fix the elections there and was only defeated by the Orange Revolution. Today, Moscow's candidate is in power, the revolution has failed, and Ukraine's future is undecided; whether it is to be part of Western democratic culture or fall back under the influence—perhaps more than that—of Russia.' He waved the cigar then pointed it like a weapon. 'So far this has been largely a propaganda war instigated by Russia against Ukraine. But is it just propaganda? In this case—as in most others—we should always listen to what the world's leaders actually say. In the twentieth century that would, perhaps, have avoided several catastrophes. And what did Putin say about Ukraine? In April 2008, he said to President Bush, "Ukraine is not even a state." He described how large parts of it were a "gift" from Russia. My belief is that we should listen to what our leaders say, particularly those who don't have to appeal to a fully democratic electorate. What I believe is that Putin wishes to take back this so-called "gift" of Russia's. The question is, How will he do so?'

Burt leaned back in his chair, finally placed the cigar into his mouth and, with his head tilted slightly back, lit a long match that ignited the end of the cigar until he eventually sat blowing clouds of blue-grey smoke towards the ceiling. Then he looked down again at the table.

'So let me begin by assessing what we can be expected to believe of the recent events I've just described,' he said. 'And, of course, what we should not believe. First of all, the plans for the enlargement of Novorossiysk's port are negligible in terms of the facilities that the Russian Black Sea fleet needs to operate. In other words, despite Moscow's assertions at international conferences and private meetings that it is planning to relocate its fleet to the Russian port and away from Ukrainian territory, no such intention exists. It plans to remain in Sevastopol, come what may. I call this Russia's Strategic Aim One. From the plans themselves, I think we can believe this aim.

'Second, the canisters, which arrive on Ukrainian soil backed by rumours and some evidence of Russia distributing its passports to Ukrainian citizens in the north of the country, and by stories of weapons caches there.' He looked up at the watchful faces of the group at the table to indicate something momentous. 'For weeks now our labs have been conducting tests on the canister you brought back from Ukraine, Anna,' he announced. 'Now, at last, we have the results. It's taken so long because they couldn't quite believe it. What the canister contains is a mixture of Georgian mineral water, iodine, camphor and a small amount of sulphuric acid. The mineral water was the hardest ingredient to identify.' He paused again to let this sink in. 'In other words, there is no poison, no secret weapon, no threat to Ukraine— at least from these canisters,' he added darkly.

This revelation seemed to throw all of the party into confusion except, mysteriously, Burt.

'Then why did the Russians spend so much time and subterfuge smuggling them into the country in the first place?' Bob Dupont asked reasonably.

'Exactly,' Burt said. 'Why?'

Mikhail looked up from his usual position of staring at the table, as if in some form of deep meditation, and said in a level voice: 'So they wanted us to think it was important. They hadn't anticipated that Anna or anyone else would actually capture any of the canisters. What they were expecting—requiring, in fact—was that our satellites and any other observation would pick up their movements, the military vehicles, even the special forces personnel involved. They wanted us to see the smuggling operation, without knowing that what they were smuggling was harmless.'

All around the table pondered this for a moment before Burt spoke.

'When all this began,' he said, 'it was against a background of Russia ramping up its hostilities towards Ukraine in the northern sector of the country. Handing out Russian passports, the so-called weapons caches and planned strike action and revolution. Then came the canisters in a highly-organised, obviously subversive smuggling operation across the border. All these things were taking place in the north-eastern sector of the country along the borders with Russia. But if the canisters can be shown to be a charade—a lie, effectively—then may we assume that all these actions in the north-east of the country are so much chaff the Russians are throwing up in order to divert our attention?'

Nobody replied.

'I think we can assume that,' Burt said. 'Which is what makes Sevastopol and the Crimea all the more relevant. The Crimea is where any action the Russians are planning will take place. That's where the tipping point is.'

'What about the terror ship?' Dupont said. 'That's off the Crimean coast. They'd know we could see it from satellites too.'

Burt looked up at him and studied him for a long time. 'The so-called terror ship,' he said, emphasising his distrust of identifying the *Pride of Corsica* as such, 'that's an interesting question, isn't it? Yes. Where did we learn to call it a terror ship? From the man with the severed head. Who was this source? The CIA didn't know. Yet the CIA have always believed what he told them. The CIA now talk of this "terror ship" as if they'd discovered it themselves. It is now a fully fledged terror ship, simply because it's *called* a terror ship. Not for any other reason. No other reason exists.'

'We need to know what's on board,' Larry interjected. 'We can't assume anything until we know.'

'I agree,' Burt said. 'And I'm arranging a little trip to view it. Logan, as it happens, will be in charge.'

He looked at Anna.

'Tell us about the CIA's source, Anna,' he said. 'The severed head.'

'He's an occasional the KGB sometimes uses,' she replied. 'An ex-convict, drug addict and sometime assassin.'

'Whom the KGB used to plant this terror ship information,' Burt completed for her. 'And then they got rid of him. A criminal. An occasional. One job only—but one vital job. After that he's surplus to requirements. They kill him and they make his death look like a Chechen killing. Yes?'

'Maybe, Burt,' Anna answered.

'The ship may be a double bluff,' Mikhail said. 'They may actually intend for us to find out the identity of the source. That he was KGB. When we know who the dead man is, we see the CIA's source is likely to be a fraud. And then we don't take the ship seriously. But perhaps the ship is a real threat.'

'That is true,' Burt said. 'The ship could be a double-bluff. It might indeed contain dangerous substances, weapons . . . God knows what. And we need to know, as Larry says, what's on board before we write it off.'

At this point, a telephone by Burt's elbow rang. He picked it up.

'Send him up,' he said. 'Logan has arrived,' he announced to the room.

Through the windows in front of where she was sitting, Anna could see Logan talking into a phone in the driveway. It was the first time she'd seen him for two years. But there he was, exactly the same: the cream suit, the long, lanky gait and, though she could only see him briefly, the shoulder-length hair. The hair was the only difference. It was a lot

275

longer than it had been the last time she'd seen him.

Earlier in the day, Burt had taken her aside to tell her that Logan was coming here—and that he'd been doing some 'special work', as he called it, also in Ukraine.

'You want us to work together,' she'd asked him. 'I can't do that, Burt.'

'He's been in Ukraine for three months already.'

'I don't trust him,' she said. 'I don't want him anywhere near what I'm doing.'

'That's OK,' Burt had said. 'You'll be working in parallel, both of you in Ukraine. Different assignments. You'll only meet by your arrangement, or not at all.'

'You know he's not to be trusted, Burt. Why do you give him so much rope? He's a danger. Larry knows, you know, Bob . . . we all know. Why do you trust him?'

But Burt hadn't given her an explanation.

As she watched him now, Anna recalled the last time she had seen Logan. It had been at the ranch in New Mexico where they'd last met, two years before. She had discovered that Logan, the disgraced ex-CIA officer and now Burt's man, was the snake who had almost got her kidnapped by the Russians. Logan had been working as a freelance before Burt had hired him, selling secrets to the highest bidder. He'd sold her location in France to the British, the Americans and the Russians. And then she'd discovered what he'd done. She'd vowed to kill Logan then. But he'd disappeared and, it later turned out, had gone to Russia and killed the man who'd murdered her husband, Finn. It was his attempt to atone for what he'd done.

That was an incredible feat—even she had to admit it—to kill a KGB-trained crime boss in Moscow and get back alive. But if he'd thought it was an atonement, he'd been wrong. At the ranch after his return, he'd told her he loved her, and she'd told him to get out of her sight. Two years ago—it was their last conversation and back then she'd watched his tail lights disappearing across the mesa. She'd hoped never to see him again.

Now Logan entered the room. She watched him walk across it, avoiding her eyes—the sloping walk she remembered, as if one foot slightly dragged behind the other. It was a laziness rather than any injury that his walk originated from. She thought Logan cultivated an attitude and a physical presence that betrayed a sort of concealed narcissism, one that he hid behind his sloppiness, tangled hair, distressed clothes and dragging feet. She could think of nothing about him that didn't distance her from him and it surprised her normally steady consciousness.

He nodded to her. 'Anna,' he said. 'It's good to see you.'

'Logan,' she replied.

Then he nodded to the others in the room without speaking.

'Please sit down, Logan,' Burt said.

Logan took a chair next to Anna.

'Seen Theo?' Burt asked.

'Yes. And he sends news.'

'What's he got for us? More news of the terror ship? Do you call it the "terror ship" too, Logan? Have you fallen into Theo's ways?'

Logan looked completely relaxed. 'You know I

277

have access to Theo,' he said. 'It was you who sent me under his auspices to the embassy in Kiev.'

Burt looked away and left his question and Logan's answer hanging in the air.

Then his face changed from its usual soft amiability. 'I don't think the so-called terror ship is worth a twopenny fuck,' he said in an unmistakably aggressive tone of voice.

'But we have to know,' Logan said levelly.

'We do, we do,' Burt replied. 'So what have you brought us from Theo?'

'News from Ukraine. According to our embassy in Kiev, President Yanukovich has just signed a deal with Moscow. The Russians get to keep Sevastopol as a base until 2042. It's been extended from 2017 for another twenty-five years. In return the Russians are giving Ukraine cut-price gas. In addition to the lease's extension, there will be no expulsion of Russian intelligence officers from the area. The cause has been removed, Burt. The Russians are getting what they want in Ukraine without having to lift a finger.'

There was a breathless pause in the room. 'So,' Burt said. 'Ukraine is saved,' he added sarcastically. He turned the sound on for one of the television screens on the wall. They all listened to the Ukrainian announcer relaying the news live.

'There were violent scenes in Kiev's parliament, but the deal's gone through, yes,' Logan replied, ignoring Burt's sarcasm. 'Street demonstrations are expected, but they don't anticipate much trouble.'

'So Russia has got what it wants,' Burt said, turning the sound off again. 'And why would they ask for more now? Why would they exacerbate a situation further, since they have what they want—Sevastopol?' He looked around the room, taking in those present one by one. Larry first, to his right, then Bob Dupont, Logan, Anna next to Logan, and finally Mikhail. 'The Ukrainian president has given the Kremlin a gift.' He looked back at Anna. 'You said once, dear Anna, that when someone rejects a part, it's because they want the whole.' He refrained from looking at Logan, who was the context of her remark. 'But what if someone—in this case a spy elite in Moscow driven by an overriding desire to recapture its old empire—what if they *do* get a part of what they want? Does that mean they're satisfied? Does that mean the game's off?'

Anna didn't respond.

'No,' Mikhail answered for her.

'So are the CIA going to stand down in Ukraine?' Dupont said.

'Yes. But there's more,' Logan said.

'Tell us,' Burt commanded.

'Theo says there's evidence that the *Pride of Corsica*—the terror ship—is under the command of Qubaq in the Crimea. Also evidence that the bomb that blew up the Odessa nightclub is their work.'

'Evidence from where?' Burt asked.

'From Moscow. The CIA and the Russians are going to work together. Once we've had a close look at the ship, assessed its potential, we, the Russians and the British are going to make an assault on the ship.'

'Evidence from Moscow, you say,' Burt said. 'And you call the ship a "terror ship" now too, Logan?'

'That's what she's being called.'

'By the CIA and the Kremlin.'

Logan didn't respond.

'Ah,' Burt continued. 'So it's all very neat, isn't it? All the focus now from the White House is on your terror ship, Logan,' he said, and looked hard at Logan. 'Theo says that the terror ship is under the control of Qubaq,' he intoned, making Theo's voice appear like an oracular prophesy. 'Theo says that the bomb that went off at the Golden Fleece nightclub in Odessa the night before the elections was also a terror attack by Qubaq.'

'A man has been arrested,' Logan said.

'Then a conviction will be certain,' Burt replied. 'The Russians are being very clever indeed,' he said.

Logan cleared his throat and sat forward in his seat. 'Burt,' he said and stared into the big man's eyes, 'Theo said that Cougar also needs to stand down in the area. After we do the recce of the ship, Cougar needs to stand down. Those were his words.'

'And he sent you to tell me, rather than tell me himself.'

'He knew I was coming here,' Logan replied amicably. 'It's just convenient.'

'Everything about this is a little too convenient, wouldn't you say, Logan? Evidence from the Kremlin. Islamic terrorists. Sevastopol handed over on a plate. Double agents with their heads removed. And all the rest. It's all convenient. And now the CIA and the KGB are linking up to fight this new manifestation of the people we fear the most, the people who have inspired our war on terror. The CIA and the KGB are buddies again, just like in the nineties.' He looked at Mikhail now. 'All very convenient, wouldn't you say, Mikhail?' Then he looked back at Logan. 'Everything is convenient here, isn't it? Everything except Cougar. Cougar is inconvenient.'

'Why the sarcasm, Burt?' Logan interjected. 'Look at the evidence. Then say the evidence is not good enough for you.'

'What evidence, Logan?' Burt replied, and everyone around the table saw the hard vein of granite beneath the regular bonhomie. 'Evidence from the spies in the Kremlin? OK, so I've agreed with Theo's request to second you, Logan, to a CIA team working with the British. You'll shadow and assess this so-called terror ship. I hope that's fine by you.'

'And then Cougar's finished in Ukraine?' Logan asked. 'Theo wants to hear it from you.'

'Thank you for relaying that,' Burt said. 'There's a boat waiting at the port of Burgas in Bulgaria. You'll be on it, in command, as will some boys from the CIA and a British special forces team.'

'And the Russians too,' Logan said implacably. 'Theo's agreed to have them come along.'

'Well, I think that's a good idea,' Burt replied. 'As many of you on board Cougar's spy ship the better. Let's have the Russians on my ship.'

Logan sat back in his chair and looked back at Burt. There was a new fearlessness in him; an idea that it was he who was making the play, not the great Burt Miller any more.

'While you trash the idea of Qubaq being a terrorist organisation, Burt, don't forget that it was you who sent me to Kiev in the first place. The whole point of the meeting with Sam MacLeod was that I float Qubaq with the CIA station there. That was your plan, not mine, not Theo's, not the Russians'. So why is it you who's now pouring cold water on it?'

Logan sat forward in his chair and leaned on his elbows. He recalled that in the report he had delivered to Sam MacLeod, the name of Qubaq had been explicitly left out. That had bothered him then, and it bothered him now. Burt had made the reference to the organisation only verbal.

'I wanted to see where everyone would jump,' Burt replied. 'And you've all jumped the same way, haven't you, Logan? You, Theo—and consequently our own president—and, of course, the Russians too. All of you have seized on what you call the terror ship and all of you have seized on Qubaq. Coincidence? No, I don't think so. It's exactly what the Russians wanted us to do.' He looked around the table. 'We're being led by the Kremlin,' he said. 'I wanted to see how easily the CIA would fall in with their lead. Nobody wants to help Ukraine, that's the truth of it. And now the CIA will actually help the Russians get what they want there.'

Logan looked down at his hands. All he could think was that it was him Burt had assigned to encourage such disinformation—if that's what it was. He would never have asked that from Anna.

CHAPTER TWENTY

Taras walked down a long airless corridor on the third floor of Sevastopol's naval military hospital, turned left past more armed guards, and continued along another identical stretch that traversed the front of the building. Neither the occasional view through barred and sealed windows of the port on a sunny morning in spring, nor the antiseptic cream of the hospital floors and pale yellows of the walls did anything to soothe the confusion in his mind.

As his chief evidently suspected, Taras knew that his cousin Masha was involved in some subterfuge and it was now he, as her relation, who had been despatched to find out what it was she had been doing at the barn. His confusion seemed to be without a solution. If he succeeded, then Masha would undoubtedly be in worse trouble than she was in already. But if he failed, they would send in the proper interrogators again, this time to force it out of her.

There were the unanswered questions he had turned up in his investigations so far; was there a connection between his cousin Masha's predicament and the murders of two KGB agents on the very same day that she'd been wounded and then arrested three months before? His chief clearly thought so and Taras had to admit that the coincidence seemed too great to ignore. The Russians were angry at the loss of two men on Ukrainian soil but were angrier still, apparently, at Ukraine's refusal to hand Masha back to them. But still the SBU were jumping to fulfil all their other demands. It was a tightrope—to please Russia and to retain some semblance of independence. And then there was the question of the gun she was carrying and why she had used it if she were merely on a vacation.

Two nurses walked past him without looking at him. He stepped aside as a trolley with tubes attached to it was wheeled past by an orderly. Everything in this area had the appearance of a normal hospital, but this was an illusion. He was now in the prison wing. There were guards in the corridors and at every junction, as well as outside the elevators and on the stairs, and there were bars on all of the windows. He'd had to show his pass five times already. Security was tight and the guards were nervous and imperious at the same time, despite his security clearance to enter.

He reached the final, prison door to the ward and hospital cells. There was an officer here, as well as two more regular soldiers from the Ukrainian army. The officer checked Taras's identity papers, took a scan and shone a thin torch into his eyes. He studied the special pass that had allowed him into the prison wing with a deliberate slowness that made Taras's face twitch with irritation, and then he made a call to Kiev. Eventually satisfied, he handed Taras's papers back to him and a guard opened the locks on the door and let him and the officer inside.

Were the guards there to prevent escape, Taras wondered, or to guard against the intrusion of outsiders? What was Masha most in danger from—kidnap? assassination? or both? The security in the hospital was on Red, his chief had told him, but he hadn't explained why. The only certainty was that his little cousin—an innocent, as far as he was concerned, whatever she was involved in—was currently its most precious inmate.

The officer had personally been waiting for him to arrive and accompanied him through a ward as he heard the door slammed and locked behind them. There was no one in any of the six beds in the ward and they passed through to another locked door and on down another corridor that was distinctively a prison now, not a hospital. Bare concrete floors, one solitary high window at twice the height of a man, with more bars. Cells lined this corridor on either side, and were equipped with minimal comforts, judging from the open door into one of them that was empty. Three others had their peepholes shut and he didn't know if anyone occupied them. There were two guards on the inside of the final door, sitting slumped in hard wooden chairs with the varnish peeled away. Like all guards, they were evidently bored, until they sprang to attention at the sight of the officer. Then Taras and the officer proceeded to the last cell on the right.

One of the guards who'd followed them jangled keys until he found the right one and opened the cell.

Taras looked inside into a harshly lit cell that had no window. Against a wall, Masha lay on a bare cot, a grey blanket pulled over her. Taras stopped in shock before he could enter. He hardly recognised her. She looked terribly thin and pale. The wires had been removed from her jaw but one side of her face was heavily bandaged. Her eyes were filled with fear.

He turned to the officer. 'That'll be fine,' he said.

Grudgingly, the officer closed the door behind him and locked it. Where did they think this terrified, wounded twenty-four-year-old girl was going to flee? Taras wondered. There were three locked doors behind them already.

Alone with her now, he looked again. They'd weakened her beyond her wound, he could see that, once he was closer to her. She was deliberately underfed, he thought. The bare light bulb with its high-watt power glared down from the ceiling at her and he knew they would leave it on round the clock. He knew too that she'd been interrogated by others in the past fifteen days, ever since she'd been able to speak for the first time.

He tore his eyes away from her and looked around the cell. Eight feet by six, there was a concrete toilet in a corner that stank. Otherwise just the cot. No table or chair, no window, airless. At least it wasn't a concrete bench she had to sleep on, he thought. He looked up at the ceiling and saw a camera behind him above the door that covered the whole cell. The cell would be wired too. Did they think he could get something out of her that others couldn't, when both he and Masha knew that other ears would be listening anyway? But his chief had said that she was more likely to talk openly with him. Whatever coercion they'd used so far clearly hadn't worked. Before they tried anything stronger, his chief had told him—as if to threaten him with the fact that he held the fate of his cousin in his hands—they would try this softer approach. So Taras knew he had to make some progress with her in order to make this meeting

286

worth another one. And he felt the burden crushing his hopes of being able to help her.

'Hello, Masha,' he said.

She was silent, staring up at him, the fear in her eyes the same as when he'd entered.

'It's Taras,' he said.

She stared back. Then he saw her eyes flicker a little and tears forming. Her desperately thin body shook spasmodically and then quietened.

'Taras,' she said finally.

'We'll soon get you out of here,' he said breezily, but heard the encouragement in his voice had a hollow ring to it. He looked down, embarrassed now by his inability to really help her. 'How are you feeling?' he said, and didn't need an answer. None of the soothing phrases you heard in a normal hospital were any good in here.

Carefully, he sat down on the cot very close to her head so that his back was between her upper body and the camera. He judged that his body would obscure her from the lens. But she flinched at his closeness and a noise came from her mouth that sounded like inarticulate terror.

'It's OK,' he said. He bent down slowly and kissed her forehead, feeling the bandage on her face brush his cheek. Then he sat up slowly again. Her right arm was by her side, he saw, and the left one she'd moved slightly, so that it crossed over her stomach and made room for him when he'd sat on the narrow cot. He gently picked up her right hand in his and moved it away from her side in front of his body and out of sight of the camera. It was a simple gesture of affection, a straightforward holding of hands. But he didn't know if this was going to work, even if she complied. At least she'd let him move her hand.

'It's spring,' he said. 'The flowers are all out along the mountains. The trees are their wonderful new green. You remember?'

She seemed to nod slightly.

'At the farm this was our favourite time of year,' he said lightly. 'New life, the end of winter, warmth. My mother would start to cook properly again after all that tinned food we used to eat over the winter. I remember the first spring you came to the farm. You'd never seen so many flowers, never seen a southern spring.'

The farm. The barn at the farm where she'd been ambushed by Russian intelligence and tried to kill herself.

'It wasn't a good time to visit in January, darling Masha,' he said. 'What on earth were you doing?'

He'd read the transcripts of their interrogations so far. All she'd said, repeatedly, was that she was visiting an old place from her childhood, where her cousin Taras's family spent their summers. He thought back to her one statement which he knew in his heart was the only place any hope for her lay. It was a statement from the Russian officer who'd led the ambush party. 'It's not her,' the Russian officer had shouted that night in January at the barn. 'It's not her.'

In her interrogations at the hospital in the past fifteen days, all she'd been able to say, apart from repeating the nostalgic reasons for her visit, was this phrase of the Russian officer. 'They must have been waiting for someone else,' she'd told her interrogators so far. 'Or why would he have said it? I just happened to be in the way.' Was it a really chance in a million—her visit—Taras wondered?

288

Was it a case of mistaken identity? Not necessarily the same answer applied to both questions. Her reason for entering the barn was thin, at most. And if the Russians had been waiting for someone else, who was it? In his own mind—though thankfully his chief didn't seem to have considered the possibility so far—another person could only be the person making a pick-up. The barn was a dead letter box, chosen because . . . why? Because Masha had a reason, an alibi, to visit it. And that made his cousin right in the frame for making the drop. A surveillance team had found a strip of tape on the inside wooden frame of the only door to the barn. They were treating it as a signal sight.

But then there was the most damning evidence of all: her possession of the gun and her subsequent attempt to use it on herself. They all but knew—his chief included—that Masha was there for a specific purpose—even if she herself didn't know what that was. That was the only approach Taras could think of developing—that Masha was unknowingly caught up in something, that she was an innocent bystander.

Now as he sat and held her hand he lifted his arm slowly, just enough to gently slip a two-by-three-inch notepad out of his sleeve with a pencil following it. It slumped off the end of his hand on to the grey blanket beside their joined hands. As he did so, he continued talking to her. 'I know how much you love the place,' he said. 'But January, for God's sake! And on your own! I'd have come with you, Masha. We could have stayed the night, opened up the house, built a fire, eaten some of those tinned "rations" together.' He tried to laugh, but it came out as more of a grunt. 'Why the devil didn't you call me?' He smiled down at her, a big wide smile that he realised was the first genuine facial expression he'd managed to make since he'd entered the cell.

Then suddenly she spoke. Her voice was weak, faraway, as if she were at the farm back then, ten years or more ago. 'I remember the spring there, Taras,' she said, and her deep grey-blue eyes in the sunken face never left his.

He loosened his hand from hers a little so that her fingers were free. 'Tell me, Masha, what took you there in January?'

She didn't reply at first. Then slowly she picked up the pencil and spoke at the same time. 'I was unhappy, Taras,' she said.

'Unhappy?' He felt her fingers turn the pencil round in her hand so the lead faced the right way.

'Yes. I was unhappy in my marriage. I needed to be on my own. I needed a place of safety.' She laughed a hollow, ironic laugh that rattled in her thin chest.

'But you've only been married for a few months, darling Masha,' he said and laughed so that the movement in his shoulders covered the slight withdrawal of his hand. 'You haven't made a mistake, have you?'

'I was very unhappy, Taras. It wasn't what I thought. He changed as soon as we were married.'

'Your husband. Has he tried to visit you here? Has he contacted you?'

'He's filed for divorce. As soon as he heard I was in trouble. He's afraid for his career.'

Everything she'd said until the last sentence he saw had been a lie. She hadn't been unhappy. She was unhappy now. Her husband had deserted her, threatened perhaps in Moscow with his connection to her. But her unhappiness he saw in her new tears was that he was leaving her, that her marriage had so easily been thrown away as soon as she really needed help.

'You want that? A divorce?' he said.

'Yes,' she replied, but he saw in her tears it was the last thing she wanted and that her husband was the last hope she'd had in this cell. At the same time, he felt her fingers brush his as she began to scrawl on the paper. But her eyes still never left his.

'The reason I'm here is to help you,' he said. 'So you were unhappy. That's why you came to Sevastopol?'

'Yes,' she replied. 'I was lost. My husband wasn't the man I'd thought he was. I was in turmoil. I couldn't go to my parents. They would have taken his side, told me not to be so stupid, that he was a good man, et cetera, et cetera. I felt so lost, Taras,' and he saw her tears were genuine, though they weren't for the reason she was giving, but for its opposite. 'I wanted to connect with something I was sure of, a happiness, a happy memory, something to secure me from back in the past. That was the time I spent with you at the farm.'

'So you went to the farm, yes?'

'Yes, but it was all locked up for the winter and I just went to explore around it. The places where I used to play. You remember, I used to jump off the straw bales in the barn, high up from the piled-up bales down on to the loose straw on the floor.'

'I remember,' he said and felt her slide the notebook and the pencil back inside the cuff of his jacket. He fixed her with his eyes now. 'I need you to help me, Masha. It's not that I don't believe your story, but just that it's awkward to believe it. It's awkward for them,' he said, and indicated his superiors with a throw of his head. 'You can see that. It's awkward because of what happened. We know what you do, we know about your job, and your husband's too. We know about your FSB graduation—everything, you see. It's awkward that you just happened to be there, on that occasion, because of all those intelligence connections in your life. And the gun . . .'

'It's just a standard issue,' she replied.

'I know, but you shouldn't have carried it with you. Not into Ukraine.'

'I'm glad I did. When the shouting started and the lights blinded me, I thought I was being attacked. It was an automatic reaction.'

Taras was silent for a moment, wondering how he could at least appear to be useful to his chief. Then he looked at her. 'Before you entered the barn, did you see anyone else? Anyone around our farm, or on the land? Anyone near the barn?' He stared at her, willing her to understand his meaning.

She watched his face and seemed to think deeply about his questions. Then spoke. 'I saw a woman,' she said. 'She was walking along the road, up from the centre of the town, then she turned up through a gap between some houses towards where the farm is.'

That was good, Taras thought. She'd understood. The Russian officer had said, 'It's not her.' So they'd expected a woman, another woman, and Masha had supplied him with a fictional one, but it was more than she'd said to the interrogators who'd come before him. It made Taras seem useful.

'What was she like?' he said.

'I don't remember much,' Masha replied. 'She was just a woman I happened to see.'

'What was she wearing?'

'A black coat. I remember that. And a wool hat, but I don't remember the colour.'

That was good, a description, but not a description that suggested she was looking hard at anyone, that she was making an observation.

'Did you see her afterwards?'

'No. I just saw her turn up towards the farm. I was already on my way back, before I decided to look in at the barn.'

She'd helped him, Taras thought, and he hoped it was enough to justify another meeting with her.

As he walked back through the corridors of the hospital, he took care to thank the officer, so that he would remember him, on what he hoped would be another visit. When he was clear of the area surrounding the hospital he walked for a while, down towards the port. He saw a café and entered. He ordered a coffee. Then he went to a toilet which was lit by a wan light bulb and dropped the notebook from his sleeve and read what she'd written in the dim light. It was hard, not just because of the light, but because she hadn't been looking at the pad when she wrote and her scrawl was bad, falling off the side of the paper twice. He made out a name, 'Volkov . . . my boss. He gave me a package.' Then he finally managed to decipher the only other words. 'A tree,' it read. '400 metres above the barn.' He tore the paper and flushed it down the toilet.

When he left the café he took a taxi to the centre of town. He decided to be open, on the assumption that they might be watching him. He took a bus up to the western end of town and then walked the route Masha had told him she'd seen the woman walking, until he came to the farm. He let himself in with a key and opened up the locked shutters and then the windows. In the kitchen he found an old jar of coffee and boiled some water and piled five spoons of sugar into a cup, before going outside and sitting on the porch in the sun, sipping the hot coffee where anyone could see him. When he'd finished, he put the cup down and walked towards the barn a quarter of a mile away. That would be normal.

He reached it. Surveillance and forensic teams had already turned the place over several times. He glanced at the door jamb where the single rotten door hung loosely and saw the lighter shade where the signal sight had been left in the form of a strip of adhesive tape. He walked around the barn and then turned to the left, heading up the hill behind him. He saw the tree, but sat down halfway to it and looked out over the bay and the Black Sea beyond, taking the sun in on his face as he lifted it up towards the sky. But all the time he watched for eyes.

He walked the remaining part of the way to the tree in a roundabout way, giving no hint that it was where he was heading. When he reached it, he swung his leg on to a knot in the trunk and hauled himself up into a crook and sat again, as if to get a better view of the town below and the sea beyond. But he noted the two sets of footprints that had been left when the ground was wetter. They'd stopped at the foot of the tree, then one set headed up the hill—the woman's he supposed—and the other set—Masha's led down the hill towards the barn. But there was nothing in the tree. The woman, whose steps he saw before they disappeared in the harder ground above, must have picked up whatever Masha had been carrying. Someone good, then; someone who could work out what a courier would do. Someone who looked at the possibilities and saw that a courier really only had one place to lodge a package while they reconnoitred the barn. Someone highly professional.

Back in the centre of town, Taras took a taxi to Simferol airport for the flight to Odessa. He turned over in his mind the scenario that seemed most likely to him. Masha had been asked to make a drop. Another woman had been making the pick-up. Two KGB officers had been killed on the same day, one in Odessa, the other on a remote road in the Crimean peninsula. Had the woman been the killer? He suspected so.

And then his mind went to where his chief's hadn't gone—not yet, in any case. If the Russians were sending something secret into Ukraine—which her boss, Volkov, evidently was—they wouldn't have used something so obscure as a drop in a barn. Something so small that Masha could carry and would have been brought in on a military vessel from the Russian side, and then handed over in a more straightforward way in the town. So that suggested to him that the woman making the pick-up wasn't from Ukraine at all and that the message or whatever it was that was being transmitted from the Russian side was intended for a person or people or organisation outside Ukraine. Ukraine was just the drop. And if it was intended for someone outside Ukraine, that must mean it was intended for someone from the West. Her boss, Volkov, was sending something to the West. Was he a double agent, then? Everything suggested that.

As he sat on the plane and watched the coast of the Crimea unfolding beneath him towards Odessa, he knew what he had to do. Check the entry points, the airports, the ports in southern Ukraine on that day, 16 January, and the days before, and identify a woman travelling on her own; a woman who had killed two Russian intelligence officers and then disappeared, presumably with the package.

CHAPTER TWENTY-ONE

Up above the city, in an area of desolate waste ground, there were signs of bulldozer tracks. Anna paused at the side of the earth road and looked at where they criss-crossed the landscape, gouging the earth and ending in piles of smashed wreckage that were once makeshift shanties. Then the tracks were reversed in order to continue their destructive work. She turned and gazed down the hill behind her from where she'd come. A solitary lark was singing above a green meadow immediately below the stripped landscape and a few brown and white cows grazed on a slope. Beyond the meadow, the city of Sevastopol lay in its long bay, with other bays that branched off it.

The blue waters reflected the clear, deep colour of a cloudless sky.

She turned again and looked up ahead in the direction she was walking. There were green-tinted mountains rising beyond the waste ground that were topped with tooth-shaped crags. She was near the new shanty town now, and saw how hastily it had been erected after its predecessor had been destroyed by the bulldozers. The waste ground was dotted with the shacks and shanties made from odds and ends found in the city's dumps or on the beaches. The scrawny habitations had an unmistakable impermanence about them. They looked like the scum and refuse left by a falling tide. The bulldozer tracks marked where the inhabitants of the shacks had last put up their bedraggled homes and where the homes had been unceremoniously crushed a few weeks before. Twelve weeks, she'd heard, that was how long the people here were left unmolested before the bulldozers arrived again. The length of time had nothing to do with leniency, it was merely the time the creaking bureaucratic machine of the Crimea parliament took to grind into its destructive action.

She walked on again and, as she approached the first of the shacks, she saw it was made up of mostly cardboard boxes, a torn awning consisting of a plastic sheet that probably came from the city's waste dump nearby or had been washed ashore from a freighter, and bits of twisted iron pipe that supported the rickety structure. Two dark-skinned boys were playing outside, rolling a metal wheel hub along with a stick. One of the boys was naked, the other wore a pair of torn and filthy shorts. There was no water or electricity up here on the detritus-strewn land. The inhabitants had to walk half a mile across the hill and take their water from a stream in plastic cans that had been washed up on the beaches. As a refinement of the bureaucrats' cruelty, each time they bulldozed the shanties they moved them further from the water source. And it must get very cold up here in winter, Anna thought.

A woman stared at her from what passed for a doorway in the jumble of boxes and crates. There was no greeting, just a blank, narrow stare that concealed, perhaps, fear or suspicion, or both. Anna had the Slavic features of the persecutors who bulldozed the shanty town's Tatar inhabitants from their homes. Unusually for children, the boys ignored her and she walked on. Perhaps they had learned to avoid the Slavs. The lark's song rose above their shouts and cries as they beat the metal hub.

The density of the shanties increased as she approached the notional centre of the derelict habitation. They were all Tatars who lived here, it was a refuge for Tatars who continued to return from the lands of Central Asia and from Siberia where Stalin had exiled their forefathers. The sons and daughters, grandsons and granddaughters of Stalin's slaves were returning to their own land and had been returning in fits and starts since 1991 when Ukraine won its independence. Their former homes in the cities of the Crimea had long-since been requisitioned or just stolen from them at the end of the Great Patriotic War in 1944. Stalin had chosen to ignore the contribution of the vast majority of Tatars who had fought in the Soviet Army and punished the whole group for the errors of the few who had joined the Nazis. They had done so in the forlorn belief that Hitler would give them an independent Crimea. Once a majority, the Tatars were now a disaffected, unwanted minority who were viewed with suspicion and hatred by those who'd stolen their land and property.

Anna came to a rough circle of shanties. Most had prayer mats laid outside them on the ground. In lieu of a mosque, this was their prayer centre where they turned towards the south-east and Mecca. A few cooking fires were burning, sullen men without work smouldered beside them. They stared blankly at her or continued to squat or whittle sticks—empty activities without a purpose. The women seemed to be inside the makeshift structures. There was a smell of stale coffee and vegetable waste that mingled together in the warm morning air.

Anna approached a group of men who were smoking and talking in low voices, leaning against a stripped World War Two truck. They looked at her with a mixture of hate and curiosity. A 'white' woman never came here at all, let alone unaccompanied.

'I'm looking for Irek,' she said.

'Who shall I say is calling?' one of the men said with an insolent pretence at formality.

'A benefactor.'

The man laughed scornfully and drew on the last grains of tobacco from the cigarette that was clamped between his front teeth. He had a wild flame of black hair that fell across his face behind which the intense whites of his eyes glittered angrily.

'What have you brought us? Bread and liberty?'

He laughed harshly again and threw the cigarette end to the ground.

'Where is he?' Anna said.

The man looked at her, studying her without speaking, surprised at her assurance in so hostile an environment. Then he snapped some words to a boy playing nearby, some instruction spoken in their language, and the boy raced off up the hill and disappeared behind the irrational turmoil of the shanties. Anna made no further attempt to communicate. She sat down on the ground, removed her pack and crossed her legs. She was hot. The sun was climbing and by midday the temperature looked set to rise to a summer heat up here on the hill. By adopting this submissive position, she guessed the men would relax and ignore her.

In a short while, the boy returned and spoke to the man who'd given him instructions. The man turned to her and switched to speaking Russian, telling her to follow him. Three other men joined him and as she got up from the ground they surrounded her and walked like a guard escort, shielding whoever they were taking her to meet at the top of the camp.

They reached a traditional, tent-like structure which had a few rugs laid out on the bare earth and two poles that supported several plastic sheets. It was a larger place than the rest of the shanties. One of the men went inside, bending beneath the low, plastic sheet that served as an entrance. From inside, Anna heard the Tatar twang, its Turkic origins dating back from when the Huns swept west and assaulted the Roman empire. Finally, the man emerged from the tent and beckoned to her.

When she entered, she saw there was an attempt at making a home of sorts. Cushions were strewn around a rug that was frayed and eaten with holes. An ancient radio that looked like it had been salvaged stood on an upturned fish crate. A couple of metal pots and some cooking utensils hung from a string. But only the old man who sat on a cushion facing the tent's opening didn't have a temporary look about him.

'*Selam*,' Anna said and Irek motioned to her to sit on a cushion facing him. With his other hand he irritably waved away the men grouped by the entrance to the tent.

'*Selam*,' he replied.

Anna watched his expression closely. Irek, the senior man in the community, had fierce dark eyes set deeply in a face that was nut-brown and lined in generous gouges of flesh that stretched tightly over high cheekbones. His cropped hair was grizzled and grey and his ears stood out from his head unnaturally large against the veined and shrunken skull.

It was true, he must be ninety years old, Anna thought. That was what she'd been told in the briefing, although there was no record of his birth.

Nearly every trace of Tatar culture in the Crimea had been erased by the Russians after the Second World War. Ancient texts and even Marxist-Leninist tracts in translation had been burned. Mosques and cemeteries were destroyed, records obliterated and whole villages were razed. All the Tatar place names in the Crimea had been changed. Irek was one of the oldest of a people who had been brought to the brink of extinction, both literally and culturally, and one of the few still

301

alive from those times. He had been crammed into a cattle truck in 1944 and sent on a ten-day journey without food and barely any water, to be left with the less-than-half of his people who survived the journey. They were simply thrown out of the cattle trucks on to the winter steppes of Kazakhstan to fend for themselves. He'd had four sons and four daughters, as far as she knew, half of whom died in infancy and the rest in the years of brutal hard labour and starvation.

'You are Russian,' Irek stated.

'I'm an American now,' she replied.

'Russians . . . Americans . . . what's the difference? You say you are a benefactor. Neither are our benefactors. We are a hounded people.' He shrugged. 'What brings you here?'

A thin plastic curtain inside the tent was pushed aside and a large woman in a single piece of shapeless brown clothing that reached to her ankles entered carrying a plate of biscuits which she laid on the rug between them as if it were a rare speciality. A tea urn bubbled in the background and when the woman returned she brought two tin cups with a leaf tea the aroma of which Anna didn't recognise.

'I've come with a request,' Anna said when the woman had gone, 'and an offer of help.'

He lifted his mug of tea and indicated for her to do the same.

'Giving and taking at the same time, is that it?' Irek said, but without acrimony. 'First, what are you offering? What justifies your claim to be a benefactor?'

She watched the shrewd eyes watching her and sipped from the tin mug. That he had seen her at all was a testament to how desperate these people were. But she knew he would examine what she had to say carefully and reject it if he had no trust in her.

'The people I represent believe they have uncovered a conspiracy,' she said quietly. 'It concerns an organisation called Qubaq.'

She saw him stiffen. 'What about it?' he said sharply.

'There are people who wish to implicate it in terrorist acts,' she replied. 'The bomb at the nightclub in Odessa, for example. Back in January. These people wish to hide their own deeds by blaming Qubaq for them.'

He didn't reply. He reached his arm behind his back without turning and brought out a hookah pipe that had been hidden from her. Without responding to what she'd said at all, he began to flake a sweet-smelling tobacco into the bowl and lit a small piece of charcoal which he then placed over it. He fitted a mouthpiece over the pipe and drew the smoke through the water deeply. Then he replaced the mouthpiece with another and offered it to her. As she smoked, he began.

'We are not extremists,' he said. 'The Tatars have never been extremists for Islam. We are like the Turks, a Turkic people. We do not share the aims of the extremists. What we want, quite simply, is justice. We are not looking for the restoration of our property, we are not looking for financial compensation for the evils of the past. We want a new start. We want political freedom in the parliament of the Crimea, within Ukraine, not separation. We are too worn down to be used for anything by anybody.'

'You will be made the scapegoats,' Anna replied. 'That is the conspiracy. Your weakness is no defence against that. It simply invites it.'

She passed the hookah back to him and he took another draw.

'Why should I believe this?' he said when he had finished.

'I'm not from the American government,' she replied and he laughed out loud for the first time.

'People don't usually boast that they are,' he said.

'I'm not from any government. The people behind me are a private group of Americans,' she replied, fixing him with her eyes. 'They have the interests of a free Ukraine in mind. It is also in their own interest.'

'What is their interest?'

'Business in Ukraine. Peace in the Crimea is important for the peace in Ukraine. The Crimea is Ukraine's Achilles' heel. That is why the trouble is beginning here. We believe that Qubaq has been identified by certain forces who don't have Ukraine's interests as an independent nation at heart. They want to use you as a scapegoat. You will be blamed for acts of terrorism not committed by you. That will provide an excuse for . . . intervention by these forces.'

'By Russia,' he said.

She leaned in towards him. 'You, or someone close to you, has been approached. Or maybe you soon will be approached. The purpose of this approach is to offer you, the Tatars and Qubaq, funding. It will be said that it is to build you proper homes, educate your children, provide work . . . whatever they say, it will be appealing, perhaps

304

couched in humanitarian terms, or coming from a charity.'

'And?' Irek too now leaned in towards her.

'But when the money trail is examined by governments who are fighting terrorism, as it will be, it will be found to lead not to any humanitarian or charity organisation but to known terrorist accounts.'

Irek lit a cigarette.

'We don't know what exactly these malevolent forces are planning, only that they are intending to use you as cover.'

'That's what you have to offer,' Irek replied. 'What is the favour you wish?'

'I'm looking for a blind man,' Anna said. 'He may be the man who approaches you or one of your religious leaders.'

Irek didn't reply.

'I will come back in three days,' Anna said.

Anna descended the hill from the shanty town, down into the meadow, and sat on a knoll that gave a good view of the bays and Sevastopol's harbour and dockyard. There were nearly a hundred warships of various kinds, either at anchor in Sevastopol's bays or on the quays or under repair in dry dock. It was an ageing fleet. In an agreement in the nineties, the Russians had bought most of the Ukrainian half of the split Soviet fleet, but none of the ships she could see was less than twenty years old and most of them were far older and heading for the scrap heap. What she was staring at was, according to Burt, the touch paper to set off a conflagration intended to destabilise the whole country, yet the ships she looked at were a sorry sight and a pale comparison to the once mighty Soviet Black Sea Fleet. She stood up. She wondered if, for once, Burt had got a crossed 'line to God'. Russia had what it wanted now—a pro-Kremlin leader in Kiev who had extended the lease at Sevastopol to Russia's fleet for another twenty-five years. There was nothing, so it seemed to her, that could advance Russia's position further, nothing that the Kremlin could want more than that. With a friend in power in Kiev, surely Moscow would now exert its influence by stealth not confrontation.

Above her, the lark hovering stationary over the field continued its trilling song.

CHAPTER TWENTY-TWO

The Bulgarian-registered trawler *Mira* was motoring at a steady eight knots eastwards, on a course of 85 degrees. The vessel was around twenty-five miles from the Crimean shore.

Logan stood on the foredeck. He was dressed in a thick sweater, over which he wore seaman's oilskins and dungarees against the cool sea air. Despite the sun in the clear blue sky it was still only April.

Behind him, he saw the other 'fishermen', dressed like himself and going through the motions of preparing nets on the stern deck. They stood against a deep blue background of water that stretched away to the invisible coastline of Bulgaria two days' journey behind them and the dim purple outlines of the mountains of the Crimea on the boat's port side.

Ahead of him he watched the bow of the *Mira* cut through the water, sending up gouts of spray around his head that were caught by the sun in an endless display of sparkling motion. He turned finally, tearing himself away from the comforting motion and the dancing water, and checked the bridge. Although on the roof of the trawler's bridge there was displayed a regular radar that was slowly turning in dutiful observation of the empty sea, beneath the decks a whole array of sensors, imaging equipment, infra-red monitors and computers were set up in the holds which would normally have held the day's catch. The *Mira* was converted to being a regular spy vessel of the old, Cold War type.

Burt Miller had fallen out with Theo Lish on the significance of the *Pride of Corsica* and its unknown cargo. Burt's protégé was making a stand and he, Logan, knew which way he would leap if it came to it. The CIA chief saw in the mysterious movements of the *Pride of Corsica* an incipient threat to stability in the Crimea. Lish was adamant that the 'terror ship' must be positively identified as such and, if necessary, boarded by force. Burt had been defeated, as Logan saw it, at a high-level meeting in Washington between the Intelligence Committee, with Theo on its side, and Cougar.

And so the *Mira* was to be the first contact with the terror ship, the probe that would bring more conclusive evidence. Though Burt disagreed on the subject of the ship's importance, he had nevertheless laid on this entire operation. That was mysterious too, to Logan's mind. To him, Burt wasn't a man who wasted Cougar's resources on operations he disagreed with, and the speed and ease with which he'd done so made it doubly suspicious. In Logan's opinion, Burt's agreement to lend the vessel to the CIA therefore couldn't be taken at face value. But the CIA had no such ship at its disposal anywhere near the Black Sea. Burt was perhaps showing his generosity in defeat, Logan thought. But this didn't exactly fit with how well he knew Burt Miller. Burt had suddenly come up with a fully equipped spy ship of Cougar's in the Bulgarian port of Burgas, which he'd offered to provide. The equipment was already installed— and the CIA had brought a few more state-of-the-art accessories of their own. And now, here they were, steaming across the Black Sea on a day in mid-April.

Burt's openness about lending the vessel was, as ever, irrepressible. Lish had been concerned about getting too close to the *Pride of Corsica*, but Burt urged an all-but-actual physical contact with the ship. 'Charge it,' he'd advised Logan. This was to be for the purpose of 'provocation' only, Burt had argued. A spy ship was now a less relevant piece of equipment to a nation's intelligence arsenal with the ever-increasing development of satellite technology and the World View satellite could see everything the *Pride of Corsica* had on show without the need of such a close-up encounter. So the point of the operation was to test the *Pride of Corsica*'s defences. Provoke a reaction. See what hardware would be brought to bear against the *Mira*.

'Let's see what cannons they point at us,' Burt had told Theo Lish in an ops. room in Harper's Crossing. 'That way we'll have an idea of the worst they can do if you need to make an assault. It will

308

help your boys in that event.' Burt was handing the whole operation over to the CIA lock, stock and barrel. And with the Russians added to the manifest at the last minute.

'The worst they can do is blow us out of the water,' Lish replied anxiously. 'What do we do then?'

Burt had erupted in laughter. 'Then you can send in the marines, Theo,' he replied and added, in order to dampen Lish's alarm, 'Don't worry, Theo, they won't attack unless you attempt to board. They'll just warn you off for now.'

And so, at Burt's request—and the more Logan thought about it, the more Burt's sudden helpfulness was odd—Logan was hosting a party of the CIA, as well as British, French and Russian 'observers' on 'one of Burt's Cruises', as Burt jokingly called it.

Why the Brits and the French had to be invited, Logan didn't have a clue either. It was to be a joint operation, as Theo described it. But that too seemed odd to Logan when he'd thought about it, though he'd dismissed his misgivings quickly when he couldn't find a reason. It's a CIA-run trip, Burt told Lish, carefully acknowledging the CIA boss's position and stroking Lish's sense of priorities but, as Logan knew, Cougar was paying for the whole operation. We like to help our friends in the CIA, Burt had told him. Another diversion from Burt's usual line.

Logan looked back and up at the bridge. The Brit, Philip Holyoake, Special Boat Service, was standing next to the wheel and talking to the skipper. He was one of those seemingly quiet, retiring types who said little and Logan found him uninteresting, difficult to take seriously. He was something of a naval historian, it turned out, and had already pointed out to the skipper the formation of the British and French fleets when they'd steamed up the Kerch Straits between Russia and Crimea in 1855 in preparation for war.

Then Logan checked on a couple of the Agency's operatives who were standing around the nets, one of whom was one of the terriers he'd met at the Kiev embassy in January. Logan looked around the decks for the Frenchman, Laszlo, but he couldn't find him. He needed to talk to Laszlo later, in private, and that would have to happen once they'd returned to port in Burgas. Finally there were two Russians who were keeping to themselves so far. One of them watched him from the stern of the *Mira*.

As Logan looked out ahead of the trawler again, he weighed up a situation that was unfolding, as he saw it, in favour of anyone but Burt. Despite Burt's doubts about the significance of the *Pride of Corsica* to any plans Russia might have, Logan thought that Burt Miller had blown it this time. With Burt's increased obsession with Ukraine over the previous months, Logan felt that his boss, and hence Cougar, had become blinded by this one-track policy that saw Russia as simply the enemy. Perhaps, after all, he thought, Burt was just another Cold War hero who couldn't see the way the world had changed in the past twenty years; someone whose life's work had been pulled from under them and who couldn't accept it. Laszlo knew the world had moved on—and his French masters too. Lish was rightly interested in the ship, however. And Logan supposed the CIA needed to cover all the bases. Their fear of leaving any stone unturned was paramount when the word 'terrorism' rose above the shit that accumulated from their stations across the world. Either Lish believed the ship was a danger, or he was just covering his arse with Washington. Burt's dogged refusal that you could do business with the Kremlin didn't necessarily fit with Lish's world view, Logan knew that.

In fact, now Logan thought about it, it was people like Burt who were becoming the chief danger to peace in the modern world, not the old enemies from the Cold War. He held on to the guard rail, then leaned his elbows on it and watched the water gush past the trawler's bow. If he could further win Laszlo's trust, then it might be that he could parlay a deal over Ukraine between Lish and the CIA and Russia. Then he could do without Burt and become a star with the agency as he'd been before.

His mind turned finally to Anna Resnikov. Was it Burt's obsession with her, too, that drove his anti-Russian position? It seemed she wouldn't rest until she'd taken her dying breath striking against her old country. She had all Burt's attention. To Logan, it was almost embarrassing. He was like some senile, rich man who'd fallen for a pretty woman half his age. Then Logan thought back, as he had done so many times before, to the night he and Anna had spent in New York, before she'd cut him out of her life for good. 'Maybe in another life, Logan'—those had been her exact words at the ranch to end a relationship that had only just begun. One night with her, for Christ's sake! Well, if Burt fucked up over Ukraine, maybe she

311

wouldn't enjoy Burt's protection for much longer, and Logan wouldn't be sorry to see her star fall. She'd become an irritant under his skin.

He buttoned the oilskin up higher to his neck and walked to the stern of the boat. Then he climbed some steps up on to the bridge.

'We should have her in sight soon,' he said to the skipper, an ex-navy Seal, and then he nodded to the Brit Holyoake.

'We have her on radar.' The skipper showed him the radar map. The *Pride of Corsica* was the only other vessel in the area apart from them.

'Has she moved at all?' Logan enquired.

'Been there for two days. Same spot, near enough.'

'Any supplies brought in?'

'Nothing. No physical contact, according to the satellites.'

Logan looked across at Philip Holyoake. He'd provided no analysis so far, made no contribution of any kind, in fact. He guessed he was there just to keep Adrian Carew, his MI6 chief, in close touch with Burt. It was a known fact that Adrian was looking for a soft, well-paid job once he stood down from the British intelligence service, and Cougar could provide that if anyone could.

A half-hour later, they could see the *Pride of Corsica* appearing from the horizon through powerful binoculars and, shortly after that, her outlines appeared to the naked eye.

'She'll have been following us for as long as we've seen her,' the skipper said. 'How close do you want to go?'

'Head for her,' Logan replied. 'We want to see what she points at us.'

At a distance of just more than a mile, the techs below the deck in the fish hold began to pick up a missile guidance system from the *Pride of Corsica* that was trained directly at the *Mira*. They relayed it to the bridge, with some guesswork attached as to the type and firepower.

'Bit over the top for a merchant ship, wouldn't you say?' the skipper said quietly.

'They've got a Russian Helix helicopter on the deck,' Holyoake said, looking through a scope. 'You can see its coaxial rotors. No markings. Probably bought on the open market. Armed with Aphid missiles. That's what the sensors are picking up. They're fixed.' He turned away from the telescope, as Logan moved beside him and put his eye to it.

'Are they locked on?' Logan asked, and the skipper relayed the message below decks, to receive a reply in the negative.

At that moment, a ship-to-ship communication crackled over the radio. 'To fishing vessel *Mira*. To fishing vessel *Mira*. This is the commercial freighter *Pride of Corsica*. This is the commercial freighter *Pride of Corsica*. Over.'

'Reading you, *Pride of Corsica*. This is *Mira*. Over.'

'We request you alter your course immediately. We are carrying toxic materials. Over.'

Logan put his hand on the skipper's arm. 'Don't reply,' he said. 'Not yet.'

There was a silence that seemed like an age, but it probably lasted no more than a minute. Then the communication crackled again over the *Mira*'s radio. They were just over half a mile away from the *Pride of Corsica* now.

313

'This is the *Pride of Corsica* calling the *Mira*. Alter your course immediately. Immediately. Over.'

'Take her a couple of degrees off,' Logan ordered the skipper. 'No more.'

The *Mira* didn't seem to alter course unless you looked closely at the bow. They would now miss the *Pride of Corsica* by a hundred yards or so.

'This is the *Mira* to the *Pride of Corsica*. This is the *Mira* to the *Pride of Corsica*. We have altered course and will be passing on your port side. Have a good day. Over.'

There was a short pause, then the radio crackled back at them. '*Pride of Corsica* to *Mira*. This is the final request. Repeat. This is the final request. Alter your course by at least ten degrees. Over.'

They were six hundred yards from the *Pride of Corsica* now and Logan, Philip Holyoake and the skipper saw men on the stern of the vessel which the *Mira* was approaching. One of the Russians and one of the Americans joined them on the bridge.

'They're wearing balaclavas,' Logan observed.

'Against identification from satellites,' Holyoake said. 'Nothing to do with us.'

Logan picked up the radio that connected the bridge with the hold below. 'Are they locked on?'

'No . . . no . . . wait. They're locked on now. Something on the deck.'

'The Aphid missiles on the chopper,' Holyoake said.

Logan looked at him. He seemed completely calm as if they were enjoying a day out game fishing.

'How long have we got?' Logan said, and felt a

314

sweat break out on his forehead.

They were four hundred yards from the *Pride of Corsica*.

Suddenly there was an explosion from the vessel ahead and a spout of water shot up almost simultaneously about fifty yards to the right of the *Mira*.

'*Pride of Corsica* to *Mira*. *Pride of Corsica* to *Mira*. The next firing will be aimed at you. Over.'

'Turn away now,' Logan said and the skipper swung the wheel sharply to the left until they were far to the left side of the *Pride of Corsica* and passing between it and the distant mountains. Logan found himself trembling. When he looked at Philip Holyoake, he was amazed to see a small smile playing around his lips. Holyoake clapped the skipper on the shoulder.

'Beers all round, Rick,' he said.

CHAPTER TWENTY-THREE

Balthasar stooped to come out from beneath the hanging plastic sheet that served as a porch. The heat through the plastic roofs in the shanty town was intense, even now in early spring. It must be unbearable in high summer. Once he was outside, he straightened up and stood for a moment, welcoming the cool air on his face that came in from the sea. He stayed still for a moment, listening to the sounds around him from the encampment on the hill, orienting himself. The speech of the inhabitants was a mix of Tatar and Russian, a sort of pigeon language that owed a

315

great deal to the Russian language after centuries of rule from Moscow.

Balthasar heard a man shouting about a missing goat, then a boy replying, who in turn was told finally to go and find it. He picked up the sounds of pots and pans jangling together on a woman's back, on her way to the stream for cleaning. An old motor was turning over and over, sounding less healthy each time, until it died—a Neva jeep, he decided. There were random shouts of men, a kick against something metal. Tinny music was playing on a radio, an old Tatar folk song.

But what he sensed over and above the smells and sounds of the shanty town on the hill was the deep air of resignation, which was occasionally ignited by anger, then doused again by despair. The river of the camp's collective psyche contained little else in its flow but these three elements. He turned to his left away from the lean-to and went to find Irek. When he found the old man's home, he stooped again under more plastic and entered.

'How long ago was she here?' Balthasar asked when they were sitting on cushions and facing each other.

Irek looked up at the sightless eyes of the man opposite him. It was true what their mutual friends in Ingushetia and Chechnya had said about this man. He saw more than the seeing did.

'Around four hours,' he replied. Then not being able to completely believe the man could have known of her visit without some information, he said, 'Someone told you she'd come?'

'I felt her. I feel her now,' Balthasar said. 'She sat here, on this cushion where I'm sitting.'

'You know her well?'

316

'Once. But not for many years. Not for decades.'

They sat in silence for more than a minute. Balthasar sipped water from a metal cup, a round copper mug without a handle, not the tin cup that Irek had served the tea in, four hours earlier. Balthasar was in no hurry.

'My acquaintances said you are a Muslim,' Irek said finally. 'Yet you come on behalf of Russians. Which Russians?'

'Money is money, old man,' Balthasar replied. 'What does it matter which Russians?'

'Maybe it matters a great deal.'

'We are offering to build you a mosque,' Balthasar continued. 'But that's just the beginning. There will be more mosques, madrassas for learning. Eventually, we'll get you out of this camp into proper homes. My sponsors wish this to remain anonymous.'

'The woman said you would offer us good things,' Irek replied.

'Did she? What is her interest in what we offer you?'

But Irek didn't answer his question.

'Why are you making gifts?' he said at last.

'Why? We are all Muslims. We should all stand together. We understand the treatment of your people. It was the same with us.'

'But you . . . ?' Irek said quietly. 'I don't think you are a religious man.'

Balthasar stirred, shifting slightly on the cushion, and put down the copper cup, very precisely but with an ease of purpose, on to the small level space beside the rug.

It is as if he sees everything, Irek thought. Sometimes he wondered if this man Balthasar was

317

even blind at all.

'Religion is just man's imperfect attempt to see God,' Balthasar replied. 'But religion doesn't always look in the right places.'

'Then you and I are similar in our views of religion,' Irek replied. 'But that doesn't explain why you wish to finance mosques for us. What we want is homes. First homes, then we can see where religion fits in.'

'My sponsors who are providing the finance are offering mosques and schools,' Balthasar said. There was a pause, as if he were waiting for Irek to show his gratitude, but none was evident. 'You haven't reached the age of ninety, I see, by believing what you're told without doubting its truth. It's the woman, isn't it? She has made you wary.'

'Everything has made my people wary,' Irek replied.

'You're concerned about the origin of the money,' Balthasar stated.

Irek was silent. This man could see inside his mind, he thought.

He reached for the hookah and flaked apple tobacco into the bowl, lighting it with a piece of charcoal that he put in place with his hand though it was burning. He took two or three puffs, then passed it to Balthasar without putting a different mouthpiece on to the pipe as he had done for the woman. Balthasar received it easily and took a long draw and the water in the glass bowl bubbled. Then he exhaled slowly, tilting his head upwards to the roof of the dwelling. A dog began to bark outside, then squealed and fell silent; a kick or a stone must have been aimed at it. In the pecking

318

order of human anger there'd always be someone or something to beat up that was less than you, he thought. Even these people who were fixed by history and circumstance in the drainage system of humanity needed something to oppress, something to feel superior to.

'What did she tell you?' Balthasar said. 'No. Wait. First, tell me how she appears.'

'Physically?' Irek said.

'What is your impression of her? How does she present herself? And what is her disguise, if you could penetrate it? Then, yes, you can tell me what she looks like if you wish,' he added, as if that were not important.

Irek told Balthasar what Anna had told him earlier; that she represented an American company with business interests in Ukraine. For those business interests to be successful, the Americans needed Ukraine to be free, or at least not a vassal of Russia's. Her disguise? What did the blind man in front of him mean by that? 'She didn't tell me everything,' Irek continued, 'if that's what you mean. And neither do you,' Irek added. Then he finished by saying, 'She is a beautiful woman whose beauty seems to be irrelevant to her. Maybe she even feels it gets in her way. Maybe she's met too many men who don't see beyond her physical beauty.'

Balthasar smiled. To Irek, it was unexpected. Did the blind man not know that she'd warned him against Balthasar?

As if to answer his thoughts, Balthasar spoke through the smile that hadn't left his lips. 'She knew about me, didn't she?' It was a statement and Irek saw he was still smiling.

319

'I don't know. All she said was that someone would offer to help us. That money would be given.'

'And not to trust this offer of friendship?' Balthasar said, the smile still playing around his lips. 'This money?'

Irek wasn't afraid to say the truth. 'She said it would link us to terrorism,' he said flatly.

'And who do you believe?' Balthasar replied. 'Her or me?'

'Her visit was unexpected. Yours was not. I have to think it over.'

'There's no hurry,' Balthasar said.

'Tell me,' Irek asked him, 'do you yourself really know what is behind this offer of help you bring? Or are you just the messenger?'

Balthasar considered what he knew. He saw that all he really knew was what he'd been told by his bosses in Department S, his father included. 'We want these people on our side,' his father had said. 'That's the reason for help.' Why did it come from Department S, then, Balthasar thought? Why not as part of an aid package from the government? But he didn't communicate his misgivings to the old man.

'Is she returning?' he asked Irek.

'She said in three days.'

As he walked down through the camp, the smell of long-cooked vegetables wafted across the hill. Over and above it was the smell of intense, but temporary human activity, of fleeting lives, but that was not a smell in the conventional sense. It was a sense. It was something only Balthasar could feel.

He walked easily through the creaking shanties, avoiding pitfalls and the structures themselves.

320

Children approached him without fear. He held a small boy's hand. Nobody challenged him. He attracted reverence from the men, the women cast their eyes down. The boy looked occasionally up at the blind man as if trying to ask a question that never came. Balthasar left him at the end of the camp and pressed some Ukrainian bank notes into his hand, small denominations. 'Buy some sweets for your friends,' he said and turned down the hill on to the bulldozer tracks. The old smell of burned-out wreckage from the destruction of the previous shanty town hung in his nostrils until he reached the meadow. He walked steadily down towards the town.

CHAPTER TWENTY-FOUR

Taras sat in a wooden swivel chair in his office on Deribasya Street and looked curiously at the list that lay on the pale, peeling veneer of the desk. Outside, though he couldn't see much from the office window that overlooked the tiniest of courtyards, Kiev was bathed in spring sunshine. Soon the heat would be demanding air conditioning, but so far that was beyond the reach of Ukraine's intelligence services.

He finally had a list he felt he could work from and one name on it stood out, to his way of thinking, in any case, that was screaming every kind of alert. To be more accurate, it wasn't so much the name, which was evidently a false one, but the profile of the woman behind it which he had now constructed loosely in his mind. It was more of an X-ray picture than a full portrait.

From back in January, in the three days that led up to the killings of the two Russian KGB officers and the arrest of Masha, Taras had been able to positively identify thirty-four foreign women who had almost certainly entered Ukraine alone, but he knew this didn't include any women who had entered apparently accompanied—in other words using a man as a cover. That was something he would never be able to ascertain. But he believed anyway that a courier would have arrived alone— and so he concentrated on the thirty-four women.

Of these, twenty-nine had flown from various parts of the world into the capital, Kiev. And Taras had by now decided that—whoever the woman was whom the Russians had been expecting at the barn—she must have entered through Odessa, not Kiev. Everything pointed to that; the first of the killings took place there, and the second in the Crimea where, presumably, she was making her way to Sevastopol for the pick-up. Why would she have come through Kiev? It made no sense for a courier to enter the country so far away from a pick-up, when time and the speed of exit would be of the essence. So, for the purpose of his more focused inquiries now, he was looking at five women who had entered Odessa, apparently unaccompanied. And only one of these had entered the country on the day itself, 16 January.

Taras picked up the list from the desk and thrust them into a briefcase. He shouldn't have brought them in here to the office, he knew that. Everything had to be concealed from his chief for now, at least until he'd worked out what was going on, until he had a thesis of some kind that would help Masha. He took the list out of the briefcase again. There was always the possibility of having it searched on the way out the building. He screwed it into a tight ball and jammed several chewed bits of gum into the squashed paper, then closed the paper over them. Then he thrust it casually into the pocket of his jacket—his chewing gum disposal. He decided this would be the last day that he used his office to pursue the woman.

The second question that still preyed on his mind was Masha's boss in Moscow, Volkov. The more he'd thought about it, the more he'd reached the conclusion that her boss had used Masha to deliver a package to a Western intelligence service. Therefore Volkov was a double agent working for some Western agency. That was useful to know and might, perhaps, be of paramount importance if he needed leverage in Moscow at some future date. It might also be extremely dangerous for him to possess the knowledge.

But in the present, part of him was enraged that his cousin had unwittingly been made a part of such an operation by her boss, while another side of him—once his anger had subsided—began to think of what use Volkov might be to him—and indeed to Masha and her eventual freedom. She was undoubtedly in the safest place for now, even though her imprisonment, on top of her self-inflicted wound, was making her more ill by the week. But if she left now, her life would certainly be forfeit by her boss. For that reason, Taras knew he had to devise a way to let Volkov know that she wasn't the only person he would have to kill, that he, the Moscow agent for some Western interests, was blown unless he played ball with Taras.

The woman his mind now focused on was named in her American passport as Natalia Simmonds. She had passed through Odessa's border control at 7.35 in the morning of 16 January. Eight hours later a KGB officer was found dead and jammed behind some builder's material in an alley off Odessa's boulevard. The time of death was estimated at somewhere between an hour and two hours after the woman's arrival. Sometime later that day the body of another KGB officer was found at the side of a remote road in the Crimea near Vihogradovo. Taras had ascertained that a youngish woman travelling alone had been on the bus from Odessa to Sevastopol that morning, but had got off at a stop past Nikolayev. So she could have been in the vicinity of where the second body was found too. Later, on the evening of the same day, the senior Russian intelligence officer at the barn had shouted 'It's not her', when he'd seen Masha.

Taras considered the possibilities as he walked down the corridor and poured himself his third coffee of the morning from the machine that was leaking the thin sludge they called coffee here on to the linoleum floor.

A female courier arrives by boat from Turkey. But whoever Natalia Simmonds was, she was evidently more than just a run-of-the-mill courier. The Russians know about her arrival, she is pursued, perhaps? At any rate, she kills two of her pursuers or watchers and makes her way to the barn by that evening. When everything goes wrong she nevertheless finds the crook in the tree where Masha had hidden the package while she reconnoitred the barn. The woman Simmonds takes the package. And then she disappears. Two Russian spies dead, a pick-up achieved successfully from the jaws of defeat and in extreme danger—and all the while the Russians knew she was expected and had her in their sights.

Taras returned to his office and sat and sipped the foul-tasting coffee. He wanted a cigarette and, opening the window on to the courtyard, he leaned out and against regulations lit a cheap Eastern European-manufactured Marlboro. But the woman didn't leave his mind for a second. Somehow this woman going by the name of Natalia Simmonds had left Ukraine while never leaving Ukraine. For there was no customs record of her departure. She'd arrived on a week-long visa, with a return boat ticket, also of a week's duration, and then she had disappeared. There was only one likely solution. Unless the Russians had subsequently apprehended or killed her, she had left the country by clandestine means. Possibly even the same night as she picked up the package. If not, it would have been the following night or the one after that. One thing he was certain of was that the woman was no longer in Ukraine.

Taras sucked on the stale-tasting tobacco. Who was this woman, he wondered? To enter Ukraine pursued by the KGB, kill two of their officers, pick up a package that wasn't left at the assigned place, and then disappear . . . that took some balls, let alone skill. An immense amount of skill. Whoever Natalia Simmonds was, it was clear she was a professional. And probably a native Russian speaker who could move with ease without attracting attention—if you discounted the Russian intelligence services who'd anyway known she was entering the country.

There were several things that bothered Taras about this scenario. The main question in his mind was why the Russians had waited for her to get to the barn rather than simply killing her when they could. But other questions spun out of this one. How did they get two of their operatives killed? What did they gain by waiting for her to reach the barn, since it appeared that it was her they were waiting for? Perhaps they wanted her alive—but why? What was her importance beyond being a courier picking up a package? Taras couldn't think of an answer, or at least the answer was somewhere buried inside the confusion in his head and he hoped it would surface later like a bloated corpse from the bottom of a river.

He left the office and the building. Nobody challenged him to open the case. They were too sloppy, the internal security people, he thought. First he walked, deep in thought, working out his next move. When he found he was near Slavi Park, he entered and saw the first of the spring leaves scattered on the branches, like a magical picture of summer emerging from the blank sheet of paper that was winter.

He took the list from the bag and put it into a waste bin behind some toilets, then dropped a match on it. It flared a little but there was nothing else in the bin to catch fire and only a small plume of smoke which rapidly disappeared announced the list's destruction. Only the blackened gum remained.

Then he went home, still on foot. The question he needed to work out now was how to make contact with Volkov, Masha's boss. It was far too dangerous to go to Moscow—it was dangerous enough to bring pressure on him from Kiev. He was a powerful man. But Taras knew he would only find more answers by applying pressure to Volkov. A high-risk strategy certainly and he would have to think of a way that distanced him from Volkov as much as he could. A third person, a cut-out who could threaten Volkov, or an anonymous communication, another drop arranged for Volkov to communicate with him. But he could think of no one he could trust. Either way, he would to some degree have to put himself in the firing line.

When he'd walked for half an hour, he took a bus to the west of the city and walked again to the small apartment he shared with his wife and two children. He was just reaching to put the key into the lock when he felt his phone vibrate. He lowered his hand from the door and answered it. It was a message from Logan Halloran. Just a suggestion for a drink, Logan was in Kiev—unexpectedly, he said. But nothing about Logan—nothing in a sense about any of this—was unexpected. Logan wanted something from him, even if the American didn't really know what it was he wanted. And perhaps—now he thought about it—Taras wanted something from Logan too but he knew what that was.

Taras turned away from his own front door and took a bus back into the centre of the city. He went to an Internet café near the cathedral and opened an account. Then he googled the American company Cougar. There were tens of thousands of sites. He scrolled down through pages of information, official sites, unofficial blogs, news reports, comments and attacks on the American

327

security company, and began to read some twenty pages further on, a small, official announcement from two years earlier. No names, no details—just the carefully controlled information that concerned the 'defection', as it was called, of a female Russian colonel in the KGB who was in some way connected to Cougar and the CIA.

He closed and erased the account and walked swiftly back to his office. He would need SBU search engines to find out more. He walked through security and upstairs to his office. One message from his boss. Come to the fourth floor.

Taras opened his computer and logged in to search for wanted persons on the SBU list. Nothing there. He looked at requests from Moscow from two years before asking for help with 'missing' Russian nationals. Then he put in 'Logan Halloran' and came up with what they knew of his CIA background in the nineties when he was stationed in Bosnia. Nothing of interest that he hadn't seen before. Finally, he found a small note that concerned an approach Halloran had made to the KGB station head in Montenegro from two years ago. Halloran was offering the whereabouts of a KGB defector for money. The KGB had alerted their friends in the SBU and the security agencies in other Eastern European countries who looked with favour on Moscow. Money had been paid, but the woman had evaded capture. The Montenegro station head had been recalled, replaced. A high-level colonel—the youngest colonel in the KGB—and whose father had been the station head in Damascus in the seventies. He could have checked that, but then the name came under strict red security alert: Anna Resnikov.

There was a photograph attached. Taras stared at her picture for a long time.

Then he closed the computer, took two packets of cigarettes from the drawer, and descended to the exit without responding to his boss's order. When he was clear of the building, he texted Halloran and arranged to meet in the bar where they had arranged to meet three months before, when Taras was in Odessa and had to cancel. He detoured from the direct route to the bar, stopped at the railway station and bought a ticket for the night train to Odessa.

CHAPTER TWENTY-FIVE

There were three tents pitched in the canyon. Anna casually watched the three groups who were occupying them. It seemed they were all travelling youths from Western Europe, talking in Western European languages. One group was building a fire in a pit near the river and looked like they were preparing to make something to eat as the day drew to a close. A guitar played from somewhere behind one of the tents. It was just after five o'clock in the evening. The sun had disappeared behind the high walls of the deep canyon but it would be light for another few hours.

It had taken her a while to follow the forest track that began in foothills some distance behind the city of Sevastopol and led into the mountains. The camp site was a little too far from the city, but here at least she would pass unnoticed by the forest rangers, or by anyone else who might be inquisitive.

She walked over to a group of Swedes—two men and two women—and asked if they had any milk. She told them she would bring some back from the city in the morning. To the other campers around the tents, she was just another backpacker, waiting for her boyfriend to arrive. But she wanted to establish an easy relationship with them. It might be necessary to link up with them if her 'boyfriend' didn't arrive.

She decided to forego making something to eat herself. She was heading into the city, she told them. Long before it was dark and while they were becoming enthralled by their own experiences of the lonely place, helped by the quantities of beer that seemed to take up a large part of their travelling equipment, she would leave them and walk back towards the city. Where the track emerged from the mountains, she would find a vehicle that, for a small fee, would act as a taxi and take her to the hill right above Sevastopol that looked down over its bays. If she timed it right, she would be able to reconnoitre the shanty town while there was still enough light and then approach if she judged it safe. It was three days since she'd seen Irek.

At just before five-thirty she began the walk back up the canyon. It was gloomy down here now, but there the sky was still bright above the canyon's edges where the sun lit it as it slowly began to sink towards the west. By the time she entered the forest, you couldn't have seen that there was light anywhere. When she was well away from the camp, she ran for four miles until she came to the small dirt road that led along the edge of the mountain.

It connected a few farms and small holdings above the city. Below her, Sevastopol's bays glittered in patches of white light from the sun, which was now heading for the horizon. It looked like there would be another great orange sunset that filled the sky and turned the sea below into a flame of water.

She turned to the right and walked along the track. It was unlikely she would find a lift here, but as she was set for another two-mile walk, she heard a vehicle bouncing along the road behind her and finally saw it coming in her direction. She crossed to the other side and waited with her thumb out.

With a grinding of gears and hissing from its overheated engine, the truck drew up alongside her and she looked through the open window on the passenger side. The driver was a farmer. There were hay bales in the open truck bed and two dead chickens hanging upside down from a metal bar.

'I'm going to the east of the city,' she said. 'Ten dollars?' It was a sum that she knew would divert anyone along this road from their course. He nodded and leaned over to open the door which was impossible to open from the outside.

They drove in silence for a mile or so. But he kept looking sideways at her and eventually his curiosity needed an answer.

'Tourist?' he said.

'Yes. From America.'

'You speak Russian well.'

'My mother emigrated.'

'Are you alone?' His voice expressed concern rather than unwelcome curiosity.

'No. I'm with a party of friends. I went for a walk and got lost. I'm meeting them back in town.'

'You shouldn't go into the mountains alone.'

'I won't make the same mistake again. I thought I was going to be there for the night.'

The outskirts of the city began with potholed roads and grubby houses. Away to the east, she knew, was the shanty town, a mile or so from here. She looked across the wide seat.

'And you? Are you Russian?'

'Half and half. Maybe quarters or eighths.' He laughed. Then they reached the main road into the centre of town.

'Please drop me here,' she said. 'There's a bar where we're meeting.'

He didn't seem to mind about her safety now that they were on the edge of the city. She took a single ten-dollar bill from her trousers and gave it to him before they reached a small intersection on Shovkovychna, where he pulled into a truck park.

'Down that way,' he said. 'You'd better find your friends. You attract too much attention.'

She climbed out of the cab without a word and turned down the hill.

When he was gone, she turned back up the hill again and ran up towards the rising ground that looked down on the shanty town. Away from the road now and invisible from it, she found herself on a rise that gave her a view in both directions—back to the city and ahead to the shanty town below the hill where she was. She took binoculars from inside her jacket and laid them on the grass. Various bird-watching society badges in different states of disrepair hung from the straps. Burt's boys had done a good job with all her equipment. She unscrewed one of the long lenses from the binoculars and extracted a small, powerful scope with a night-vision lens and opened it up. There was still some light but the night lens would make the faces down below her clearer. She was about a quarter of a mile away from the shanties. Around her were thick coarse grasses and a single granite rock behind which she crouched out of sight.

First she swept the area from below the shanty town down towards the road she had walked up three days before and that led to the city. She was looking for unmarked vehicles parked or waiting with running engines, but the road contained only a few cars mostly heading in the direction of the centre of the city. Then she trained the scope on to the slopes above the shanties. Up in this direction she was looking for human signs; no vehicles could make it above the shanties. The ground was too steep.

They would be in a group, if they were waiting for her at all, or perhaps individuals who would be scattered at intervals above the shanty town.

After ten minutes studying the landscape, she saw no movements, but it was possible that any reception committee could be concealed by the rocks. She would check again a second time and maybe a third.

Then she swept the sides of the camp, first on the far side up towards the stream which the women used for washing and then back in the direction on the side of the camp from where she was looking. She saw nothing that caused her any alarm.

Finally she began to study the shanty town itself, dividing it into sectors that were defined by the area of the scope itself. She trained the scope steadily on each area, watching the movements of the mainly men and children going about their business or playing in the failing light. Each section of the camp showed the same sluggish, purposeless movement of a people caught in limbo. They were Tatar faces, some mixed Russian and Tatar, and these she watched more closely. It was possible that any special forces squad would simply intimidate the inhabitants of the shanty town in order to infiltrate men disguised as residents. That would be harder to gauge. Ultimately, it would be impossible from this distance to be sure.

Finally she focused the scope on Irek's hut. She held it absolutely steady for more than five minutes, seeing no movement around it. Then she rolled over on her back, rested her eyes for a few minutes and began the whole process again.

On the third sweep of the camp she saw a man emerge from the entrance to Irek's makeshift home. He was taller than most of the men and had a similar dark skin colour, though it was hard to see colour now in the fading light. The man had more of a Middle Eastern look, she thought, than the Tatar faces around him. But it was something else about him that arrested her attention. He carried himself with an air of complete calm—a restfulness and self-containment that was alien to the other men she observed. He stood still, seeming to observe without observing, sensing rather than seeing. And she knew then the man was Balthasar.

She descended from the hill back in the direction from where she'd come. It was time to leave Larry a sign. She'd decided by now to go in. Out of sight of the shanties now, on the far side of the hill, there was an ancient, broken wooden fence that ran along a field near the road at the foot of the hill. On the fourth post away from the road she left a piece of black tape stuck on the side of the post away from the road. Larry would be somewhere near, perhaps even observing her, but the black tape was the sign that she would enter the camp. Green was the sign for postponement. Then she walked back up the hill and took another sweep of the shanty town. There was nothing that caused her any more suspicion than before and she waited behind the rock until darkness had fallen completely.

At just before nine o'clock she skirted around above the shanties, keeping at least a quarter of a mile away and in the shadow of the hill, until she reached more rocky ground above the camp where it was easier to conceal herself. She put a shawl around her head that reached below her waist and changed her shoes for some cheap, broken, plastic sandals of the kind the women wore. She took a gun from her pack and wedged it in her waistband and covered her upper body and the gun with the shawl. She stuffed the pack into a crevice between two rocks. Then she began to pick her way down a steep rocky slope towards the edge of the Tatar encampment.

In the darkness, it was easy to enter the fringes of the camp without being observed. But Anna was past the first few of the dilapidated homes when she had the sensation of being watched. She didn't turn or look up, keeping her head bent with her eyes looking where the light of open fires illuminated the rough ground. It was a male voice that challenged her, but she walked on, and either the man couldn't be bothered to challenge her again or his curiosity was satisfied.

335

Ahead she could see Irek's home, a paraffin burner inside catching the edges of the plastic sheet at the entrance and its glow penetrating a tent-like roof. She stopped and squatted on the ground so that her heartbeat became calm and she could allow herself to blend with the surroundings and let the scenes around her become normal to her.

She must have been there for more than ten minutes in which she'd taken in everything in the camp she could see by the light of the small fires. She was aware of the presence she had seen from the hill earlier. He seemed to have a life force about him that dominated the pallid energy of the camp. Either that, or she was in a state of heightened consciousness herself at his proximity. She hadn't thought about him for over twenty years, since she was a child, yet suddenly he seemed very vivid in her mind, very close to her, as if they were old friends rather than childhood acquaintances, someone she had seen maybe a dozen times only.

She stirred herself to get a different perspective on the camp and heard a footfall nearby.

'You are wearing blue this evening,' came a soft, Russian voice. The voice came from behind her to the side and about twenty feet away. He was keeping his distance, she thought, so as not to alarm her. But what dominated her mind was that beneath the shawl she wore a blue sweater and blue jeans. She could feel his presence strongly now and, turning her head, she saw a pair of boot-clad feet some way to her left.

'And you?' she asked without turning round again. 'What are you wearing, Balthasar?' She felt

336

the gun digging into her stomach and moved her right hand beneath the shawl and around the butt.

She felt him approach. He squatted down beside her and, looking straight ahead and not at her, said, 'I'm wearing jeans too, a black smock, wool hat, also black. It's OK, you won't need the gun. Not now, anyway,' he added.

She looked sideways at his profile and he still didn't turn. She saw a soft smile playing around his lips. Then she looked ahead as he was doing.

'It's been over twenty years,' he said at last.

'How did you know?' she replied. 'How did you know the colours? How is it done?'

'I'd know you,' he said. 'You have the same smell as when you were five years old,' he continued. 'But you're right, it's more than that. Seeing colour without eyes is a simple trick. At least to me.' Then he turned and she felt his face on hers and she turned towards him too. He was apparently looking at her, if you didn't know he was blind. 'Maybe I can teach you sometime, Anna,' he said.

'Are you alone?' she said, looking into his face that flickered with amusement in the soft glow of a fire to their left.

'Apart from a couple of hundred Tatars,' he said.

'Why are you here?' she said.

'I might ask you the same thing,' he replied good-humouredly. 'But there are other things first. I want to hear about you. I see your mother from time to time, but she doesn't see me. I know she hates the KGB. Maybe she always did, even when she was married to your father and living at the KGB station in Damascus. So I don't embarrass

337

her by visiting.'

'You know all about me,' she said. 'I'm a wanted traitor. They've tried to take me back to Russia at least twice. You must know about me.'

'I know those things,' he said vaguely. 'But what is it you're doing with your life? What is the picture you are painting? Avenging your husband Finn? You think you are going to bring down the regime in Moscow, perhaps? What about your boy?'

She stiffened.

'Why have you chosen this life for yourself?' he said. 'There are better things in the world for a woman like you.'

She paused. 'I have a whole life to clean out before I can begin again,' she said. 'I made my choices and now my choices are changing again.' She looked at him. 'And you, Balthasar? What choices are you going to make? You can be a great hero by bringing me back.'

He laughed. 'I'm already a great hero,' he said. 'And it's the heroes they don't trust most of all.' He paused and bent his head towards the ground. 'If we ever truly make choices, it's not for a long time,' he said. 'We have to be rid of the automatic, the compulsive, the careless, the stupid—then we can make choices if we can at all. So I, too, am at a turning point in my life.' He turned his head towards her. 'You are pleased to see me?' he asked, and the question came at her out of the blue.

She didn't need to think, but she paused anyway. 'Yes,' she said finally. 'I'm pleased to see you, Balthasar.' That was all she could say for now. She felt a confusion in her mind to see this blind man whom she hadn't seen since they were both children. She didn't understand the confusion. But against it, she felt that everything she was doing here, in Ukraine, for Cougar, paled in comparison.

They sat in silence for a moment, then she spoke again. 'The reason Finn died is that he forgot how to act in his own best interests. He forgot he could choose.'

They squatted in the dim light of the distant fire. Above the camp, the waxing moon was three days away from its fullness.

'We must decide in the next few minutes how it's going to be with us,' he said finally.

Without speaking they stood and they walked side by side to Irek's home.

Balthasar pushed back the flap of the tent opening and beckoned her to enter. His arm pointed her towards the rugs and the paraffin lamp that swung slightly with the movement of the sheet flap and the light breeze that followed it. She bent and walked into the hut and saw Irek sitting in the same position where she had left him three days before. She looked around to check for any other presence, but could see nothing. The woman who had been in the closed-off section of the home and had brought tea was absent. Irek was making a pipe, patiently filling the bowl and lighting a charcoal fragment in his hands. He didn't look up as they sat down on the cushions in front of him.

'Enemies or allies?' he said and, when neither of them replied, he said, 'How does a poor people like ours—the poorest of peoples—become mixed up in the world's affairs? We have no voice, no place that is home, no living to make and, maybe, no future. Yet here were are, with suppliants from America and Russia who perhaps both wish to

339

engineer our final destruction.' He looked at them, leaning his pipe against a crate next to him. 'We have nothing to give you and we are wary of your gifts, whether of money or information.'

Balthasar leaned forward and took the pipe, as if he were an equal to the man whose house they were in. Then he handed it effortlessly to Irek. 'Let's smoke,' he said. 'Then I'll tell you what we can do.'

Irek lit the pipe, took several puffs and then passed it to Balthasar who did the same. Finally, Anna sat and smoked. It was stronger than the time before and she felt her head swim. The small space seemed to swim in front of her eyes before she could focus again. She wondered if soon the flap of the entrance would be thrown back and Russian *spetsnaz* would drag her from here and she fought down her fear.

Finally, it was Balthasar who spoke. 'I have been instructed to offer you money,' he said to Irek. 'The purpose of the money is for you to build a mosque, a school—later some houses, perhaps.' He paused. 'But that is not the real purpose.'

Anna turned to study his face. It was completely at peace. She saw the face of someone who had made his choice.

'The real purpose is to implicate you in some Russian action against Russians in Ukraine,' he said calmly. 'Then you will be blamed first. After that the Ukrainian government will be blamed for not protecting Russian interests here. I know all this, but I wasn't told it,' he added. He looked at Anna. 'The lady is right, Irek. She and this company she works for by the name of Cougar have found the purpose behind this offer from the

Russians.'

Anna looked at him and felt a wave of astonishment. This was the moment of truth. If the whole game with Irek and Qubaq, and Balthasar's presence was simply to capture her, it would be now. But there was no movement that she could detect outside the shanty and inside all three of them were completely still. It was as if breathing had stopped.

'Why do you tell me this?' Irek said at last.

'Perhaps we can stop it happening,' he said simply.

CHAPTER TWENTY-SIX

Taras decided to meet Logan Halloran at a roadside café restaurant called Karmaliuk twenty-five miles east of Kiev. It was a place owned by a reliable friend of his wife's from schooldays and who Taras knew well. He and Sasha occasionally went fishing together and, more often, left the rods in the car and stayed drinking in the yard if it was summer or by the fire at the rear of the café where Sasha kept a private room for friends. Mainly it was sufficiently far outside Kiev where he was afraid he might be spotted meeting Halloran by chance.

He was early, parked his wife's car at the rear, away from the road, and was enjoying a cold beer when Sasha told him that an American had come into the bar. Taras downed the half-glass that remained and walked through to the front.

'Follow me,' he said, without greeting Logan.

'I'll meet you in the front. A blue Fiat.'

Taras drove around to the front and watched as Logan pulled out on to the road behind him. He kept his eyes in the rearview mirror and slowed twice to allow vehicles to overtake. When he was satisfied that Logan had come alone, he chose a dirt track to the left off the road that wound along the banks of a small river and through two villages before Taras turned again to the left and up to the edge of a wood. He cut the engine and stayed in the car. He watched Logan in the mirror as he slammed the door of a hired Toyota Land Cruiser and walked slowly up behind him. The American was twirling the car keys round and round his forefinger and, to Taras, looked altogether too relaxed.

When Logan stepped into the passenger seat and had shut the door, Taras began to talk without letting him speak first. At the same time he patted down the American, turned out his jacket pockets looking for wires or mikes.

'We want your help before I can give you anything,' he said. 'Whatever it is you want, I'll give you information for an agreed fee paid into a bank in Austria, details to be provided, either on a monthly basis or as a one-off, depending on the type of information you require.' He finished checking Logan and was satisfied. Then he looked straight out of the car's windscreen ahead of him. 'That's my side. But before I commit to anything, I want something from you.' Taras kept looking straight ahead into the car's windscreen, as if he were embarrassed by what he was saying. And he supposed that he was. Despite the insincerity of the offer he was making to the American, he still felt dirty doing it. But now he turned and faced Logan. 'That's the deal, no negotiation, no questions, nothing—until you give me what I want. And I have to see the results of what I'm asking before I commit to helping you or Cougar. Either way, we don't meet again. We set up a drop if we're to do business.'

He sat back, realising his shoulders and back had been tensed as soon as Logan had stepped into the car. He felt his back was rigid and a heat was coming from inside him. He didn't know if the American was going to laugh in his face, if Halloran's interest in him had never been about anything other than some lonely social reason. Maybe he was just a foreigner in Kiev, a spy with a knack for making contacts who might help him. Halloran's background, Taras knew, suggested otherwise, however. After he'd been sacked by the CIA twelve years before, Halloran had been selling whatever he could get his hands on to anyone who would buy it. For a moment, Taras didn't understand why someone of Burt Miller's calibre ever employed Halloran. He seemed a busted flush. So, either the American wanted something from him for his own reasons, some private game he was playing—and that was highly likely in Taras's opinion—or he had been assigned by Cougar to befriend Taras and make an approach.

Logan sat in silence. The silence lengthened and Taras tried to remain cool, but he felt this heat inside him intensifying. He wanted to open the car's windows, but he knew it had nothing to do with the temperature. It was him. He thought of Masha and the risks he was taking. He thought of what he would do even if he managed to free her.

They would never let her go voluntarily, he knew that. And he knew the most likely outcome was that—once they'd got everything out of her they thought she knew—they'd make a deal with the Russians and hand her over. And then it would all begin again for his cousin.

'I can do that,' Logan replied languidly at last. 'Even if I don't know what the answer you're looking for is.'

He looked at Taras and Taras turned away, uncomfortable in the company of Halloran. It was going against all his better instincts to be talking to the American at all.

'If you don't know, then it's no deal,' he said. 'If you don't know, find out or get out.'

'You'd better ask me, then, Taras,' Logan replied, and smiled at the Ukrainian.

'What was Resnikov picking up in the Crimea in January? Outside Sevastopol?'

Logan was taken aback, but he sat completely still, maintaining an expression of relaxed calm. How did Taras know about Anna? Even he knew only because Theo Lish had told him. Logan had become closer to Theo since he'd begun to give the CIA chief some oddments about Cougar's operations. 'Blueprints,' he said. 'Blueprints of extensions to the port of Novorossiysk.'

'Did she get them out of the country?'

'As far as I know, yes. Burt Miller seemed pleased that they showed the Russians weren't serious about expanding the port sufficiently to take their Black Sea fleet.' Logan's mind was racing. He felt a rush of power giving away this information. He felt it redressed some kind of balance he'd lost in Burt Miller's considerations.

'Why was he pleased?' Taras asked.

'Because Miller has a theory the Russians are never going to leave Sevastopol. That Sevastopol is some kind of beach head for their further encroachment into Ukraine.' Logan shrugged. 'That's not the American view,' he said. 'The CIA view.' He felt the sense of power again, a rush of excitement that he could give Taras not just Miller's but the CIA's opinions, that he was at the centre of power.

'She came into Ukraine a second time,' Logan volunteered. 'I'm not sure what for. And I think she's in the country again,' he added.

'Where?' Taras said.

Logan looked at him. 'Come on, Taras, that's information the Russians would pay a lot of money for. You don't think that even if I knew I'd just give it away.'

'The Crimea?' Taras pressed him.

'Probably. That's where Miller sees the Russians making their move. If they intend to make a move at all,' he added dismissively.

'What identity is she travelling under?'

'I don't know. And anyway, if you want to hand her over to the Russians, why would I tell you?' Logan answered. 'Whatever it is you can give me, it won't be worth as much as that.'

'It doesn't sound like you care one way or the other what happens to her,' Taras replied, and this time he turned and looked at Logan and didn't like what he saw at all.

Logan sat with his hands in his lap, the fingers gently crossing each other. Did he care what happened to her, he wondered? For a long time, he'd been ambivalent about her. First, two and half years before, he'd slept with her—just for one night. Then she'd discovered that he'd previously sold her location to the Russians, as well as to Miller and the British, and she'd told Miller she was going to kill him. After that, he'd risked his life to kill the Russian mobster who had killed her husband. He'd expected forgiveness then; an eye for an eye. He'd redeemed himself in his own eyes, but not in hers. She'd told him to get out of her sight.

'She's already killed two KGB operatives in the Crimea,' he said. 'I'd be careful of her, if I were you, Taras.'

'I know what she's done.'

Taras felt a fury rise up in him. The American worked with this woman and evidently couldn't care less what happened to her. It reminded him of Masha's boss in Moscow; casually using someone to pass highly dangerous information she knew nothing about. He felt the prospects of Masha hanging on to life diminish in the face of such cynicism.

'Tell Burt Miller,' he said, 'that I know who his source is in Moscow. At any rate, the source who provided the blueprints. Tell Miller that I'll reveal this source to the Russians unless I have his help. And unless I get to see Resnikov. Here. In Ukraine. Tell him I'll leave a message for Resnikov at the drugstore in Ochakovstev Street in Sevastopol. If I don't hear from her in three days I'll reveal his man in Moscow.' He looked at Logan and handed him a scrawled note. Logan read, then screwed it into a ball and put it in his pocket. Instructions. He'd dispose of them later.

'Now get out,' Taras said.

CHAPTER TWENTY-SEVEN

The first thing Logan noticed from the launch as it crossed the harbour was that a surface-to-air missile system had been fitted to the stern deck of the *Cougar*. Burt Miller's vessel lay at anchor—and apparently at peace—in deep water on the fringes of the port of Piraeus.

But as Logan stepped off the launch and on to some steps dropped specially for him, he noted that the crew appeared to be in a state of readiness to depart. He guessed the *Cougar* would be leaving before nightfall, as soon as his meeting with Burt was completed. Rumour on land at the harbour master's office—which Logan had taken his usual meticulous care to discover before he stepped on to the launch—suggested that Istanbul was the vessel's next port of call and from there, he assumed, it would be heading up through the Bosphorus and into the Black Sea. If that were the case, then Burt was breaking his agreement with Theo Lish.

As his ambitions grew and his formless resentment served as fuel for that growth, to Logan everything was information now, and all knowledge might—at some point—be used to his own advantage.

It was an unseasonally hot and sultry afternoon at the back end of April, but the sea breeze made the boat an infinitely pleasanter place to be than on land in the port itself. He came up the steps and arrived on board the *Cougar* and looked across the blue haze that joined the sea to the sky. Logan paused on the deck, admired the gleaming missiles, observed the crew going about their business, sniffed the breeze as if there might be some useful message in that too, and then descended stairs towards the operations room.

It was less than twenty-four hours since he'd made the meeting with Taras and the time for making a decision was running out. There were now just forty-eight hours before the Ukrainian said that he would hand Cougar's Moscow agent to the Russians. But if Logan had anticipated Burt being in a state of anxiety at having a possible spoiler thrown in the works to upset his plans—whatever they were—he was proved wrong.

Now, from across the huge, polished wood desk in the deck-wide operations room of the *Cougar*, Burt stood, hands in the pockets of immaculately ironed white trousers, a cigar blowing its occasional, arcane signals from an anchor-shaped ashtray next to him, and with the air of a man who directed events rather than being directed by them.

Logan had been urged by a butler to sit in a chair on the far side of the table where he now half slouched, sipping a glass of water and contemplating how this approach from Taras Tur had suddenly and, perhaps, fortuitously, put him at the centre of events. Burt turned from studying some papers Logan couldn't see and rested his eyes for a minute on his brilliant, if sometimes wayward operative.

'Do you believe him?' Burt asked mildly. 'That's what I want to know. What does your instinct tell you, Logan? How could this SBU officer possibly know the identity of our agent?'

As Logan looked back into Burt's eyes he saw

348

they contained an expressionless stare that was unusual for him, but there was none of the hostility he'd received at their last meeting. Burt was the picture of calm, his genial self apparently unruffled by the prospect of time trickling away towards the deadline.

'I don't know if we can afford not to believe him,' Logan replied. 'It seems he has all the cards. We disbelieve him at our peril.'

'But that isn't the same thing,' Burt replied with what seemed to Logan a deliberately exaggerated patience, like a long-suffering schoolteacher's. 'It's not the answer to the question I asked you, in fact. Never mind "affording not to". Do *you* believe him?' he repeated. 'That's what I most want to know. You were there, my boy. As always, I value your judgement of human character.'

Logan thought for a moment about his meeting with Taras and the two times he had met the Ukrainian before. If you forgot he worked for a foreign intelligence service, Taras was an honest man, at least in Logan's opinion. He found he liked him, despite his recent—and out of character—aggression towards him at the meeting in the car. There was a quality of innocence in Taras that, perhaps, reawakened some lost innocence of Logan's own. But if it did, he drove it underground again; it was too painful to look in the face. Nevertheless, Taras's obvious sincerity had made Logan feel connected in a way that he hadn't felt when he'd met Taras on previous occasions. In fact, in his opinion—and now he thought about it more closely—Taras seemed to be operating at a personal level rather than being the dumb automaton of the SBU. Logan didn't

349

understand why he thought that—or why the Ukrainian would be acting outside the parameters of his job at all. It was just an instinct. There was something about Taras's brand of anxiety in the car that went beyond the regular strictures of a job and into the realms of the personal. It was a fine distinction, but it made all the difference.

'If I *had* to say one thing or the other,' Logan said carefully, 'I'd have to say I believed him. He knows, though God knows how he knows.'

'Good,' Burt said and stood up to his full five feet nine inches, his eyes alight with possibilities and a beaming smile fixed once more on his chubby face.

Why the news that a Ukrainian spy knew the identity of one of Burt's Russian agents in Moscow should make Burt content, however, Logan couldn't fathom.

'Good?' he queried, in genuine incomprehension. 'How is it good?'

'We know where we stand,' Burt said. 'If you're right—and I trust your instincts—we know what's happening. Let's say he knows exactly who our agent is. That's very valuable to him. And it's valuable to us that we know it about him. We can use this Taras, perhaps.'

Logan didn't ask Burt how he intended to do that, when the boot seemed to be firmly on the other foot. Taras was in a winning position, in Logan's view.

'Are you going to let Anna make the contact with him, then?' he asked.

Burt stroked his chins. 'We must,' he said at last. 'We must treat it as good fortune. We must see what happens when they meet.'

'But revealing the agent's identity is going to be a threat he'll always be able to hold over Cougar's head,' Logan said. 'Not just this time. If we deal with him now, he can use the threat again and again.'

'Oh, I don't think so,' Burt said, and he evinced an almost complete lack of concern at the prospect. Then he turned to Logan. He looked at him for a long time until Logan began to feel uncomfortable. 'Logan, I'm going to ask you something very important,' Burt said. 'A change of plan. It's something of personal importance to me, not just to Cougar's business. I want you to go down there, to Sevastopol. I can't withdraw Larry to brief him, he's needed there, on the spot, looking after Anna's back. So I want it to be you, Logan. Let's say I want it to be you anyway, Larry or no Larry. This could be the most important assignment of your life.'

'She won't like it. Neither will Larry. You know that. Neither of them trust me.' Logan's voice betrayed some bitterness, despite his attempt to be unemotional.

'Maybe they won't. She doesn't trust you, that's true. But she has her reasons. Here's a chance to start rebuilding that trust. Look at it that way.'

'What's she doing in the Crimea?' Logan asked bluntly.

'That I can't say,' he replied. 'It's unimportant. It's not relevant,' he added, correcting himself.

'I'm not in the need-to-know loop, you mean.'

Burt raised his eyebrows slightly, but his voice was regulated, friendly, paying Logan compliments he hadn't paid him in some time. 'Look, Logan. I'm doing everything possible to square a

351

complicated situation. You can help me. I will value it highly.'

'Theo wants Cougar out of the area completely. You know that. We shouldn't be there at all.'

'I'm glad you said "we",' Burt replied slyly. 'Theo will also want to be squared about the situation—and other things—shortly. But we'll come to that later, when this is over.'

'They're going to board the *Pride of Corsica* by force,' Logan said.

'I had heard. Who's they?' Burt said, ignoring what the CIA chief wanted Cougar to do, to vacate the Crimea and leave it free for the CIA, the Russians, the Brits . . . anybody, it seemed, as long as it wasn't Cougar.

'Us—the CIA, the Russians and the British. It's going to be a joint assault team just like the recce was.'

'Of course,' Burt said, and appeared deep in thought. 'The Russians have got the CIA and the British involved in a joint operation.' He looked back at Logan. 'That's the way they'd do it,' he said mysteriously. 'Do we have a date for this assault?' Burt asked.

'No,' Logan said. 'Not as far as I know.'

'Then I'll speak to Theo,' Burt replied. He looked hard at Logan again. 'You think you can do this right?' he said. 'Meet with Larry and Anna? It's you who will pick up Taras's message at this drugstore in Sevastopol, then relay it to Anna. I don't want her walking into an ambush, so it has to be someone else. You're ideal, Logan. You've always been one of the best.'

'Why wouldn't I be able to do it?' Logan said, ignoring more of Burt's easy flattery. 'It's just being a messenger boy, isn't it? Just the usual job of Burt's bagman.'

Burt leaned down to the table, putting his big hands palms down flat against the surface. 'It may be the most important thing you ever do for Cougar, Logan. For me, too. And certainly for Anna. Not to mention our agent in Moscow, of course, whose life may well depend on it.' Burt surveyed Logan once again, before continuing. 'But it also may be the most important thing you ever do for yourself. Think about that. Understand where your best interests lie. This may well be a moment of truth for you. You understand the importance of this? It's not just conveying a message to Anna so that she can meet the Ukrainian. It's about the implications of the message and the actions that will follow. In my opinion, we're nearing the point of explosion.'

'If you say so, Burt,' Logan replied and stood up to peel off the top of a cold beer that was standing in an ice bucket.

'At times like this,' Burt said, 'we all behave in character, no matter what happens.'

Logan had no idea what he meant by this, but he automatically felt himself under some critical glare and it made him defensive.

'When do I go?' he asked.

'At once,' Burt said. 'Talk to our travel people, they're expecting you.' He handed Logan a ship phone. 'Get a flight to Odessa, then a flight to Simferol. A car from there.' He took out a pen and wrote a coded number on a scrap of paper. 'This is Larry,' he said, indicating the number. 'I'll tell him you're on the way.'

'I'm sure he'll be delighted.'

353

Logan took an afternoon flight from Athens to Istanbul and then connected to a flight for Odessa. He checked into a small hotel on Odessa's waterfront, drank at several bars along the strip that were just waking up for the summer, chatted to two pretty teenage girls who said they were dancers, slept a little, and took the first flight to Simferol on the following morning. From there it was a long taxi ride to Sevastopol.

Somewhere in the city, he thought as the old Mercedes approached the edge of town, somewhere, he knew that Taras would be waiting for him, and for Anna too. He'd have left his communication at the drugstore by now. It was already two days since their meeting in the car and they had twenty-hours before he blew the whistle on Cougar's Moscow agent.

When he'd paid off the car and found a suitably wide open space away from buildings, he contacted Larry on the coded number Burt had given him and heard the sour tone in Larry's voice. Logan felt his hackles rise immediately. Larry had briefed against Logan to Burt, ever since it had been discovered that Logan had sold Anna down the river two years before. When they met on this sticky afternoon in Sevastopol—the heavy air seemed to stretch from Greece all the way to the southern borders of Russia—Larry was terse, monosyllabic, and conveyed an almost tangible sense of disgust.

'Just pick up the message,' Larry said. 'Then come straight back. And give it to me.'

'I'm to give it to Anna,' Logan replied. 'Those were Burt's orders.'

'Then they've changed, Logan. She's not

354

available. And anyway, she doesn't want you anywhere near this.'

And so at four o'clock in the afternoon—and with fifteen hours now remaining—Larry and a surveillance team reconnoitred the street outside the drugstore on Ochakovstev. It seemed to be clear, according to the watchers' signals.

Then one of the team entered the store and took up a position at the back as Logan entered. Logan walked to a dilapidated booth with a barred window over it and asked for the pills being held for Stanislas Lavrov, the name Taras had instructed him to say. The grouchy woman behind the counter eyed him warily and took off her glasses as if to distance herself from the significance of what she was doing, but she handed over a packet, sealed at the top. From its sound as Logan picked it up, it seemed to contain pills. Logan paid her more than the cost and left.

He walked out on to the bright street and saw the sea arcing away below him. The warships of the two fleets were tied up against quays, or hung at anchor close-to, or lay dotted in the bays that disappeared into the slight haze that deepened with distance.

And fifty miles off the coast was where the *Pride of Corsica* rode the sea lanes that led towards the south of the Black Sea and on to the Mediterranean. When he was finished here, Logan thought, it would be time to rendezvous with the teams for the assault on the ship. They were gathering at Burgas in Bulgaria from where the *Mira* had also set out. By now, Theo had arranged everything, with the Russians' guiding hand behind it all. It was being billed in Washington as a joint, international effort in counter-terrorism.

Logan looked up the road in both directions. The watchers would be out there, but they were well concealed. He turned to the left and walked briskly down a slight hill before catching a bus to the rendezvous Larry had given him.

The holiday villa Larry had taken for two weeks under the name of Philip Ames and Family lay in some hills to the east of the city. The team had all arrived there before Logan: Larry, his 'wife', a former CIA veteran called Lucy, and their two 'children'—stretching it a bit, in Logan's mind, for Grant and Adam were in their early twenties, though dressed like teenagers they could have passed for a lot less. It was Adam who let Logan in and he stepped into a thinly furnished room with cheap red floor tiles and bars on the windows— against normal, opportunistic thieves, Logan assumed, rather than Ukrainian security agents. Larry was in a kitchen at the back, making coffee in a machine whose red light flickered on and off with the failing electric current only to receive a sharp slap from Larry when it was off. Larry turned with his hand already out and Logan hated him for the insulting peremptoriness of the gesture.

'Here,' he said, as if he couldn't care less, and handed over the package from his pocket.

At that point, Anna walked into the room.

'You got it?' she asked.

Logan nodded. He couldn't wait to get out of here now. The atmosphere of criticism that seemed to him to be aimed unfairly in his direction was beginning to stifle him.

Anna took the package from Larry's hand and opened it. She extracted a small piece of paper from among the pills and held it towards the light from the kitchen window.

'It's a number,' she said.

'Bastard.' Larry hit the coffee machine again. 'He wants you to call about a meeting, not just meet.'

'It seems so,' she said.

'You'd better do it far away from here,' Larry said. 'I'll send Adam and Grant with you. Best to go up in the hills. Here.' He gave her a phone— one of many mobile phones—which he took from a cupboard. 'Chuck it as soon as you've used it.'

'It's OK, Larry. I know what to do.'

Anna looked at Logan now. 'And you, Logan?' she said. 'You're done here. Best to make yourself scarce.'

And that was it. He was out of the villa in less than fifteen minutes after he'd arrived, the delivery boy. Lucy drove him in a hired jeep into the town and directed him towards a square where he could pick up a taxi back to Simferol and the airport. But when Lucy had waved goodbye—the only friendly gesture he seemed to have received from any of them—Logan first put in a call to Laszlo before heading north.

CHAPTER TWENTY-EIGHT

Balthasar left Anna at the foot of the steps that led to the monument. The monument stood at the top of a hill at the place called Balaclava and looked out over the city and beyond it to the sea from where invaders had always come until Hitler attacked Sevastopol from the land. To the left, the mouth of the Kerch Straits was at its widest before the straits entered and split the land like an axe, and separated Ukraine from Russia. To the right, the mountains descended towards the Crimean steppe as the coast turned to the north.

Anna looked down at Sevastopol's perfect harbour. There was one long bay called Sevastopolskaya Bukhta, and then five or six perfect bays for anchorage off the main bay. In the main dockyard below her, she saw a train, loaded with submarine batteries, Balthasar had said. At the end of the dock where the train stood, the Russian aircraft carrier *Moskva* was moored broadside against the quay.

It was a hot day, the air completely still up here, and there were few people who were willing to climb up the ninety-five steps to the monument.

Larry had chosen the place for Anna to meet Taras. 'It's a dead end,' he said. 'Normally I don't like that. But once you're at the top by the monument, no one can come up easily except by the steps and the road. We can watch that.' But by now, Larry and Anna had firmly decided that Taras was acting alone. Larry and the surveillance team were out in full force to watch—and if necessary follow—anyone who decided to make the trip to the top.

Anna began the long climb up the steps. She wore a cap against the sun and carried a small pack on her back and a guidebook in one hand. But inside her jacket there was a Thompson Contender handgun. She watched up ahead of her as she climbed and, from time to time, glanced to the sides of the steps, looking for anything on the steep slopes that shouldn't be there. She felt the sun on the right side of her face as it rose towards its zenith and heard only the scuff of her shoes on the stone steps and the occasional hoot of a ship's horn from Sevastopolskaya Bukhta. Taras had said he would be waiting at the top, behind the monument at 11.30. It was now 11.45.

It took her ten minutes to reach the top. The monument was made of a soft stone, weathered by the Black Sea winds, and the engravings in Russian Cyrillic writing had lost their knife sharpness. She turned once when she reached the top and looked back down from where she'd come; at the glittering bays and the grey warships and at the black hulls of submarines. All were absolutely still in the water, as if they were two-dimensional images stuck to a diorama of the scene rather than real ships on a real sea. Then she moved carefully around and behind the monument, her hand on the butt of her gun inside the jacket and her finger poised close to the trigger.

She saw a well-built, stocky man sitting on a bench, his hair ruffled—habitually un-brushed, she thought—and his hands resting clasped but relaxed in his lap. He was looking ahead to where she appeared from the far side of the monument and the sun caught the side of his face and showed her a man with weary eyes and a patient expression which seemed to hold the expectation of nothing very much. He didn't move his head when she appeared, but looked into her eyes without fear.

'So you're the great Anna Resnikov,' he said softly. 'The great *Colonel* Anna Resnikov.'

He made no move to get up and, once Anna had checked the slopes that fell away behind the bench where he was sitting, she sat down, an arm's length away from him.

In the previous hours between her phone call to Taras and this moment, Balthasar had discreetly run checks in Moscow on several SBU officers, including Taras Tur some way down on the list. The Russians had a note in the FSB archives of Taras's father and his murder in Berlin. They also had a mark against Taras as a 'Ukrainian nationalist—to be discussed'. Balthasar interpreted this as the KGB's obsessive listing of possible enemies in Ukraine and its anxious distinction between pro- and anti-Russians in the Ukrainian secret service, but he'd said that this distinction was crude and not necessarily to be trusted. Taras might be a Ukrainian nationalist, that was true, but that did not mean he would necessarily act against the Russians. He might also fall in Russia's direction, depending on the alternative. It was known that Taras—using his father as an example—had no great respect for the harsher capitalist practices in the West—and Cougar was likely to be viewed by him as the unacceptable face of capitalism. But most of all, anyone—Russia or the West—whom he perceived to be interfering with Ukraine's sovereignty—was likely to be viewed by him with distaste at best, and, at worst, as an enemy.

'There's a great reward out for you in Moscow,' he said.

That too was considered to appeal favourably to Taras's general distaste for Moscow's politics.

'Burt Miller would like us to work together,' she said softly. 'For the good of Ukraine.'

Taras gave a short laugh. 'It's good to know we

have such a great friend in the West,' he said, but it was without the harshness she'd expected. 'But it's me who's here to help Burt Miller—not the other way around,' he added. He turned to her, his body language unthreatening, his upper body pulling slightly away from her on the bench. 'They say you killed two KGB officers in Odessa and the Crimea on the sixteenth of January,' he said. 'Me? I've never killed anyone. Neither has my baby cousin who's now lying in a prison hospital cell down there'—he indicated towards the city—'with part of her face blown off and a posse of interrogators who want to know what she was delivering and aren't afraid to ask.'

So that was how he'd worked it out, she thought. The woman was a Russian relation of his. He'd pieced together her story, found out the name of her boss in Moscow, and worked out that the package was being delivered, not within Ukraine, but to someone in the West. Therefore the woman's boss was a traitor in Moscow. Smart of him, she thought.

'What's your cousin's name?' she asked.

'Her name is Masha. She's twenty-three years old, she's caught up in a scheme devised by Ukraine's friend, Burt Miller, and executed by you. If she isn't handed over to the Russians and dispensed with after they hollow her out, body and soul, she'll probably meet the same fate in Ukraine. Either way, if she lives she lives with a beautiful face destroyed by a bullet and an innocent mind destroyed by people who only wished to use her.'

'Maybe she shouldn't have joined the KGB,' Anna said and looked him directly in the eye. She saw him reel slightly, astonished perhaps by her directness or lack of sympathy. Then his face hardened and he gripped the back of the bench until his knuckles whitened and she saw him trying to control his anger.

'What Masha left were blueprints of the development of the port of Novorossiysk that came from the Naval Ministry in Moscow,' she said, without allowing him to respond. 'They show that Russia never had any intention of moving their Black Sea fleet there. Now your new president has given them Sevastopol for another twenty-five years anyway. Your new Moscow-friendly president Yanukovich has handed the facilities to Russia for nothing except some price concessions on gas that will bind Ukraine closer economically to Russia than before. Even with the same hand that gives, the spy elite in Moscow also takes. That is their way. There is no stick and carrot, just the stick. A concession from them is merely another chain around Ukraine's neck. So they have the port and now they also have a tame Ukraine bound to them more closely with economic ties. I was betrayed when I came to Ukraine in January. That is how they were waiting at the barn and how they caught Masha. That is why I killed two of their operatives. And I'll kill more of them if they get in my way.'

'Fighting on the side of the right now, are you?' Taras replied mockingly.

She stared him in the eyes and he felt the cool, blue gaze penetrate his mind and throw him off balance, but this time it wasn't anger that welled up in him but a kind of blank astonishment. He seemed to see only her face, her eyes. The whole world around him, the hill on which they sat, the city below and the sea and the ships were beyond his concentration. There was only her.

'When I defected from Russia,' she said, 'I thought it was for love, but even then I knew in my heart that love was the excuse for doing what I'd wanted to do anyway. Does that make my love for my husband any less? I don't think so. But he's dead now, murdered by the KGB. He let himself be killed because he couldn't, finally, step away.' Her eyes bore into his. She sat perfectly still, with a relaxation that belied her readiness to use any method necessary to defend herself. 'Don't believe that when I defected I thought my friends lay in the West. I'm not naïve. All I knew was where my enemies lay and that was in Russia, in the Kremlin, in the KGB and Department S, where I worked so successfully for so long. And even my own father. The question is—or was then for me—not Who are my friends? but Who are my enemies? When that was clear, as it had been becoming clear for many years, I knew what I had to do. And for you too, Taras, that is the question. I don't offer you Burt Miller's friendship—let alone the West's. I could not do that and, in any case, I don't consider I have either of them myself. The question for you is the same as it was for me. Who are your enemies? And what do you stand for that makes them your enemies?'

'Alas, I have no one to love in the West to give me the thin excuse you had to make so fateful a choice,' he replied.

'The choices, all the major choices you make in your life, are emotional ones,' she replied. 'How you apply those choices later to reality is rational.

You don't need someone to love to make an emotional choice. That was just how it was for me.'

'I have the name of Miller's agent in Moscow. I also have a cousin who is a prisoner and whose life is in danger. What can you do for me?'

She looked down at her hands and then up towards the panorama of city and sea and ships below. This time she didn't look back at him. 'If your emotional life is bound to your family and your cousin and your country, and all three are, I believe, the case with you, then I can show you something and you can make your choice. I'm not here to prevent you revealing the identity of Miller's agent. That is up to you. But I can show you another side of the picture.'

'You're playing a very dangerous game,' he replied.

She looked back into his eyes again. 'And you are, too. You are acting alone, aren't you? Your bosses know nothing of this.'

'They're only a phone call away,' he said.

'Perhaps you've left it too late for that. They'll wonder why you didn't report to them earlier.' She paused. 'You know what they're like as well as I do. They won't trust anything you say.'

'And you expect me to trust you.'

'If I thought you wanted money, Miller has plenty of it.'

'No. No, I don't want Miller's money,' he replied.

'I want to introduce you to someone,' Anna said. 'Do I have your permission?'

Taras fell silent.

'He is someone who will make the picture of Masha's predicament more clear. He is someone who will make your country's endangered position more clear. He's Russian. Like me in another life, he works in Department S.'

'Why is he to be trusted any more than you?'

'I'm just asking you to listen to him.'

'Just one man?'

'Just one.'

Taras thought for a moment.

'Here?'

'Yes.'

He stayed with his thoughts for a while longer. 'OK,' he said. 'And then?'

'If you agree with what he has to say, we can help Masha together.'

She stood and walked around the monument. He didn't see the gesture she made. But after she'd returned and they'd waited for ten minutes, a man appeared. He walked around the monument and sat cross-legged on the ground in front of the bench. Balthasar began to tell the story of the Kremlin's plans for Ukraine and of Qubaq.

CHAPTER TWENTY-NINE

Logan stood in a room at the Kerch hotel. It looked out over the bays that spliced the city like a badly stitched wound. It was twenty-four hours since he had picked up Taras's coded message at the drugstore and he had returned to Sevastopol, against orders, undecided, caught between conflicting emotions that threatened to destroy his fragile state of mind.

By now he should have returned to the *Cougar*,

as Burt had told him to do, and then moved on to join Theo's and the Russians' assault team in Burgas. But he'd stayed behind and, as at many times before in his life, he found himself in the soulless limbo of a foreign hotel room, in the no-man's-land of a decision not made and, free floating in this non-state of disconnection, he felt caught in a kind of purgatory of his own making in which he wished for a decision to be made for him, but also hated the fact that he was helpless himself to make it. He had his orders, he knew the path he should be walking on, but this knowledge embittered him. He was a man trapped in the impossible bind of wishing to possess personal control over his future and at the same time wishing for some divine or semi-divine purpose that would absolve him of that responsibility. Neither satisfied him and both now filled his head with a painful confusion of motive, ambition and fear. But what he hated most was the fear that stripped him of all but his humanity, and this hatred he projected outwards to all the people he held responsible.

Behind him, sitting on the edge of the worn and scraggy sofa which had lost its once-green colour many years before, Lazlo waited patiently. It was he, Logan, who had invited the Frenchman down here from Kiev. The reason he had done so, Logan could only put down to the compulsion that possessed him now, and had done throughout his life, never to close down any option—but the option he had left open in asking Laszlo to Sevastopol was one too fateful for him now to act upon. Not with clarity, in any case. He felt constrained by the choices that he had let unfold

366

before him rather than liberated by them.

He brushed his hand through the long, unwashed hair that hung well over his shoulders. The shutters of the room were open and a light breeze fluttered the ageing, grey net curtains. Then he turned from the bright, sun-bleached view of ships and dockyards, glittering sea and—nearer to the hotel beneath his gaze—the cacophony of small buses and trucks that stretched three-deep and bumper to bumper along the waterfront as if they were an unbroken train. He had been silent for some time and had felt the Frenchman's patience turning to irritation or perhaps confusion behind his back.

Putting his hands back into the pockets of the rough, cream-coloured jacket that had become, he thought, like some uniform when it should have been a sign of his devil-may-care individualism, he turned to find Laszlo watching him. He saw that the Frenchman's stare was uncertain, as if he were beginning to think he'd made a mistake flying from the capital down here to the Crimea. But Logan had told him that it was something for which his boss in Paris, Thomas Plismy, would thank him. That had been enough. Logan and Plismy went back a long way and Plismy knew that Logan could deliver if he kept himself straight. Now Laszlo waited, eyeball to eyeball with Logan, for whatever the American had summoned him here for.

Logan tried to read his mind and all he saw in the maelstrom of his own guilt and feelings of a wasted life—and love—was another human being exercising yet further control or criticism over him. He suddenly felt desperate, suicidal, and he wanted to sleep, to forget who he was but most of

367

all to excise the why. Why did he feel like he did? Why was he alone? Why was he lost and why had he always been lost from the very beginning? But he found no answer.

Laszlo cleared his throat slightly. 'My government will be very grateful for something that helps to advance Franco-Russian relations,' he said smoothly. 'That, I understand, is why I'm here, why you called me.' He paused and smoothed the lapel of an expensive dark-blue blazer that didn't need his attention. 'There are contracts to be signed imminently between our two countries. Ten-year, twenty-year contracts that will put France in a very favourable position in Europe. A symbiosis of Russian raw materials and French technical expertise that will guarantee our energy needs amongst other things. To bring a little gift to the Russians at this time would be opportune, Logan—for me, my boss, our government, and, of course, for you. To bring a big gift . . .' he exhaled a sharp breath through pursed lips, 'well, that would bring great advantage to everyone concerned. What is it you have for me? Do you want money?'

He looked carefully at the man in front of him and wondered whether, under the washed-up, frightened and bitter exterior he saw there was anything that Logan possessed apart from his own delusions. Maybe it had been a mistake for him to come here? But his boss Plismy had told him Logan could deliver and he had insisted Laszlo make the journey. Laszlo felt safe that the result of his trip was comfortably out of his hands. He was following Plismy's orders, that was all.

'Why don't we have a beer?' he suggested.

Logan looked back at him. 'Whisky,' he replied.

When a waiter wearing a stained waistcoat and trousers that were too short for him had brought up a tray containing a cold Czech beer and a bottle of Scotch, and left the room with a hefty tip, Laszlo first poured Logan two fingers of Scotch and then delicately half filled a glass with beer for himself. As he raised his glass to Logan and watched the American down more than half the measure, he asked himself—not for the first time—how a man like Logan Halloran had ever found his way into the circle of Burt Miller. He seemed so obvious, he lacked so much finesse—and he was clearly a man who had worn the thread that attached him to any clear, guiding purpose very thin indeed. In some respects he was ideal, in fact, from Laszlo's point of view. He was a shell, an empty vessel who put his value only on what he could give, on what knowledge he possessed and on how well he could impress his peers. He was a man Laszlo viewed as satisfactorily on the edge—but this only mattered if he possessed anything of value.

Logan sloshed some more whisky into the glass and glanced briefly back through the window, as if looking for an answer in the bustle below or in the deep calm of the sea beyond. But he looked back at once and drank greedily. The information he possessed, which should be making him feel like some master of the universe, only made him feel ill, hollow. He suddenly wished Burt were here and not this Frenchman, whom he didn't like, but he was afraid, too, of his own feeling of being less than Burt. And Theo had as good as said that he would restore Logan to his once-important and highly respected role within the CIA. So perhaps that was his goal today.

As if his self-loathing hadn't dragged him low enough already, he summoned up the masochistic thoughts of Anna that had plagued him now for two years and they tugged him still lower. He'd betrayed her once, was it so difficult to betray her again? He'd had her for one night in an apartment in New York. He wouldn't say she had exactly given herself to him—it was more the other way round. She'd taken him, dominated the occasion, used him for sex. She'd practically said as much to him before they'd had sex. And then, within days, she had discovered his previous betrayal from before either of them had ever met. Feelings of desire and disgust, anger and inadequacy swirled in his mind as they always did when he thought of her; so confident, efficient, so effortlessly cool— and so cold towards him. He turned to Laszlo.

'Miller is conducting an operation here. In Sevastopol,' he said.

'What is the operation?' Laszlo asked.

'I don't know. The Ukrainian secret service is involved. And so is Anna Resnikov.' He'd said it. He felt a temporary wave of relief come over him.

'Resnikov?' Laszlo said, and Logan saw that he had caught the Frenchman's interest. 'Here? Now?'

'Yes.'

'She would be a fine gift for our friends in the Kremlin.'

Logan walked over to the table by the bed and scribbled with a pen he took from his jacket pocket on a sheet of hotel paper. 'There,' he said, giving it to Laszlo. 'That's where Burt Miller's team is holed up. It's to the east of the city.'

'She's there?'

'I've seen her only briefly, at a distance. But that's where Cougar's people are.' He drank and filled the glass, but he felt the drink was doing nothing to help him.

Laszlo stood and pocketed the piece of paper. He walked over to the window. Standing right next to Logan, he looked sideways at the American. 'And I thought you only worked for money,' he said.

Logan felt the crushing effect of this deliberate insult reach into the pit of his stomach like a knife. He summoned up what remained of his tattered opinion of himself and looked back at the Frenchman. 'I expect a different sort of reward from your people,' he said. 'And from the Russians.'

'And what is that?' Laszlo said sarcastically. 'The Légion d'honneur? Hero of the Russian Federation?'

Logan wanted to scream 'Respect!' back into the Frenchman's face, but all he saw in Laszlo's eyes was contempt.

'Why not?' was all he replied. 'But you won't find her on your own,' he added. 'You need me.'

'Then we'll make a deal,' Laszlo replied. 'I'm sure we and the Russians will reward you financially when we hand her over to them. Very handsomely indeed.'

He stepped away from the window.

Logan drank more steadily from the glass. He felt a sense of power now that smothered everything. Maybe the drink was steadying his nerves.

'What do you need, Logan?' Laszlo said. 'What can we provide you with that will ensure her delivery?'

'I'll tell you when the time comes,' he replied. 'In the meantime, don't scare them away from the address I gave you. Put up a watch, not the Russians, but the French. We don't want the Russians taking all the glory, do we? She's smart and very deadly. I'll tell you when the time is best to take her.'

He had taken the first step, but he hadn't given her away. That power still lay in his hands.

Laszlo sat down again on the bed and made a call. He decided he couldn't leave Logan alone now. The man needed watching. He had the feeling that Logan wasn't being entirely open and that once he was out of his sight he might even change his mind. The American's skittering motives were evident in his every movement, and in the partial revelation he'd just made.

He spoke fast into the mobile and Logan listened to him ordering up a surveillance team from Kiev to be despatched at once to Sevastopol. He then called Paris and Logan heard him talking briefly to Plismy, and heard Plismy's growl in the background. 'Every urgency' was how Laszlo left it. Then when he'd clicked the phone shut, the Frenchman looked up at him and smiled his smooth smile.

'Why don't we have some lunch sent up here?' he said. 'We have until this evening before we can stake out this house.'

Logan didn't reply.

CHAPTER THIRTY

The news that Logan had gone missing was conveyed to Larry and the team within hours of him failing to show up at the *Cougar*. The ship was by now laying at anchor in the Dardanelles, waiting for permission to pass through the Sea of Marmara and then into the Bosphorus and the Black Sea.

Later, according to Bob Dupont, it was as if Burt seemed to have factored in Logan's disappearance. 'He almost seemed to welcome it,' Dupont reported to the Cougar internal affairs committee after the events that were to follow. 'It was as if a decision were now made, written in stone, and there was no turning back.'

Burt personally put through the call to the villa in Sevastopol. The message was curt. Using the code name for Logan, Burt told Larry that Logan had 'gone on holiday' and it was likely 'he wouldn't be back'. Larry was furious. After the call, he stormed around the villa, cursing Logan—and Burt for ever trusting him in the first place—'and again, for Chrissakes!'—until Lucy pointed out that they had no time for displays of emotion.

Larry, Lucy, Adam and Grant had cleared out from the villa within twenty minutes of Burt's call. The house was swept of prints, the garbage and any extraneous possessions burned, until no trace remained of their visit. The team was now heading up towards the mountains behind the city where they would be out of contact from the *Cougar* except for two times a day, morning and evening, when one of them went back into the city to make or receive a report. But it added to the strains and difficulties of the operation and made Larry madder with Logan than he had ever been. 'I should have broken him two years ago,' he commented, 'when we found out what he'd done to Anna back then.'

But before they had left the area's mobile network and entered the first of the canyons, Burt put through another call to Larry who had by now mastered his fury.

Again in code, Burt conveyed the message he had apparently been waiting to receive before the *Cougar* entered the Black Sea. It held an importance for Burt that was a mystery to Larry and even to Dupont who, as ever, concealed his frustrations with Burt's methods. The message was simple, just a date. 'It's the first of May,' Burt told him. And it was the date of the planned assault on the *Pride of Corsica*. 'This has great significance,' Burt added to impress Larry in an unusual outburst of explanation. 'I believe it is the day we, too, need to act.' But act in what way, Burt did not reveal. His explanation of the significance alone was judged by him to be enough. 'Just tell Anna,' Burt said, and abruptly ended the communication. There were to be no questions.

It was afternoon by the time the four members of the team, kitted out now as campers, entered the canyon which Anna had made her base. When they arrived, it was agreed they should move on; a change of camp every two days. That way they would keep apart from others and the curiosity they might conceivably arouse. Larry also judged that, in order to avoid the park rangers who occasionally came into the park to check if

374

campers had the correct licences, they should decamp to a more remote place where there were no footpaths. On a satellite map provided by Cougar he'd already found a narrow defile, with a seasonal stream, that was difficult to reach and even more difficult to negotiate. But it was far enough away from anywhere that they would be able to have a fire here. The nights were still cold in the mountains and the temperature had gone below freezing two days before.

When Larry informed Anna of the date of the assault, she walked away from the new camp for half an hour to be on her own. She seemed to be calculating the time between now and the assault—just three days—and to need this time now, alone, before making a decision that would turn out to be irrevocable.

'What's so important about the date?' Larry asked her when she returned.

'I don't know yet,' she replied. 'Just that it's when they'll make their move.'

'The Russians?' Larry asked, and took her silence to be an affirmative.

But she explained no further and when she announced in the early evening that she was going to the city, and that she was going alone, Larry guessed that it was to rendezvous with Balthasar.

'I should be there,' he said. 'There's too much risk. We don't know if he's sincere.'

'He's had the chance to betray me,' she answered.

'That doesn't mean he won't now,' he replied. 'We know nothing about him.'

'I know enough,' she replied. Then added, 'I have to take the risk. There's no time left.'

And whether Anna had any loss of nerve beneath her cool exterior, Larry couldn't tell. 'It's as if she dares them to take her,' he said to the others after she'd left, and as he settled into a night of wakefulness and tension that he didn't share with her. He took on, in a closely adoptive way, the anxious feelings he thought she should have in the current circumstances, and he tramped around the perimeter of the camp until dawn rose. 'Worrying makes him calmer,' Lucy said to the others. 'He wouldn't know what to do without anxiety. It fills some hole in him.'

By the time Anna descended into the city, darkness had fallen. She walked away from the embankment by the city's harbours and kept to the smaller roads above it. She was unwittingly within two hundreds yards of Logan's hotel at one point and she continued up the hill to a small café bar which was her rendezvous with Balthasar at nine twenty-five every evening if they could both make it.

She saw Balthasar sitting in an alcove at the far end of the bar. He looked as composed as she felt, sipping occasionally at a cup of coffee, a local newspaper opened in front of him, the pages of which he turned as if he were reading it. He was like the other occupants of the bar, just another solitary man at the end of a day's work and comfortable with being alone. She sat down in a seat opposite him and ordered a coffee.

'The date is the first of May,' she said.

'I found out the same thing this afternoon,' he told her. 'From our side.'

'Then that's when we can expect something to happen in Sevastopol. According to Miller.'

376

'I agree,' he replied.

He picked up her hand suddenly in his and appeared to study it, but it was his own hand feeling hers that was his 'vision' of it. 'You have a great tendency to independence, Anna,' he said, running his thumb between her thumb and forefinger. 'We're alike in that way. How is it we've spent so much of our lives doing the bidding of others?'

'It takes time,' she said, 'to overturn a lifetime.'

And then he said, 'It's my birthday. The first of May. A good time for change. To close the book on my beginnings.'

And then they paid for their drinks and left the bar to walk up the hill further from the port, he sometimes holding her hand, she watching the long slope of his step or the back of his brown neck as they walked up a narrow stone stairway. Neither of them spoke. Once, he stopped and turned to her and put his hand on her cheek. 'I've a lot to thank you and your mother for,' he said, but he turned and walked on before she could reply.

When they reached the Trinity Church with an ancient, round, ruined wall tower on a small cliff above it, which was called Kalamita, they both turned and she surveyed the city below. For a long while, neither of them spoke. The lit dockyards were spread below them. The *Moskva* was still moored at the end of the main quay, and the train that contained the submarine batteries waited like a sleeping monster further down the same quay.

'Wait for me up here,' Balthasar said at last. 'I have one thing to do this evening. My contact at the base is expecting me to check in. I must see him, even more so now. We need to find what is out of the ordinary about the first of May.'

He let go of her hand. She watched him standing and apparently watching the sea. Then he turned to her. 'Don't think that I won't come back alone,' he said, 'but I don't need to tell you that, I hope,' and then he turned to retrace their steps to the city.

*　　　*　　　*

There was a bar on the embankment where the Russian sailors went. The Ukrainians tended to go to another one, further along the front, since fighting between the two had become a regular occurrence. Military police were evident on the stone embankment leaning against motorbikes or chatting on the wall. An uneasy agreement between Moscow and Kiev had been reached in order to keep the peace.

Balthasar flashed his KGB identification at two Russian marines who stood guard at the door. They saw its 'Special Purposes' elite stamp and the implication was immediately noted. 'One of you come with me,' Balthasar said.

The inside of the bar was noisy and close, the smell of beer and men and smoke mingling in a wash of stale air. Music was playing loudly in the background. For a moment Balthasar felt disoriented, the noise and crush of people interfering with his fine instincts.

'Is there a table at the back?' he said. The marine walked away a little, then came back and said to follow him.

When he was seated, Balthasar dismissed the man. He sat still, collecting his hidden senses, and

378

began to form a mental picture of the mass of sailors around him. A waitress came and he ordered a beer, sitting at the edge of his seat, his antennae working overtime until he felt he could comfortably 'see' the layout of the men and the bar's interior. Then he sat back and waited, taking a short sip of beer, careful not to draw the attention of anyone.

At just after 10.30 he felt someone sit down opposite him. There was a coded greeting, softly spoken, which he returned. It was all correct, as it should be, as it had been on three occasions already before. He sensed his contact's mind and began to focus on the man's thoughts and behaviour. The man was scared of him, Balthasar noted, but he also felt a thread of contempt to be deferring to a blind man. He couldn't understand Balthasar's importance. It made little sense to him, and by now it was late in the evening, he didn't want to be here. He was tired, perhaps. The man was bored, Balthasar realised. There was nothing much happening in Sevastopol and there hadn't been since the early 1990s when the nuclear submarine bunkers had been closed and then reopened as a tourist attraction, and as the steady decline of the Russian fleet continued, apparently without concern to the Kremlin. Earlier in the day, in fact, Balthasar had noted that there were just two modern warships in the port, the *Moskva*, an aircraft carrier built at the beginning of the 1990s, and the *Lazarev*, a destroyer built just before, and two submarines. The rest of the fleet was past its usefulness.

'Your superiors at The Forest want to know why they haven't received the go-ahead from you,' his contact stated with a hint of defensive aggression. 'What's the problem?'

'The group is suspicious, that's all,' Balthasar replied. 'They're worried that taking money may link them to something undesirable.'

'As it undoubtedly will—but only you people know what. Why do they think that?'

'Maybe they're just cautious.'

'And maybe something else.'

'They haven't survived this far without being careful,' Balthasar replied. 'The Qubaq are a clean organisation and they want to hang on to that reputation.'

'There's been a change of plan. The payments need to be made on the second of May,' the contact said. 'That's four days' time. Not before and not after. The second of May exactly. We need account numbers and we need a document from them that requests the money be paid.'

'I always said that a document was unnecessary,' Balthasar replied. 'The money could be simply paid into their accounts without them even knowing. They're still implicated.'

'Nevertheless, The Forest wants it done this way. They want it to look like an approach was made. That ties it up neatly. No one can deny it afterwards.'

Balthasar didn't reply. He sipped his beer thoughtfully and waited.

'So when are you going to overcome their caution?' the contact said impatiently. 'It's a matter of days, we haven't any leeway.'

'What's so special about the second of May?' Balthasar replied slowly.

'It's the first of May that's special,' the contact

said. 'The payment on the day after is crucial so that it looks like a reward.'

A reward for what? Balthasar wondered. But he didn't pursue his line of questioning. He felt the man lean in across the table.

'I spoke to the fleet commander this morning,' the contact said. 'In Moscow, Putin is holding the biggest May Day Parade since 1989. And here? Nothing. The Black Sea fleet might as well not exist. All they're doing on the first of May are special drills on land and maintenance work in the harbours.'

Balthasar shrugged. 'Oh yes?'

The contact didn't say anything further. Balthasar's head was thumping from the music, he couldn't focus as he was used to doing. But he knew this would be his only chance, to keep the contact talking.

'There are special operations in the harbour that day,' Balthasar said matter-of-factly. 'They're a celebration of Russian power in themselves, surely.'

'You'd know,' the contact replied.

'And the Fleet Commander would know most of all.'

'All right,' the contact replied. 'So you know all about it. On the first of May they're switching off all the sonar in the harbour for an hour at midday. Something to do with maintenance on the sonars, they say, but I don't believe it.'

'Why not? It seems perfectly logical to me,' Balthasar replied.

There was a further silence. Then Balthasar felt the contact lean in towards him again.

'What am I to tell them at The Forest?' he said.

'Tell them that arrangements will be made. The account number, the document—they'll have everything they want by the end of the day on the first of May.'

When the man had gone Balthasar sat and sipped the beer in the now half-full glass. He listened and with his acute hearing picked up conversations. He felt his sensory powers begin to strengthen and a map of the bar room and its occupants—their feelings and thoughts—began to take shape in his mind. After a while, by now thoroughly oriented, he rose from his seat and walked carefully past groups of men and to the side of the bar on the left where there were tables. He stood and listened to two or three conversations at different tables and then went to the middle one. He stood over it, felt the eyes and attention of its occupants slowly turn towards him, and took out his KGB identity card. They saw the special clearance and the note at the foot of the card that all knew—though it didn't state so—as the imprimatur of Department S.

Balthasar felt an intake of breath from the four men at the table and then felt their attention was completely caught by his presence.

'Which of you is with the PDSS?' he asked.

There was a slight pause. Finally one of the men spoke. 'The two of us here,' he said, and pointed to the man sitting next to him on the bench. In his mind's eye Balthasar formed the picture of the two of them.

'I'd like to talk to the two of you alone,' he said. Then turning to the other two men on his side of the table, he said, 'Excuse me. I'll just be a few minutes.'

382

He felt the two men drag themselves to their feet. A thumping Russian dance track reverberated across the bar as Balthasar took a seat opposite the remaining two men. He sipped his beer again and relaxed back into the seat. The PDSS were the special *spetsnaz* group of frogmen that every naval harbour possessed. They were there to protect Sevastopol's harbour. Once, there had been submarine nets, but they had been taken away in the 1990s. Now the PDSS and the fixed sonars in the harbour and in the sea lanes leading from the Black Sea into Sevastopol were the port's main defences.

'I'm here for the first of May,' Balthasar said. 'Will you all be on duty?'

There was a pause. The men were reluctant to divulge their orders to someone they didn't know, even someone as important as a colonel from Department S.

'No,' one of the men grudgingly replied at last.

'No sonars and no frogmen,' Balthasar said. 'My department thinks that's rash.'

'You're from the SVR,' the second man said. 'That's your view, maybe. But we're with the GRU. Nothing's going to happen in an hour with them switched off.'

'All the sonars—passive and active—all the way down the coast?' Balthasar said. 'It's very unusual.'

'Unprecedented. But those are our orders and you have no jurisdiction with the GRU.'

'General Antonov should know,' Balthasar said, and felt the men stiffen at the mention of the GRU boss. 'It's irregular.'

'I imagine he already knows,' the first man said.

'What will you be doing on the first of May?'

Balthasar said.

'Screwing and drinking, most likely.' The second man laughed. 'What's your business here, anyway? Why don't you get lost?'

But Balthasar had got to his feet. 'You may find your orders will change,' he said.

'Not by you, they won't,' the first man replied.

Balthasar walked away to the bar and finished his drink as his mind turned over the possibilities. He felt one of the PDSS men brush past quite close to him and take the attention of another man at the far end of the bar. He felt the eyes of both these men fix on him. Then he put down the glass, empty now, and walked out of the bar into the street.

After walking for thirty yards or so, he felt three men following behind him.

CHAPTER THIRTY-ONE

'Now listen carefully, Logan. Eric is a veteran of the war in Algeria. He pulled out countless fingernails there, didn't you, Eric?' Laszlo paused and surveyed the bound, gagged and terrified Logan who sat upright in a wooden chair, his eyes wild and his head raging with whisky and fear. 'It may be forty years ago,' Laszlo continued, 'but he's lost none of his old skills. And believe me, the fingernails were the soft end of his talents.' Logan's eyes rolled sideways at the hulking figure of Eric who stood over him like an attack dog, the sleeves of his T-shirt rolled up over his shoulders and his big fists clamped together so that the knuckles were white. 'Claude is much younger, maybe even stronger, and has more—' Laszlo paused—'more modern techniques, shall we say. And he's even more effective. Claude has spent a great deal of his life being punished and now— once we found him and took him under the wing of the DGSE—now he likes to deal it out. Get his own back.' Laszlo stood up and walked over to a window. The curtain was drawn but he stood as if he were gazing out at something. He'd changed his suit since the three of them had got Logan out of the hotel three hours before, hanging half-drunk between Claude and Eric and fully stunned. Now Laszlo was wearing a crisp, dark-blue, fitted designer suit of the kind worn by multimillionaire footballers. 'OK, do it,' he said.

He heard the blows raining in on Logan and stayed turned to the curtain. No sound came from the gagged figure of Logan, but the snap and thud of knuckles on flesh and bone.

'That's enough,' Laszlo said, and turned when the beating had stopped.

He saw agony in Logan's eyes. 'Untie the gag,' he said.

The two embassy security men carefully undid the knot, one handling the gag, the other ready to clamp his hand over Logan's mouth. But Logan hung in the chair as if suspended from the ceiling and his breath came in agonised rasping pants followed by a death rattle noise from the bottom of his throat.

'That's what happens if you do nothing,' Laszlo said. 'If you fail to give me what I'm asking for, however, it will be a lot worse. Got it?'

Logan couldn't speak. A long, low moan

escaped from his lips, but the job Eric and Claude had done on him was expert and there were no marks to his face. Sweat poured down him and he'd urinated in his trousers.

'Give him some water,' Laszlo ordered.

Claude held a bottle to Logan's lips and poured it as if he were filling a bucket until Logan choked and screamed, but the sound was simply the noise of vomit and water and whisky spilling down his chin.

'So,' Laszlo said. 'Why did you give me a false address? Where's the right one?'

Logan groaned.

'We haven't got time to stroke the information from you,' Laszlo warned. 'Where's the house? Where's Resnikov?'

'That was the house,' Logan rasped falteringly. 'I swear. That's where they were.'

'But they aren't there, are they?' Laszlo snarled now.

'Then they must have left. What was there?' he said, looking at Eric with terrified eyes. 'You must have seen something. Were there signs of anything burned? Did you check the rental agency? You'll find it was rented, but I don't know under what name.' Logan talked in staccato sentences, and then repeated himself, anything to keep in the game, to keep them from hitting him again.

'Well?' Laszlo said to Eric.

'There was a metal barrel outside at the back,' Eric said reluctantly. 'Signs of stuff being torched, I'd say.'

'And the rental company?'

'It was too late by the time we got there. We'll have to find out in the morning.'

It was eleven o'clock in the evening, according to Laszlo's watch which he looked at now. The watch was a Piaget, Logan noted blearily, the same type that Putin wore, he thought feebly.

'You have a few more hours of comfort in that chair, then,' Laszlo said to him. 'But then the hammer really drops if I find you've been lying.' He looked at Eric and Claude. 'Don't hurt him too much,' he said, and left the room.

CHAPTER THIRTY-TWO

When Balthasar had left her, Anna didn't remain up on the cliff at Kalamita as they'd agreed. She watched Balthasar descend the hill past the church and then, some while later, she walked down the hill herself, also past the Trinity Church, until she found a place where she could find reasonable concealment for herself and where she could study his return. There was a wartime memorial park halfway between the church and the embankment by the harbour. From here she would be able to see him coming back up towards Kalamita and confirm that he was alone.

At just after 11.30 she saw him ascending the road. He seemed alone but then, a hundred yards behind him, she saw three men. When they walked under a street light, she was certain they were special forces or KGB operatives. They wore light-blue berets and shoulder flashes—VDV airborne uniforms—but she was sure they weren't regular forces. They had the same unit patches as the Russians had worn back at the barn in January, and the patches were cover, she guessed; they were using a locally based unit's insignia.

At first she could barely believe it—that Balthasar should have tricked her so well—but then she realised that the men weren't following him with his approval but out of suspicion.

She saw him stop near the entrance to the park. He knew he was being followed, she saw. Then she saw further down the hill the men melting into shadows away from the street lights. He'd half turned and then she knew he was aware of their presence. To her consternation, he walked on, turning into the entrance of the park and towards a memorial stone a hundred yards away from where she was concealed behind a cabin. The men were closing now behind him.

Anna drew the Contender handgun from inside her jacket and screwed a silencer into place.

When Balthasar reached the stone monument he sat down on a step and took a packet from his pocket. She couldn't see clearly but it looked like a paper bag with food in it. He held it in his right hand and removed an apple. He began to eat the apple, still holding the paper bag, and facing directly towards the entrance.

The men walked abreast now in the open space of the park. They were a yard or so apart and had evidently decided to no longer track him from a distance, but to make their approach. She saw the sides of their faces, and the positions of their heads told her they were staring straight at him. The distance closed. Balthasar sat perfectly still apart from the movement of the apple between his left hand and his mouth. He ate it in a slow, measured way, chewing each bite with great care. Down from the direction of the harbour, a bell chimed midnight. The air was still and—down here in the city—retained some of the warmth from the day even now.

Anna came out from behind the cabin and stealthily walked at an angle from behind the men towards where Balthasar sat. There was no cover except the thin protection of a wood and iron park bench halfway between her and the monument. She decided to make for the bench and crouch behind it. But she knew now she was committed. There was no way back without exposing herself. Attack was possible, defence almost out of the question. She reached the bench, crouched behind the short end of it, leaving its full length between her and the men, and watched them now approach Balthasar and stand a yard away from him in a semicircle that blocked his escape. He put down the apple. One of the men had asked a question and drawn a handgun. Slowly Balthasar put his hand inside his jacket and withdrew his card identifying him as an SVR colonel.

The second man took out a small torch and also received the card, which he proceeded to study in the torch's beam. The first man held the gun, hanging lightly and looking as if it wasn't trained anywhere in particular. The third man just stood, arms by his sides, completing the semicircle. Balthasar picked up the apple from the step and stood up.

Anna watched a conversation ensue, sharp, abrupt questions from the man who still held Balthasar's ID and slower responses from Balthasar. The third man now held a phone in his hand and was tapping a number into it slowly.

389

Anna watched Balthasar slowly raise the paper bag in his right hand towards the man with the gun. It happened very slowly, a simple gesture, the offer of something in the bag. Instinctively, the man leaned slightly over the bag and then pulled back as if realising an instinct had got the better of training. As he did so, Balthasar's hand that held the bag shot straight up towards the man's neck. Anna heard a strangled cry and raised the Contender on to the back of the bench.

She saw a knife flash, perhaps just in the light of the moon, its blade swinging away and the knife handle wrapped in the paper bag still clutched in Balthasar's hand. The blade had swung upwards with great force, cutting the Adam's apple in two and slicing the man's neck from just above the chest to the throat. Before the man had started to topple, Anna fired a single shot at the third man who was reaching for a gun. He dropped instantly. The one who held the ID card was suddenly distracted from drawing a gun of his own as he saw his colleague drop like a stone. In an instant, Balthasar flashed the blade sideways and sliced his neck halfway to the man's spine.

There was a gurgling sound from the ground and one of the men thrashed his legs for a minute. Then there was absolute silence. Anna and Balthasar stood frozen in position for a second that stretched into ten before Anna stood up from behind the bench and walked towards the monument. When she arrived, she just looked at Balthasar's face. He still held the paper bag in one hand, the knife protruding from it, and the apple in the other. Slowly he raised his left hand and took a last bite, before putting the core in his pocket.

'Now I know you're real,' she said.

'You didn't before?'

'No. I'm not like you, Balthasar. I have to see things.'

They carried the three bodies across the grass towards a heap of composting grass from the previous year. Anna began to shovel it away and placed the first body on the ground, the other two on top of it. Then she shovelled the compost back over the bodies.

CHAPTER THIRTY-THREE

Anna and Balthasar sat on a high rock above the canyon camp. The dawn was rising from across the Kerch Straits and Russia and, below them, the derricks lining Sevastopol's dockyards and harbours and the superstructures of warships were catching the first light in the city. For a long while they sat in silence and watched the coastline revealed on another clear blue day.

On their exit from the city into the mountains neither spoke, but both were thinking of the implications of the dead men buried below them. There would be a massive manhunt if the Russians persuaded their Ukrainian allies in government that it was necessary.

But most of all, it was the intelligence that Balthasar had brought back with him from the bar that preoccupied their minds; the sonar in the harbours and their approaches being cut off in two days' time and the standing-down of special forces frogmen. At last, Balthasar broke the silence.

'Miller is right,' he said. 'The fake attack is going to happen down there on the first of May. The payment on the second is to be the supposed reward for the attack.'

Anna looked at the hulks of warships dotting the bays. Then she paused at the aircraft carrier, *Moskva*, and the other relatively new ship and submarines.

'They won't want to damage anything that's worth something to them,' she said. 'They'll stage this attack on one of the ships that's past its usefulness. And that will be the cause for Russian anger, their casus belli. The destruction of a useless ship.'

'Provocation followed by its reaction,' Balthasar said. 'They set up the attack themselves, then say they are under attack. It's the way things are done. Our terror experts know exactly how to make it work and how to make it look.'

'And then?' Anna said.

'Then the Kremlin will demand that Crimea becomes Russian again. In order to protect its own interests. After that? I give Ukraine itself a few more years at most of independence. Putin is binding the country ever closer to Russia with economic ties. It's the end of Western ambitions for Ukraine to join Western Europe. It's the end of Ukrainian nationalism and independence from Moscow.'

She turned to look at him. 'You must get out now,' she said. 'You're the only witness.'

'And you?' he said, returning her gaze with sightless eyes.

'I have to finish things here,' she replied. 'I've made a deal with Taras.'

He didn't ask her what it was, the deal. He merely looked back towards the sea and felt the sun's first warmth on the side of his face. 'Then I'll stay too,' he said. 'Until it's finished. We'll take our chances together.'

She studied the side of his face. It was a new experience, to feel a man looking at her, when he couldn't see her with his eyes. She felt the novelty of being next to a man who didn't see how she looked but only felt her as a woman through some power that was inexplicable to her. The feeling was good and it made her strong. Her usual distrust of a man's motives in her presence was entirely absent. It was as if the twenty odd years since their last meeting at an orphanage in Damascus had never existed. A feeling of comfort, simplicity, inevitability even, invaded her mind and she didn't resist it. There was nothing about Balthasar that aroused her suspicions or defensiveness. It was the most natural feeling she ever remembered happening, more so even than with Finn, whose early relationship with her had been one of recklessness. There was no recklessness about sitting beside this man. She felt that they had been destined to meet again.

'Why, Balthasar?' she asked him. 'Why now? After doing so much destruction to Russia's enemies, why did you decide to come over now?'

He didn't speak for a moment. Then said, 'The necessities of acting for oneself develop only over time. At first, events and other people dominate our lives. It was the same with you, I believe. We do a job—it doesn't matter what the job is, even. It's a life moulded to other people's rules. And, like you, I was good, very good, at my job. That

393

made me question it less. And I didn't stop to ask whether I believed what I was doing. The job too was exciting,' he admitted. He bent his head. 'That perhaps is the most shameful excuse, the compulsion of excitement. But when you've done the same thing for many years, it suddenly loses the compulsion. You become a machine. If you're lucky or merely not entirely stupid, you begin to question the machine-like qualities of who you've become. Suddenly, it's as if the child in you returns, the voice that speaks for itself and not for others. You want that again and not the machine.' He turned towards her. 'And then treason is easy,' he said. 'People become traitors to their country for many reasons; excitement plays a part in that too. But with me it was the futility, the futility of doing something I didn't want to do and had never really wanted to do. I will do this one thing for the West; be a witness to what is happening here. But I'm not changing sides, just being on my own side.'

He stopped and by now the sun had broken over the bays below them.

'You have a plan, Anna. I know it,' he said.

'Yes.'

'Are you going to tell me what it is or do I have to tell you?'

She laughed. 'I'm sure you have a very good idea, Balthasar.'

'You're right.'

'If the Russians are planning to blow up one of their own ships, why don't we do it too?' she said. 'But with a ship that really matters to them.' She stood up. 'It's time to get some sleep. We only have a few hours now. Then we'll explain to Larry and the others. After that I have to square everything with Taras. I need his help.'

They descended into the canyon along a pathless scree slope that finally brought them up above the camp and then followed the stream until they saw tents. But it was Larry who saw them first and who looked with alarm at the presence of Balthasar.

'It's OK, Larry,' she said. 'We'll all work together until we get out of here. Where's the *Cougar*?'

'It's to the west of the Crimea. About sixty miles away. Along this coast between here and Odessa.'

'Good. Wake me in a couple of hours.' She looked at Balthasar. 'You can sleep where you wish,' she said.

The invitation wasn't lost on him or on Larry, who turned away in confusion and perhaps frustration.

'I know,' Balthasar stated.

Anna laughed. 'Of course. Of course you know,' she said.

Balthasar followed her into her tent.

After two hours, Larry called through the flap of the tent and she emerged first. Balthasar followed a while later. Lucy and Adam were making breakfast over a charcoal fire, reduced to ashes in order to limit the smoke. They ate in silence and then Anna laid out the plan.

'This depends on Taras?' Larry said and failed to conceal his deep scepticism.

'It does,' she replied impassively.

'You trust him that much?'

'I believe what he says about this, yes.'

'Why?'

'His interests coincide with ours. If he helps us,

we help him. Don't forget, he has to believe what I told him too. There's a mutual gain.'

'Well, OK,' Larry said. 'We don't have nearly enough ammunition. Not for what you're planning.'

'I think plenty will become available,' she replied.

CHAPTER THIRTY-FOUR

At five minutes past two on the morning of 1 May, when darkness was reaching its greatest intensity over the sea, the American frigate *Lafayette* was exactly fifty miles to the west of the *Pride of Corsica* and on a bearing of thirty-nine degrees. The engines were now idle and rubber boats were being lowered from stanchions on the deck into the calm waters. In each boat there were eight marine commandos and there were five boats in all. Four helicopters waited, with airborne commandos milling around them, waiting themselves for orders to board. They would leave when the boats were well on their way.

The majority of the boats were manned by British Special Boat Service teams and it was the British who had the command of the operation in a compromise between Moscow and Washington. One boat was under the individual control of Russian special forces and the other under American control, but the operation was planned by the British and all were agreed that the British should command the assault, from the sea and the air. At sixty knots—which it was agreed could be achieved in the calm waters—the boats would reach the *Pride of Corsica* in just under an hour. The helicopters' departure was timed to be ten minutes before the boats reached the target vessel and the assault would come from the sea and air simultaneously. Three boats were to approach the starboard side of the target, drawing any fire in the priceless seconds before they boarded. The other two would remain out of sight and below radar and approach the port side as the choppers swooped in. The plan was to split the defenders' attention three ways.

The boats began their rapid passage across the black waters, planing at speeds that sometimes went over the required sixty knots and sometimes under, but always maintained as close to the average they were aiming for as possible. When they judged they were within ten minutes of the strike, there would be a radio call to the *Lafayette* and the helicopters would leave.

The British teams were made up mainly of M Squadron members, the SBS maritime counter terrorism squadron, of whom the Black Group provided one officer and three men and there were two members of 14 Intelligence Unit, briefed on what to look for, assuming the assault was successful. They were all trained in multiple weapons use and hand-to-hand fighting at the highest level and were all practitioners of Brazilian ju-jitsu.

It was two days after the new moon, and the darkness and below-the-radar approach of the rubber boats enabled them to reach within two hundred yards of the *Pride of Corsica* before anyone on board the ship saw them. The boats

397

swerved violently in see-saw motions over the remaining distance to avoid providing a steady target and as soon as they'd drawn aside—so far without a shot being fired—pulleyed abseil equipment was fired over the decks of the vessel and the first four-man team shot to the deck level. The other two boats attacked simultaneously from the port side and then the helicopters were heard and the deck was suddenly flooded with intense spotlights that blinded the defenders and left the attackers for the moment in shadow.

Lines fell from the helicopters and marines abseiled down in seconds. The defenders had drawn towards the bow of the ship, up towards the bridge, when the helicopter and boat teams opened an intense burst of fire that ripped the night apart. 'It was like a firing squad,' an SBS officer was quoted later as saying. 'They were up against the white steel wall of the bridge, spotlights on them, in a row and hands over their faces. Some had their hands in the air. They were surrendering. They had no guns that we could see, there was no return of fire.'

After a minute of firing, one of the helicopters landed on a deck space cleared by the assault teams. Then all fell silent as the other choppers flew to stand off the ship and await instructions.

Above the silence came the groans of the wounded.

Two teams of four descended steps into the ship's belly and began a section-to-section search. The captain was turfed out of bed and a few bemused crewmen were similarly awakened who hadn't already heard the firing. All were brought to the deck, hands strapped in plastic cuffs behind them. It was a scratch crew, only five in all. The rest of the ship's occupants—twelve in all—were on the deck and all but two were dead. As the SBS teams and their American and Russian counterparts stripped masks from the faces of the few who had managed to don them in time, and looked at the unmasked dead and wounded, there was a stunned silence, the occasional shout of a man's name, curses and swearing that rose in anger and distress as the identities of the defenders who had put up no defence was revealed. In each case, faces were recognised by the British and the Americans as former colleagues in their own special forces, in one or two cases, friends. It was a massacre of their own. There were no Russians among the defenders. And it was noted later that none of the Russian *spetsnaz* present bothered to look at the faces of the dead and wounded.

The captain of the *Pride of Corsica* was interrogated in a chair on the deck while the teams searched the vessel and brought up five wooden crates from the hold. The captain repeated over and over that there was no cargo of a dangerous nature.

'Why the missile system? Why the helicopter?' The SBS interrogators were not sensitive in their methods. The captain was weeping, and repeating the same phrases over and over. The Russian special forces stood back and watched.

It was said by the captain and his crew that the bodyguards were a defence against pirates. But he didn't know, none of them knew, why they were there, why any defence against pirates was needed.

Eventually the SBS got tired of asking the same questions and the Americans moved in, without getting any more from the stricken captain than that he was a Filipino with five children back in Mindanao; that his crew were a scratch collection of individuals from a shipping agency. They finally finished with roughing him up as the crates were opened carefully with jemmies.

Inside the crates were boxes and the boxes contained bubble wrap and the bubble wrap contained nothing. Nothing at all. The *Pride of Corsica* was void of incriminating material. All it contained after the assault were five crew, the assault team and ten dead colleagues of the British and American assault force. Two others were saved.

Later, at the inquiry at which Theo Lish was the principal defender, it was asked why British and American special forces teams had been induced by the Russians to kill their own kind—albeit former colleagues—and why nothing was found on the *Pride of Corsica* that pointed to a terrorist or any other plot. Lish was able to come up with no adequate answer. Burt Miller, called as a witness, explained that he'd informed the CIA head that he believed the *Pride of Corsica* had been a bluff all along; that he'd tried to warn Lish, in fact. Miller regretted the loss of life—and the tragic mistake made on the morning of 1 May. But the central question to which Lish continued to flounder under questioning from the Senate Intelligence Committee, was why on Russian evidence alone the assault had been made at all.

CHAPTER THIRTY-FIVE

Anna sat at the far end of a cave at the foot of the cliff on the north shore of the city. Below her feet, the sea water lapped sluggishly at the rock. Where the sea ended, where she sat in the darkness of the cave, was also the final resting place of the harbour's detritus of oil and chemical waste, metal and plastic cans, polystyrene and fragments of wood and rope that created a six-inch scum on the lapping surface. The insignificant tides of the Black Sea never scoured the cave clean and the smell was one of vegetable and toxic rot and chemical and oil waste that over decades had stained the cave's walls in a black, glistening film. Drop a match in here, she thought, and the whole place would go up in flames.

She and Larry had descended from the part of town on the north shore after dark and then he'd left her. She'd watched the light grow at the tunnel's entrance as dawn rose across the heaving channel of the Sevastopolskaya Bukhta, listened to the horn of a ship that entered from the sea through the breakwaters of Sevastopol's perfect natural harbour, saw its surface lines as it cut through the channel into port—though the cave's low entrance obscured the superstructure—and listened to the tight chug of a fishing boat and the nerve-jangling cries of seagulls.

Now she fitted the aqualung with its de-breathing apparatus that would eliminate bubbles rising to the surface as it recycled her own oxygen. She fixed the full mask over her face and ensured the tight dry suit that concealed a Russian GRU uniform, the Contender handgun and two sticks of Semtex, was fastened into an airtight position. She checked her watch again. Then at midday exactly, she descended into the filthy slime of the cave's waste, sunk beneath it and swam towards the entrance of the cave.

It was a swim of just over two kilometres—at an angle across the channel—until she could come ashore on the long naval quay inside the Russian fleet's protected zone. Somewhere beneath the same waters where she swam she knew other divers were at work, Russian frogmen who had come to set off an explosion that would rend some unwanted fleet vessel apart and at the same time rend the uneasy peace between Russia and Ukraine that clung on in the Crimea.

The waters where she swam were dirty with industrial waste and visibility was low. That would be a help, if by some fluke she and they should cross paths.

All along the shores on the north and south of the Bukhta the fixed and passive sonars were now, she prayed, disabled.

She swam fast, looking at the compass on her arm from time to time. Accuracy at her landing point was crucial. There was a set of steps that descended from the nearest of the two quays she was heading for. They came down at a protected angle which meant that anyone surfacing at the foot of them was visible from only one viewpoint and that was a kilometre away as the crow flies, on the north shore. Unless someone was actually standing on the quay above where the steps emerged, it was the best hope of remaining undetected.

From a ship, the narrow entrance to the dockyards within the main harbour, and to which she was heading, was signalled by a cathedral tower and a monument on the western side of the entrance and a chimney on the eastern side, as well as the usual array of navigational marks, the illuminated reds and greens and whites that gave a vessel its position. But beneath the surface all she could rely on was the compass. If she missed the steps it would be a question of feeling along the walls of the quay until she found them.

She swam strongly and knew she'd entered the dockyards after fifteen minutes. It was a short distance from here to the end of the first of the quays that jutted out from the land into the deep water where big ships could dock. Then she reached the green slime of the quay wall and waited twenty feet beneath the surface while deciding whether to go left or right along the wall. She chose the left and was rewarded after twenty yards with the sight of stone steps that descended beneath the surface. She checked her watch. There were still forty minutes to go while the sonar remained inactive. She imagined that the frogmen would plant whatever device they were using and then get clear of the harbour and away. The explosion might not happen within the hour's planned lapse in security. But it wouldn't be long afterwards if it didn't.

She came as close to the surface as she dared and, through the water now lighter from the sun's glare, tried to spot any movement on the quay that betrayed a human presence nearby. After five minutes when she'd seen nothing move, no shape

403

or outline apart from the quay's wall, she came out on the bottom step above the surface. She took another quick look around, then stripped off the mask and aqualung, the dry suit and fins and, weighted with the gas bottle, watched them sink slowly into the grey water. Then she stood and walked up the steps towards the top of the quay.

When she was halfway up she heard a deafening explosion and stopped in momentary shock. Then she saw a ball of flame that reached thirty feet into the air. She crouched down, feeling the Contender digging into her ribs. She saw now that the explosion had come from the main channel, to the north of the dockyards through which she'd swum only minutes earlier. The victim of the blast was an old Russian naval vessel, anchored outside the dockyards. It was just as they'd thought when she and Balthasar had sat on the high bluff above the city.

Now she ran up the remaining steps on to the top of the quay. It was a piece of luck that they'd exploded the vessel now. There would be pandemonium and, in the confusion, it would make her task more easy. Immediately, sirens tore through the low hum of the city and klaxons began to scream their message here, inside the Russian fleet's highly protected zone.

She looked up along the quay towards the high steel gates that shut her in on the inside of the protected zone and unwanted visitors out. There she saw the train on its tracks that led along the quay and, at the end of the quay where the tracks ended, she saw the aircraft carrier *Moskva*, broadside on, its towering superstructure dead in line with the train tracks.

There were uniformed men running along the quay pointing at the stricken ship, shouting orders. She heard a man shout at her but she ran past and shouted an order in return. She kept running and was concealed in her speed by the desperate reactions of the few people left inside the protected zone. She reached the engine of the goods train and saw the twenty goods vans trailing behind it and carrying three hundred submarine batteries, most of which weighed half a ton each. With the weight of the train itself, there would be well over two hundred tons of weight.

She climbed into the cab. She heard shouting, but it wasn't directed at her. Not yet. She started the engine of the train and released the brake. Slowly it ground into action and began to rumble along the quay the quarter of a mile before the quay ended at the *Moskva*. Once it had reached nearly thirty miles an hour, she jammed the accelerator into place, crossed to the other side of the cab and flung herself out on that side where there was no one. All the people on the quay were on the other side of the train, watching the aftermath of the explosion.

Anna rolled hard on the unyielding concrete and got to her feet. Beside her the twenty goods vans were gathering speed and she heard the engine roaring with the strain of reacting to the jammed accelerator. She ducked down and ran to the far side of the quay, away from the train and the burning ship. She wanted to be far from the train when the last of the vans passed her so that she and the train's catastrophic run towards the *Moskva* were dissociated as far as possible. When the final van passed she saw that all the military personnel were now turned from the burning ship and watching in horror as the train reached forty, then fifty miles an hour and still kept adding speed.

She didn't watch but kept moving at a fast walk now towards the steel gates that protected the quay from intruders. She heard the smash as the train broke through the concrete buffers at the end of the track and then the squeal of tortured metal as it swung itself clear of the tracks and on to the bare concrete of the quay. It must be going at seventy or eighty miles an hour now, she thought, and increasing all the time. When she did stop so that, like all the others now on the quay, she was looking at the impending disaster, what she saw was two hundred tons or more of roaring steel crash into the superstructure of the aircraft carrier *Moskva* and keep on going. The train was like a massive bullet, the thickened steel of the ship's superstructure no match for its onslaught. It sheared the side of the superstructure away completely on the quayside and kept on boring into the ship until by the time it stopped half of the train was hanging into the harbour on the far side of the carrier and the engine finally exploded with the unrewarded effort of forward propulsion. The entire superstructure toppled and swayed and crashed over itself and on top of the train. Then a sheet of flame erupted from the bowels of the ship.

Anna turned away. She ran towards the steel gates, her right hand arming one of the Semtex tubes, her left waving the Contender. She hurled the explosive at the centre of the gates and rolled away to feel the flash of the explosion on her back and the searing pain of the heat that tore off the back of her uniform. She kept rolling behind a watch hut and gathered her breath. Then she leapt to her feet and ran through smoke and falling debris out of the protected zone. Behind her a ton of steel from one of the gates crashed to the ground and she was through.

The approaches to the gates were now a mass of troops and security personnel, military vehicles and fire trucks that raced towards the gates from the land side. She dodged in and out of them, losing herself in smoke and terrified humanity until she reached the embankment. There was the Ukrainian military ambulance, exactly where Taras had told her it would be. She ran towards it and stepped into the cab, discarding the jacket of her Russian GRU uniform and slipping on the jacket of a Ukrainian military medic. As she turned the ambulance she saw the aircraft carrier *Moskva* heave a huge sigh that released another wall of flame, then it keeled over to one side and rolled into ten metres of water.

CHAPTER THIRTY-SIX

From a window of a house in the foothills behind the city, Laszlo watched the pyrotechnic disaster unfold in the harbour below. First a rust bucket of a ship exploding in the main lane of the harbour, then the train hurtling towards the *Moskva* and the carrier's total destruction. In the moments before the train's impact with the carrier he focused on the train itself as it began its apocalyptic race to mutual destruction and from the window of the engine's cab he saw a figure hurl itself and land hard on the concrete quay. He saw the GRU cap roll away as the figure itself expertly went into a crouch and a roll to lessen the brutal impact. Then he saw the figure rise up, temporarily dazed and scraping her hair back under the cap and he knew it was her. His face twisted in fury and he shouted at Eric to get another set of binoculars from the table behind them and train it on the figure, running now, swerving along the quay towards the steel gates of the exit from the protected zone. Then Laszlo saw the explosion at the gates and furiously trained the binoculars on to the swirls of smoke billowing outside them to see in a patch of clearer vision, and still running through falling debris, the figure still there, and escaping.

When Eric had her in his sights, Laszlo told him to keep her there and to radio her movements. He unlocked a door into a back room, summoned Logan from the bed he was lying on and reading a newspaper, and half dragged him from the chair. Then he took a spare gun from his coat pocket and jammed it into Logan's hands.

'What's happened?' Logan said laconically. 'A nuclear attack?'

'This is your moment of glory, Logan,' Laszlo snarled. 'We have her. Follow me.'

The two men ran down the stairs to a Cherokee jeep outside. Claude started the engine, looked in surprise at the gun in Logan's hand, checked with Laszlo for instructions, and revved the jeep through the gears as they hurtled down the hill.

'To the harbour,' Laszlo screamed at him.

His radio crackled and Eric's voice came clear over the headpiece. 'Follow it as far as you can,' Laszlo shouted in return. 'Then follow us.'

The jeep raced around two curves in the steeply falling street to see the embankment ahead.

'It's a Ukrainian military ambulance,' Laszlo said, quieter now. 'And it's heading west.'

Once they were on to the embankment, Claude drove the jeep up on to pavements and on to the wrong side of the road, past oncoming military and fire vehicles until, at a distance of some four hundred yards, they saw the rear of the ambulance travelling at a steady speed towards the end of the harbour where the sea finally ended and abutted the city. It followed the curving road around towards the north side.

'Bring the other car,' Laszlo shouted into the radio to Eric again. 'She's going to the north side. Cut off the route from the top of the city if you have time. Keep your radio on.'

But by the time Eric had got the second car on to the road that descended at an angle above the embankment, the ambulance was round the corner of the harbour and heading at greater speed along the north side. Behind it, the jeep travelled fast enough to gain a little without alerting Anna to the fact that she was being followed.

Halfway around the north of the harbour, the ambulance took a sudden right turn, up a street that climbed away from the sea. The jeep followed and Laszlo radioed again to Eric, giving him the track of the ambulance.

The jeep was now two hundred yards away from the ambulance and Anna caught it in her mirror.

'She must be heading for the military hospital,' Logan said, bemused. 'Why do you think it's her? Why would she be driving an ambulance to the military hospital, for Chrissakes!'

'Never mind why. It's her. Eric saw her getting into it.'

'Unless there are two ambulances,' Logan replied.

But then, as the jeep began to gain again on the ambulance, he saw her hair free from the cap and knew it was her.

'Load up,' Laszlo said quietly. 'But shoot to wound, to disable, not to kill. The Russians want her alive.'

Ahead of the jeep, the ambulance swung to the left up the incline of a hairpin bend and suddenly it was broadside on to the following jeep. Logan saw Anna level the barrel of the Contender on to the ledge of the door and fire. There was an ear-splitting crack in the jeep. The bullet made a neat hole in the windscreen, the jeep veered violently to the right across the road and bounced against an earth bank, ricocheting back and twisting on itself so that by the time it reached the bend it was facing in the opposite direction to that in which it needed to go, the rear tyres squealing against tarmac and the smell of rubber rising into the car. Claude screamed at the wheel. His left arm hung uselessly by his side and he was fighting the spinning steering wheel using only his right hand.

Laszlo grabbed the wheel and steadied it, the tail-spinning slowed, and Claude gunned the accelerator up the hill.

'The bitch! The bitch shot me!'

Ahead of them the ambulance swung up and around another bend and in the rearview mirror Laszlo saw the black Toyota truck right behind them, Eric at the wheel, his face gripped with a stone rage.

'Wrap this around his arm,' Laszlo shouted at Logan in the back and handed him a white silk scarf.

'Jesus!' Claude bit his lip and the blood ceased pumping where the scarf tightened around his bicep. The jeep had fallen back after the encounter but now they were gaining again when they saw the grim façade of the military hospital on a rise in the hill above them.

In the ambulance Anna reloaded the Contender. Ahead of her she too saw the hospital and prayed that Larry and Taras and the others had made it. But still, when she was five hundred yards below the hospital, she knew the ambulance wasn't going to make it. In the mirror, she saw the jeep and another car behind it gaining all the time. And from the windows of both cars she saw gun barrels levelled at the ambulance and she knew now that her only chance was to fight.

As she swung the ambulance sharply to the right she spun the wheel back until the vehicle screamed on its rear wheels and suddenly it was facing the way she had come up and the two cars slowed to a halt, one beside the other, blocking any route to her from above or to anyone coming up from below. She saw the doors swing open on both sides of the cars for some slim protection and a man from the second car dipped below the sill and ran into the cover of an earth bank. And then she saw Logan.

At the sight of him, Anna was gripped by the cold anger of revenge, but she was enraged not just by him but by Burt too, for allowing Logan to jeopardise everything and all of their lives. At some point, they'd all warned, cajoled and almost threatened Burt on the subject of Logan. She couldn't believe that Burt—out of some uncharacteristic generosity of spirit—really wished to give him every chance at redemption, or that in some way he even saw much in Logan worth redeeming. She was distracted now at the sight of him and the first bullet from a pistol in the jeep thwacked its way through the dashboard of the ambulance and missed her by an inch.

Anna rolled on to the floor of the ambulance cab and reached up to open the connecting door to the back. She crawled through and cautiously opened the rear doors. The first thing she saw was Larry and Adam, who had heard shots from higher up the road. Their short machine pistols were drawn. She silently motioned them with her hand to take cover and held up four fingers to indicate the number of assailants. The two of them fanned to either side of the road and, once away from the cover of the ambulance, rolled behind earth banks and began to crawl down the hill.

Logan slid painfully out of the jeep below the window, knowing that the car's panels would offer little defence against Anna's Contender. He began to retreat to the rear of the car, crouching and facing forwards all the time. He saw Laszlo indicate to Eric to move up behind the earth bank towards the rear of the ambulance. Then he saw Laszlo himself drop over the other side of the road, taking advantage of the lull in any sight of Anna. And as he stopped now, seated on the road and with his back pressed against the bumper of the jeep, his gun cradled and loaded in both his hands, and a bead of sweat making its way between his eyes, his mind took one of its revolutions that had always—as long as he could remember back to childhood—spun his senses from confusion to clarity or clarity to confusion. But this time it was the former. Through the turmoil and resentments of the past, through the unnameable grief at the waste of his existence, and from the depths of his self-tortured soul, emerged a clear vision of what he had to do.

His eyes blurred for a brief moment, but he knew he could rely on the cold and deadly killer inside him that had got him into Russia two years before when he had killed the KGB-trained Moscow mafioso who had butchered Anna's husband, Finn. His hand was steady, his heart was still and hard and the clarity that now burned in his mind was like a drug that swept conflicting thoughts from his head and left one clear and conscious sliver of knowledge remaining. All that he had done—from his years in the CIA and then his abandonment by them, from his days as a mercenary collector and seller of secrets and his original betrayal of Anna, from his restless and inconclusive sojourn at Cougar under Burt's eye— all his confused and hopeless past, in fact—could be wiped away by this sliver of knowledge. The confusion that had led him to even think—let alone suggest and act upon the suggestion—of betraying Anna a second time, to Laszlo and the Russians, was swept away. The only thing that remained in Logan's mind was that he had to save her.

He looked carefully round the side of the jeep to where Eric was crawling up the hill behind the bank, then to the other side where Claude was similarly ascending the hill at a painfully slow

413

speed, and decided that he would kill Laszlo first. Then he would take cover and shoot whoever put his head above the earth banks. Laszlo was ahead, crouching, then rolling, crouching again, and all the time his eyes were on the spot where they'd last seen Anna. He was now ten feet from the ambulance.

Logan gripped the pistol in both hands, got up into a crouch and then, with a swiftness that would have momentarily dazzled any normal observer, he whipped his body around from the rear of the jeep, arms locked in a V-shape with the gun in his hands at the end of them and levelled directly at Laszlo's back.

But Anna was no ordinary observer. She had emerged from the rear of the ambulance and then crawled back underneath it towards the front. She'd seen Laszlo's progress towards her, but couldn't get a fatal shot from beneath the ambulance, only a wounding blow to a shin at most. But as she saw Logan's sharp movement, only his feet and lower legs visible, she decided to act instantaneously. She rolled over twice and emerged on the right side of the ambulance, totally exposed and, without a pause, shot Logan through the heart.

At once, two short bursts of automatic fire which burst from behind the earth banks crashed into her consciousness. She saw Laszlo, confused at the sound of weapons he knew his people didn't possess, turn for a second to the right, just as he'd seen her prone form on the road. Her second shot entered the side of his head, just in front of the ear and, travelling upwards from her position on the ground, blew his brains out.

414

'Anna?' It was Larry's voice.

'All dead?'

'If you got two, yes.'

'All dead,' he said and was suddenly beside her.

'Where's Taras?' she asked him.

'He's waiting.'

They left the two cars blocking the road from below. Their exit route was in the other direction. They left the bodies splayed on the road or contorted in death behind the earth banks, as Anna turned the ambulance and headed the remaining five hundred yards up the hill, with Larry, Lucy, Adam and Grant in the back.

Taras had heard the gunfire. He was already inside the hospital where there was sufficient mayhem from the sight of the ships ablaze and sinking down below in the harbour. His message had already been relayed to the guards inside. 'A terrorist attack. Get down to the harbour.'

Some went, others refused to leave their posts without orders from a direct superior. As Taras emerged on to the front steps, he saw the ambulance approach, then swing around to the side of the hospital to the bay where the dead or wounded were admitted.

He tore back inside, shouting that he needed all the men they could get who remained to guard the front of the hospital. He himself went to the rear, down three corridors and across an instant surgery room, and swung the lever that raised the metal curtain between the emergency bay and the hospital's rear entrance. The ambulance doors were open, he saw all five of them, Anna putting a new clip into the Contender. The others had reloaded, he half thought, with the dim,

415

professionally automated sub-consciousness born in extreme moments of action. The ambulance was backed up right to the ledge where a trolley could be wheeled straight on to it.

The six of them took the service lift. Anna led, the only one of them with a silenced weapon. As the doors opened on the fifth floor, she shot dead two of the guards to the prison wing. Taras took the keys and they entered, racing through the empty ward. The two guards were bemused. One began to raise his gun.

'Don't shoot!' Taras said. 'There's a terror attack down below.'

But the guard armed his gun and Anna dropped him with a single shot by the time Larry had punched the second guard and then struck him hard on the back of the head with his pistol butt.

They unlocked the second door, and this time only Taras ran down the corridor of cells. The others began to take up stations staggered outside the cells, in the ward, outside the lift and along to the end of the corridor, where another corridor joined it.

Taras fumbled with the keys, trying first one then a second. He'd gone through five keys and the sweat was pouring off him by the time the sixth slid the lock and he pushed the door open. He crossed the room. Masha lay staring in horror at him from the cot.

He scooped her up.

'It's all right. It's all right, Masha. It's me.'

Then he heard a fire fight erupt from somewhere beyond the ward. He guessed it was from the end of the corridor. Adam and Grant were holding off a concerted attack. He lifted the emaciated body of his cousin from the cot and ran out of the cell, past the others and into the ward.

The lift was waiting, its doors jammed open with a trolley. Taras saw a body at the far end of the corridor. It was Adam's, he thought fitfully. Suddenly a loud explosion ripped the plaster from the walls of the corridor and splintered shrapnel at four hundred feet per second into the body of Grant. He fell immediately.

They couldn't risk the lift now and they began to run down the stairs, Anna ahead, Taras holding his cousin in the middle, while Larry and Lucy brought up the rear. They cascaded down the steps, rather than ran. It was a pell-mell hurtling of bodies broken only by Larry who crouched at each turn and trained his gun back up the stairs, firing at will at their pursuers. They reached the bay, descending five floors in under a minute. By the time the ambulance pulled away, they were all present apart from their two dead comrades and the metal curtain had been jammed shut behind them.

CHAPTER THIRTY-SEVEN

Three and a half miles offshore from the flat coast north of Sevastopol, the navigation lights of the ancient, twenty-six foot wooden fishing vessel *Lyubimov* were comfortably anonymous among the lights of a pack of other small commercial fishing boats strung out along a two-mile stretch of water. On the fourth night after the full moon, the red and green and white lights bobbed in the lazy current that drifted along the coast and the swell was gentle, unremarkable.

Balthasar leaned against a guard rail on the starboard side of the vessel facing northwards, the boat's prow pointing out towards the Black Sea. A small sail at the stern kept the fishing boat pointing upwind. Already he sensed that things were moving as they should. But he knew too that people had been lost. He felt Anna on the wind and in the salt smell of the sea. He felt her approach. He felt the invisible lines that linked him to her. The darkness was his favoured time. He felt the darkness as much as he felt the light, though neither made any difference to him. For the benefit of the rest of the world, in the pocket of his fisherman's jacket, he held his orders from Department S that were the proof the world needed. He also kept in the same waterproof package the minutes of meetings that started at The Forest back in January, the last time he'd seen—or would see—his father, as well as the notes from his briefing sessions with both his father and the GRU boss. The rest of the world needed to see, he thought with amusement. They needed to see because that was their impoverished version of knowledge.

He turned away from the rail and walked along the deck to the wheelhouse. A nineteen-year-old boy was reading a rock magazine in the thin light from the ceiling and listening to the radio.

'We need the channels open now,' Balthasar told him, and he heard the music stop as the boy tuned the radio to the Open channel. 'Start the engines,' Balthasar told him. 'We'll be heading further out in a short while.'

This time he walked to the stern of the vessel and heard the steady hum of an engine half a mile away. It was them. But he'd sensed that too, long before the sound became public.

The small motorboat nudged alongside the *Lyubimov* and Balthasar already had the gate open in the guardrail to receive them. There were five of them, two were missing, as he'd known.

Larry lashed the motorboat to the side of the *Lyubimov*, Taras carried the inert form of Masha into the wheelhouse and laid her on a thin bed, while Anna and Lucy walked to opposite ends of the vessel and leaned against the rails. Anna stood next to him at the stern. They didn't speak. Behind them they heard Larry ordering the boy to set a course of 180 degrees. Then he took the wheel and they heard the old engines grind up to full throttle.

The *Lyubimov* pushed through the black swell for another three miles towards the open sea where the lights from the fishing pack were left behind them and finally lost. Nobody spoke. Anna and Balthasar stood at the stern, Lucy and Taras with her now, at the bow, while Larry pulled back the throttle and cut the engines again. The silence was complete. Only Larry's footsteps as he came out of the wheelhouse broke it briefly before he, too, stopped and scanned the sea.

It seemed a long wait to the tense party, but it was no more than twenty minutes at most. Only Balthasar seemed completely at ease. He didn't even turn when the submersible emerged four hundred yards off their port bow and wallowed sluggishly in the rolling water. Larry walked back into the wheelhouse and called for him.

'What about the boy?' he said.

419

The nineteen-year-old was staring at the black shape in astonishment, then fear. He looked at Larry now and decided it was finished with him. Larry's face was set in grim determination. But Balthasar smiled at the boy and put his hand on Larry's shoulder.

'We leave him with the motorboat,' he said. 'No radio, enough fuel to get to shore. And some money,' he added, and took out another waterproof package from a pocket of the jacket. 'You did well,' he said to the terrified boy. 'If we hear you've kept your mouth shut, in a week you'll receive the same amount again.'

'We can't let him go,' Larry said through gritted teeth.

'I already have,' Balthasar said.

Larry started the engines and took the *Lyubimov* with great care a hundred yards from the submersible and downstream from the current and the swell and Lucy untied the motorboat and held the lines tightly so that it still kept closely to the sides. Taras carried Masha first into the motorboat then the others climbed in, Larry keeping hold of the boy's arm tightly. He frisked him to make sure there was no hand-held radio concealed anywhere, found nothing, and cursed under his breath at Balthasar's methods.

Balthasar descended to the engine room of the *Lyubimov* and opened the seacocks and heard the seawater slowly flooding the scuppers and felt it overlap his feet. Then he climbed back up the ladder and down into the motorboat. By the time they reached the submersible the *Lyubimov* was wallowing low in the water and would disappear altogether in half an hour. On the submersible a hatch was opened and, to the astonishment of everyone, Burt's bare head appeared.

'Reminds me of Cam Ranh Bay, 1969,' he said cheerfully. 'But that time it was the Russians under our ships.'

Anna smiled at him, despite her low-level anger. She didn't believe that Burt had ever been anywhere near Cam Ranh Bay. But Burt's mythologising of himself was, as ever, for his own personal entertainment. He required nobody to believe it.

Inside the submersible there was room for six, eight at the maximum. Burt's presence didn't exactly help the seating arrangements, but at least he seemed to have realised that it wasn't de rigueur to smoke on submarines. Balthasar was the last to descend. He pushed the boy away from the submersible and told him not to start the engine for twenty minutes after the sub disappeared.

'Remember what I told you,' he said. And he felt the wave of relief in the boy's smile. 'We'll look after you well,' he said. Then the hatch was shut and the chambers began to fill with water for the descent.

The sub was based on an old model, but reworked by Cougar's scientists into a piece of equipment Burt proudly stated was a stage beyond anything any nation possessed. It was designed for infiltrating frogmen on to enemy shores and for small-scale assaults into enemy territory. Data systems took up nearly all the space, there was real time imagery and advanced sonar, high precision echo sounders, as well as optronic masts carrying thermal pictures of their surroundings. The sonars could listen up to a thousand miles.

'Even the US navy has nothing quite like this,' Burt boasted. And then he frowned briefly, like an actor remembering his lines. He said, 'The others?' He was looking at Anna now.

'They're not coming back,' she replied. 'And neither is Logan,' she added.

Burt seemed uniquely stumped by this information. But there was nowhere to pace in the confined space and, for once, he had to face an unpleasant situation without covering it with any histrionics.

'How do you know Logan isn't coming back, Anna?' he said finally.

'Because I saw my shell going into his heart,' she replied brutally.

Burt suddenly looked stunned. He was speechless. His thick, pudgy hands flickered at the fingertips and finally came to rest at his sides as if he were trying to stand to attention. His face was white.

'Why, Burt? It's the question we're all asking, not just me. Why did you let it happen? If you'd listened to any of us—*any* of us—Logan wouldn't be dead but maybe running one of his own nasty little operations out of harm's way.' She stared at Burt's face and saw he couldn't meet her eyes. His face was losing its paleness and taking on a livid red colour. 'Logan is dead because he teamed with some French intelligence officer from Kiev and the accompanying thugs to kidnap me. Again. A second time time, Burt! You let it happen. You endangered all our lives. For what? You're smart, Burt, but in this you were a fool. Why?'

In the confined space, the only sound was Burt's harsh breathing. Everyone but Balthasar was staring at him. Finally it was Balthasar who spoke. 'Why don't you just tell them?' he said. 'It's finished now.'

Burt breathed deeply. The others were silent and the anger that flowed from Anna, Larry and Lucy was as palpable as a monkey wrench. In the sub, descended now to the limits of its operating depth in the blindness of the Black Sea, Burt wrung his hands and his head seemed to sway. Finally he looked up and faced his accusers. 'I'm sorry,' he said. 'I wanted him to come good. I thought I could make him come good. I thought if I gave him my trust, he would change. I thought I could *make* Logan. Logan was my son.'

Before dawn, the submersible entered the dry dock of the *Cougar* and the ship set course for the Mediterranean.

EPILOGUE

The view from the parade ground-sized sitting room at Burt's ranch in New Mexico took in the low mountains to the north-west and, in the foreground, a stretch of scrubby mesa of cactus and sagebrush that petered out in the red rock foothills. Any observer who admired the grandeur of the sweeping panorama would see that, and would also see the low hangar half a mile distant, where one of Cougar's jets simmered in the eighty-degree heat. They might pick out the perimeter fence nearly a mile away and, on closer inspection, spot the guards and watchtowers at the entrance to the vast compound. And they would undoubtedly be awed by the richest blue of a sky that domed this corner of the world in what was, to some, a spiritual embrace. But would they have seen the trillions of details that existed in this brief landscape that led to the line between mountain and sky?

'Between here and that peak,' Burt said, without turning from the window, 'the insects alone can be counted in billions.'

Anna didn't reply.

Burt finally turned towards her. She sensed that he'd been building up to making this explanation he was about to make for some time.

'Intelligence—and the people engaged in it,' he stated flatly, 'are only feeling their way in near-perfect darkness. The great intelligence operator is the one who is concerned with the greatest number of hypotheses. The person who has only one cherishes and promotes that one of his own, and is blind to its faults. That fatally limited hypothesis means he observes very little—almost nothing, in fact—and therefore his crucial observations are marred by prejudice. And the triumph of truth is postponed.'

Burt picked up a bottle of Krug '87 champagne and nipped the edges of the foil until he could untwist the wire and open it, gently and purposefully towards an antique champagne coupe on a fine antique Persian marquetry table. He picked up the glass and placed it on an identical table next to where Anna was sitting, before pouring himself a glass.

Burt raised his glass and drank.

'Lish's mistake,' he said, and she noted that it was now 'Lish', not Theo, no longer the friend and colleague of thirty years' standing, 'Lish's mistake', Burt repeated, 'was to be the latter, the man with a single hypothesis. The Blind Spy. Yes.' Burt seemed to gaze into the distance. 'Lish is the Blind Spy.' Then his mind focused again on Anna before him. 'But Lish's mistake is a mistake every agency makes, including, thankfully, the KGB. Lish is the perfect bureaucrat. No wonder that he found such common cause with the Russians.'

'You mean . . . ?' Anna began, but Burt cut her off.

'No, no, I don't mean that Lish is a traitor,' he said. 'Not in the big sense, anyway. But we'll come to that in a moment. What I mean is that he feels more comfortable with any bureaucracy, even the dead hand of the Kremlin machine, than he did with me, with Cougar. He's a man who hides behind the safety of organisations.' Burt sighed

426

expansively. 'But now he's hanging upside down from a piano wire in Washington, I guess he'll be thinking about his mistakes.'

Anna saw that this was one of Burt's melodramatic figures of speech. The Senate Intelligence Committee in Washington didn't yet, as far she knew, interrogate their intelligence chiefs that way.

'And you, Burt?' Anna said. 'You kept all the hypotheses in your head at the same time?'

Burt looked at the floor. 'All of them but Logan,' he said. 'Right up to the final days, I was prepared for my own prejudices to be proved wrong. But at least I left the opportunities alive in my head until the last.'

'Except Logan,' she said.

'Logan was always a project,' he said quietly. 'I wanted to make him in my image. It was a deep personal failure of mine. I will think about that mistake for a long time. For the rest of my life.'

'He betrayed me once,' Anna said. 'Then he betrayed me a second time in Odessa back in January. And then you gave him the opportunity to betray me a third time. And now he's dead. But it could have been me.'

He looked up at her sharply. 'It wasn't Logan who betrayed your trip to Odessa to the Russians,' he said.

'Oh no?'

'That's what I meant a moment ago,' he said. 'About Lish and treason. Lish didn't commit treason against his country. He committed it against me, and, by extension, against you. It was Lish. He told Logan, but Logan didn't take it to the Russians, Lish did. I have the documentary

427

evidence to prove it and we'll see before this enquiry is over that it will be the final nail in Lish's coffin.'

Anna sat silent. She was stunned that Burt's man at the CIA, the boss himself, could have betrayed her.

'You see, what I also failed to see was Lish's fundamental resentment towards me. His deep-seated jealousy. He wanted to damage Cougar. Now it's the CIA that's damaged. The *Pride of Corsica* was ultimately registered to a letter-box company in Omsk with KGB connections. The Russians set the whole thing up. The CIA go off on some Russian-inspired wild goose chase in the Black Sea and end up killing their own former colleagues on an empty ship. The British too. It's not just a PR disaster, it has deeply damaged the relationship between the CIA and the military in my country. No doubt in Britain too. Adrian will shortly be looking for a job, I don't doubt.' Burt paused. 'On the plus side, all that's happened in the Crimea will, in time, add another billion or so to Cougar's government contracts.' He looked at her. 'And you, Anna, you should have a stake in that.'

'That's your motive, Burt, not mine.'

'And you? Dear Anna, what are your motives?'

She didn't reply.

'The Senate Intelligence Committee is very pleased with Balthasar's damning evidence against the KGB. They don't intend to use it—as long as the Russians play ball. As long as the Russians drop their plans to implicate Qubaq in the events at Sevastopol, we'll keep the world from knowing what those plans were. You've read the newspapers. The Kremlin is talking about a rogue group of special forces soldiers of their own who went on a psycho rampage in Sevastopol's harbour. All good. They can't go back on that now, even if we didn't hold the cards against them that Balthasar brought.'

Anna picked up the glass on the table next to her for the first time. She drank half of it.

'And who will you put forward to be the next head of the Agency?' she said.

'I'll wait until I'm asked.' Burt grinned.

'I'm not sure you're going to find anyone who doesn't end up resenting you and wanting their freedom from you,' she said. 'You don't give someone their freedom, they resent you. It's written in stone.'

'Maybe. But I can't help what other people think.'

To see and not to know, to know and not to see. Anna thought of Balthasar.

'Because you were right?' she asked. 'Is that why you're so full of yourself?'

'I think you know I'm always full of myself.' Burt guffawed, then he became serious. 'Every time I'm right,' he said, 'I get richer and more powerful. But every time I'm right it also becomes more difficult to be rich in hypotheses. Being right—or just thinking that—is an open invitation to prejudice. That's what I try to guard against in every waking minute.'

*   *   *

As Anna rode away from the ranch house, the sun was dimming to the west. She opened the throttle